WELCOME TO THE CLUB

A novel

Lee Jorgenson

ISBN: 197785351X
ISBN 13: 9781977853516

DISCLAIMER

Welcome to the Club is a work of fiction, and is therefore a product of the author's imagination. All names, characters, places and incidents are used fictitiously. Any resemblance to actual persons, living or dead, events or locales is entirely coincidental.

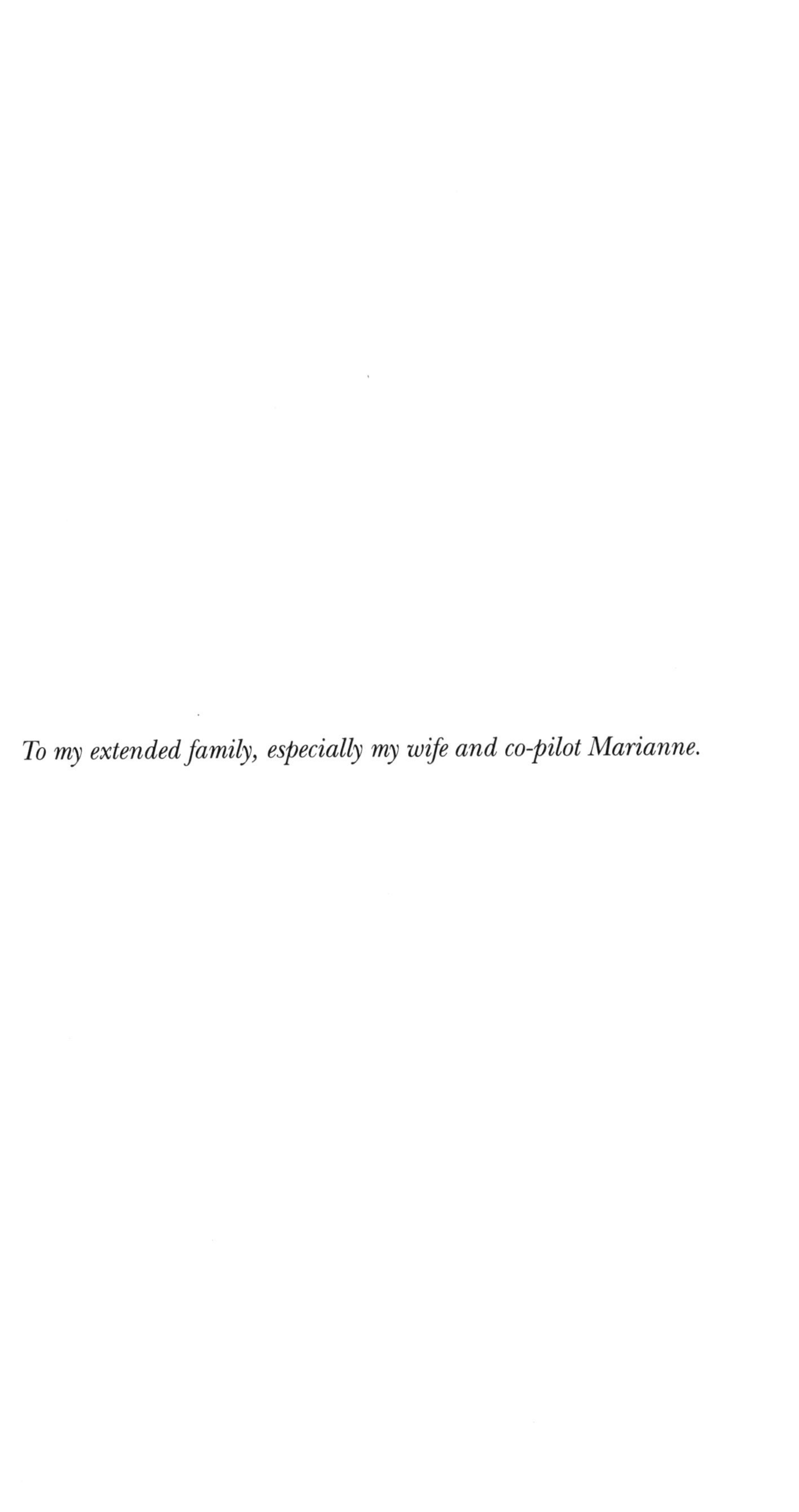

To my extended family, especially my wife and co-pilot Marianne.

ACKNOWLEDGEMENTS

Rex Olsen, Esquire, author, friend and generous contributor of his time in helping this book get to print; Jeanine Jorgenson, always willing to lend an ear and computer support; Lauren Jorgenson, Cover Photography, and expert technical and copy support; Under Sheriff Robert A. Edmonds (Ret)Los Angeles Sheriff's Department, technical advice and support; Rosalie Edmonds, Steve and Deborah Hadrych, transportation and lodging services, Paul O'Dowd, professional hospitality industry related consulting; Jarett Jorgenson, contributed sharp perspective and strategic input, Brian "Disco Dog" Warner, official choreographer, Don Audleman, copy review and input, Morton and Marguerite Kondracke, copy input and encouragement.

CHAPTER ONE

Rosewood Golf and Country Club sits on a handsome bluff about fifteen minutes north west of downtown Vancouver, Washington. The club is located on the crown of a large knoll amid rolling foothills. There is a view of town and on west to the majestic Columbia River, as it rolls north of Portland, and continues on to its mouth at Astoria, Oregon and the mighty Pacific Ocean. To the west are sloping plots of fruit orchards, mostly apple and cherry, which please the eye, and create a most bucolic setting. We use "Come play with us", for our marketing hook. Sounds good, doesn't it? Well, please stay tuned.

We are very proud of the history of our club. Having been founded in 1923, near the start of the roaring twenties, we have been going strong for eighty-five years now. Our inception was around the time when the west was beginning to civilize. The aristocratic game of golf was slowly moving our way from the bastions of the great courses on the east coast and Europe. Local lore says membership in Rosewood in those early 1920's, paved the path to renown and social prominence.

People say many a business deal materializes on the golf course. But just as many if not more, are culminated in the bar with your peers, over drinks. At our course, like any private club worth its' salt, your peers are lawyers, bankers, accountants, architects, doctors, dentists, CEOs., big time agriculture, fishing, shipping, railroad, etc. types.

We were one of the first courses in Washington to offer eighteen holes of golf, albeit, those old folks were forced to play on sand greens. The early practice facility, included both a driving range and a short game practice area. There was also tennis, a swimming pool, and a stately old club house. This project was largely driven by cheap land prices of the day, and the fact that when one hundred or so of the finest put their minds to it, just about anything was possible. According to club archives, the whole project was launched for around one and a half million dollars. From early club records, the terms for the original members was a $10,000 buy in, then $5,000. a year payment for ten years. Fulfill these obligations, and you were a proud founding father, with a full share of equity membership in Rosewood G&CC. The investment of the founding fathers bought 150 acres of prime real estate, designed and built the course, and the corresponding clubhouse and related amenities.

Of course, like any private club, there were also monthly dues. Without which operation of the new clubhouse, the pro shop, pool etc. would be impossible. What a thrill it must have been back then to sit on the warm veranda in the summer time after a morning's round of golf, with your colleagues. Even though nationwide Prohibition was staunchly in effect, you could still sip a Gin and Tonic, with a wink and a grin to your barman. Such was a benefit of belonging to the local elite. And if you got lucky, you could win a quid or three playing gin rummy with the boys. The wife had her games of tennis or badminton or bridge. Some of those early pioneer women even took to the game of golf. The children always had the swimming pool to keep them occupied.

Evenings were more formal. Members dressed in coat and tie for dinner, except for the men's grill, which was more a bit more casual and accommodating. On Saturdays, there was always men's club golf or designated tournaments, followed by either a formal dance with a big band up from Portland, or an awards dinner. Perhaps there was a wedding or celebration of another sort, which would necessitate inviting most of the membership. All these activities made Rosewood a busy place in its' early days. It was truly the hub of society in our growing little, northwest city.

Now, we are much less formal. Our elitism has worn off to a large degree. Although it is still a thrill and a pleasure to motor up the tree lined drive of our Club's pastoral entryway, it doesn't seem to be the be all and end all that it once was.

As golf continued to expand, and peaked during the Tiger Woods years, it oversaturated itself. And now Rosewood, like many private clubs is merely surviving, rather than flourishing like days gone by. Don't get me wrong, Rosewood and those old boys made it through the great depression and World War II with their industriousness and work ethic. So, I think we can suck it up and find a way to keep going forward.

But modern times are also dramatically different. And there is no question that those old founding fathers would be rolling over in their graves, if they had any idea of all of the confounding troubles we were about to get ourselves into. Not the gut wrenching, water boarding type of troubles just yet. Unbeknownst to us however, they would become more of the, help, I'm going down for the third-time type of thing.

Part of the problem modern golf clubs experience is universal, and it is addressed by the simple fact of their aging demographic. The younger generations don't seem as anxious to join up, unless there are special incentives and/or sweetheart deals offered.

This annoys the older members, who then want a sweet deal of their own. Couple this with inflation and competition, and while our membership is very successful on a relative basis, the bigger, newer clubs across the Columbia River in Portland, Oregon have taken a significant toll.

Rosewood was lucky to have owned it's land all these years, which was/is our salvation. And while we may not be the crust of the crust anymore, at least we pretend to be most of the time. Hey, we didn't tell Portland to go and develop Pumpkin Ridge and Waverly GC, and all of those upscale new courses.

As far as operating the club, our impediment in addition to the aging factor, seems to be the challenge of getting along with each other. Rosewood's organizational structure is like that of a lot of other clubs. With a governance system consisting of a Board of twelve Trustees, who each serve a three-year term, with four new Trustees rotating in every year. We elect a President every year. There is a Vice President, Secretary, and a Treasurer (the Executive Committee.) Then there are the remaining eight trustees who man the club's designated sub committees: House, Greens, Golf, Membership/Marketing, etc.

We have bylaws to guide us along, but often personalities get in the way. Once you are on the board, peoples' priorities can change, egos kick in, especially for the A types. And if you are affluent enough to join a private club, trust me, you are an A type. Then there are the Presidents to deal with. While some of them work hard, and do a good job, it is, of course, a volunteer position. They can often get sideways. Somehow, they come to believe Rosewood is their own private Idaho, and if people will just get out of their way, they can create a lasting legacy. Rosewood will build a statue of them, and install it by the first tee box. But, in truth, a lot of them don't have a real idea how to run a hospitality related organization.

A club is a social institution. It is your home away from home. It provides you with privacy, status, and entertainment. It feeds you, and can serve you a cool beverage. It will host your special occasions and gatherings. It is more intimate than a public facility, and because as it is private, it serves only a limited number of regular clientele. You generally know most of the staff, and they in turn know you, and most of your wants and needs. They will admire your wife's new diamond earrings, and compliment you on your golf game. You can freshen up in the locker room, and buy equipment in the Pro Shop. If you want a golf or tennis lesson the pros are there for you. Here's to the faithful staff, who mow the course, clean the pool, cook, serve, pour, and take care of your every need.

What does a new President, who is a busy executive at Lockheed Martin Corporation in Portland, Oregon, know about running a private country club? Not much, experience has told me, but this is where the fun starts. They all seem to have an Agenda. Usually their Agendas revolve around the golf course. The guys golf in the morning, and come into the bar to have drinks and a sandwich, and settle up the bets. I really think they could sit just about anywhere, and do this, and remain oblivious to their surroundings. They are loath to spend a dime on the clubhouse, but if the eighth tee has a bald spot, God help us. Here is ten grand for the greens keeper to build a new tee box. Even though our stately old club house is no longer so stately, and in sore need of an upgrade. The President usually has just enough of a majority on the board to maintain his or her priorities.

And oh, you forgot to inform the Board or the membership of your Projects and Priorities when building your new tee box? No problem, it was just routine maintenance. Unfortunately, the General Manager is often caught in the middle of all this. Usually the Good Old Boys are politically aligned with the Greens Keeper, and the GM will of necessity go along, to keep the peace.

He, after all, has a family to support, and waves can be dangerous to one's health. So, the boat keeps floating downstream, mostly of its' own inertia. It's kind of like the Labor Unions in our state of Washington. They help elect the Politicians, and then the Politicians award nice, big fat contracts to the Unions. And everyone is happy, especially the union leaders and the politicians. Except that, of course, this process can get expensive for the rest of us.

In addition to having a novice as a president, often there is a calumnious type of intrigue involved with the selection of the board in general, and the officers in particular. Alliances are formed, usually back at the nominating committee for future board membership. Who is this person? What are their qualifications? Most importantly, will they play ball, and be good soldiers for the cause? And there always seems to be just enough of a majority to keep the furtive status quo large and in charge. Always calling the shots.

The Rosewood women's club has learned this general principal of club life very well. Consequently, they are the best organized group in our club. They generate enough respect and a power base, to keep the men's club off of their backs. They have learned how to protect their turf, and survive without creating significant issues. But they keep records of everything, and their attitude is: Leave us well enough alone guys. If you want trouble, we will give it to you. Just go google the Spokane Country Club, and see how poorly their little conflict with the women members worked out.

Me, I am just a hospitality guy, a foodie. I started working in restaurants at the age of thirteen, and have been employed in about every type of joint you could imagine. After working my way through school, I did time in the hotel business with the Hyatt Corporation. They were a very fine group with which to gain management experience. Very professional, and very systems oriented. And although I am not personally fond of the hotel business, I have been Food and Beverage Director at several big city hotels and also managed at City Business Clubs, at Country Clubs, Resorts, etc. My wife and I have owned and operated our own Steak House here in Vancouver, for twelve years now. The game of golf is very near and dear to me, and while no longer an ultra-low handicapper, I still get a great deal of exercise and enjoyment from the game. Even with all my institutional experience, I am more of a speck on the wall at Rosewood. It is the flashy attorneys, a honcho at Nike, or CEO of a fast-moving new Tech start up, that have the most money, the most cache, and naturally so.

Still, I get no small amount of entertainment watching our curious little circus stumble along. It can be extremely amusing, but also understandably frustrating to an industry professional. The Good Lord knows there are a lot smarter people around than me. Still, I have worked with some pretty bright people in my day. And we have run own business for some years now, so I think I have a fairly good idea of how to keep the beast moving forward. Maybe I should just go on the board, and get elected President. I could have the old place straightened out in no time. And when that was done, a moderate sized statue in my likeness, might not be a bad idea either. But there you go.

The Private Club industry, reminds me a lot of our Federal Government bureaucracies earnestly plodding along. Doing their best, but inevitably fumbling the ball at a critical moment, or painstakingly crafting policy, only to have the next regime come in and do a one hundred eighty-degree turnaround on them.

Similar to our government and its' tax revenues, Private Clubs are subsidized by the members' monthly dues. Both of these support systems are a lot like being a trust fund baby. No matter what happens, oh well, just another bump in the road. No stake in the game for us, we'll just try harder next time. We'll get it right. Of course, if you don't know what you are doing in the first place, that is often easier said than done

CHAPTER TWO

My wife and I joined the club in 1998. An investment company had acquired land adjacent to Rosewood's western border, and wanted to develop a new residential community. Rosewood wanted to add a third nine holes. They thought it would help attract new members, and add to the club's options and operational flexibility. A deal was cut with the developer, who donated some of the land for the new subdivision. The part of the deal we liked, offered a free membership with the purchase of a residential lot on one of the new holes.

We were living on two and a half acres north of town. It was a fine little homestead, but two and a half acres is a lot of work. There are lawns and fields to mow, weeds, pruning, vegetable gardens to tend. We had to maintain the well house, the access road, the apple tree orchard, etc. It was a nice four bed room rambler, but keeping up with all of this, in addition to operating a restaurant, was very time consuming.

One day I was playing golf with some friends at one of the local muni courses. It was a hot day, and play was excruciatingly slow. The course was overgrown, and not in very good shape. It was noisy, too expensive, and overcrowded. My friend Michael Elliott says that the job of any respectable foursome, is to hate the foursome in front of you. And that was very easy to do on this day. They were zig zagging back and forth across the fairways, endlessly chasing errant balls. And the slower the play, the hotter it seemed to get. We were in the middle of a five and one-half hour round, and the more we waited on the group in front of us, the more balls were being hit into us by the group behind. Then, the mosquitos started to come out, and the golf cart was running low on juice. We finally finished playing, but when we got to the snack bar, the refrigeration wasn't working, and there was no cold beer. It was the round straight from hell.

I finally got home, and my wife, Jeanine, had just come in with the mail, which she was perusing. There was a brochure sent out by Rosewood Golf Club. It advertised a free Proprietary membership with a purchase of one of the new residential lots. "Hey, check this out," she said to me.

Her timing couldn't have been better. I read the brochure, and told her, "Let's move to the golf course. Instead of having to endlessly manage maintaining this property, and play golf on a muni dog track, we could be playing at a private club. We would actually have some leisure time. Plus, the kids will love the pool, and there will be some nice young families buying in over there."

I didn't have to do much to persuade her, nor the kids. Especially since our son who was now nine years old was beginning to be interested in golf. I used to take him to the driving range on Sunday afternoons, and it was obvious that he was going to be a pretty good junior stick. Daughter liked the social side of the idea best, and all in all the move was a unanimous family decision.

If you ever have the opportunity to get your kid hooked on golf, I would advise you to go for it. They will spend much of their summer days at the course playing and practicing. They will work on their games, they will play from dawn to dark if they can, stopping only for a sandwich and a milk shake. They will willingly go to the gym, and pump some iron.

Even though my dad was a preacher, and I grew up in a very religious home, I am not sure, I myself, or any one, especially an impressionable kid, won't learn as many values on a golf course, as they do in Sunday School. There is honesty, patience, respect, humility, courtesy and etiquette to absorb. You learn to do math, you have to be responsible for your equipment. You learn to compete, and the values of winning and losing with grace. You often develop long term relationships with your peers. Who knows, you may even be a PGA or LPGA star someday. Isn't this a more healthy, productive environment, that sitting around all day playing video games? Plus, when is the last time you heard or read about a professional golfer getting busted for drunken driving, or domestic violence, PEDs, or drugs? We leave those kind problems, except for Tiger's little hiccup, to the NFL and he NBA.

At any rate, moving to the golf course was the best thing we ever did. We were so excited to build a beautiful new custom home. We made many friends and acquaintances, which was good for us, and also for our business. The kids loved being closer to town. They were around middle school age, and made many new buddies. I played a round of golf on weekends, and could usually sneak in a game or two during the week, when the nine to fivers were busy at work. Jeanine even decided to take up the game. We were now dues paying club members, which included golf for the entire family, so she said why not?

We already knew lots of Rosewood members from our restaurant contacts. And as Vancouver is not a huge town, we integrated pretty quickly into the social structure of Rosewood. There were the older members, who could be a little crotchety sometimes, but there were also a fun younger set and we fit right in.

If there were any problems with our move, they revolved around the club, rather than our new home and community. The development added about sixty new members to Rosewood's roster. And the existing driving range and practice areas, not to mention the antiquated clubhouse were now clearly overwhelmed. They had had only minor upgrades since their inception, and any kind of a popular, well attended tournament, seriously taxed the place. Most of the members saw these problems as the Board of Director's next priority. It was fixable we all thought. Although no one was quite sure what the progression of these capital projects would be.

Rosewood was managed then by a fairly serious gentleman whose name was Edgar Cordoba. He was from some type of eastern European stock, and I'll give him this, he was a very hands on General Manager. Much more so than his successors have ever been. He ran the Dining Room, and Food and Beverage department himself, and had one assistant. She was his catering manager, but had a weight problem, and was not very professional looking.

I think this didn't help his cause any, as members didn't say much, but just did not respect his staff. This, of course, transferred onto him to some degree. He was also pretty rigid, and as we are no longer an uptight, elite private club from a large city, he could never seem to adjust to a more casual style of clubhouse operation. He was also very, very loyal to his people. Which is great if you are surrounded by the right people. I'm pretty sure he wasn't.

With the new nine holes, and all of the freshly minted members, Rosewood was enjoying some of their busiest times. Especially in the high season summer months. Our Greens Keeper was a rather quiet young man, who was actually an amateur hockey player from Canada. How they learn to grow grass in Canada, I'm not quite sure, but he seemed adequate for the job. The course was in decent shape, and he had won a couple of awards for environmental stewardship relating to his work stocking our golf course ponds with food fish. The local Bald Eagle population loved to feed from our ponds. And everyone loved to see the eagles around. There is just something about observing this majestic bird in such close proximity, either diving for their dinner, or bathing by the side of one of the ponds. So, Mr. Greenskeeper seemed to have made the right moves there. Otherwise, no one paid him much attention.

Our club president at the time, was a rather corpulent corporate attorney. He worked in downtown Portland for one of the big banks. I believe he was in land use/real estate law, and was in his third year on the Rosewood Board of Trustees. He had been quite helpful and influential to the club in the permitting process to get the new nine built. He was of course very proud of that, and also quite proud of the added activity for the club. He possibly could even have been entertaining thoughts of where he would like his statue placed.

Back on the home front, things were also developing nicely. Our new neighborhood was filling in rapidly, with a good roster of seemingly compatible families. One lane over from us, on Magnolia Street, we met some new friends. Actually, I met them at our restaurant one day when they came in for lunch, and Danny was wearing a Heavenly Valley ball cap. Heavenly Valley on Lake Tahoe's south shore is one of my all-time favorite ski resorts. It boasts long graceful runs overlooking the huge, but pristine alpine lake. We immediately formed a new acquaintance, as well as a mutual love for alpine beauty.

Danny had gone to Washington State University over in Pullman, and then went to work in Portland as a stock broker. Being a bright young man, and being in the right place at the right time, he took advantage of emerging technology, and invested as heavily as he could in Microsoft type tech stocks. He made a killing, and retired from the market. After investing in several apartment houses in Portland, he and his wife were now living in Vancouver, and he was amusing himself by building custom houses in our development. He used an interesting style of Hawaiian Pole Architecture, which people seemed to like. He kept as busy as he cared to be.

His wife, Susan, was a statuesque brunette who was also a Washington State grad. Turns out Danny and Susan had known each other as kids in Seattle, and had finally hooked up at college. Susan didn't officially work, but helped Danny with his projects, and did a lot of decorating type stuff for the new homes Danny was building. Susan was also an excellent golfer, and was very helpful to Jeanine in getting her game going. Danny and Susan were the main catalysts in the bonding of our new residential community.

There were other couples as well, such as Calvin and Marisa. She was a Chicana, and he was in regional sales of some kind. He had lost the middle finger of his right hand in a car accident. This caused his golf grip and his game to suffer a bit, but they were a fun couple, and Marisa was also a good golfer.

Seems Calvin was out driving one day, doing his sales thing. He was following along on the freeway behind a construction truck that was carrying supplies. Suddenly a long piece of rebar flew off of the truck, pierced Calvin's windshield, and severed his middle finger, as he was holding onto the steering wheel. Weird huh? Actually, he might have felt a little lucky to only lose a finger, because if that piece of rebar hadn't hit his finger and the steering wheel, it would have fatally impaled him right through the chest. I don't think the truck driver even realized what had happened, and just kept on going. Probably wondered why his rebar was one short when he got to the jobsite.

Another nice couple lived across the street from Danny and Susan. Bjorn, an accountant, and his wife Tammy, was a twin.

Then there was Hugh and Bunny. OMG. These two were out there. Free love, open marriage, casual sex, hot times in the hot tub, all of the above.

Bunny used to do stuff in the late spring, summer, and early fall like go out and work in her rose garden. Trouble was, she only had on a pair of skimpy, thong panties, and was hanging out everywhere. She was a tall woman, enjoying, not a beautiful face, but handsome. Handsome, in a happy and friendly way, but experienced with a bit of a hard edge around her large, hazel eyes. She was long legged, extremely buxom and quite congenial and chatty.

If the mailman happened in or UPS, whatever, she was absolutely unabashed by visitors. "Come on in," she most cordially invited anyone in to do their business. She and Hugh owned some kind of a mail order company, so there was usually a lot of traffic coming and going from the house. Bunny loved every minute of exposing herself. Hugh as well, seemed quite proud of his wife's voluptuousness, and had no qualms about sharing it with other people. I'm sure their home was the postman's favorite stop.

As Hugh was self- employed, and therefore available during the week at odd times for a golf game, he and I used to play together a fair amount. But I found him to be a bit of a braggart and a bore. Jeanine also drew the line with Bunny, as it seems she was sometimes out in the garden au natural, when her son would come home from school with a couple of buddies to hang out. And there was mom literally hanging out. It didn't matter if she was outside in her panties or not, because there were naked pictures of her and Paul all over their house.

We are no prudes, but this kind of stuff was not our thing, and we didn't see them much, other than on the golf course. But this was their life style choice, and they seemed very happy and comfortable with it. So, who am I to judge? I should say their son was a great kid throughout all of the interesting influences on his young life. He played on our son's junior basketball team, which I coached, and I always found him to be an intelligent, hard-working kid with a great attitude.

The social event of the year was the annual party at Danny and Susan's house. Danny was a bass player, and sang vocals in a Portland rock and roll band. Every Halloween, he would line the band up for a gig at his house. It was always a come as your favorite musician/rock star person. We would go as Dolly and Willie, or John and Yoko, and there would be everyone there from Elvis to Robert Palmer replete with the Palmer girls (Susan and three of her pals), partying into the wee hours. There were lots of other fun parties throughout the year, often with the band, but Halloween was always the best. We were also able to supply a lot of the food through our restaurant at cost. Ribs, rib eye steaks, Pacific North-West King Salmon, etc. Fun food. So, we fit right in back then in the early days, and were having the time of our lives.

Who knew Halloween would become such a significant day in our community?

CHAPTER THREE

We had quite an eclectic, established membership at the Club as well. Your usual barrage of professionals, plus stock and insurance brokers, money managers, scientists, educators, corporate sales people. The computer people were starting to roll in. Tech startups and tech support was the thing. There were land freight shippers, international cargo shippers, a couple of wine makers, and one gentleman who owned a yacht for charter out of the Inland Empire and Alaskan waters.

Some of our membership was ultra-wealthy, some not as much, and then there was everything in between. We had Asians, Hawaiians, Brits, Aussies, Kiwis, Jews, Gentiles, Blacks, Latinos, seniors, juniors, women, a local Municipal Judge, a couple of retired Generals and Admirals, and numerous mayors and city council members over the years. Probably pretty typical of a private club of those times, but Rosewood was somehow a little bit different. Just a little off center somehow.

Still, and not to sound like an elitist, but it was certainly more fun playing golf here with a British CPA, an Aussie airline pilot and a local doctor, rather than a pickup game on the Pabst Blue Ribbon muni circuit.

If you have ever visited a more affluent, major city club, East or West Coast, and I mean a really top of the line, venerated club, you will find a certain prevalent aura. It is second nature to know who is who at your club. Who they are, what they do for a living, what their background may be, what their personal wealth is. If you are an unfamiliar, i.e. a visitor, often members will evaluate you, usually indiscreetly looking down their nose at your posture or some element of your attire. Who is this guy, what the hell is he doing in my club? Or for the women, what kind of jewelry or accessories is she wearing? How about makeup, shoes, and who does her hair? A sort of visual third degree, that can't be a little disconcerting, or for that matter quite annoying. It is a very interesting social phenomenon, but by this time, was just not as true of Rosewood GC. Or, we were less obvious about it. Not that we didn't have our substantial members, our swells, but we are apparently just more relaxed. Pretty confident apparently, of our little place in the golfing universe, and therefore not so critical and conservative.

There is an old story about the Augusta National Golf Club, probably the grandest old Club of them all. It is a great illustration of these types of differences.

Augusta was co-founded by Bobby Jones, a scion of the game of golf, and Augusta National hosts the annual Masters Golf Tournament. This information is offered, just in case you are one of the few people on this planet who don't have this information on file. ·This club is so exclusive, even Presidents of the United States of America must be invited by a member if they would like to play.

One day a new, younger member was asked to join a group of three long standing members for a round. The new member asked about the stakes of the game, and was told that they were playing for a two-dollar Nassau. Someone might win or lose as much as ten bucks at this type of game.

"Well, at my last club, we played $500. Nassau's." His comment seemed to have littler if any effect on the older guys.

After golf, the gentlemen went into the Men's Grill, ordered drinks, and started up a game of Gin Rummy.

"What are we playing for?" asked the new member.

"Nickel a point" was the answer.

"Well, that's nothing. At my old club, we played for ten bucks a point." Again, no response from the rest of the foursome.

"And we played no limit Stud Poker every weekend for a thousand dollar buy-in".

"Say" one of the older members finally responded, "What is your net worth anyway?"

The younger man thought for a minute, and replied "Oh, probably six or seven million, depending on the Market."

"You want to cut the cards for it?" he asked.

Now it was the new member's turn to be quiet.

The great thing about golf is, simply, it's golf. It is the great equalizer, and once you tee it up, no one cares who you are, what you do, or what your net worth is. Just hit the damn ball, man.

Anyone can play with their son, daughter, wife, father/mother, grandson, granddaughter, employer, employee, your client, your pals, strangers, or other club members.

With all of the above potential playing partners, there are also an unlimited number of playing options. Stroke or match play, nine or eighteen holes, bets, creative games, or just working on the game-long or short, tournament, non-tournament, etc.

Often, you are walking, and in some very pleasant surroundings, which is healthy for you. And don't let anyone tell you golf doesn't involve athleticism. I have seen adult men, in reasonable shape, quit playing after nine holes of golf, bent over double with back or knee pain. And another adult of the same age, play 27 holes a day, six days in a row.

I'm not saying a sixty-five-year-old golfer could go out and run a marathon or triathlon. But there is a certain tenacity and toughness to golf. It is a learned skill, which requires not only physical, but extreme mental concentration as well.

But getting back to Rosewood, my favorite members are more the self-made, rather than the trust fund or entitled ones. There is just something about a person who has succeeded through initiative, hard work, brains and good luck that is appealing.

One of our most self-made guys is Davin Harris. Davin grew up in Astoria, Oregon and started working the charter fishing boats at an early age. Rugged, aggressive, determined and a damn good fisherman, Davin migrated up to the Bering Sea, and began his career in earnest as a commercial Salmon fisherman. Alaska, it turned out was his cup of tea.

These guys are Bad Ass. They work days on end, and if they got four to six hours of sleep, it was a banner night. Those were the good old days of Salmon fishing, where with the right captain and crew, and in a long, toilsome season, a man could come home with some serious money.

Now days, fishing seasons are shorter. A lot of it is done with seine nets, hydraulics and processing boats. In those earlier days, you could be down in the hold, up to your waist in fish slime, sorting and icing wild salmon for twenty hours at a time. Up top, the crew was pulling in more salmon, on more lines. It was a grind.

And when you came ashore, the fish camps were rough spots, also. No bargain at all. The bars served Miller beer and shit whisky. There was no happy hour. But there were dice and card games to separate you from your money. Not to mention loose women, drugs, and long runs of just you and your hired-on crew. You had to be tough and smart to survive.

The mentality of a lot of the guys was to go through three or four months of hell. Then go home and live like a king for eight or nine months. Soon enough, it was time to go back and do it all over again.

Not Davin Harris. He came back to Astoria and took his hard-earned money, got an additional credit line, and started buying commercial boats of his own: Sport fishing boats, commercial salmon and crabbing boats. In time, he had branched out into the exotics like geoduck, octopus, etc. and developed his own markets in China and Japan. He became the largest, sustainable exotic exporter in the USA, frequently traveling to Asia on business, or getting up at three in the morning to take calls from his Chinese buyers. These exotics, being aphrodisiacs in Asia, were commanding top prices.

The mystique of the fish camps must have rubbed off on him, because he still loved a high stakes golf game, and would travel down to the deep south every year. He was gone for week long, big money golf and fishing tournaments.

He also managed to meet and marry a beautiful young woman, who was up from San Diego working in Alaska on a processing boat. This in itself is very difficult to pull off, as guys outnumber attractive woman in those parts, by at least a hundred to one. But Elisa must have recognized a keeper when she saw one, and she kept Davin for her own.

He hosts his own annual event at Rosewood, a golf tournament called the Harrasment. After the game, he invites all of the players over to his and his wife's riverfront spread. The tournament is called the Harrasment because Davin and the greens keeper go the course the night before the match, move all of the tees back, and put the pins in the absolutely most diabolical places. Not a new concept in tournament golf, but one that was certainly moaned about every year by all of our players. I think the entry fee was a couple hundred bucks. But even if you didn't win a dime, right after the tourney, Davin put on a feast. Fresh Alaskan crab legs, Dungeness crab legs, smoked salmon, fresh shucked oysters, a complete sushi bar, roasted baron of beef, side dishes, dessert, and a fully stocked and hosted beverage table. Our head barman at the club, Leon, would come over and tend bar, and usually bring his top cocktail girl with him. There was a waiting list to get into the tournament, but this was Davin's way of saying I love this game, and I love you guys. He was also very generous in the community, especially to people who might be a little down on their luck. He is just a prince.

Another rags to riches type, is Lance Dixon. A bright guy, who grew up in Southern California. He was working for one of the big electronics firms, when the wireless phenomenon started to happen. So, he took a chance and quit his day job. He got a couple of lines of credit, and started buying up wireless leases in geographical areas. Not like cell phone leases, but commercial leases, like for fleets of commercial trucks, or anyone that would have need of short wave commercial communications. The last I heard, he was heading north of 25 mill. Only trouble was, he kept getting married. Even with a prenup, divorces can be expensive, but he was a good-looking guy, and sometimes it is hard to say no to the ladies.

He used to come in our restaurant a lot, and we got to be pretty good friends. I told him to be careful out there. Funny thing was, as wealthy as he became, he was very liberal politically. Usually, the more money someone has, the more conservative they get. Not Lance Dixon.

Probably, one of the most interesting characters at Rosewood, was Charlie Strong. Charlie was an ex-Marine, a Union Executive, and a recruiter for the trade unions. He was a quasi-mobster type, and told a lot of stories. Tall tales. No one quite knew if his stories were 100% legit, yet they were very entertaining. After a round of golf, and over a few beers, he would hold court in the bar, telling of the time he had to bust some heads in Philly. Or where Jimmy Hoffa had been cremated, maybe how he had to take the Viet Cong down a peg or two, etc. Guys love this kind of macho shit. They eat it up. And Charlie knew how to work a room. He and I would later serve on the Rosewood Board of Trustees together. What a ride that was.

Some people, you just couldn't make up this stuff about. Such was Dane Knutson. He was yet another Southern California import, who migrated north. He played baseball as a collegiate athlete in the SoCal state university system. Long Beach State I think. He married a comely young woman, got going in the wine business, and started a family.

His wife was pregnant with twins, and they were very excited. They were gifted with a baby boy and a girl, but something wasn't quite right. The little boy turned out be happy and healthy. The little girl was also happy and healthy, but was a little person. Dane and his wife were wild with anxiety, and couldn't seem to get any medical help in Southern California. They were not coping well with their situation.

Finally, the University of Washington in Seattle, proved to be their salvation. They got the counseling and medical support they needed, then just stayed on in the Pacific Northwest.

Incidentally, their daughter is now in her thirties, and is a lovely, charismatic young woman. She recently married another little person, and they live in Las Vegas. Her husband does unique marriage ceremonies and other corporate events. Her twin incidentally, is six feet five inches tall, and weighs two hundred and sixty pounds. Little sister is three feet tall, and weighs fifty-five pounds.

The Knutson's are neighbors of ours, and Dane is one of the few guys at Rosewood that has shot his age. We sometimes go to Cabo San Lucas in the spring, as do Dane and his wife Julie. Occasionally, little Larin and her husband come south to spend time with the parents in the fabulous Cabo climate. When we go out to dinner together, no matter where it is, Larin and her husband will light up the room. Within an hour, they will know half of the people in the restaurant or bar. They will be dancing on the bar top by the time we leave, and the drinks will be flowing.

As are many North Westerners, Dane is a Nordski. He has a bumper sticker on the back of his car that reads, "The few, the proud, the Norwegians." But Norwegian or not, his timing, which is often everything in life, has been impeccable.

While Jack Nicklaus was busy supplanting Arnold Palmer on the PGA tour in the early nineteen sixties, and creating his own amazing golf legacy, the neophyte wine regions of Oregon and Washington were just beginning to stir.

Oregon had been hard hit by Prohibition, being one of the first states to embrace dryness, and also one of the last to abandon it. Consequently, the development of their viticultural heritage, in spite of incredibly rich alluvial deposits in the Willamette Valley, south of Portland, didn't emerge until the around the same time as Nicklaus' growing visibility.

Washington's wine production, on the other hand, had been retarded by their state beverage control system. For political reasons, it supported the liquor distributors, to the disservice of wine production.

This advantage by the liquor industry maintained their control, until the nineteen sixties, when a group of alumni from the University of Washington, known as Associated Vintners, began producing wine in Eastern Washington for their own consumption. More or less, an early version of a do it yourself wine club. Several entries into blind tastings by A/V members, won national recognition for their unique qualities, and an exciting new industry was born.

Although the terroir of both regions varies greatly, outstanding, internationally recognized wines are produced in both regions. It is almost surreal to note the progress in these new territories, when compared to California's more established history, or better yet, see them winning awards when competing with French Vintners who have dominated the wine industry for centuries. And as both of these novice regions developed exponentially, before our very eyes, Dane Knutson was there on the forefront of a tidal wave.

He formed a distributorship of his own, promoting the newly emerging markets, which included California's larger and more established varieties as well. As successful as he became, he remained one of the good guys. Friendly, always supportive of a new club member or novice golfer, and most generous with his time and product. He was always there for anyone who needed a case of wine for a fundraiser or wine tasting. A model Rosewoodian.

CHAPTER FOUR

When you go over to Davin Harris' house, you will usually see a few crab pots sitting around in the yard. These are somewhat ubiquitous to coastal areas in the Pacific Northwest, and as far south as Northern California. Much like the Lobster traps you might find, while traveling the coast of Maine.

Although indigenous tribes have harvested crabs for centuries on both the east and west coasts of the US, the modern crab pot was first invented by Benjamin F. Lewis, of Northumberland, Virginia, in 1920. It was later improved upon, and patented by him in 1928.

There are numerous types of crab and lobster traps in the industry, but the common principle of all of these traps is very simple. Once you venture in, you cannot get out.

Recreational traps are either cylindrical or square in design. They have a floor with ingress doors, and bait is attached to the upper level of the trap, known as the parlor. Upon entering the trap, the crab can't exit, and floats up to the Parlor area. At least the crab will hopefully, have an enjoyable last supper in the Parlor of the trap.

Crab pots are baited with any appropriate, appealing editable you might have available. Often, turkey or chicken parts, but you can also use canned pet food, frozen sardines, tuna fish, shad, etc. If you use canned cat food, poke holes in the top of the can, and bait it on up. There are also spray attractants you can use to enhance your bait. Always set your pot in saline waters.

The pots are dropped via a stiff nylon line called a Blue Steel Crab line. Which line is attached to the pot, and once dropped, the line is attached to a buoy with your identification grease penciled onto it. This will hopefully deter poaching, but unfortunately theft in the industry is common place. Crabbing beds or territories, are highly contested and closely guarded secrets spots. The pot locations should then be visited later in the day, or the next morning, and retrieved, hopefully with some keepers trapped inside.

For Dungeness crabs, keepers can vary, but must be males, and are usually in the minimum of 5 to 6" range, depending on local restrictions and guidelines. Keep a metal caliper on board to measure the shell of the crab. Non-keepers are tossed back overboard to return to their milieu.

Commercial Crab Pots are much larger than their recreational brethren. Their frames are constructed out of heavy steel bars, and then covered with netting or galvanized wire mesh. They can weigh up to 600 or 800 pounds, when loaded, and ready to be set for Alaskan King Crab in the Bering Sea, the Pribilof Islands, etc.

Crabbing in these northern waters, can be extremely hazardous, and have claimed the life of many an able seaman. The crews fishing these waters are experienced veterans, with the best of equipment available to them. They are connected by the latest in communication technology, and still a boat and crew, can be lost due to conditions of the sea (rough), wind (high) and weather (extremely cold).

These courageous crews have inspired hit television shows like the Deadliest Catch, and spawned numerous folk heroes in fishing ports throughout our region.

It is even conjectured that Alaska's march to statehood in the late 1950's was fueled in part by the Crab Pot. The strong desire to gain control over their local fishing territories, and prevent the incursion of profitable forays by international fishermen into Alaskan waters, was one of the motivations to seek admission into our Union of States.

It seems Japanese crabbers liked to congregate and set pots around some of the larger cod fishing processing boats in the Bering Sea. The crabs enjoyed feeding off of the by-product of the processing boats, and these were very lucrative fishing grounds. But native Alaskans, of course, took issue with this foreign competition, and several ensuing confrontations sparked some almost lethal international incidents. All of the crabbers had apparently armed themselves. Fortunately, Statehood alleviated most of those potential problems.

As crabbing is a very hearty endeavor, crab pots are subjected to the most challenging of conditions and climates. This has created an emerging related industry in ecological circles. It is the reclaiming of "ghost pots'. Ghost pots, are pots which have escaped their buoys, their drop lines, have been lost, taken away by rough seas, etc. They often congregate in collection areas, guided by current patterns, and if in sensitive areas, will cause significant damage to ecosystems and local crab and fish populations.

Often, left unattended, these crab pots will continue to fish, whereby, they become self-baiting, and perpetuate the depletion of the general crab population. Once the pots cease to function, they are still littered on the ocean floor, or over time become embedded. Their lines can tangle both whales, and other marine craft.

There have been numerous efforts to reclaim these derelict pots, in part by local tribal organizations, educational groups, the Nature Conservancy, and the NOAA. The effort of reclaiming the ghost pots, will help maintain a sustainable a crabbing industry. It has become a recognized sport of its own, among the environmental groups.

These reactive organizations within the industry, are also strongly advocating sturdy, but biodegradable crab pots. The improved pots, as they decompose, will be an invaluable assist to a sustainable and healthy future crab population.

Did old Ben Lewis ever imagine that his invention back in 1928, would have utilized the harvest of over 25 million tons of Dungeness Crab last year (2016) in the states of Oregon and Washington alone?

I would personally like to thank him. **B**ecause, is there anything better than freshly boiled or steamed Dungy Crab, right out of the pot, with drawn lemon caper butter? Or eaten cold with a tangy southwestern cocktail sauce? We particularly like a combination of cocktail sauce, and a creamy watercress aioli at our house. Or how about warm, golden, crispy Dungeness Crab Cakes? Maybe a bit of Hollandaise or Béarnaise Sauce as a topping? Delicious!

The cuisine of the Dungeness Crab aside, one of my former Accountants loved to make an analogy of the C Corporation to a Crab or Lobster Trap. He would say, and quite often, "Once your ass(et) goes into that trap, it is hell to get out." From an accounting standpoint, this means double taxation, and an aggravating loss of resources.

Golf clubs are similar to Crab Pots. Once you are in, which is not always an easy process, you are invested. And you are invested financially, socially and emotionally until you buy your way back out. Even if you encounter difficulties, aggravations, expenses, commitments, changes of circumstances, you are still invested. And much like a crab can't just elect to exit at will out of a crab pot, very few clubs will allow you to just walk away without a pound of flesh in return. From a private club standpoint, members walking away means replacement costs, and short-term loss of revenue. Ergo, the pound of flesh on the way-out concept.

In hindsight, some of us would have been better off biting the bullet, and buying our way out of the Crab pot early on. I'm not sure we or anyone else would have understood why we left so prematurely. We were all having too much fun, and walking away back then, was not even a consideration. For better or worse, we stayed. But enough about the bounties of the North West. This is the background, now let me tell you what happened.

CHAPTER FIVE

By 2007, I had been recruited onto the Board of Trustees. We had an interesting President, who was an attractive, youngish woman from a local Engineering firm. She was very popular with the members, especially the women, and her husband was a low handicapper. But, as she was a breast cancer survivor, she was mostly concerned with raising money for Breast Cancer Research, and didn't seem to care much about anything else at the club.

She had large shoes to fill anyway, as her predecessor, Pete Collins, had been a very well-liked and dedicated chief executive for us. He was a brilliant attorney, and was a one-man band of a law firm, doing lots of business, land use, divorce and driving under the influence cases. He was a tireless worker, and in addition to his law practice, he donated huge chunks of pro bono work to our club. He had a very even disposition and could navigate his way through just about any club issue. He was one of the drivers (no pun intended), behind a new driving range project at Rosewood, and helped convince the membership of its necessity.

Charlie Strong was also new to the Board, and was Chair of the Greens Committee. I was assigned to the House Committee, and had made it known that my primary interest was in putting some long overdue resources into our aging clubhouse.

One Thursday afternoon in May, I got to the club a little bit early for the monthly Board meeting, and went into the bar for a beer, to kill some time. Charlie was sitting with some of his golfing buddies, one of which was another Board member, who was also waiting for the meeting. Charlie joined the group that went out every day at 10:30 for eighteen holes, usually two or three foursomes of the diehards, whenever he could. Trouble was they usually got in around three, and headed for the bar, but the Board meeting didn't start until 5:30. So, he was usually oiled up pretty well by the time the later meeting kicked off.

I joined Charlie's table. He was sitting with Rick Ferin, who was on the Green's Committee but was not on the board, Bruce Cranston, who was the other Board member, and some other guy. They were arguing over a bit of golf scoring minutiae. I began to look aimlessly around the old bar. It was obviously too small. The acoustics were bad, so it was always overly loud, especially on weekends when it was busy. The draperies and carpeting had seen better days. Especially the drapes, which looked like something from a thrift store. The paneling was dark stained wood, and made everything seem dated and claustrophobic. It was the kind of bar that was at best tolerable in a private club, but would never make it on the street as a public establishment. Unless it was a complete dive bar.

There was a group of four or five women sitting next to us. The women were chatting, obliviously. "Well, she got her breast implants, and couldn't have been happier with them. Then, after a couple of years, they detected breast cancer." The girls were talking about one of their friends in absentia.

"She said the implants had actually helped prevent the spread of the cancer cells. But her doctors still had to do a radical mastectomy. When they did the reconstruction, they had to use some cadaver skin to support the implant inside her breast. But the cadaver skin was too thin and elastic, and her breast became indented on top, and poorly supported structurally. This made the breast noticeably sag, and then her nipples were asymmetrical. She was soooo upset and depressed." The woman droned on.

"To repair the problem would require another complete reconstruction, which was costly, not covered by insurance, and might also leave visible scar tissue. She thinks that rather than go through all that again, she should just leave well enough alone, and just sue that hack of a doctor." Etc.

"Hey, if we had a bigger, newer bar, you wouldn't have to sit around and listen to this poor girl's problems," I said to Charlie.

"Forget it, man," he fired back at me immediately. "You know we need to get the new driving range up and running this year. The membership just approved the assessment for the new range, not the Clubhouse. And after that, we need to get the computerized instruction equipment for the golf pros."

"There is no way they are going to approve another major assessment for a new clubhouse," chimed in Bruce Cranston. He was another Greens Committee flack.

So, there it is, our diametrically opposed, entrenched positions. Greens vs Clubhouse. Golf vs Sociability. Control vs Flexibility and Democracy. Why couldn't you just have both worlds I wondered? How could a new clubhouse that would totally upgrade our facility be a bad thing? What was the problem with having a Food & Beverage program that might actually make us some money for a change?

I think it is strictly a matter of who's in control, but it is obviously a much more complex issue than meets the eye. And in the meantime, the existing order wasn't about to give up anything resembling control.

After the. Com and Real Estate eras calmed down, the economy took a pretty good nosedive in 2008 as it readjusted to more normal times. The reality of the new nine turning seven years old, meant the novelty had largely worn off there, also.

Edgar Cordoba, was a good operational manager for us, but he proved to be less talented at managing the financial side of the club. His shtick had always been to pack the Board with as many housewives from within the membership as he could, and thereby keep the Board under his thumb, and as reigned in as he could get it.

But, when the cash flow got stretched, when the financials started showing too many red numbers, the housewives weren't much help in driving new membership sales, creating member promotions or interpreting much of the financial nuts and bolts.

It can be brutal to stand in front of an annual meeting, in an overcrowded room full of angry lawyers, who all want to know why the books are in the red, etc. And most of them have a pretty good idea of how they could do things a lot better than you. So, Edgar pretty much bought the ranch and moved on.

When he left, Bud Schmidt the greens keeper went along with him.

Edgar did leave us a nice (sic) little legacy behind though. It seems he had been feuding with some of the neighbors, especially on the new nine side of the club. This might have been inevitable to some degree. Not all those neighbors were golfers, which meant they were less than thrilled with the mowers droning on the greens at six in the morning. Or the maintenance trucks rumbling down their Magnolia Street every day, replenishing us with supplies.

If you are a golfer, these things don't bother you. Usually, they even go largely unnoticed. But to non-golfers, a dump truck full of sand, wheezing down a residential street, was not only a nuisance, but was dangerous to the kids playing on their rustic, little family cul-de-sac.

Without giving it too much forethought the club had designated Magnolia Street to be the main access point to the west side of the course, and a lot of people didn't like it.

To make matters worse, the more they bitched, the more Edgar Cordoba dug his heels in, and ignored and insulted them. His philosophy was, so you bought and built your home on a golf course, but you don't want to see or hear any golf course activity? Get over it. Live with it. This made people madder, and the more they bitched at him, the worse the cycle of animosity got.

Whether this whole little feud was just some normal venality between neighbors, or whether everyone was just a little bored, and needed some stimulation, I don't know.

I always did think it was a little unwise of Mr. Cordoba to enjoy fighting with his membership, because while many of these people weren't proprietary members, a lot of them were still Social members. Which certainly gave them a voice in things.

I had had an excellent exemplar of the kind of animosity that had been going between Edgar and the Magnolia Street neighborhood. One afternoon Hugh and I had just finished playing a round of golf, and were sitting in the bar drinking a beer. If I remember correctly, Hugh hadn't played particularly well, so he was a bit snitty anyway.

Edgar Cordoba came through the bar, and stopped for a second to chat with us.

"How do you like the new fence we built?" he asked Hugh rhetorically. He was very proud of the new divider we had recently installed at the end of the Magnolia cul-de-sac. This side entrance to the course, also came with a large, powered gate.

"I think it will give Magnolia Street more privacy, and the power gate will also get the delivery trucks off of the street quicker.

We want to be good neighbors you know'" he said with seeming sincerity. Maybe he was turning over a new leaf, who knew.

I know I was absolutely shocked by Hugh's response.

"Good neighbors?" he said. "You are the worst fucking neighbor anyone could have. You bother, endanger, and annoy us nonstop. We are forming a neighborhood group to bring our issues with you to the city. You break the law and the noise ordinances every day, and don't give a damn when we call you on it. You take pleasure in abusing your position as General Manager here. We wish to God you would leave tomorrow." Etc.

Edgar's face turned pale, and he spun on his heel, and walked away. Good for him. I wouldn't have blamed him in the least had he turned and cold cocked Hugh, knocking him off of his barstool, and on his snitty ass.

I finished my beer, and left. That was the last time I ever played golf with Hugh.

On the way out of the club, I stopped by the GM's office, and apologized for Hugh's behavior.

"I was embarrassed to have witnessed that," I told Edgar, "but you handled it very well. I had no idea these people were so vitriolic."

"Oh, it was nothing. You should hear Kudlach when he gets going. He's the worst."

Bob Kudlach was kind of like the mayor of Magnolia Street. He was an Ivy league guy, Cornell I believe, so he felt entitled. He was also a retired military pilot, and now flew commercial jets out of Portland International, for one of the major airlines. He'd flown a fighter jets in Vietnam, which made him fearless and tenacious. This guy was an absolute beast, and for some reason, he viewed Rosewood as a mortal enemy. We were like the Viet Cong to Bob Kudlach. And not just the Viet Cong, throw in the

North Koreans to boot. Perhaps he had transferred some of his frustrations over the war onto us.

I should have said the Commander of Magnolia St., because as a pilot, Bob called the shots. He ran the ship, and you were either with him, or he would get you. One way or another.

Bob was not an overly large man, but rather a solid six-footer. He was beginning to gray at the temples, but was trim enough to pass his annual airline physicals. He dressed preppy, from his Ivy league days. He was a Polo, and penny loafers' kind of guy, always with pressed Kahiki slacks.

I knew Bob well, as we had brought our restaurant staff in and had catered a couple of parties at his home. He could be a fun guy if he wanted to be. He and his wife Lillian were also regulars at Danny and Susan's parties. A couple of years ago, he came to the Halloween party dressed up like Courtney Love. He was made up all trashy looking, and was wearing women's underwear, with a huge padded bra, and a corset over that. Lillian came as Kurt Cobain. I wish I still had the pictures.

Not only was Bob tough, tenacious and street wise, he had the unique ability to attract people to himself.

Once you were with him, he was the commander, and you were one of the troops. He gave the orders, and you took 'em. Of course, he did it in such a way, like all good leaders, you thought it was your idea in the first place. But don't ever cross him, remember this fact of life. It was kind of spooky, on a more mundane scale, almost Charles Manson like. Thank God, we lived the next street over, and weren't right in the middle of all those local politics.

In addition to Hugh and Bunny, Bob's main allies were his next-door neighbors, a married couple named Neil and Carol. Carol was an attorney who worked in Portland, and Neil was in the freight forwarding business. Carol was certainly the brains of that outfit. She was also tall, leggy, and above average in attractiveness. She and Bob were particularly tight. She was his second lieutenant, and neither of them ever passed on an opportunity to take a shot over the bow of Rosewood. Carol played on his midlife insecurities, and they could often be seen with their heads together, strategizing.

The rest of the Magnolia St. players were not nearly so hostile. They rather remained neutral, but on Commander Kudlach's side. Neutral until it was time to be heard on an issue, then they would happily weigh in behind him.

Interestingly, all of this hateful odium was in the fomenting stage. Not that many people on the Board, certainly in the general membership, were even aware of it. But, I had a feeling it was going to rear its ugly head, and much sooner rather than later.

After some down time, we hired a new General Manager, who was from Bermuda Dunes Golf Resort in Palm Desert. His name was Larry Easton, and he seemed like a good fit. He was a younger acting older fellow, and this was probably going to be his last club management job. He was a good golfer, and he ended up staying around for five years before he retired. Sure enough, he was hell on wheels for his first couple of years, then kind of faded off into the sunset a bit. In between, he appeared to know just about every club management trick in the book, and always seemed to stay just a step or two ahead of everybody.

Larry's first order of business, was bringing in a new greens keeper. I don't know where he found Frank Davis, but Frank immediately set to assessing our course issues. Within months he had the greens in the best shape they had ever been in.

When we built the third nine, we did it on the cheap apparently, and didn't lay enough drainage down under all of our new sod. Our grounds being predominately clay in composition, and with the plentitude of rain six months out of the year, the new nine proved to be quite soggy all winter and in the cushion months. Frank set about aerating the fairways post haste. He did this every spring, summer and fall, three times a year, and in five years, he had built up a solid foot of impacted sand beneath the fairways.

Needless to say, the members loved this. Instead of the mushy, winter ground sucking the golf shoe off of your foot, we were now on pretty solid turf all year around.

This was the good news. The only bad news, if you want to label it, and again remember our laid-back style of club culture, was that Frank, who was also an excellent, low handicap golfer, was soon one of the boys. He could be found in the bar after the Thursday afternoon money game every week, sitting with the big hitters, enjoying a cold one. But he was a total hands on guy, and he worked so hard for us, the members grew to respect and trust him. Especially the men's club members, so if he became a little more cocky and aggressive, so what, most people just ignored it.

If he felt like we needed a new sand trap on one of the holes, in it went. If anyone said anything, it was always, "there was a maintenance problem, and while we fixed the drainage, I thought you would like a new trap too."

Or move a tee box, or lengthen a fairway, or plant fescue grass, whatever, he pretty much did as he pleased, and always with the blessing of the Greens Committee. They became a mutual support group, and if anything was ever said, the GC or the General Manager always had his back at Board meetings.

Some members resented Frank's style, but in a relatively short time Frank had created so many improvements around Rosewood, nobody ever really confronted him much. And he seemed to be able to go about his business pretty much as he pleased.

CHAPTER SIX

The Board of Trustees meeting later in the evening went a little longer than usual. We had the normal reports: President's, House, Membership, Treasury. Nothing unusual. A big fund raiser for the Susan B. Komen Foundation after the women's Member Guest Tournament was discussed. The house committee had no real issues, but had little money in the budget to do anything, anyway. Membership was also quiet, in spite of the prime season for signing up new prospects being upon us. It was announced that the sell list for the club was now over forty members who were seeking to release their memberships. The member buyout policy was discussed, and it was agreed that it would remain at the current amount of five thousand dollars. The Treasurer, was a young, very brilliant guy, a CPA, and was pretty concise. Nothing earthshaking, either good or bad. We were current on our accounts, and only a couple of members were in arrears on dues.

But Greens were another matter. It had taken a lot of lobbying, and calling a special meeting last September, but the membership had finally approved a thousand-dollar assessment to grade out a new driving range on the west side of our property. It was the last developable plot of land we owned, and the Greens guys were committed to getting our new range installed and upgraded. It was a necessity. This would include building covered stalls on the near end of the range where we could also add technical computer equipment for a new golf teaching facility at a later date.

The assessment was offered with options. You could either pay the thousand bucks up front, or starting next year, pay one hundred dollars a month for twelve months. Most people just wrote a check for the assessment, and were done with it, so the monies were largely collected, and deposited in a dedicated account, as our brilliant, young Treasurer was happy to report.

Trouble was, by the time everything was approved and collected, it was too late in the year to start any clearing or constructing on the project.

Now, we were into a new calendar year, and the Board thought it prudent to go ahead with the formalities of officially applying for a land use permit. But much to the surprise of the Greens Committee, the neighbors on Magnolia St had formally contested the findings of the City Land Use Department. They engaged an attorney (Bob's neighbor Carol), and filed a formal challenge of our conditional use permit. And on the last day of the appeals period, yet. This was received with no small amount of indignation by the GC, and the Board in general. But one thing was certain, it was going to grind any immediate progress on the project to a halt.

Especially after our board Secretary, Mr. Scott Walton, an attorney, explained the process of a land use hearing before the Examiner to us non-lawyers on the Board. It appeared to be a three or four-month process, barring delays and postponements, and it was proposed by the Secretary that we should realistically set a goal of sometime in the fall, as a wrap up date. We would also have to hire an attorney, which would cut into the assessment funds. No one was excited to go back to the membership for more monies, which meant that Frank Davis and his greens crew would have to shoulder more of the day to day work, once the project was finally approved. This was doable, as Frank was usually very hands on when he was needed, or when he got the opportunity to operate any heavy equipment.

It was decided the Executive Committee would begin a search immediately, and there were several viable and qualified attorneys right in our own membership. We had lots of options concerning who to interview, for our representation issues.

Aside from this annoying legal hurdle, no one really anticipated any problems. I mean it was our land, wasn't it? And fortunately, the Board had had Edgar Cordoba file for a land use permit in the first place. With the Magnolia neighbors filing their challenge, we would really have had some problems, if we had just gone ahead and started breaking ground, like we might have done in the past.

Charlie Strong, as Greens Committee Chair, was particularly annoyed with some of our own members taking issue with the club's operational plans.

"Those assholes live on this course, their property values are driven by the way we manage and maintain this course, yet they have the audacity to proceed this way against us. We should kick their sorry asses out of here." This is pretty much the colorful way Charlie talked, and he was never the least bit afraid to share his opinions with anyone. Even though it was a ridiculous assumption, that we would start arbitrarily kicking members out of the club every time there was a disagreement of some kind.

The news of the Land Use appeal by the Magnolians spread pretty quickly through the membership, and with much grumbling.

We began to see less and less of Hugh and Bunny. Danny and Susan already were in the process of moving to Bend, Oregon and Mount Bachelor country, so they were pretty much out of there. The rest of the Magnolians were Social Members, and didn't matter much anyway. Bob Kudlach was a social member, but he had no qualms about showing up at the bar whenever he felt like it. He liked to rub his adversarial presence in our collective noses, and Charlie's blood pressure would just about blow, whenever he saw Kudlach around the club.

After a couple of weeks, the Exec Committee recommended the hiring of a big land use guy, who was indeed one of our members. His name was George Richardson, and he had worked on some pivotal developments in the Portland area. Even some golf course stuff. He had done one very cool development, where they had gone right over a land fill, and developed a stunning golf course, replete with residential homes. They really brought that property back up to its highest and best use, and we all were very impressed with Mr. Richardson.

In a special conference with the Board, immediately after we ratified his employment, GR shared his strategy with us. Requesting our complete and utter confidentiality, he was very informative about time lines and delegating specific functions to individual board members.

Mr. Richardson's only reservation, seemed to be with the selection of the Hearing Examiner. She was a veteran of these proceedings, and George knew her well. He had actually appeared before her bench on several occasions. She was apparently of a liberal bent, and as Washington's land use laws and interpretations seemed to be drifting in that direction on a statewide basis, her ruling as our Examiner was a bit of a concern to him. Yet as he explained to us, this was a conditional permit application and hearing. There would be no actual hard development of this land. In effect, it was being preserved for posterity through the restricted use of the property that we had defined. Although the property in question would be stripped of any meaningful vegetation, there would still be no residential development. This relatively harmless and conforming use to the rest of the property, should take us home with little if any problem. He would see to it personally.

And who wouldn't believe him? Although he wasn't a large guy stature wise, he was well tanned, and had a hundred-dollar haircut. His gray flannel slacks were perma creased as if by an Asian specialist. He wore button down collared shirts, a snappy blue blazer, and designer ties from the Nordstrom men's department. His black, shiny loafers even had tassels. We knew we had our man.

Our biggest job as a Board, was to beat the drum, and collect as much support on behalf of the project as we could. Especially from long term members, who could attest to the precedents already long established by the club in its ongoing land use function. And also by members who lived near the proposed driving range. Many of us would be more than willing to testify on how little impact there would actually be on our day to day lives. How we would much prefer having open space there, rather than the club deciding to build town houses, and block our views of the course.

Heck, I didn't care. Our house abutted the far end of the proposed range, with our property angled away from the landing areas, and the front of our house facing the street. That driving range wouldn't affect us much at all.

Whereas, one whole side of Magnolia St. abutted directly onto the proposed range. That amounted to about a dozen houses whose yards would back right up to the range, including the Kudlach's and the Horn's.

I have never met anyone with a burning desire to live right next to a driving range, as they are basically pretty ugly to look at. What with all of the stripped balls laying around, the obnoxious netting, and then the sound of golf balls being whacked at all hours of the day. Not to mention the evening ball whacking, and the night lighting. So, I could see their problem with the proposal. Not to mention the fact that Magnolia Street seemed to hate our guts anyway.

So, this was the reason Rosewood was magnanimously proposing to plant a fifty-foot barrier of vegetation of their choice between ourselves, and the Magnolia Street properties. We all seemed to think this was a pretty generous offer. Heck, plant a redwood forest back there, and have a green belt behind you for life. We also offered to eliminate any artificial lighting, and limit the range to operation only during the natural daylight hours. Plus, use state of the art fencing that would muffle and mute a lot of the golf ball striking metal pole noises.

George felt that with these mitigating offers, the Magnolians and Mr. Kudlach, would come to their senses, and withdraw their appeal. Or at the very worst, we would proceed with the litigation, and the Examiner would find in our favor.

Our first item on the punch list, was to get the pre-trial hearing scheduled, and begin recruiting our support team. GR would tend to the first task, and I was on the committee to help with the second matter of business.

CHAPTER SEVEN

While we were busy getting ready for the pretrial hearing, life kept moving along at the Rosewood.

One of our members offered to donate some wine for a tasting dinner. The member was another brilliant attorney, heading up the Labor and Anti-Trust Division of the biggest law firm in all of Oregon. This man had put himself through his L3 studies working at a pulp mill in his home town of Aberdeen, Washington. He had then gone on to his illustrious career, and achieved glory, through hard work, long hours and one of the most pleasant dispositions I have ever encountered.

Mark and his wife were probably the nicest members at our club. Just genuinely fine, good people. Always a wine aficionado, Mark decided to start his own Winery. He purchased grapes for a couple of years, and had one of the best vintners in Walla Walla, Washington, blend his end product for him. The wine was an immediate success.

Next, he purchased eighty five acres of fertile land in Milton-Freewater, Oregon, which is just south of Walla Walla. We went over and inspected his first crop of grapes on the new to him property, and enjoyed dinners with Mark and his lovely wife. It was indeed a special weekend in the sun dappled wine country. Within three years, Mark's Syrah was rated one of the top twelve wines in the freaking world. I swear everything this guy touches turns to gold.

Mark wanted to donate a couple cases of his Syrah to the club for a wine tasting dinner. As I was heading up the Rosewood wine committee at the time, we planned a beautiful event for the end of June. It is a time when our weather is getting close to perfection.

Champagne on the deck to welcome everyone. A lovely Lobster Bisque, accompanied by an incredibly deep Washington Chardonnay, with the most pleasant dark cherry tones from Kystrel Vintners in Prosser. Our club Chef at the time was a young woman, who was very creative. Her second course was an organic greens salade. Fresh from the gardens, with seasonal garni, and the best salad dressing I have ever tasted. It was a Pomegranate vinaigrette, rich with virgin oil, yet light and fruity. It was accompanied by a perfumed Viognier varietal, again from our prolific state. I must have had a dozen people come up to me after dinner, and compliment the salad dressing alone.

For our entrée, Chef presented us with Seared Filet Mignon. Oh, and oops, the purveyor had made an error, and sent us Kobe beef by mistake. No problem, we were very helpful in taking it off of his hands.

The Syrah and the Kobe were an inspired combination. For desert, Chef served some divine chocolate concoction. Utterly heaven. The whole dinner.

If your club does wine dinners, they are almost always a great value. The club has already purchased or planned out the wine, the food is usually above grade, and the club must keep the prices affordable in order to sell out the event. In order to promote their event, the club is happy to break even on this type of function. Which means good deal for the member. The event sells out, which is good for the club, the Chefs and Winemakers get to show off their stuff, etc. Everyone is happy.

Unfortunately, Larry Easton wasn't at the dinner, and didn't get to sample the greatness the rest of us enjoyed that evening. Even more unfortunately, when I came back to the club the next Tuesday afternoon for a committee meeting, Larry had fired our Chef. I couldn't believe it, and was not hesitant to tell him what I thought.

"There were other problems in the kitchen," he said gruffly to me.

In talking to some of my sources in the kitchen, they said the Chef had some ongoing problems controlling a few of the male line cooks. They told me when she got frustrated, she talked incessantly. Just a real nonstop chatterbox, nothing but nervous tension. But maybe with more support from Larry, she wouldn't have gotten so frustrated with her staff in the first place.

It turned out Larry Easton wasn't a real big F&B fan from the get go, and wasn't too supportive of that department no matter what was going on. He had another plan up his sleeve anyway, and within a week had hired a new chef, a Frenchman, as a replacement.

I was very peeved with him, and tried to hire his ex-Chef at my own Restaurant, but she was apparently burned out on kitchens. She went off, and started a new career in commercial food sales.

Larry's new Chef was a classically trained, turned nouvelle Frenchman, but a club is different from a French Restaurant or even a Bistro. Maybe it is more like a Gastro pub. Where gourmet wine dinners are certainly appreciated, but the members also just want to have a good, old fashioned burger or club sandwich for lunch a lot of the time. And with fries please, hold the fermented Lentil Salad. As stated, dinners were pretty well received, even so, the staff was really not trained in formal Continental service. And Larry Easton was certainly no service trainer.

To help bridge the gap between regimes, Larry and the new Chef decided to offer some cooking classes to the members. The first set of classes were to be classic appetizers, paired with appropriate wines for the ladies, right after their Tuesday golf activities. The first couple dozen or so ladies to sign up every week were in. If this first series of classes went well, the girls would graduate from appetizers on to more complex concepts.

The second group of classes, were geared toward the men, if any were interested. They would be held on Tuesday evenings, and would also be basic in nature. How to braise a roast, how to prepare some starter sauces, make chili, make your own barbeque mops and rubs, etc. Of course, there would be adult beverages involved.

The women's classes were very well received. They were sold out a month in advance. The men's classes, too, were enthusiastically supported.

Soon, there emerged some star pupils in the lady's groups, and apparently the ladies were smitten by the handsome young Frenchman. He, with the gorgeous accent, and the misty, soft Gaelic eyes.

Many of the wives found the petite food and selected wines, combined with the chef's personal instruction somewhat overwhelming. They began to spruce up their appearance for the cooking classes. They all seemed willing to come early, and stay late type of thing. There was almost the undercurrent of competition for the young chef's attention.

Maybe it was the fine, silk blouses with the scooped necks. Maybe it was the professional level make up, or the dangling, diamond earrings. Perhaps it was the subtle fragrances, or the slight blush of their cheeks in his presence, but it was quite apparent the new chef was a huge hit so far. Mais, helas! Our nouvelle chef was more interested in the men's personal instruction, and began to show a particular interest in one of our older members. A gentleman and social member, with substantial means. The attention was reciprocated, and began to be the talk of the club. Unfortunately for the chef, it is most difficult to maintain one's privacy in either a small town, or a private club.

In due time, word got back to Larry about what was happening, and he was obligated to fire his new, overpaid chef. Even as casual as we had become, fraternization was strictly prohibited in our Rosewood employment contracts.

What did the Frenchman care? There is always work for a properly trained chef. If he should get a temporary layoff, for inappropriate conduct so be it. Especially if it is in the summertime. A French chef will always find a new position when desired. And in the meantime, his new friend was comfortably positioned to soften any financial hardships he might have suffered.

And, if anyone was left holding the bag, it was us, the faithful. And I guess, the crestfallen ladies club. Now it was going on August, with the member guest golf tournaments coming up, as well as a busy summer season, and we were Chefless in Vancouver. Larry was forced to promote the sous chef to the number one spot. No bargain there, as the sous was a local boy, with limited training, and with no real experience running a busy kitchen. So, we all had to lower our standards for the rest of the year.

On the legal front, we were proceeding along nicely. The membership was only too happy to bear witness on behalf of the club.

We had even more than we needed of fresh, friendly faces who were ready to step up for our committee. Besides, the Magnolians didn't even seem to have their own attorney.

The pretrial hearing came up just before the men's member guest tournament, which was always the first weekend in August.

I will never forget how professional George Richardson looked in his charcoal Armani suit. His posture and bearing in the courtroom. His starched white shirt, and the polished silver necktie. Silk, of course. Even his flourishes and gestures were superb, and seemed designed to win the Judge over to our side with nonverbal communication alone.

The courtroom was packed. Standing room only, and apparently, the Magnolians had gone out and recruited all of their own friends to come and sit in on their behalves. This was seriously high drama to them. To us, it was just a driving range. An empty field in which to hit golf balls. What was the big deal?

Opening arguments were made with Kudlach acting as attorney for them, and George Richardson, of course, representing Rosewood. George made a very impressive opening argument, using many whereas' and wherefores', and generally outclassing Kudlach by a mile.

The Magnolians first witness was Carol Horn, Mr. Kudlach's neighbor and protégé, who got on the stand, raised her right hand to take her oath, and then actually started crying. She explained in a tearful, halting voice to everyone, that we were trying to kill her children with our errant golf balls. Her performance was compelling. It was worthy of an Oscar nomination.

Then Kudlach marched in from the back room, wheeling a 55 gallon steel drum on a hand cart. While he was coming in, he was bouncing a golf ball off of the steel barrel, and catching it only to slam it down again off of the barrel. This made such a godawful racket that immediately, he got everyone's nerves on edge.

"This is what we will be forced to endure, in our own homes on a daily basis," Kudlach explained to the Judge, and all of assembled in the courtroom. The Rosewoodies were stunned by this gross exaggeration, and manipulation of the truth. We had absolutely no intention of putting anyone through anything remotely resembling Mr. Kudlach's vivid presentation. Yet the damn Hearing Examiner sat there shaking her head and staring at Kudlach in deepest sympathy. The gravity of this situation has finally been exposed, was the expression on her face.

Even George Richardson seemed taken aback, and in my opinion fumbled his delivery several times while making a rebuttal.

"Our netting support poles will be extensively padded and protected," Mr. Richardson explained. But he just didn't seem to have made the same impact as Mr. Kudlach.

The rest of the pretrial proceeded rather uneventfully. Numerous parties from both sides testified succinctly, and the input seemed to be well balanced. We certainly had the precedence of an extended land use track record on our side. Also, numerous expert witnesses swore there would be no major injury or personal intrusions caused by the new range.

But the Magnolians were very sincere and convincing when they cried about their children's survival. And about the hordes, mobs really, of fanatics who would be out at the range from dawn until midnight noisily slugging golf balls. They would also surely be drinking heavily, laughing loudly, and swearing uncontrollably.

Hugh and Bunny got on the stand and lied their asses off. Hugh actually had the nerve to suggest that, while we said we wouldn't have artificial lighting, as soon as the permit was granted, we would do whatever we wanted.

Bunny cried, and told how we broke the law every day with our lawn mowers running full blast at sun up, our sprinkler system going on at all hours of the night. Both of these inexcusable intrusions, rudely woke her up, and gave her terrible migraine headaches almost every day. She had tried to get Rosewood to change their maintenance schedule. But they were so very big and overpowering, and she was just one little person. She forgot to add that to get rid of the headaches, she had to go out into her rose garden, with virtually no clothes on, to assuage her painful condition.

The pretrial finally ended with a thud. No more real drama, but for all of Barrister Richardson's courtroom maneuvers, the other side seemed to have grasped the momentum. By all appearance, they were ready to spring a stunning defeat, unless we could think of something pretty fast. No luck there, and so we all adjourned.

The Judge said she would post her decision by the end of next week, and we trudged off to go work on our golf games. To do anything really, to get out of the Hearing Examiner's presence.

CHAPTER EIGHT

As we rolled into August, the Board was obligated to elect new officers for the operating year which began September 1. This is an interesting time on our board, because some members have no desire to serve as an officer, while others are chomping at the bit to gain the title and enjoy the notoriety of representing the membership. Still others are interested in serving, because they have an agenda. And the chance to be the President of the board brings an excellent opportunity to fulfill that agenda, if it is at all reasonable in scope.

Such was the case with our elections for the coming year. Charlie Strong badly wanted the Office of President, as he was totally committed to the concept of the new driving range, and wanted to see this project to fruition. Charlie had Bruce Cranston nominate him, and since no one else really wanted the job, he ran unopposed.

Our hotshot young CPA's term on the Board was ending, and so I volunteered to take over as Treasurer. No one else wanted that job either. Therefore, I figured getting close to the books, and the accountings of the club, would prepare me to run for the Presidency next year. After the eventual passage of the driving range application, then maybe I could convince people to put some resources into the Clubhouse. Also, I would be on the executive committee, which was a ticket to the inner circle.

The Board members were a little skeptical of Charlie's ability to perform as President of the Club. With his very reckless style and colorful language, which seemed to worsen exponentially as his frustration or alcohol level rose, there were definitely issues. But he toned his act down around election time, stopped coming to the Board meetings all tipsy, and cleaned himself up pretty well. So, he was elected unanimously, with Bruce Cranston ratified as Vice-President, Roger Taylor, another attorney as our new Secretary, and myself as Treasurer.

Rick Ferin, Charlie's golfing and union buddy, was coming onto the Board, and he was going to serve as Chairman of the Green's Committee.

This lineup was very satisfactory to Charlie, as he now controlled the Board, the Exec Committee, and also the Green's Committee. Larry Easton, the general manager, had been around long enough to understand well insulated Presidents, and his style was to be supportive of the President anyway. So, Larry would see that he and Charlie got along famously. I mean, who but the President can really cause a problem for the GM on a day to day basis? And unless everything fell totally apart, taking care of the President was a very good business/survival strategy.

I figured to lay low, and be in a solid position to get my clubhouse redo going. If not a total remodel, then certainly the visible installation of some strategic elements. And depending on the driving range, who knew what might happen.

George Richardson attended our Board Meeting in September. After the election of the new Slate of Officers, which was the first order of business, he brought us all up to speed on the Hearing Examiner front.

It was a common practice, he told us, for Examiners, barring a preponderance of evidence to the contrary, to go ahead and remand the prehearing over to a formal hearing. Especially when there was a strong showing from the involved community, and in this case, there certainly was lots of pushback.

He reminded us how we had already been approved by the Planning Commission, the Department of Land Use, and we had made a serious effort to mitigate the concerns of the community. The testimony of the Community had largely been emotional, and therefore, should prove ultimately ineffective.

Without being able to guarantee us 100% approval at this second upcoming hearing, George's felt it was as close to a slam dunk as could be expected. And of course, his billable hours kept adding up, while he was working every angle of our case.

Someone from the board reminded us of Rosewood's long-standing commitment to Junior Golf, and how we donated use of the course every year to both the High School Boys and Girls Golf Teams. How beneficial this was to the kids, and how many exemplary kids we had helped by our support. I think this topic was raised for our consideration by Bruce Cranston, who was totally in Charlie's back pocket, but he was a retired Professor of Economics, and therefore no dumbbell.

George Richardson loved this idea immediately, and as a current club member, was embarrassed he had not thought of it himself. We appointed a subcommittee on the spot, to contact the coaches, the High School Athletic Director, and as many players, both current and former, who would be willing to appear at the hearing on our behalf. As an adequate driving range is critical to the performance of any golfer, especially young men and women, who are in the learning phase of the game, who could possibly deny the kids, our own kids, the virtual community's future, an opportunity to master our noble game.

The date for the Hearing had been scheduled for the last week in September, and George was positively beaming as he left our meeting. We were all much more comfortable about the possibilities of the range. This new and expanded strategic breakthrough, and George's optimism on our behalf, had swung the tide back over to our side.

Rosewood's golfing couples usually take a trip in early September. We try to take advantage of the last of the optimal weather, and with school having restarted, most courses are starting to calm down from their busy summers. This can usually mean some pretty good golf and lodging rates for medium sized groups such as ours.

This year we were all going down to the fairly new Bandon Dunes Golf Club on the southern Oregon coast. Some of the guys had already made it down there, but the majority of us were Bandon virgins. We were all excited to experience this recently developed area, which had burst onto the national golfing scene in such dramatic fashion. It had basically taken the golf world by storm. It was world class, and it was right in our own backyards.

You could hardly pick up a golf magazine, be it Golf Digest, Golf World, etc. without finding a first-hand narrative of Bandon's magnificence. The breathtakingly spectacular views, and the painstaking attention to detail, in recreating a significant tribute to the authentic links style courses of the old world. We were all anxious to get down there and try it for ourselves. And as it is only about a four-hour drive from us, it is a local treasure.

Couples' golf trips can sometimes be a challenge, especially when the destinations are not too dramatic. Some of the less committed players, or couples who have played poorly early on, or maybe someone who has incurred a back injury or something, can lose interest. They drift away to the spa, or a movie or anything else, which of course screws up all of the pairings. It is usually the hardest on the organizers, and it seems like you certainly can't please all of the people all of the time. Most organizers are good for one year, and the general attitude afterwards, is never again.

But Bandon was going to be different. This was first rate, a deluxe trip, and we had twelve couples who were our better club players going. We were committed to a great three and a half days of tournament golf.

Bandon itself is very impressive. The grounds are expansive, and well appointed. The entry road winds through tall, majestic fir and cedar trees, to the large, substantial Lodge. The Lodge area and pro shop sit up on high bluffs overlooking the Pacific Ocean. After checking in and receiving our room keys, we met in the bar to have a cocktail. We got there in time to enjoy the sunset, and set up pairings for the next morning's round.

On these outings, a golf pro will come along to oversee the scoring. Since a few of the gals' husbands don't play, or they are widows, the golf pro will partner up with them and be a part of the group. As the Pros are PGA professionals, they don't pay greens fees, and the group pitches in and pays for the pros lodging. Our attendant Pro this year was Jerry DePietro. He was actually one of the assistants, who had been with us for about a year. He was an ex ball player in the Dodger's system, had actually been up to the major leagues for a cup of coffee. Obviously, he was a great athlete. Big and strong. He could hit the ball a mile, and was also a good golf teacher.

The next thing you realize about Bandon Dunes, is that it is all about golf. Just golf. There is no swimming pool, let alone kiddie pool. There is no spa, no ballroom, no concierge or recreation director. There is quite a nice restaurant, and plenty of bars. There is a golf library on the second floor of the main lodge. The main lodge is highly desirable, because it is closer to the main bar, and then there are cabins spread out on the property. The cabins are nicely appointed, and all include stately river rock fireplaces. They are comfortable and cozy, substantial, and perfect for a couple's get away.

Our package included breakfast and dinner for three days, with one last breakfast on Friday morning. We teed off at nine am Tuesday morning, and it was truly a spectacular day. There are now four courses, the last I heard, but at the time there were only two. We played the original Bandon Course and half the holes are in the sand dunes, and the other half run adjacent to the cliffs. They are about one hundred feet high, and the views of the ocean are outstanding. They look straight down on the shores of the Pacific, and then out to sea as far as the eye can behold. Our weather was great, which is sometimes not the case. The Oregon coastal winds can kick up at any time, or rain can also come in in force. Neither of those options are optimal. But those conditions can also closely simulate the conditions of the British Isles, which is the birthplace of the game of Golf.

After our morning round, we had lunch in the bar, and some of the guys elected to go back out for another eighteen holes. Lunch was great, and Jeanine and I had done well playing together. She is a lot of fun to go out with, as she has worked hard on her game. She hits the ball very well off of the tee, and therefore we usually do pretty well in couple's competitions.

We had lunch with Charlie Strong and his new girlfriend. He was lively as ever, regaling us with stories of golfing in the Bahamas on the union's nickel. Sounded to me like nothing was too good for those guys, and that the union, which ever one it was, certainly liked to keep up the morale of its troops. I think his new girlfriend was duly impressed. She was certainly amused by his stories, smiling broadly, and flashing her cleavage, and her perfect, pearly white teeth at all of us.

So, it went for our three and a half days. Another thing about Bandon, is that it is pretty isolated. Just some small Oregon coastal towns around, so when you get to Bandon, you stay at Bandon. But there are lots of practice facilities to work on your golf game, lots of good beer on tap, plenty of scotch whiskey, the golf library, your daily spectacular round of golf, and then a great salmon or steak dinner to look forward to at night.

I think we won some money at the end of the week, but everyone had a good time, and we headed back up the beautiful Oregon coast for home. Jeanine's mom had volunteered to watch the kids for us, and so we stopped for one last getaway night in Cannon Beach. Cannon is another fantastic spot up the coast from Bandon. It has gorgeous beaches and huge glacial rock deposits all along the shoreline. The beach is flat and firm, solid for jogging and beachcombing, and goes on and on seemingly forever. We had another quality night, thanks to mom, and headed back to Vancouver, after a leisurely morning, and a stop in town for a hearty country breakfast.

Getting home late the next afternoon, I immediately went over to the restaurant to get my desk caught up. September is still a busy month, and apparently, Vancouver continued to enjoy the products out of the new smoker we had invested in this summer. Having lived in Texas for three years while I was with the Hyatt Corporation, I fell in love with Texas Barbeque, and we were bringing parts of the Texas smoking tradition to the northwest.

I went out to the bar to see our bar manager, when one of the Rosewoodies came in for happy hour.

"Did you hear what happened at the club?" he asked me.

"No" I replied. "I just got back about an hour ago."

"Larry fired Nate Tucker," he told me. Nate Tucker was our golf pro, and I had thought it really odd that he wasn't on our Bandon trip. Especially since Charlie was there.

"Really," I was shocked, and knew that Charlie Strong would be greatly upset. Nate and Charlie were the best of golf buddies. They had even traveled to Europe with a group of guys to play some of Great Brittan's finest old courses. They all drank world class liquor and Guinness beer, fresh from the distilleries and the brewery in Dublin. Charlie probably even told a few tales for all of their entertainment.

"Wow, what did he fire him for?" I asked. Thinking to myself, it must be bad, especially for Larry to act out of character like this.

"I don't know" was the response. "Something to do with the books I think."

CHAPTER NINE

Turns out Charlie had gotten the word on quicker than anyone. He had stopped in the Pro Shop to shoot the bull with the guys upon arriving back at Rosewood after the drive home from Bandon Dunes.

"Where's Nathan?" he asked curtly, to one of the cart boys, a little annoyed that Nate wasn't in the shop.

"Uh, he doesn't work here anymore," the kid replied.

"What???" Charlie screeched. "What do you mean he doesn't work here anymore?"

"He left a couple of days ago," the kid informed him. "Some kind of a problem with the General Manager."

Charlie stomped off for Larry Easton's office, with fire in his eyes, and malice in his heart.

"What the fuck is going on around here" Charlie hissed at Larry, when he finally found him in the back-bar area, checking on the weekend's wine order.

"Calm down" Larry implored in a chastised voice. "I assume you are talking about Nate?"

"You damn right I'm talking about Nate, you asshole." Larry and Charlie were now standing face to face. Larry told me later, he felt like Charlie was going to take a swing at him.

"He quit," Larry told Charlie.

"He quit?" said Charlie. "How is that possible. They said in the Pro Shop there was a problem."

"There was a problem. And it is a big problem. You know we are starting the Capital Budget process for next year, and you also know the membership authorized the Board to lease equipment for the Greens crew last year. Well Frank was starting to check on terms and prices with some of the equipment reps, and they said our credit rating was terrible."

"What are you talking about" snapped Charlie. "This is Rosewood. We've been here for sixty years. We pay our bills."

"I know," Larry assured him. "But the problem is not with the Golf Club. It's in the Pro Shop. Nate hasn't been keeping current on his invoices. He pays the bills, but he is always in arrears, and therefore, our credit rating is bad."

"This is no reason to fire the guy," Charlie fumed.

"I didn't fire him," Larry responded. "I told him this was serious stuff, and we would have to have an Executive Committee meeting when you got back. He just told me he was resigning. He said his wife had gotten her dream job in Seattle, with some new tech firm up there. Amazon, I think he said. Plus, it was a lot closer to her family, so they were going to relocate."

"You better be telling it like it is," Charlie snapped at Larry, and turned on his heel and left.

This type of confrontation was not foreign to Charlie. He was truly a man with a short fuse.

Charlie grew up in Akron, Ohio. He was the middle child of three brothers. His mom, Alice, was a stay at home mom, and did her best to keep up with her rowdy sons. Charlie's dad, Cliff, was a working agent for the United Auto Workers Union at the local Firestone Tire factory.

Cliff supervised a team in the machinery section of the plant. He was also the shop steward, and helped take care of problems with the rank and file. He made sure everyone knew how to vote if there were ever any agenda items at the annual meeting. Collections were his specialty, and he rounded up the weekly numbers money due from within the plant. He dutifully passed it on upstairs. It was a fairly significant amount, maybe five grand a week, so he was a trusted soldier for his Union bosses. Once in a while there was a collection problem, which Cliff and a couple of his boys would take care of as quietly as possible. But life was fairly calm in Akron for the most part.

While all of Cliff and Alice's boys loved sports, Charlie was the star athlete of the three. He played both ways on his high school football team, center on offense, and middle line-backer on defense. He was also honorable mention all-state catcher on his baseball team. But football was his first love. He just enjoyed hitting people. And it was all legal. Charlie's life was basically the All-American Midwest diet of sports, cars and girls.

After high school Charlie went to Junior College. He took classes for a year, including some in the College of Business, which would prove useful to him later on. But he had never been much of a student, and to tell the truth, college bored him to death. Despite the fact Charlie was going to school in the middle of the flower power/free love era, or of the fact that major social rumblings were sweeping the country, he wanted to be in the middle of more intense action. So, he turned down several athletic scholarships, went out and volunteered for a four-year hitch in the United States Marine Corps. The few, the Proud, the Marines. Semper Fi. This is what appealed to him.

If anyone was born to be a Marine, it was Charlie. He was six feet tall and solid as a fire hydrant. He was tough, athletic, and smart enough to get what he wanted, without questioning orders and authority. He actually enjoyed boot camp, and soon became a favorite with the non-com instructors. Plus, he was stationed at Camp Pendleton, in Oceanside, California.

Charlie made Private first class, E-2, out of Basic training, and volunteered for a month of leadership training, before going on to his post boot camp, advanced training. With his preferred status with the non-coms, Charlie had his weekends mostly off, which meant that he could head for the beach at Carlsbad or San Onofre. He learned how to hang with the surfer crowd.

Charlie was strictly a novice surfer, and the locals didn't take much to the occasional Jarheads that came around. But Charlie could have cared less. He kept to himself, was fearless in the water, lounged on the beach, and enjoyed watching the girls in their skimpy string bikinis. Hell, he thought, this beats the crap out of life in Akron, Ohio.

Charlie picked up another stripe, to E-3 Lance Corporal after leadership school, and began advanced training as a platoon leader for the two-month session that would try and teach him how survive in Vietnam. Again, he excelled. Almost everyone in the Marines is a volunteer. There are occasional recruits, but since almost everyone signed up to be there, everyone is on the same page. And since Charlie was one of the toughest guys in his Company, no one gave him any lip. He became a respected and effective platoon leader. He had the makings of a classic Marine Soldier.

After prelim training was over, Charlie once more volunteered. This time to go back to Fort Benning, Georgia for training with the 101st Airborne Division, and become an Airborne Ranger. After two months of jumping out of airplanes, Charlie was promoted again. He was now an E-5 Buck Sargent, and was a trained fighting machine for the United States of America. No one could have been prouder than Charlie in his Marine Dress Uniform at Airborne Graduation.

After a two-week furlough, Charlie shipped out to Ton Son Nhut Air Base in Saigon, Vietnam, and he couldn't wait to get there. Charlie was in Heaven. He was seeing the world, and he was in superb physical shape. He loved what he was doing, and now he was ready and trained for some real action. As it was spring in Akron, and still crummy weather-wise, Charlie elected to go spend his furlough in Florida, before leaving for the war. Compare those beaches to California's finest. Charlie's parents flew down to Pensacola, to spend a week with him before he was to report back to Ft. Benning and fly overseas.

Charlie processed into country, and after a few days on detail, was assigned to a Marine Infantry Company in Da Nang, Vietnam, just south of the Demilitarized Zone in the heart of Vietnam's infamous, mountainous, central jungle.

The jungle suited Charlie to a tee. No matter how bad things got, Charlie thrived. He had the unique personality to suffer adversity. It stimulated him.

"You want to kick my ass," Charlie would say to himself, "Well come on, motherfucker." Charlie's platoon saw how tough he was, and loved him for it. He was fair with everyone, but tough, and allowed no slacking.

Hacking base camps out of the jungle is no bargain, but Charlie led the charge. It was hot and humid, the work of humping and clearing logs, and making a perimeter was tough, hard work. The choppers would bring in supplies, and blow gritty dust like tiny glass shards everywhere. In the afternoons, the monsoon rains would come, and soak everything down, turning the camp into steamy muck. And then at night, the real fun began. Guerilla Warfare!

Jungle patrols were the real deal for Charlie. As base camp was usually set up in proximity to a village, the Marine company would send out four squads a night, trying to patrol in the four directions if possible. The adrenaline rush for Charlie was just what he had hoped for when he signed up.

Stealth was the code-word. The columns would file out of camp in single order, as heavily armed as they dared. Proceeding either on the outmost margin of the one lane dirt roads, or through lightly vegetated terrain, crouched, silent, but hyper alert. A false move or lapse, could mean disaster. If and when contact was made with the Viet Cong, a firefight would ensue, and the Cobra Gunships were called in.

Gain as much cover as possible, use a surge of fire to suppress the enemy, and pray the choppers got there quickly. Charlie loved those Cobra choppers, but he also felt by being the best of the best, he could meet the enemy on his own terms and survive. He had been in country for six months, and hadn't been proven wrong yet.

Charlie particularly loved the mornings after a firefight. He would take his company, go back out to their patrol location, and observe firsthand in the light of day, all of the carnage the firefight and the Cobras gunships had wrought the previous night. It was eerie to see uniformed grown men, shot down in place. Some sprawled out on their backs, some on their faces. Some dead, but still crouching with their weapons, and in a few cases, with their eyeglasses still on. These were the enemy, and the more of them Charlie saw dead in the light of day, the better he liked it.

Nerves could get a little strained out there in the jungle, and one time there was a new second lieutenant assigned to Charlie's company. This guy was straight out of Officer's Training Academy, and was pretty green. Apparently, he was a by the numbers soldier, and took issue with the casual style of dress in base camp.

He didn't understand the rugged nature of life in the jungle, where any day you woke up, could be your last, and where things become much more relaxed than back at Headquarters. Soldiers wear wife beater t-shirts, and sloppy fatigue pants. They have towels around their necks at all times, to cover their heads when the supply choppers drop into camp. There are no personal physicians around to help them keep the biting dust out of their facial cavities. They may or may not be wearing proper head gear. If they are wearing head gear, it may be on backwards or sideways. Boots are far from being shined daily.

The new second Louie carped at the guys for a week or two about this mundane kind of stuff, until finally Charlie had had enough. One morning, he motioned the Louie, who was out on his morning rounds of camp, over behind one of the perimeter guard post bunkers.

"Hey asshole, which do you prefer, a bullet up your ass or in the back of your head? Because if you don't stop fucking with my men on all of this regulations shit, I will kill you. Do you understand me?"

The second Louie was mortally insulted, not to mention alarmed at Charlie's direct insubordination.

"You are going to the brig for threatening an officer, Strong" the Louie shot back at him.

"Yeah, we'll see about that" Charlie grunted at him, spit on the dusty ground, and walked away.

The Lieutenant reported immediately to the Commandant's tent.

"Sir, I am reporting a case of gross insubordination. I would like to have Sargent Strong served with an Article Five reprimand, and confined to base camp, until this matter is adjudicated." He proceeded to explain the confrontation to the Captain.

"Well now, son" the Captain drawled to his second Louie. "Haven't you figured out yet that Charlie Strong is the best soldier I have in this Company? You do know I am recommending him for a Distinguished Medal of Honor, don't you? Let's say we all calm down, and just forget this little swivet ever happened?"

Within two weeks of carefully watching his back, the Second Lieutenant was out of there, having been assigned to an administrative post back at Headquarters.

After a year and a half in the jungle, and another eighteen months back at Headquarters, processing fresh recruits into the country, Charlie Strong mustered out of the Marines in Oakland, California. He had been promoted to E-6 Staff Sargent, received his Medal of Honor, been on R&R to Australia and Bangkok, Thailand, and was ready to go home.

It wasn't so much the killing that got to him, as the too frequent losses of his own men in battle. That ate away at his guts. And those losses for what, he wasn't quite sure of anymore.

Charlie liked the West Coast. After taking some time off to travel and regroup, he got work through one of his dad's union connections with the International Longshoremen and Warehouse Union. They were based out of San Francisco. The irony that Charlie had just returned from fighting to protect our country from Communism in the jungles of Vietnam, to go to work for an organization that had once been accused of strong Communist affiliations after the Second World War, was of little significance to Charlie. He was a man of action, not lofty principles or conceptual ideals.

Starting as a gofer in the union offices in San Francisco would prove to be another windfall for Charlie. The ILWU offices managed labor unions from Southern California, to Alaska, to Hawaii, to British Columbia, Canada. The ILWU's membership included dockworkers, fishermen, cannery workers, any number of seagoing vessel operators, hotel employees, warehousemen, and even book store workers in Portland, Oregon.

Charlie quickly moved up through the union ranks. He worked for the ILWU in San Francisco for ten years, he fought wild cat strikers. He recruited faithfully for the ILWU, busted some heads here and there, unionized new markets, collected bad debts, worked his butt off, and basically paid his dues.

Charlie married once, but was always on the go. He didn't prove to be much of a family man. He never had any kids, and divorced after a few years. As a reward for time well served, the ILWU promoted Charlie up to the Portland, Oregon office as Head Agent.

He moved to Vancouver, joined us at Rosewood Golf Club, and dedicated himself to his new job in the Rose City.

There is an old golfing story of an unnamed Chicago mobster, who was a member at a prestigious windy city club. The mobster had plenty of time on his hands, and used to enjoy a daily game of golf with his cronies. After golf, they took lunch and drinks in the club's venerable grillroom.

The pro shop got a new head golf professional, and the new young man seemed very serious. He was dedicated to helping provide the membership with the finest golf experience available.

About half a year into his new job, after analyzing the outcome of some six months' worth of tournament and daily play results, the new pro began to see some unusual scoring patterns. He decided that some of the members golfing handicaps needed to be adjusted. Making the proper corrections, the neophyte pro posted the new handicap roster on his shop's bulletin board.

Unwittingly, the new pro had dropped the mobster's handicap by four strokes. This was not a smart move.

The mobster sent a couple of his men around to correct the situation with the new pro. They explained that the gentleman in question wished that his long-standing handicap be restored to its original state, and that the pro's over-all health might be better suited to the sunny climes in Florida. Wisely, the new pro understood the message, and was on the train out of Chicago within a couple of days.

For some reason, this story reminds me of Charlie Strong.

CHAPTER TEN

They say opposites attract, and this was certainly true of Rick Ferin and Charlie Strong. While Charlie was outgoing and gregarious, Rick was morose and ill tempered. While Charlie was the life of the party and a master raconteur, Rick was a man of a few words. He did not suffer fools gladly. Yet the two men were best of friends.

Charlie had no immediate kin nearby, but Rick had grown up close by, and was connected. He was a small-town guy, from Castle Rock, Washington, just up the road to the north of us here in Vancouver.

Rick's father was a logger, and worked for Weyerhaeuser Corporation. Rick grew up on ten acres. He was the oldest of five boys, and there were also two sisters in the family. His dad was often gone from Monday to Friday, somewhere in the northwest on his logging jobs. Maybe even for a couple of weeks at a time, as logging became more scientific and political, the jobs were often situated in more remote lumber areas. So, Rick was the de facto dad, and his mom's sergeant-at-arms a lot of the time. The family raised some half a dozen head of cattle, chickens, several milking goats, and kept a large family garden. There was always work to do.

Obliged to fill in for his father, Rick did what he had to do, but muscling as much help from his younger brothers as possible, put him in an adversarial relationship with them. And because of that, he was never very close to his siblings. The family required most of Rick's free time, which eliminated just about all of his participation in normal high school activities. There were no sports, girls, or hanging out, etc. While all of the cool guys drove bumped up Chevy and Ford two doors to school, Rick drove his absent dad's pickup truck. Not exactly a chic magnet. Maybe it would be passable without the chicken manure in the back bed, but he certainly didn't have time to clean out the truck out every time he drove it to school. He seemed to be permanently pissed off about his Spartan life. Maybe this was the reason why he turned into such a dour adult.

Rick wasted no time in joining the US Coast Guard, as soon as he graduated from High School. After his six months of training was complete, he was hoping for a tour in the Hawaiian theater, but of course, he was sent in the opposite direction, to Long Branch, New Jersey.

He patrolled the Lower Harbor of Manhattan, on the Jersey side of the bay, and the northern stretches of the Jersey coast. While he enjoyed being out on the water, in Jersey or New York, babysitting amateur boaters wasn't his cup of tea. He lived on base for his entire tour of duty on the east coast, and saved his money, unlike most of his fellow Guardsmen, who rented apartments, brought in wives or girlfriends and tried to have a life. After two years, he again requested Hawaii, but was ordered instead to Homer, Alaska.

Well, at least he was going back to the west coast, but Alaska in the dead of winter? That is certainly no bargain. Rick just didn't seem to have the right personality to cultivate the kind of relationships who could help him get where he wanted to go. But the hell with it, he didn't ask any favors, nor did he give any. If they wanted him in Alaska, then that's where he would go. He knew he only had a year and a half left to serve in the Guard anyway. He could handle it.

Charlie Strong got called into the old man's office one morning in early June.

"Good morning, Sir," Charlie greeted the President, Harold Edmonds, of Portland's International Longshoremen and Warehousemen's Union Local #40.

"What can I do for you today?" Charlie, as Head Agent of local #40, was pretty much the personal assistant to President Edmonds.

"Book us into the Glacier Port Inn, in Homer, Alaska, Charlie. I want to go Halibut fishing."

"For how many people, sir?" Charlie asked.

"There will be four of us. Myself, Ben Harris, Sam Conklin from Seattle and you. Get us the same guide we had the last time, if you can. And bring those two Casual girls along. So, we should need five rooms."

Ben Harris was the Secretary-Treasurer of local number 40 in Portland, and Sam Conklin was the President of ILWU number 19 in Seattle. Casuals are people who work as part timers for the union. They have no contract, and no benefits, but the work pays well, and of course, all the casuals want to get permanent tenure with the Union. Permanent tenure pays north of a hundred grand a year, with a pension, and lifetime benefits. Hopefully these two Casual girls would have an inside track when permanent job postings came up, which wasn't often. But then, it also would depend on how much fun everyone had on the trip.

Charlie's predecessor had told him about the annual June fishing trips before he retired. "Harold likes to go fishing in Alaska during the summer solstice every year," he'd told Charlie.

"It's either Halibut fishing in Homer, or Salmon fishing in Sitka. You need to pre-book two five-day trips, with lodging, guides, and don't forget the girls, and the licenses. Then, whichever way he wants to go, just cancel the other one. If you don't pre-book, you will never get reservations down in time, and of course he will be pissed off at you."

"What about the deposits?' Charlie asked

"Benny understands what is going on, and will cut whatever checks you need."

So, Charlie was pretty much ready to go after his visit to Harold's office. But he still had to make things seem like they took a bit of time to co-ordinate. Harold had maybe a couple more fishing trips on Local 40's dime before he retired, and Charlie intended to make sure that they were good ones.

Ben Harris was eight years older than Charlie, but was a CPA, and also came from a ILWU family. He wanted Harold's job, and Charlie was gunning to take over for Ben as Secretary/Treasurer when Ben moved up. Provided, of course, that everything went well for the next couple of years, and Headquarters in San Francisco didn't jump someone in from outside the local jurisdiction.

Charlie called Tricia Martin. "Are you and Kelly ready to go catch some big fish?" Charlie asked.

"Hell yes," Tricia said, without even thinking. This gave herself and her girlfriend Kelly a great getaway from the daily grind, and Tricia a break from her kid. Her mom would help take care of him while she was gone. This would be Tricia's third trip to Alaska with the boys. "Just let me make a couple of phone calls, and I will be ready."

"Harold is going to take care of me this year, come posting time, right?" she asked Charlie. She wanted permanent status with the Union, and Harold's retirement was getting close. If she missed this shot, she knew she would have to start all over with the next guy. Something which could take another five years.

"Hey Charlie, we will need some dough to get ready, you know," Tricia purred.

"How much?" Charlie asked.

"Oh, I think four grand will cover us," Tricia said back to him.

"Damn," Charlie said. "You are getting expensive."

"Plus, a grand for Mom to take care of my kid," Tricia added.

What could Charlie say, Tricia was Harold's favorite.

"You want us to look nice, don't you? Plus, I have get my Jeep fixed."

"Okay," Charlie told her. She could have gotten more Charlie thought to himself, as she was calling the shots. But she is paying her dues the right way, he thought, if she wants to get on permanent status.

Getting to Homer entailed a flight to Anchorage, Alaska, then taking a puddle jumper over to Homer. No one on the trip cared, as Portland to Anchorage took the better part of three hours, and was booked first class, and they just drank champagne all of the way. Charlie slipped the Alaska Airline stews a couple hundred each, and they tromped off to the connecting flight. The in-state hop took only twenty-five minutes, but being a prop plane, there was no first class. Still, Charlie had made special arrangements, to have some Moet White Star on board. It was Harold's favorite bubbles, and while the rest of the passengers drank Alaskan Amber beer, Harold was able to high-life it, and keep his buzz going.

"Nothing's too good for old ILWU," Charlie said to himself.

Their flight was uneventful if a bit bumpy. Tricia was sitting with Harold, and was all over it, so to speak. The van was there to ferry them to the resort.

"I love it up here" Harold said to their table that night in the resort bar. "The view is magnificent; the air is so fresh. The sun won't set until almost midnight tonight."

"We have reservations at Captain Pat's in an hour," Charlie reminded everyone, "and then a five am wakeup call tomorrow. Dress warm, because it will be crisp in the morning."

"Right on," Harold crowed. "We are going to hook us a barn-door this year. I can feel it." Then he ordered another Sapphire Martini.

If Local 40 dues paying members did get any benefit out of underwriting this trip, it came from Harold's benevolence. Because after he had filled his own large freezer upon arriving home, he always donated the rest of the catch to the annual docker worker's barbeque, back down in Portland every August.

Dinner at Captain Pat's was delicious as always. Pat's was one of the few Alaskan restaurants it seemed, that specialized in both beef and seafood. You would think Alaska would be crawling with exotic seafood restaurants, especially in the summer. The truth is, until the commercial fishing season opens in July, the local catch is pretty limited. And once the commercial season comes on, a lot of that catch is exported to mainland markets down south. But Captain Pat's actually would buy commercially caught salmon from the Copper River area, and the Yukon River supply lines, whose seasons opened earlier than the saltwater seasons. They therefore, always had the best of the world's Salmon, and also thirty-day old, dry aged Angus beef. Even some fresh game from time to time.

Charlie had called ahead, and ordered a whole side of Chinook Salmon to be lightly cold smoked, then grilled over alder wood. It had a most incredible smoky, richness to it, with just the right amount of oily, tender flavor and texture. Served with fresh Hollandaise Sauce, and a couple of three or four bottles of Chardonnay, it was a walk off homerun.

The gang wrapped up dinner around ten. It was another memorable night in Homer. The meal was spectacular, the wine was crisp and delicious, and the girls looked so pretty and petite in their little low cut, sexy tops. Harold wanted to get back to the lodge to watch the sunset, Charlie had to pay the tab, and tip out, the usual fresh, crisp Benjamins for everyone. He picked up the box lunches for tomorrow's trip, and off they went.

"This place is so special," Harold said to Tricia. They were back in Harold's suite overlooking Cook's Inlet, watching the late, Alaskan sunset. Tricia was cuddled up on the couch next to Harold in new black panties and lacey, black push up bra, with a little red ribbon, right there in her cleavage.

"I love being up here with you," Tricia whispered in his ear.

"Don't worry, Tricia," Harold said quietly, but somewhat unsteadily, "I will take care of you before I go."

"I know you will," Tricia purred back at him.

"It's time to go to bed," Harold announced. "We've got an early wakeup call tomorrow morning, and it's been a busy day."

"I have to go do my girl thing before bed. I'll be right there."

By the time she was done removing her makeup, putting on moisturizer, etc., and got back to the bedroom in the suite, Harold was fast asleep. He was snoring like a sea lion. Tricia covered him up, and padded off to her own quiet bed in her and Kelly's suite.

The sun was up and running by 4:00 am, and Harold was already awake, and brimming with anticipation. He dressed and went down to the lobby for coffee. Tricia was already there.

"Good morning" Harold greeted her, "I guess I wasn't too much fun last night."

Tricia went over and kissed him on the cheek. "No problem. I just went back to my own bed so I could get some good sleep for today's trip. I can get a little seasick you know." Now Kelly stumbled into the lobby, desperately looking for the coffee pot.

The girls really didn't do too much fishing, but by having two extra licenses on board, that meant four more fish the guys could catch.

They got down to the lodge docks, and got on board. Their boat was a thirty-eight-foot, Swedish Princess motor yacht, named, what else, the Homer S.

It had a luxury heated cabin, which was good for the party, because even though it was the middle of June, it was only 40 degrees when they cast off.

They had a crew of three on board, including the captain, a deck hand, and a steward for cabin service. The first order of business was Bloody Mary's for everyone who was interested. That certainly included all the guys, as everyone was still a little fuzzy from all the travel and drinking yesterday. Plus, if Harold drank, then Ben and Charlie drank.

Fortunately, it was pretty smooth sailing, as the waters were morning calm. Everyone was still half asleep, but the Bloodies were helping, and the satellite was pinging MSNBC in on the 48" flat screen TV. The market was doing well, although some of the shippers were a little disgruntled with the Dockworker's slow-down on the handling side.

"Fuck 'em," Harold said, laughing. "We have to keep those shippers people on their toes. The new contracts are due next year, and then I can fade off into the sunset." With a pretty damn nice pension, Charlie thought to himself. Wouldn't do to say anything like that aloud, though.

Harold switched the TV to a Rambo movie. "No more business today," he boomed. "It's bad luck on a fishing trip."

They got out of the inlet, and into Kachemak Bay by seven in the morning. The sky was starting to clear from the morning, coastal inversion. The seas were relatively calm, there was a light wind out of the south west at about five knots. It looked like it was going to be a perfect day for fishing.

The deck hand had all of the rigs ready, and everyone was baited by eight am. The guys were belted up and ready to go. Belting up entails a sturdy strap harness, with a wide belt and a hollow stump to grab the butt of the pole if you have a strong Halibut hookup.

Those fish are so flat and deep, that if it is a large fish, you absolutely need the leverage of the belt, to help pull that baby up. As you pull upwards, your fish is trying to dive back down, and that creates the barn door effect.

The guys were out on deck at eight, and the girls were going to nap, and let it warm up for an hour or two, and then jig for Salmon off of the back of the boat. Whatever they all caught Salmon or Halibut, their Chef back at the lodge would be broiling it up for them tonight.

"What kind of sauce do we want on the Halibut tonight," Harold asked no one in particular. They had been fishing for about an hour, and as the sun came out through the cloud cover, were getting into the lazy rocking motion of being out on the sea. The universal wait for a bite. The Blood Mary's did nothing but help the rocking motion. It was warming up nicely, and was going to be a beautiful day.

"You want another drink, boss?" Charlie asked Harold.

"I think I'll have a beer," Harold replied. "Anyone else?" Charlie asked, before he ducked into the salon to get Harold's beer.

"Any luck Charlie?" asked Kelly.

"Nothing yet, but they are coming," he told her.

The guys had been at it for over an hour, and were anxious to get the morning bite going. It was starting to warm up, and the girls had just come out of the cabin, when Harold hooked up.

"Fish on," he yelled out, and started reeling. They were fishing a shelf, about two miles off shore, and 600 meters down, so it was a pretty good haul to bring his fish up. As mid-morning approached, the off-shore wind started to kick up just a bit, but because of the size of the boat, their craft was holding pretty steady.

Harold was about halfway up, when Ben hooked up. Harold's fish looked to be about a forty pounder, and it was too early to tell for Ben. As Harold got his fish further up to the boat, the halibut started to lose its fight. Her lungs had started to expand, and Harold was close to getting her on board.

The deck hand gaffed it, and swung it over the rail. It turned out to be just about right on forty pounds, which is the perfect size Halibut. Young and strong, full of flavor. The bigger Halibut, while they are certainly trophy fish, don't eat near as well. They are older, fleshier and sometimes a little wormy.

Harold's fish measured almost four feet long, and Charlie had had the Nikon out for some action shots of Harold landing his prize. Now Charlie had him pose holding his catch up.

"Turn it around so the belly is outward," Charlie told Harold. "The white belly makes the fish stand out more."

"I know that, you asshole," Harold laughed at him. "Do you think this is my first rodeo?"

The fish was so much dead weight, that the deck hand helped hoist the fish up for Harold, until Charlie was ready to shoot, then he stepped away.

"Nice one," Charlie praised. "I'm thinking a well balanced Beurre Blanc sauce tonight, eh?"

"That sounds great," Harold responded. He was a little tired from fighting the fish, what with all the fun times and yesterday's solid day of drinking.

Harold said "I'm going to go in and take a break. I'll be back in half an hour. Where are the sandwiches?"

"The steward has them, Black Forest ham and cheese, just like always."

It was getting lively on deck. Ben was bringing his fish to the surface, and the deck hand had the gaff out. It looked to be about the same size as Harold's, maybe just a little bit smaller. Sam had also hooked up, and the girls were now well out of the cabin, and had their lines wet.

Harold went into the salon, and asked the steward for the sandwiches. He cracked a Heineken, and took a good, healthy bite out of his sandwich. He loved ham and cheese, especially good Black Forest ham and thinly sliced, Jarlsberg Cheese. He sat down and took another slug of beer, and glanced at the TV, while he began to finish his early lunch.

Harold had been gone for about twenty minutes or so, nobody really noticed how long, when the steward burst out of the salon.

"Something's wrong with Mr. Edmonds," he shouted at Charlie.

"Holy shit," Charlie muttered, and rushed for the salon.

The steward jumped out of the way, and Charlie careened past him. Everyone else except Sam, who still was fighting his fish, dropped their poles, and crowded into the cabin. Sam threw his pole at the deck hand, and went and joined them.

"Give me some room," Charlie yelled.

He had found Harold laid back on the couch, with half a bite of sandwich hanging out of his mouth. The rest of the sandwich was all over the place, the beer bottle was in a puddle on the rug, and Harold was turning blue.

At first Charlie thought the Harold was choking, and immediately hauled him upright, and started giving him the Heimlich Maneuver. But Harold was getting bluer, and there was nothing coming out of his mouth.

"Check his pulse," yelled Ben Harris. Charlie laid Harold down on the floor, and felt his wrist. There was only the faintest sign of any pulse.

"This is cardiac," Charlie sputtered, and began to perform compression on his chest. Charlie was an expert in CPR from his days of coming to the aid of his mates in the jungles of Vietnam.

"Tell the Captain to send out an SOS to the Coast Guard, now," Charlie bellowed.

Tricia jumped in, and began to give Harold mouth to mouth resuscitation. Charlie kept up his compression reps.

Luck was smiling on ILWU local 40 that morning, as the Coast Guard was at the mouth of the gulf about three nautical miles from the Homer S's location. They immediately kicked their big rescue craft into emergency mode. It was full speed ahead.

Rick Ferin was the lead corpsman on duty that morning. He was on his radio.

"Homer S, what is your status?" his voice bulled through the static of the short-wave radio.

"We have a man down. It looks like a heart attack. He's in bad shape," the Captain replied.

"Are you giving him first aid?" Rick asked in his crackly voice.

"Yes, they're giving him Resus right now."

"Keep it up. We will be there in two minutes. We have your location on our radar."

Charlie kept up with the compression pumps. Tricia with the mouth to mouth. Ben was in a state of shock, so he just stood there and said Hail Mary's. He was fully aware that he, Charlie and Tricia all needed Harold alive and ticking. Their careers depended on him.

"Coming to your port side," the Captain heard Rick Ferin say just before he threw down his radio.

The boats pulled parallel, the Coast Guard hands threw bumpers over their side, and lines were tossed, securing the boats together. Ben Harris saw the bubble chopper leashed onto the back of the Coast Guard cutter.

Rick jumped onto the Homer S. He had the paddles with him.

"Stand back," he firmly told Charlie and Tricia, immediately taking charge of the emergency situation.

Rick unwrapped the paddles, and began the electro stimulation of Harold's heart. Harold stirred ever so slightly. The paddles were convulsing his chest cavity.

"He can make it if we get him back to the aid station in Homer," Rick announced.

"Man the chopper," he shouted to his crew. They jumped back to the Cutter, and began to ready the chopper. Rick kept up the CPR until the chopper was fired up. Harold was dazed, but slowly becoming semi-conscious again. Rick cracked a vial of ammonia smelling salts, and held them under Harold's nose.

Rick and Charlie very gently rolled Harold onto the Coast Guard stretcher Rick's crew had brought on the Homer S. The Coast Guard crew took over from there. Harold was loaded into the hatch of the chopper, and the pilot immediately lifted off, and headed back to port.

Charlie exhaled broadly. He and the rest of the group breathed a sigh of relief. Charlie watched the chopper fade off into the distant horizon.

"I love helicopters," he said to Tricia, and put his arm around her shoulders, which seemed to steady both of them. "That was a close one." Now what, Tricia thought?

The Homer S's automatic winch began to whine as it pulled anchor, and they headed back to port. It took about an hour to get in, and Charlie and Ben immediately took off for the Coast Guard Station Infirmary.

Rick Ferin was still there, when they arrived. He had just finished up his report. ILWU would be getting a pretty hefty invoice, because anytime the CG had to fire up the helicopter, it was a minimum of ten thousand dollars.

"Thanks a lot," Charlie said to Rick, and shook his hand. "You saved a good man today."

"He's resting comfortably now. We've got him stabilized, but he had a pretty serious Myocardial Infarction. They are thinning his blood with Plavix, and they've also got him sedated, he should rest for a few days with us. The doc isn't sure if there is permanent damage, so he should have a through check-up as soon as he gets home, and absolutely no strenuous activity until then."

"We can't thank you enough," Charlie said to him. "Do ever get down Portland way? Here is my card, look me up, we will definitely show you our gratitude."

"I'll do that sometime," Rick replied. "I'm from the Vancouver area, so I'm not far away. I'm just glad that we were in the area today. If it had happened an hour later, and we were out to sea, your boss would most probably be a dead duck."

"Come see me," Charlie told him again, "I owe you."

Needless to say, the fishing trip wound down pretty quickly after that. Charlie called ILWU Headquarters in San Francisco, and made arrangements for the Corporate jet to fly in on an evac back to Portland. But it would be a couple of days before Harold could travel. It was decided that Sam Conklin would fly out with him, and Harold's wife would meet them, with an ambulance, at the Portland airport. After dropping Harold off, the private jet would run Sam back to Seattle before returning to San Francisco. Charlie and Ben would stay in Homer to clean up the trip, and then head back south with the girls and the fish they had caught. They had to stay on for another couple of days, before they flew out, but it was pretty subdued around there after almost losing Harold.

Charlie was able to track Rick Ferin down, and they did manage to take him out to dinner at Captain Pat's before they left town.

The fishing trip went all to hell, but Charlie and Rick hit it off famously. Rick had saved all of their bacon, and Charlie liked the taciturn young man, who seemed overly quiet, but ultra-focused, with a kind of tiger like well of reserve energy in him.

Rick finished his last three and a half months in the US Coast Guard, and mustered out at the big Coast Guard station on Elliot Bay in Seattle. He had done his time, gotten out of Castle Rock, Washington, and saved some twenty thousand dollars during his tour of duty.

The first thing he did when he hit the streets, was book a flight from Seattle to Honolulu, with his return flight booked to Portland. He wanted to relax in the sun and the trade winds for a spell, and he was finally going to get to the Islands with or without the Coast Guard's help. When he got back state side, he would go look into the International Longshore and Warehouse Union. What better place for an ex US Coast Guardsman to work?

After a restful couple of weeks in Hawaii, Rick returned to the west coast, and headed to Portland, and he and Charlie hooked up for lunch. They renewed old acquaintances, talked a little bit about Hawaii, and Rick expressed an interest in the ILWU. By now Harold Edmonds was pretty much of a figure head at the Portland Local, and Charlie was de facto running the show.

"I need a guy up in Kelso/Longview," Charlie told Rick. "That office is in Washington, but it is so far south that Seattle doesn't want to deal with it, so it is part of our district. Seattle manages Tacoma, Seattle, Everett and Bellingham, and we run Kelso, Vancouver, and Portland. They are a much smaller outfit, but they are a bunch of independent sons of bitches. They cause trouble, and no one wants to deal with them," Charlie outlined to Rick.

"How so?"

"Well, they are from Washington, so they resent us guys from Oregon bossing them. They are small town guys, so they resent paying the same scale union dues as the city dockworkers. They bitch and complain about our executive salaries, and want to review every expense report at annual meetings with a fine-tooth comb," Charlie was now getting irate. "They are just a royal pain in the ass."

"But you are both part of an international organization with significant benefits," Rick observed.

"No shit," Charlie agreed. "You and I get it, but they don't. I need someone to go up there, a real tough guy, who is willing to stay on for a couple of years. Start out real quiet like, and find out who the trouble makers are. Then we will get rid of the assholes, and get some people in place who appreciate what we have done for them. I need a guy who can get some dirty work done, who will have my back."

"I can do that," Rick said. It didn't seem all that much worse to him from dealing with smugglers, poachers and distress calls on the waters of New York and New Jersey."

"I mean sometimes stuff happens. Stuff to be dealt with," Charlie mused. "I'm not necessarily talking about painting any houses, (painting a house is mobster talk for assassinating someone) but sometimes I just need a guy I can count on."

"I'm your man," Rick replied to Charlie. "When do I start?"

That was some time ago, and Rick and Charlie have been tight ever since. They became the favorite trouble shooters for ILWU Headquarters in San Francisco. Because whenever there was a labor problem, or an issue with some truckers, Charlie got a call.

The first-time Rick went with Charlie down to the docks in Los Angeles, the local Wilmington cops were pretty much hands off, and things were getting ugly.

"Man, these people must be big Dodger fans, because I sure am seeing a lot of baseball bats around," Rick told Charlie.

"No problem," Charlie growled. "Here put these on." Charlie took out a bag of brass knuckles, formed their guys into a wedge, pulled their watch caps down, and busted right through that picket line. Of course, it didn't hurt to have a couple of snipers on the warehouse roof, in case there were any wise guys around.

Rick stayed in Kelso/Longview for a couple of years, and he and Charlie got things restructured to Charlie's liking. When that job was done, Charlie brought Rick down to Portland and Vancouver as his Chief Agent. If the rank and file members were making north of a hundred grand, Rick continued his ILWU career making north of a hundred and fifty. He was very happy, because that is good money anywhere, especially for a local boy from Vancouver, Washington.

By now, Harold had retired. But before he left, he made sure Tricia had been taken care of. Charlie had jumped over Ben Harris to replace Harold Edmonds as President of ILWU Local # 40. San Francisco apparently liked his toughness and loyalty to the organization. San Francisco decided Charlie would run Portland with oversight over the whole district, Ben Harris would manage Vancouver, and remain as Local 40's Treasurer. Rick Ferin was confirmed as Charlie's Chief Agent and worked out of all three Ports: Portland, Vancouver and Kelso/Longview.

Rick eventually married and started a family. He actually was the first of the two to move to Vancouver, preferring a smaller city to the busy lifestyle in Portland. In deference to his hard scrabble youth, he elected to join Rosewood Golf and Country Club, and take up the noble game of golf.

Charlie visited, and liked our club. He also liked the more casual, genuine style of the people on our side of the Columbia River, and also moved north. He told Rick he didn't feel like he had to watch his backside every single minute up here.

CHAPTER ELEVEN

Back on Magnolia Street, the neighbors were busy preparing for the big Hearing. If Rosewood was taking things only semi seriously, especially, after George Richardson's prognosis of a slam dunk for us, this was not the case with Rosewood's neighbors.

Especially with Bob Kudlach leading the opposition's effort.

Bob came from eastern European stock via the east coast. His people, while not of Jewish descent, had still survived enough persecution to flee to America before the culmination of World War II. His immediate family consisted of a brother and a sister, mom and dad, and grandma on his mother's side. They were determined survivors, and tough enough to make do in Brooklyn as dirt poor immigrants in the late nineteen forties.

Bob fought his way through the New York public school system, and he and his younger brother by a year and a half, proved to be quite a tag team. They not only had to cope on their own, but they had to look out for little sis as well.

The Kudlachs lived in a five room walk up flat, in the Park Slope area of Brooklyn. What is now a quite fashionably gentrified enclave, in the late forties it was a teeming morass of humanity.

Thomas Kudlach, although he was educated as an accountant, and was an accomplished violinist, got work in a packing plant. He hauled sides of beef around in a two block long refrigerated warehouse by the docks for a living. Sometimes, Thomas felt like the refrigerated warehouse was warmer than his cold water flat at home.

Bob's mother got work as a maid across the river in Manhattan. She worked six days a week, and was glad to be employed. Grandma kept the flat clean, then she cooked and washed for the family. As tough as things were for them, they were all deliriously happy to have escaped their repressive homeland, and to experience living the American dream.

Bob and his little brother, were up, scrubbed and faithfully ready to continue their education every day. They walked twelve blocks to the public-school house with little sister, come rain, sleet, or shine. They didn't have to worry much about the local neighborhood punks stealing their lunch money, because they didn't have any lunch money. Grandma would cobble together some kind of a sandwich for them, which the kids would hide in their school bags, and this would have to get them through the day.

After school, the boys got Sissy, as they called her, home in one piece. Then they went out and did anything they could to hustle a buck. Shine shoes, hawk newspapers, sweep up for the fruit and vegetable venders. To hawk newspapers, you had to have a downtown corner. To have and keep a downtown corner, you had to fight for it.

When everyone was home at night, grandma would serve some porridge for dinner, and then it was homework until bed time. All of the kids were smart, and excelled in school. Especially Bob.

"Get your education," Thomas preached to his kids. It even worked out for him, because eventually, he was able to get off of the packing house floor. He finally made it into his companies' accounting/bookkeeping office, and was able to provide a better living for himself and his family.

Bob's tenacious European genealogy, proved up to the task of coming of age in Brooklyn, New York. He didn't seek out trouble, but was fearless when confronted. His toughness and street smarts, would have deterred most of the difficulties you might have encountered on the mean streets of New York City's second largest borough in those days.

On Sundays, the Kudlachs went to the ten o'clock Mass at Saint Francis Catholic Church. Then they would come home and have a sit-down dinner of pot roast and potatoes. At least there were some benefits to working in a packing plant. After Sunday dinner, Thomas would play his violin, and mama would sing old country songs in her pleasant contralto voice. The Kudlachs loved their simple, peaceful Sundays.

Robert, as his mother formally called him, was valedictorian of his high school graduating class. He had always been fascinated by the big planes that flew in and out of La Guardia Airport over New York City. He wanted to be an airline pilot in the worst way, and felt the skies calling to him.

His Councilor at school, so happy in her own right to have an actual, attentive bona fide student in her charge, helped him with his college applications. He received a scholarship offer to attend Cornell University, in Ithaca, New York, and upon arriving on campus, applied for admittance to the Aerospace Engineering Department.

Bob was accepted into the aerospace program, and again proved up to the task. His college experience was one of hard work, but he took just enough time away from his studies to break up his routine in the library. His was not a fraternity oriented university encounter, but Bob enjoyed playing Lacrosse with the frat boys on Sunday afternoons in the quad. He was a member of the University ROTC and Young Democrats Organizations. He graduated with honors, and came out of school as an ROTC second lieutenant. If he was destined to meet a young woman at Cornell, it would have to have happened in the library. Someone who was as serious about her studies as he was. Apparently, destiny was not interested in him at that time.

His mom got him a job during his college summers as a bellman at her hotel, the Saint Regis. It is located in mid-town Manhattan. By now she was the Supervisor of Housekeeping. Bob of course, did well in his summer job. His innate frugality helped him stretch the money he made through the school year. As soon as he graduated from Cornell in his allotted four years, he enlisted in the Air Force. His dream of becoming a flyboy, were coming true, and he was off for the Air Force Academy in Colorado Springs, Colorado.

Colorado Springs is a long way from Brooklyn, but Bob fell in love with the big skies, mountains, and the wide-open country. He had passed his pre-admittance Air Force Physical with ease after graduation, and his eyesight proved to be 20/20, and up to the task.

He worked through flight training in the normal years' time, and choose fighter jets, as his focus area. The power and thrust of these magnificent machines enthralled him. He knew he was a lucky man, and had chosen the right career path.

The Vietnam war was just beginning to escalate when Bob was through with his Air Force training. He was assigned to MACV Headquarters in Bien Hoa, Vietnam, and flew reconnaissance missions and other sorties upon arriving in country. When the war escalated further, he began to fly bombing and strafing missions as far north as the Gulf of Tonkin. He did two tours in Vietnam, and survived some harrowing close calls.

He mustered out of the US Air Force and into the Air Force Reserves when his six years of service commitment was completed. He loved the Rocky Mountain state of Colorado, and since Denver is a United Airlines hub, he applied with them and was hired immediately.

As focused and serious as Bob had been for the first twenty-nine years of his life, he was now ready to have some fun. Ergo, the gaggle of UA stewardesses would become his new center of attention. He got an apartment in town, bought a four-wheel drive vehicle, a set of ski gear, and settled in for the ride.

Bob played the field for a couple years, and had several short-term relationships. But being a serious young man by nature, he settled down sooner than later. He married one of the fly girls, and started a family. He was transferred to Seattle, and worked out of Sea-Tac Airport for the second half of his time with United. He and his wife raised three children, two lovely daughters, and a middle son. As his career was culminating, Bob's wife wanted to be closer to her family in Portland, and so they moved down our way to Vancouver. Bob would finish his career flying out of Portland, doing west coast hops for the most part. Which was the equivalent of Michael Jordan playing in the NBA's Development Leagues in South Dakota. But he was happy to have his health, and a more relaxed lifestyle. He liked the northwest, and was resigned to winding his life's work down as a lesser light.

Maybe boredom was a motivating factor in Bob's distaste for Rosewood. Maybe it was a class resentment thing, born of his spartan youth. Maybe he felt underemployed. But when he went to battle with us, there was nothing half assed about it. He was Commander Kudlach, we were the identified enemy. As far as he was concerned, it was bombs away.

Bob's crew continued fine tuning their case for the Examiner's Hearing. They formed a kind of Executive Committee of their own, which consisted of Commander Bob, Carol Horn, Hugh and Bunny, and another attorney from down the street. He worked around land use and zoning in some function, and was an excellent resource for them.

I am not sure what was fueling their avarice toward Rosewood. Was it the actual proposed driving range, or the old animosity of the bad neighbor hostilities? There were numerous issues in existence even before the driving range project arose. So, it must have been a combination of the two. And the longer our proposal continued on the docket, the more antagonistic the Magnolians, particularly Mr. Kudlach became.

To make things worse, the more any of us in the neighborhood, or at Rosewood, tried to mitigate the situation, the more the Magnolians resisted our overtures. If we invited them to any kind of social or informational gathering, they mostly obliged us by taking whatever treats we had to offer. Then just sat there all morosely, and nodded their heads like Stepford wives. It was eerie, and nothing we could do seemed to achieve any resolve. They weren't having it, come hell or highwater.

"We have to keep on with the safety issues, introduce some environmental concerns, and of course continue to pound on the fact that they are the big bullies. They are the bad neighbors, and their word is good for absolutely nothing. No matter what, if anything, is approved they will do as they damn well please, and the neighborhoods can go to hell," Captain Kudlach said.

"Bob," Carol said, "I have a suggestion. We need to get our own attorney. Rosewood has this slicked up, city guy. We need a country boy, someone who is a little down on his luck. Sharp, but the bottom of the lawyer barrel kind of guy, like he is all we can afford. We need to play on the sympathies of the Examiner. I know just the guy."

"This is genius, Carol. Who is he?"

"Bill Endicott is his name, he's brilliant. Works in our trust division. He is short and getting older. He is rather unkempt, and would fit the part perfectly."

"How much would he cost us?" Bob asked her. Although he had had a brilliant career in aviation, and had invested wisely, Bob counted his nickels to this day. He was still subconsciously hawking newspapers back in Brooklyn, on cold winter street corners for spare change every afternoon.

"He owes me," said Carol. "He would probably do it pro bono as a favor, if I asked him."

"Go for it."

"Hugh and Bunny, you two need to have everyone on the street at the Hearing and willing to testify. And bring friends. Get there early, pack the place. Make the Rosewood crowd stand up in the back of the room. Talk to the adjacent neighbors, this shouldn't just be on us."

"Got it" said Hugh

"Bob," Carol said, "you need to start to develop a relationship with the Hearing Examiner. Her email is out there. Contact her, ask her any questions you can think of, just engage her. Start a relationship with her. The evening of the Hearing, walk into the Chamber, and walk right up to her bench. Put your heads together, and thank her for all of her help. She is an older woman.

Turn on a little charm. That will freak out George Richardson, and might cause him to overreact."

They continued to talk into the night. Hugh and Bunny left for home. Carol's husband was long gone, as he was at his office at 5:00 am to deal with the east coast shippers. Bob's wife, the ex-stew, was better at serving coffee than she was at legal strategizing, and she went to bed. Bob opened another bottle of wine, and sat down on the couch by Carol. Although he was twenty years her senior, Bob loved a handsome woman with a keen mind.

CHAPTER TWELVE

September in the Northwest is a spectacular time to play golf. The air is soft and fragrant. Temperatures are still in the seventies, the light is translucent, and starting to cast soft shadows on the verdantly green courses and surrounding vegetation. Especially if you are playing a few holes in the late afternoon or early evening.

The summer crowds are going away, it is a time for relaxing, reflecting, enjoying the game for the pure pleasure of hitting a fine golf shot, and watching the ball soar down the fairway. My son and I especially enjoyed sneaking out for six holes on the back nine before dinner. We would knock it around a bit, and loved our guy time together. It was also the valued reward of living on a golf course.

Something I'm afraid Bob Kudlach never experienced, because although he lived adjacent to the course, he didn't play golf.

"Nice shot son. You are starting to out hit your old man." My kid was already in high school, had been on the golf team for two years now, and was as strong and supple as a young cedar tree.

"Thanks dad. You're two bucks down now." Not only was he hitting it long and straight, the kid could putt. I told you Jerry DePietro was a good teaching pro. Plus, I think he is going to be an accountant. He keeps track of every last bet.

"Are you ready to testify Thursday night at the Hearing?" I asked him.

"Oh yeah. That George guy came by last week and coached us all up."

"Both the boys and the girls' teams?"

"Yep. And the coaches and some of the parents."

Not only was the kid learning all of the constructive values of golf, it was now going to teach him a little about the Law.

•

Our Rosewood legal committee had had our final organizational meeting on Monday night. This gave us plenty of time for any last-minute details we needed to prepare for. It was kind of fun for me as a restaurant guy to see our strategy and planning come together. The drama and anticipation of the hearing was building for all of us. The allure of the trial, in lawyer talk. Kind of like prepping for a busy restaurant weekend, and then counting up the deposit on the Monday morning after, in my business.

"Friends of Rosewood: check. High School teams and coaches: check. WP golf pros, and managers: check. George Richardson: check." Richardson was going down the list. We were ready, especially, with the kids. The high school committee had actually recruited the Principal of the High School, who was supposed to come and thank Rosewood for our continued support of interscholastic athletics. He would emphasize how much that meant to our local high school. Particularly, in these times of strained budgets and increasing costs. He would play up just what an invaluable asset we were. Not just to the school system, but to the community at large.

George felt like we were ready for battle. Our other "in-house attorneys", were simply regular members, who were of the legal profession. They were like Sunday morning quarter-backs, but were not on the payroll, and might have been entertaining the slightest notion of professional invidiousness. As a loosely formed group, they did not seem as openly optimistic as Mr. Richardson. They appeared much more resigned. Their consensus seemed to be a feeling of readiness, but we shouldn't count our chickens any too soon.

The morning of the hearing dawned cool and bright. Although the outside temperature was now in the sixties, the sun was shining, and spirits were high. At Rosewood, anyway.

George Richardson had come over the bridge from Portland at three in the afternoon. He was an hour early in order to prepare himself for the evening's task.

"There was an accident on the bridge right after I crossed," he told us. "I was lucky to get through. This might work to our advantage."

"How's that?" someone asked. The legal committee was gathered in the Rosewood bar before going over to City Hall for the Hearing. George Richardson ordered himself a glass of Chardonnay in a chilled glass.

"I've been notified that the Magnolians have retained council," GR replied. "He is a Portland Attorney, and if he is late, I guess the trial will just have to go on without him."

"Who is he?" someone asked.

"Bill Endicott. He is a dweeb," George told us. "He is not even a trial attorney, he is a trust guy. I know him from Stanford Law Alumni Meetings, Portland Chapter. He has absolutely no presence at all. Absolutely none. Zero!"

"Won't the Magnolians request a delay?" the same guy asked.

"I have already taken care of that," said GR, smiling. "I emailed the Hearing Examiner as soon as I got here, and communicated to her about a prolonged trial I have scheduled. It begins tomorrow morning. Therefore, time is of the essence, and I hoped tonight's proceedings would be expedient and timely. Just another little lawyer trick." GR told us, amused at his own cleverness. He took a sip of Chardonnay.

Charlie Strong was excited, and seemed to be in a state of high agitation. He had a lot of confidence in George Richardson. Not only because as President of the club, he had basically had the last say on hiring him. But he just admired the guy's style. He, as well as the Board, felt as if we had the right leader for the job. Charlie just wanted to get tonight's formalities over with, and get on with building his driving range.

George was dressed in a worsted Armani suit, he was wearing black Italian loafers. He had on a matching pearl grey Brooks Brothers, Oxford shirt, and a black silk tie, patterned with a subtle silver design. His perfectly coifed hair was gelled in place, and he looked fit and tanned. He did indeed look powerful, as well as brilliant. I believe the Board and the committees were very confident in him also.

We convoyed the four miles over to City Hall, and got there ten minutes early. We were immediately shocked upon entering the Council Chambers, to find the hearing room packed. What few seats that were left, were on the back couple of rows. We could hardly see what was going on, and most of our group of supporters would be standing in the back of the room. This included all the high school kids, and it was terrible Fung Shui for us.

Just before seven o'clock, Kudlach approached the Hearing Examiner's bench. He greeted the Examiner with an outstretched hand. She grasped his hand warmly, and smiled most cordially up at him. Kudlach bent towards her, and their heads converged intimately together. He whispered in her ear for what seemed like a full minute. She nodded several times, and again, smiled up at him. She was an older, matronly woman, and Kudlach was still somewhat the dashing, silver maned flyboy pilot. He did everything but wear his damn full-dress flight uniform, and stick his tongue in her ear in that little interlude.

We all looked at George Richardson, to see when he was going to approach the bench, and join the confab. But he seemed preoccupied organizing his notes at the defense table.

After Kudlach pulled away, the Examiner picked up her gavel, and banged it on the bench.

"I call this hearing to order" she proclaimed, "and am sorry to announce that there will be a forty-five-minute delay to the start of our proceedings. Due to a fatal accident on the Interstate bridge, and the potential of numerous interested parties being detained, including the plaintiff's council. This delay is unavoidable."

"I object" George Richardson immediately responded. "We have numerous young people here to view these proceedings. All of these kids have an early school schedule to maintain tomorrow morning."

"Overruled. We will see to it that the young people are allowed to testify early, and are dismissed in an appropriate manner." Of course, this would upset George Richardson's timing. His witness schedule had now been turned upside down. He would prove to be ill prepared for this.

We were already zip for two, and off on a slippery slope.

CHAPTER THIRTEEN

We all milled about for three quarters of an hour, and the Judge retired to her chambers. The Magnolians stayed seated, as they were not about to give up any of their prime real estate. Finally, seven forty-five arrived and the Judge reconvened. Bill Endicott still had not arrived, although several other interested people had dribbled in. But the Judge had little leverage left to delay the proceedings further. It appeared that Bob Kudlach would make the opening statement on behalf of the Magnolians.

Bob was casually, but neatly and conservatively attired in his usual khaki slacks, and a long-sleeved dress shirt. He looked serious and concerned.

"Your Honor, if it please the court, I will be making opening statements tonight, due to the traffic issues, and the delay of our council."

"Please proceed," said the Judge.

"Your Honor, we as a family community, are delighted for the opportunity to present our case as to why this intrusive proposal by the defendants is a danger to our homes, our property values, our very welfare and that of our families. We intend to present evidence which will support the aforementioned issues, and will also conclusively prove the damage this proposed project will inflict on the environment. It will adversely affect our quality of life, is incompatible with the covenants and conditions for which our neighborhood was designed, and will be improperly maintained and managed by Rosewood Golf Club. The one and same institution who has a historic track record of maintaining a terrible relationship with their neighbors. They are the gorilla in this room, and we are a disparate group of Northwest families, who intend to fight this project to the death. Your Honor and the Court, our very lives do depend on your decision in this matter of grave concern."

Kudlach droned on. He was vibrant, well-spoken and convincing. It was as if he had majored in Trial Law at Cornell, instead of Aeronautical Engineering.

George Richardson objected several times to Kudlach's descriptive terminology, especially the derogatory comments about Rosewood's character, and our "track record" within the community. George was unceremoniously overruled throughout the opening statement.

"And finally, Your Honor, the absolutely asinine reality of this situation, is that as our little community is being put through all of this stress, we are intruding on the time and resources of the Hearing Examiner. The resources of this court and this community at large are being usurped, and the fact of the matter is, that Rosewood Golf and Country Club already has a perfectly good driving range in place. How much more can Rosewood impose their will on our neighborhood, and for what, etc., etc., etc." Kudlach was laying it on thick.

Charlie Strong was apoplectic while Kudlach continued his presentation. You ungrateful bastard, Charlie thought to himself. If this driving range somehow doesn't fly, I will personally see that the maintenance shed and all of those operations are moved right over behind your house. Let's see how your realtor likes that one.

About halfway through Kudlach's lengthy spiel, Bill Endicott finally stumbled in.

He was a disheveled looking man. Small of stature, and modestly dressed. His hair was tousled. He was wearing baggy corduroy pants, an old turtleneck sweater and semi horn-rimmed eyeglasses. His ill-fitting tweed coat came off when he reached the Plaintiff's table. The ensemble was completed with a pair of scuffed up, black, bus driver shoes. Carol Horn was sitting at the table, and was going to serve as his legal assistant. She smiled at him pleasantly, and gave him the - my what an ordeal you've just been through -look.

He opened his scruffy, boxcar of a briefcase, started dragging out a pile of disorganized paper files, and stacked them in front of him.

When Kudlach finally finished, he went over to Endicott and Carol Horn and conferred with them briefly, and then sat down directly behind them in the first row.

The Judge called for Rosewood's opening remarks, and Barrister Richardson rose, drew himself up to his full 5'11" stature, and approached the Bench. He actually seemed to click his polished heels together as he approached, and bowed ever so slightly to the Judge.

"Your Honor, we would also like to thank you for adjudicating this matter of serious import. We intend to demonstrate to you and the courtroom, that Rosewood Golf and Country Club is attempting to proceed within the strictest interpretation of the law. We have already been approved by the layers of proper governmental departments. We are zoned as a golfing community, and this project is well within the confines of our recognized land use. We will demonstrate how little, if any, perceivable negative impact on either the environment, or our neighbors there will be when this project is approved. To the contrary, we will attempt to demonstrate irrefutable evidence of what a good neighbor we are by bringing up witnesses from throughout the Rosewood community. These neighbors are excited to be living in a quality golfing community, that is largely supported by this Country Club. We will demonstrate through extensive testimony exactly how we are a team player of long standing stature with our local high school students. Offering them the opportunity to pursue the great, character building game of golf. That is both the boys and the girls golf teams, both the Varsity and Junior Varsity levels, at absolutely no charge for using our facilities. Regardless of their social or economic standing, we have offered these fine young people this opportunity for the last thirty years. Finally, your Honor, we will illustrate how we have made every attempt to mitigate any possible adverse effects that might perceivably affect and depreciate the quality of life, of our respected and valued neighbors on Magnolia Street. Etc., etc., etc."

George had a polished performance manner during the delivery of his oratory, of spinning on the floor of the chamber. He would be facing the Judge, then he would do a one hundred eighty-degree spin to face the assembled crowd in the gallery of the courtroom. This was part of his technique to emphasize a point to all of us. As he spun around and back, his beautiful suit, which had an unbuttoned coat jacket, and his silk necktie, would whirl and shine in the light of the courtroom. He would click his Italian heels on the linoleum floor, and he would look over at Bill Endicott with a superior sneer on his face. As much as to say, how dare you even appear in the same courtroom as me.

Finally, Mr. Endicott made his first appearance before the assembled courtroom. His voice was mousy, and weak and he seemed to be intimidated by George Richardson. However, he also seemed to be courageously willing to forge onward, in spite of the overwhelming odds he was facing.

"We would like to call to the stand Mrs. Carol Horn, your Honor."

"State your name and address," the Judge ordered. Carol gave her usual outstanding, tear jerking performance. Hell, she was a damn lawyer for Christ's sake. She lamented, she cajoled, she crossed and uncrossed her legs, she paused often for dramatic effect. She seemed so poised and committed, both sides had to agree, what a spectacular witness she was.

"We would like to call Hugh Schmidt to the stand."

"We would like to call Bunny Schmidt to the stand."

"We would like to call Neil Horn, Lilian Kudlach, etc. to the stand"

"We would like to call our environmental consultant." These are old growth trees your honor, they are owl and eagle habitats, etc.

At any land use type of hearing, the opposing sides will often use whatever traffic, noise, environmental issues that seem relevant, in order to create an issue. Anything to project an ensuing negative objection to the project in question. The Magnolians however, went to the extreme of what could be considered normal or acceptable in a court of law.

Their environmental expert, was a young woman who seemed fairly fresh out of some liberal college program. And she been coached by the master, Carol Horn herself.

There is a small stream that feeds into a ravine that separates the Magnolia Street residents, and the Rosewood property. The small stream in question, is an overflow outlet from our golf course ponds, and otherwise, has been dormant for years.

"Your Honor," the young woman began, "we as a collective neighborhood group feel that the potential habitat of migrating

Salmon is being directly jeopardized by this aggressive project." Migrating Salmon? In a dry ravine? Are you kidding me we all thought? Yet the Examiner sat in solemn and rapt attention to this charade.

"And your Honor, not only the Salmon runs are in danger, but the Inuit Hummingbird. This is a very fragile, migrating and endangered species of avian, and could be essentially threatened with not only the proposed careless intrusion into their nesting habitats, but by a golf ball. If one of these unique, and incredible birds were struck by a high velocity golf ball, the result would be beyond disastrous. Fatal injury would occur immediately, etc., etc., etc."

Again, the concept of a well struck golf ball annihilating a poor, defenseless hummingbird, was an image that seemed to appear almost criminal to the Examiner. She just sat there, and shook her head in dismay and revulsion.

The parade of witnesses continued to pile up on each side.

George called Charlie Strong to the stand as his leading witness. By this time, Charlie was beyond cranky, and in no mood to be trifled with. Charlie was used to barking orders to hapless underlings at union headquarters, not having to grovel before a smug Hearing Examiner, who was already beginning to show a prejudice for the other side.

He answered George's questions with an almost sarcastic sneering tone to his voice. Worse yet, he closed his testimony by pointing out to everyone, the Judge included, that the irony of the neighbor's environmental arguments was entirely moot. He explained how the only reason there were any eagle or aviary habitats in the area was because the Rosewood greens crew stocked all three of our golf course ponds on behalf of said birdlife. "We fill our ponds with carp, perch and bass which the eagles like to fish for and feed on. Other birds nest around our shorelines, bathe and often feed from the ecosystem surrounding our course. Please remember that we have won numerous environmental awards, for the concerned management of our grounds. And if there were any Salmon migrating up the dry ravine in question, I would personally recommend turning this western section of Rosewood, into a permanent wildlife refuge, your Honor." Charlie could make guarantees like this, because everyone in the room knew that no Salmon had been seen in that ravine for some sixty years.

While it is entirely true that we stocked the ponds, Charlie's abrasive style made us appear to be insensitive to eagles, the Audubon Society, the neighbors, and anyone else involved. It was as if we could stop stocking the ponds anytime we wanted, and the eagles could just go somewhere else. Or go hungry. And now, we were also hummingbird murderers.

One thing you don't want to do in any courtroom in the northwest, is disparage eagles, salmon, owls, or apparently, hummingbirds.

After Charlie, we all had our turn on the stand. The kids testified early and well, and were dismissed by the Judge so they could go home and get their beauty sleep. George wanted them to testify later in the proceedings for better impact. But this option had been denied to him. Our Arborist testified, our neighbors testified. We offered to increase the width of the greenbelt between the driving range and the neighbors, at no small expense to ourselves. We offered them up to one hundred feet of barrier zone, with their choice of vegetation.

This give and take went on until almost midnight. Finally, the last dog had been hung, and everyone had had their say. The attorneys made their closing statements.

George Richardson was called first as the Magnolians had led off in the opening presentations. In his typically arrogant manner, George labored on and on with his closing, knowing full well the hour was late, and the more he ran on, the less time Bob Endicott would have to speak. By now the courtroom was over half empty anyway. Finally, the judge cut him off, and turned the floor over to the neighbors.

Yes, Bob Endicott was at the other end of the lawyer spectrum, but somehow, he had saved his best for last. He hammered on about the victimization of the neighborhood, and the environment, etc. But he came off exactly as Carol Horn and Bob Kudlach had programed him. He was humble and well spoken. He was speaking for the rights of the little people. His appearance solidly confirmed his status as one of the little people.

He kept his comments short, concise, and respectful, especially to the Judge. Finally, the hearing mercifully ended at one o'clock in the morning. The Judge thanked and dismissed us. I think Kudlach might have offered the Examiner a ride home in his earlier tete-a-tete with her.

However late, what remained of us gathered back at the Rosewood bar for a stiff one. Larry Easton played bartender.

"What do you think, George?" Charlie asked our lawyer.

"I don't think we could have made a better presentation," he said. "You all did extremely well, and were very well prepared. Thank you so much for your help and support. It is in the hands of the judge now."

"When and how will we find out about her decision?" Charlie asked. "I would bet you money, she will approve us, but require so many terms and conditions, we will never be able to comply."

"I would hope not," said Richardson. "This is a relatively straight forward case. At any rate, she will email me when she has rendered her decision, and I will call you immediately."

So, we finished our drinks, and left. It was very late, and everyone was drained and tired.

CHAPTER FOURTEEN

Davin Harris hosts a Texas Hold 'em poker game at his home the second Tuesday of every month. The guys all look forward to it, and it draws a good crowd. It is a revolving game, and there are players rotating in and out every month. If Davin is out of town, someone else will host the game. So, we all bring an appetizer, and a beverage of choice. Everyone tries to outdo each other on both the Food and Beverage fronts. It makes for quite a fun evening. Especially on the wine tasting side.

There are two tables, one is a buy in for $250., and you get $2,500. In chips. Then there is a much more serious table with a $1,000. Buy-in, and $10,000. In chips. The bigger table can get pretty lively by the end of the night.

This particular evening Davin's wife Elisa, had invited ten wives/girl friends over for their own little poker game. I say little, because for the girls, it was more of a social gathering. I'm not even sure how much money they put into the pot. They all did bring wine and appetizers however, so it made for a great social hour. We were all standing outside in shirt sleeves, enjoying the beautiful fall scenery, and the late Indian summer night. The women were excitedly talking about their big Washington State Golf Tournament. This statewide event was on the calendar for the coming spring, and the women were already deep into the planning stages.

The sky was hosting a Donkey Kong game, with some very large Cumulus clouds scudding about, bumping into each other. And as the clouds floated around, the sun gilded them and the river and the fruit orchards below, with the most gorgeous sunset crimsons and golds you could imagine. It was an exquisite sight, and was the backdrop of what should have been a capital evening.

The games got started a little late because of the light show, and we were about an hour into the betting, when Charlie's cell phone rang. He was playing at the $1,000. table, and had already won a couple of nice pots.

"Hello, this is Charlie." He didn't recognize the caller's number.

"Charlie, this is George Richardson."

"What up, George? Give me some good news."

"Well Charlie, I'm very sorry to say the Examiner found in favor of the Plaintiffs. She has denied our Land Use Application."

"Are you freaking kidding me?" Charlie replied dumbfounded.

"Unfortunately, I am not, but remember that we still have the appeal process ahead of us if we choose. If we proceed down that avenue, I will request a Change of Venue, which will bring us a different hearing examiner."

"I'll call a special meeting of the Board to decide what our next step should be. Can you be at the Club day after tomorrow at two in the afternoon?"

"Charlie, I'll be there. Trust me, I am as upset about this thing as you are."

Things went downhill for everyone after George's phone call, especially for Charlie. All the guys commiserated with him about the range decision. We had all worked hard on the case, and wanted the damn range as badly as the next guy. But no one was quite an invested as Charlie. He was not a happy man, and after donating all his chips with some questionable bets, he was even less happy. He stomped off home, to send a group email out to the Board members about the special meeting. By then, he needed several stiff drinks to help calm his agitated nerves.

In Charlie's peaceful, civilian life mind, there was the appeal opportunity. But in his Vietnam, ass-kicking, non-lawyer mind there was an alternative opportunity.

He sent out an email to the Directors of Rosewood, and then he made a call to his favorite bartender in Oakland, California. The bars were just closing.

If you have never been to downtown Oakland, it is a far cry from the climes of the fine City of San Francisco, with its Golden Gate bridge, trolley cars, preserved Victorian Mansions, wharves and exceptional dining culture. Parts of Oakland are more like San Francisco's Tenderloin district. A poverty stricken, devastated and dangerous section of SF, where you do not want to be out walking your dog late at night. At any rate, while Oakland as a whole is not as bad as the Tenderloin, it is still a fine place to secure an illegal hand gun if you need one. As long as you know the right people.

"JoJo? This is Charlie, how are you my man?

"Great Charlie. How is the Northwest treatin' you?"

"Couldn't be better. We need to talk; do you want to call me back on your cell?"

"Sure Charlie. Let me get you back in a minute from a secure line."

"Charlie? Yeah man, JoJo here. What you need dog?"

"Where are you calling from?"

"I'm at a pay phone a block down the street. Can't be too careful these days."

"I need a Sig Sauer 226. With a silencer, and clip of live x nose rounds. Be sure it is filed clean, and there is no way to ID it."

"You got it pal. That will be 3K."

"No problem. Send it out yesterday. I'll be in San Francisco for the annual ILWU meeting next month. I'll take care of you then."

"It will take me a couple to days to get it off. Where should I send it?"

"Just overnight it to my office, but be sure and mark it Personal."

"Done deal, I'm on it. Good to hear from you man."

Charlie hung up, and poured himself another three fingers of Scotch in a highball tumbler. His mind was humming like a fire station with a three-alarm blaze going on.

"Hey Rick, let's have lunch in an hour," Charlie barked into his cell phone the next morning.

"Sure Charlie. Where at?"

"Let's go to the Jackson Street Steakhouse. It's usually pretty quiet in the bar during the week. We can talk."

Even though he had driven up from Portland, Charlie got there first, and grabbed a table in the back corner of the big room. Rick arrived a few minutes later. They ordered Bloody Mary's.

"That mother fucker has got to go," was the first thing Charlie said after the waitress left.

"Who?"

"Freakin' Kudlach, that's who. What have we ever done to that son of a bitch?"

"Nothing I know of, other than a few noise complaints. What are we going to do?"

"I have got this" Charlie said. "It will be a pleasure to take care of his sorry ass personally."

"What do you need from me?"

"I need you and Bruce Cranston to have dinner with me at the club on Halloween night."

"That's all?"

"That's it. That, and keep your mouth shut. You and I are the only ones in on this deal right now."

"Charlie, you know I've got always got your back. But don't you want me to get one of the guys to help out? You don't want to get your hands dirty. You need to be very careful here, Charlie."

"Like I said, it will be a pleasure to deal with this personally." Charlie in his impulsive, yet forceful style, had already made up his mind.

"Okay boss."

"By the way, how are our shipping partners doing?"

"The Asians?"

"Yep, the Asians. They paying on time?"

"Oh yeah. They pay cash on the barrelhead. The shipments come into Vancouver in marked containers every month or so. We stock it for them, and then when they come to make the pick-up, we load it up in their unmarked van. It's a brand new one. It's all very clean. They load up, give me our 25K, and they are out of here."

"Don't give those guys any slack. The shit comes in, we handle it, they pick up, pay cash, and get out of there quick. Any trouble, then something gets lost, or goes to the wrong place. Yeah?"

"You got it, boss."

"Did they call you yet?"

"Who?"

"Their guy told me they want to increase their shipments to twice a month."

"That's okay with me. Hell, that will double our fees, plus pick up more shipping volume for the company."

"What's in those crates anyway?"

"You don't know, and you don't wanna know, Boss."

"Who does the load/unload?"

"A small, handpicked couple of my personal guys. They are specially trained, and always take care of this type of thing. It comes in on Tuesday or Wednesday, we store it for a day or two, then they pick up."

"Are we taking care of your guys?"

"Absolutely. The stuff comes in marked fragile, so these are the only guys qualified to handle it. Then Ben makes up the envelopes. They each get a thousand bucks per shipment."

"And they understand this strictly on the shut up? One stupid slip, and these guys will fall off of the back of the fishing boat, eh?"

"They are good guys. Loyal and smart. They will keep their mouths shut, trust me. Especially if shipments increase. Two grand a month, under the table? Lots of the guys, especially the casuals, would kill for that kind of money."

"We play our cards right, and this is a gravy train. They are the shippers after all. We are just doing our jobs, processing freight, right? How can we get in trouble for that?"

After lunch, Charlie went back to his office. He called Ben Harris, and they shot the breeze for a while. "How's the wife, the kids, the golf game, etc."

"How well is Tricia doing in her semi new job?" Charlie asked.

Harold Edmonds had hired her on as the Office Receptionist/ Assistant in Vancouver, but as a full union member, with benefits, and retirement, not just a civilian clerical temp. He had also promised her a promotion to business agent in time. But I guess that would be up to Charlie, now that he was running the show, and Harold was enjoying his retirement.

"She is awesome. Shows up every day, and always looks like a million bucks. I think she really appreciates what Harold did for her."

"That's great. She is a good girl."

"Ben, I need to take out a draw."

"How much you need, Charlie?"

"I need forty large. Take it out of Travel or Operations."

"Do you want it on or off of the books?"

"40 cash, and make it off of the books."

"When do you need it?"

"End of the week should be fine."

"No problem."

"Thanks, Benny. Let's go golfing before the weather turns any worse."

"Anytime, boss."

"Friday afternoon then, one o'clock at Rosewood. I'll get Rick to play with us."

Charlie picked up his cell phone, and called Local 40's telephone number in Vancouver.

"International Longshore and Warehouse Union. How may I help you?" said a pleasant voice.

"Tricia, this is Charlie. You sound good on the phone."

"Thanks boss, where may I direct your call?"

"Actually, there are a several things. I'm expecting a package in the next couple of days. It should be marked personal. Please let me know as soon as it arrives, and I'll pick it up from you. Also, it's time for your six-month review in your new position. Let's go have a cocktail this evening and talk about it."

"What time this evening?"

"Well, right after work, actually. Why don't you leave at four? Have Ginny from payroll cover the phones for you."

"Sure boss. Where do you want to go?"

"I'll meet you in the bar, at the Chart House."

The Chart House was a very nice place by any standards, especially Vancouver's. It was located right on the Columbia River's bank, and had a great water view from the lounge. Tricia had been there numerous times, but never with her big boss. And never on business. She was just a touch nervous.

Again, Charlie got there first, and watched Tricia pull into the parking lot in her sleek, black, brand new Dodge Challenger. If she wasn't all muscle, her car sure was. She was still driving carefully, it was as if she couldn't believe she was able to afford her first new car.

Charlie waved to her from the deck. It was just warm enough to sit outside if you had a fleece on, but Charlie and Tricia would be the only people out there. This was not a problem for Charlie.

"Nice wheels," Charlie said when Trish sat down.

"Thanks, we should go out for a ride in it sometime."

I'd like to ride on more than your car, Charlie thought to himself.

"So how am I doing? You going to keep me around?"

"You're doing great," Charlie said. "What do you want to drink? Champagne? A Margarita?"

"Gee, let's have some Champagne."

The waitress was approaching, and Charlie already knew what he wanted.

"A bottle of Moet, White Star, and an appetizer menu, please."

The Champagne came, and they ordered Calamari with aioli sauce, and a plate of Dungeness Crab Stuffed Avocado.

"You know your pay grade is pretty much frozen, until we can move you off of the front desk, right? You are making the same money as a starting Dockworker, so I can't pay you more than those guys. You've got that, yeah?"

"I know. But still, they can't do all of the things I can."

"This is true," agreed Charlie. "But we need to move you around the office first. Get you some experience in Payroll, Human Resources, Accounting, etc., and then, we can put you up for Business Agent."

"How cool, and Charlie, I want to thank you for this opportunity. I won't let you down."

"It's all good. Because in the meantime, I have a special opportunity coming up at the end of this month."

"What is it?"

"Well, to begin with, it's top secret. If you want this job, it is strictly classified shit. Just you and me are in, get it?"

"What do I have to do?"

"Just go trick or treating with me, and keep your mouth shut."

"There's got to be more to it than that."

"Nope. This one is as easy as it gets."

"How much?"

"Twenty-Five K, in cash."

This talk made her stomach twitch. Wow. It felt dangerous, and exciting, and it was just her and Charlie on the inside. Maybe, she thought, this is what I came here for...

"Just trick or treating, for twenty thousand dollars. What's the catch, Charlie? Nothing bad can happen, can it?"

"Not if you keep your mouth shut."

"Okay, I can do that. What do I have to do?"

"I'll tell you later."

Charlie poured some more Champagne, and Tricia scooted over toward Charlie a little bid. She held her glass up to Charlie's for a toast.

The appetizers came. They thoroughly enjoyed the tasty snacks, and the balmy afternoon.

CHAPTER FIFTEEN

If you have never read anything about Ben Hogan the world champion golfer, Ben Hogan: An American Life, by James Dodson is an excellent choice.

Ben Hogan was a tough kid who grew up on the streets of Fort Worth, Texas during the depression. He caddied whenever he could and scratched his way into a career as a professional golfer. He was a diminutive man, standing 5'7" tall, and weighing in at 135 pounds.

What he lacked in size, he made up for in heart. He was renowned for his practice habits with his fellow golf pros. While they were in the bar drinking and socializing, or otherwise engaged, Ben used to hit six or seven hundred balls A DAY. He had a few close friends, but he didn't circulate much.

After a time, when he had finally conquered a devastating duck hook, he began to win on tour. And win some more. And then some more. He won tournaments in America. He won the British open in both Britain and Scotland. He toured in Europe.

He became a darling of the foreign press. They dubbed him "The Wee Ice Mon."

In those early days of American golf, the touring pros used to drive from tournament to tournament. The prizes were so small that the guys would often travel two or three to a car and share a hotel room, to save on expenses. But these resourceful, tenacious men founded the PGA tour, and kept it going forward, until television came along, and vaulted the game into the national spotlight.

As he became more established, Ben could afford to travel alone with his wife in his new Cadillac motor car. But he still hit six or seven hundred golf balls a day.

One day he and his wife Valerie, were driving from Texas to the Tour swing through Southern California. Ben loved the west coast, and used to hang out with Bing Crosby, Bob Hope and the Hollywood crowd. As they were driving west one morning, the conditions were very foggy. While crossing over a narrow, two lane bridge, their car was hit head-on at fifty miles per hour by a Pepsi Cola delivery truck. The visibility was terrible, and at the last minute, when Ben saw the truck coming he threw himself across the front seat of the new Caddy. He wanted to protect his wife at all costs.

They both survived the accident. Valerie, amazingly with only superficial injuries, but Ben was pretty broken up. He had shattered bones, a fractured pelvis, etc. The doctors weren't sure he would ever walk again. But tough little son of a gun that he was, he took his time to recover. Then he started walking. Then he started putting and chipping. Pretty soon he was hitting golf balls.

His legs and circulation would never be the same. He had to wrap and bind them up every time he went out to play in a tournament. But the stronger he got, the more he resumed his old ball striking habits. He went on to win major tournaments in the most dramatic of fashions.

As if that wasn't enough, when he retired from play on the Professional Golfing Tour, he founded his own equipment manufacturing company. The Ben Hogan Company proceeded to make another huge impact on the game of golf.

He was without doubt a leading influence on the early era of golf in the USA, the world for that matter. His relentless tenacity in pursuing the game, is an inspiration to any serious golfer to this day.

George Richardson promised the Rosewood Board this kind of dedication, should we decide to appeal our case. He was addressing the special meeting of the Board of Trustees called by Charlie Strong.

"Again, I am shocked and completely disappointed by the decision of the Examiner," George told us. "I am afraid this decision is the inception of a policy more to the left in land use interpretation and regulation by our state and our local jurisdictions. By all reasonable standards, we are completely within our rights for this application. We are proposing a golf function, on real property owned by a golf course. Not only owned by a golf course, but utilized as such for the past sixty some years. We applied for this permit more as a courtesy to the city, and this is what we get for our trouble."

"We have three options in my opinion: The first, is to appeal the decision. In order to do this, as there are two Hearing districts in our city, I would request a Change of Venue to the Eastern District. This is the more industrialized area of the city, and they tend to have a better understanding, and are more supportive of commercial applications. I know several of the Hearing Examiners over there.

The second option would be to install a teaching facility on the eastern edge of the property in question, away from the Magnolia neighbors, and begin to use the property in the desired function regardless of the Land Use Application results. Over time, just evolve into a full use of the driving range, and ignore the community. This option would necessitate additional vegetation in the buffer area, and might cause additional litigation. And this might create a possibility of punitive damages down the road. Depending on the resolve and commitment of the adjacent neighborhood. Also, depending on the amount of mitigating vegetation the club was willing to provide.

The third option, and this is strictly between the gathered representatives of the Board of Trustees and myself this morning, would be some influence from city officials. Probably the Mayor in this case. We need to help the Hearing Examiner understand the correct interpretation of the Land Use Laws. In other words, and to put it bluntly, does anyone have any connections at City Hall? And how much would that cost us? Even perhaps, a combination of options one and three, wherein we appeal, request a Change of Venue, and also have some support from City Hall."

Yet again, George's billable hours would keep accumulating in the case of an appeal process.

This was a pretty succinct analysis by George, and the Board had some discussion of the options. There were more than a few questions relating to the matter. After these interactions wound down, it was agreed, not unanimously, but agreement was reached among us, to pursue the expansion and upgrading of our practice facilities.

"I propose that we take a break for a couple of days and digest the information we have received today," Charlie suggested. "We can have another brief meeting again on Saturday morning to come to a decision, and a direction on continuing forward."

"You have 21 days from last Wednesday, if you choose to file a formal appeal," George informed us.

On Magnolia Street, the phones were also beginning to ring.

"Hi Bob, this is Carol. You called?"

"Oh yes. I wanted to get a celebration party organized for this weekend. How about a pot luck at my house, at six pm on Saturday evening? I will supply the wine. Dane Knutson is a buddy of mine, and he's got some great wines in his portfolio."

"Sounds fantastic, Bob. I will start the phone chain. Hey, we slew Goliath, we should party, shouldn't we?"

"Hi Dane, this is Bob Kudlach. I'd like to order some wine if I could."

"Sure, Bob. What do you need, and when do you want it?"

"This Friday please. Pick out a couple of cases for me. Some Oregon Pinot Noir, and Pinot Gris. A case of Rombauer Chardonnay, and some Washington red blends."

"No problem, I'll bring them by on Thursday evening."

Charlie Strong would never have been caught dead selling wine to Bob Kudlach. But not everyone at the club was going to let politics get in the way of their commerce and old friendships.

"Hey, Larin and Mylos, my little people will be here for a couple of weeks. We should get together."

"Let's do it, I'll see you Thursday."

Saturday morning's second special meeting of the Board was another lively one. The group had had enough time to sleep on George Richardson's options, and consensus on the Board was to incorporate all three.

First of all, increase the vegetation barrier in question, and start a teaching facility on the east side of the property, away from the Magnolia St. neighbors. This concept certainly wasn't a driving range, and therefore not in violation of any court decisions.

Secondly, we agreed to appeal, especially as George Richardson surprisingly volunteered to give us a reasonable flat rate for his continuing legal services.

Thirdly, Charlie revealed to us some insight concerning his relationship with the Mayor. According to him, they had been working on the proposed Oil Refinery dock and distribution station at the Port of Vancouver property. He felt like he knew the Mayor well enough to at least broach the subject with him. "Let's see if there isn't an acceptable solution for everyone in our case." We all liked Charlie's, for once, mature approach.

Motion to adjourn, second, all in favor say aye. Aye, decision reached, meeting adjourned.

CHAPTER SIXTEEN

Tricia Watson is a born and bred Vancouver girl. Her dad was a plumber, but he left for Seattle when she was ten. They never had much of a relationship after he more or less abandoned his family. She and her mom, Maggie, managed without him for the most part. He was sporadic with his child support payments and seldom visited or made contact.

Maggie never remarried. She worked as a secretary for the City of Vancouver, and tended bar on the weekends at the Red Lion Inn in Portland to make ends meet. Working for our City Administrators, she was able to keep an eye on Tricia from an appropriate distance. But Tricia was not a problem kid. She helped her hard-working mom around the house, and did well enough in school. While they weren't wealthy, or very visible in their community, they had a comfortable apartment, and a decent lifestyle.

Tricia was an attractive young woman. She was over average height, had a pretty, inviting face, with evenly situated dimples in her cheeks. She was physically solid, full figured, and had blue eyes that brightened the sky when she smiled. Or if her eyes twinkled they looked like stars. Or if she was angry, they turned cobalt blue, and could bite you. She was an all-American type girl, who loved athletics, was a tenacious point guard on the girls' basketball team, and played a mean third base on the girls' softball team. This was somewhat unusual, as she didn't have a father figure around to coach her up. But as she got older, she began to hang out with the jock guys. She was more of a tomboy than a girly girl. Maggie used to love watching her daughter fly down the basketball court during high school games. Her blond ponytail streamed out behind her, and her bright blue eyes flashed with intensity. She had that competitive spirit, which is a natural talent. It is one of the things you cannot coach into a kid. If there was a tough matchup from the opposition, she wanted it. If there was a loose ball on the floor, she was happy to dive onto the hardwood for it.

When she was a junior, she began to date Dean Wilson. He was a year ahead of her in school, but they had known each other for quite a while, and he was also a sports oriented kid. Dean's father owned the biggest Foreign Auto Repair shop in town. Consequently, Dean always had a cool ride and was very adept mechanically. He played wide receiver on the football team, and also ran the speed events in tract. He was good to Tricia, and seemed to fill the need in her life for a serious male relationship.

They dated throughout her last two years of high school. When Dean graduated, he went off to Oregon State University in Salem, to study business. He was going to take over his dad's company. She had another year left in high school, but they kept in close touch. Dean came home every other weekend, as he was only about forty miles away. He liked OSU, and did above average work in his classes.

Tricia graduated high school, and decided to go up to Alaska and work on a processing boat for the salmon season. She would have been great college material, as she had scored in the high 1300's on her SAT tests, but she was far too practical for higher education at this time. She just wanted to make some money, and help get her adult life started. She dreamed of getting married, and was working hard to build a better life than she and her mom had known.

Dean quit college after two years. He was ready to start his career. He felt like he had gotten enough schooling to prepare him for what lay ahead. After all, his dad never went to college, and he had done just fine. While he was at OSU and Tricia was in Alaska, he had partied a little bit. Smoked some weed, been with a few girls, but he loved Tricia, and wanted to settle down with her.

They got married in a nice June wedding, nothing fancy, but it was a big wedding. Both kids were popular in high school, and still had lots of friends around town. Dean formally joined his dad's company right after the honeymoon, and Tricia worked in an escrow office in Vancouver. They had an apartment pretty close to Tricia's mom, but were building a house on property Dean's dad and mom had given them for a wedding present. With help from friends and family, they were building their new dream home together.

Tricia was now pregnant, but they still finished the house in under a year, and moved in with their new baby.

Dean enjoyed his work, and was into going out with the boys for a few beers afterward. Especially now that the house was done. He loved to have a few tokes, and get a little high on the way to the tavern to meet the guys. One day some of the guys in the body shop department of his business took him out, and gave him a little something extra.

He began chipping a little bit of heroin on the side. He knew it was dangerous, but he didn't do it regularly. Also, he knew he could quit anytime he wanted to. It just felt so good.

By the time Tricia realized what was going on, Dean was well into being strung out, and was way beyond the quitting anytime soon stage. They dealt with Dean's habit for a while, with Tricia screaming, cajoling, threatening, begging, trying anything to get him straight. Finally, Dean agreed to go into rehab. Thirty days, and he would come out clean. Tricia was heartbroken.

Dean came out a new man, and all was good again. For a bit. But he started using again, and one night, he was out with the wrong guys. He got spiked with a hot shot, and the next thing Tricia knew, she was a widow.

Devastation was not the word for her. Maggie came to stay and tried her best to help out. Tricia cried for a month before she could begin to collect herself. The funeral was the worst. He was so young, and they had such a great life ahead of them. It was such a colossal waste. How could this have happened to her? How could something like this happen to anybody?

Fortunately, she had the house that she and Dean had built. And she had her memories of the good times. After an extended period, she collected herself. She had to, for her son, her mom, and ultimately herself. She still felt like it was partly her fault that he was gone. She should have done more for him. Why wasn't she enough for him?

Dean's parents were also very supportive of Tricia and their grandson. He had been their only child, and they felt the loss as keenly as she did.

Dean Junior was two years old now, and was a very cute kid. He filled a big part of the void in Tricia's life, and she was devoted to the boy. As were his grandparents. Although his dad was gone, the child was still lucky in so many ways.

CHAPTER SEVENTEEN

On Monday mid-morning, Charlie got a call in his office from Han Say Shipping, Taipei, Taiwan.

"Good morning, this is Charlie Strong may I help you?"

"Good morning, Mr. Strong, this is Joung Chang. I am in your country this week, and I would like to meet with you on Wednesday. Is this possible?"

"Absolutely, Mr. Chang. What is your location now?"

"We are in San Francisco. We fly to Portland tomorrow afternoon, and we stay at the Heathman Hotel there. I would like to see your facilities in Vancouver on Wednesday afternoon, and perhaps we go for dinner after?"

"Yes, of course. What kind of restaurant would you like to visit?"

"We eat many Oriental food, so we like to try American food, when we visit."

"I will take care of everything. How large is your group?"

"There are four of us."

"I will pick you up in a Limousine at the Heathman tomorrow at two pm. We can tour our plant, and then we will dine in Portland, and drop you back at your hotel."

"Very good, sir." Mr. Chang speaks most impeccable English Charlie thought to himself.

Charlie called Vancouver. "Hi Tricia. Can you get Ben on the phone for me, please?" She could tell by the tone of his voice that he was excited.

"Mr. Chang and the Asians are coming on Wednesday," Charlie told Ben. "Chang wants a tour of your facilities, and then dinner. I'm sure we will be talking some business."

"Wow. This is his first actual visit with us, to my knowledge. Harold always dealt with him over the phone."

"I'll tell Rick to make sure the yards and docks are ship shape. One of their guys told him they want to start shipping twice as often. How about an extra 50K a month, work okay for you? That is some serious jack, Mac."

"Yeah it works big time. But we are going to have to start to diversify some of this cash. I already have about 200K in two different safes on site. Any more than that, and we are taking on too much risk."

"We should just pay out as the money comes in. You, me, Rick, Harold's cut, and then the dockhands."

"Should we communicate with San Francisco what is going on? You know, a cover your ass thing?"

"Hell no," Charlie said. "They would shit a brick. That would cause all kind of problems."

"Well then, we need to be sure to communicate with Mr. Chang how this is our private deal, and no one knows, or works on this but us. Tell him if San Francisco is in, the handling prices will double, or possibly stop altogether. Everything would be out of our hands."

"I'll make a reservation at Ruth Chris Steakhouse in Portland, for seven. But you should go on the walking tour of the plant with us. Then we all ride in the Limo with them, back to Portland. We can have dinner, and finish up the arrangements."

"Got it."

Charlie buzzed Tricia again, he had a laundry list for her.

"Hey, we have some big clients coming in on Wednesday afternoon. I need you to do some stuff. First, call AA Limo in Vancouver, and book them from noon to midnight on Wednesday. They will need to pick up a Mr. Chang party and myself, at the Heathman Hotel in Portland. Two pm sharp. Bring us up here, and then wait for us. Tell them to have some refreshments in the car at one. Then we are going to tour your plant, and drive back down to Ruth Chris Steak House in Portland. Tell them to have half a dozen bottles of Dom Perignon in the car. Chilled and with crystal glasses. We will need a reservation at Ruth Chris for seven of us at seven pm. Then call Rick Ferin, and tell him I need him to call me ASAP. We will also need a couple of upgraded coffee breaks. Something casual, but very nice, when we arrive. Let's finish with some fruit and cheese for around four in the afternoon."

"Yes sir. By the way. Your personal package arrived this morning."

"Great, I'll pick it up tomorrow."

It took some time for Rick to get back to his office, seeing as he was at the far end of the Port when Tricia beeped him.

He called Charlie's cell. "What's up boss?"

"Big clients coming in Wednesday, Rick. Mr. Chang from Han Say Shipping, and three of his associates. They want to tour our facilities in Vancouver, and then you are having dinner with us in Portland. I think they want to formally kick up their traffic a notch."

"What do you want me to do?"

"Take two or three guys, and make sure the V-yard is in ship shape. Let's show them where we store their cargo, how we secure and handle it, and give them a general look see, and then a security tour. Afterwards, we go to Portland for dinner and drinks."

"Done, Boss."

Rick stormed out in such a hurry Tricia was starting to wonder what was going on. She called her buddy Rebecca, in accounts receivable.

"Hey," she whispered on her phone. "Something big is happening, who is a Mr. Chang?"

"I don't know the name," said Rebecca. "But he must be with Han Say. They are our major Asian clients. Let me do some checking. I'll call you right back."

Ten minutes later, Rebecca was back on her phone.

"This is odd," she said. "Han Say's VP is a Mr. Zhuen, and there is no Mr. Chang on their list of officers or shipping agents. I don't have a clue who this guy is."

"Hmmm," said Tricia, "that is odd, because Charlie is really pulling out all of the stops on this one."

"Well, let me know if you hear anything."

"Okay."

Now Rebecca's curiosity was up. The Port of Vancouver was, of course, a much smaller port than Portland. They handled more lumber and grain shipments than anything. But Han Say was also an anchor client for them. Han Say's position in their relationship with the Port of Vancouver, was always one of efficiency. Smaller port, easier in and out. Better service, easier access to the upper northwest from across the state line, etc. Han Say after all, was only a mid-sized shipper themselves.

"Trish? Hi, it's Becca again. I've checked with everyone I can think of, and no one has heard of a Mr. Chang. The only thing I can think of is a rumor going on around the yard, that there is something secret, maybe even illegal going on down there. It probably has something to do with that kind of thing."

"Wow," Tricia said.

CHAPTER EIGHTEEN

On Tuesday morning, Charlie called Tricia again.

"Can you call the Mayor's office, and see if he can fit me in for a quick meeting this afternoon?"

"Sure Charlie. What time?"

"Anytime he is available, I will be there."

Tricia called Charlie back at his office in Portland.

"He is free after four."

"Excellent. Tell him I will be by his office at four. One more thing. Can you please have Ginny cover the phones on Thursday morning, so you can drive me back to my office in Portland? I think I will just ride back with the Limo to Vancouver tomorrow night. I don't know how much these guys are going to want to drink, but then I will need a ride back to town. Plus, that will give us some time to talk."

"Sure Charlie, and you know my limo fees are some of the best in town."

"Ha, ha. See you tomorrow."

At four in the afternoon, Charlie was walking up the steps of Vancouver's new City hall building. He was kind of cranky having had to walk three blocks to get there.

"Idiots, you think they would have put in more parking." Charlie muttered to himself. "Oh, that's right. I guess I should have taken public transportation, and then I wouldn't need a parking spot. Or I could ride a bike, and could even help save the universe." The thought of leaving his classic Jaguar XF Roadster at home, and taking one of these two options almost made Charlie double over in laughter. That would be the day.

"Hello Charlie, what can I do for you today?"

"Hi Bud, thanks for fitting me in this afternoon. I'll keep it short."

"No problem. I always have time for the good guys, Charlie. How are things?"

"Great. Looks like we are slowing down at little, heading into the off season."

"Yep. My wife is already gearing up for Halloween. We must have a thousand kids come by the house for candy. And then the holidays will be on top of us."

"Wow, that's a lot of kids."

"You better believe it."

"I have a little problem, Bud, I was hoping you might have an idea or two for me."

"What is the issue, Charlie?" Although he had a bit of an idea already.

"It is your West Side Hearing Examiner, Bud. We are trying to expand our practice facilities over at Rosewood, and we just can't seem to get past that darn gal. You know how much we pay in property taxes, and that we support all of the local kid's golf teams? That means four teams for practice, all with league matches every other week. And we try to help out with as many

High School Playoff Tournaments as we can. During the summer, with the nice weather, and all of our regular member play, it is a mad house over there."

"Hmm," Bud mused.

"We just want to expand our practice facilities on our own land which is already zoned for mixed use. But we have had two hearings now, and the neighbors come in and get all emotional, and the Examiner rules against us. I was wondering if there isn't something we can do about it. Is it possible to overrule her for the good of the community? That type of a thing?"

"Gee Charlie, I really don't have any jurisdiction over land use issues. You know how it works from our time spent working on the passage of the Oil Depot permit. There are pretty specific guidelines in that area."

"Yeah, but this seems like an entirely different consideration to me. I mean the other one is a commercial proposal, with I'll admit, some sticky issues. But this is just us trying to help out some kids on our own land. Think how much better it is for those kids to be having something positive in their lives. Would you rather have them sitting around playing video games, or out getting into some kind of mischief? You know what I am talking about. We even have a Scholarship fund, to assist some of the less fortunate kids. We help them get their equipment squared away, and pay for their league fees."

"This seems like a good thing you are trying to do here, Charlie. But you know that I don't play golf personally, and from what I have heard, there are some valid safety issues involved."

Charlie's blood pressure was starting to percolate. He could feel the run around coming from this bureaucrat of a Mayor.

"Gosh Bud, I don't personally go horseback riding, but I think we can both see a lot good there for kids. We have offered to mitigate any and all safety issues that the neighbors might have, but they are absolutely intractable. Why, I don't know."

"Well, I'm sure that the Hearing Examiner has weighed the testimony pretty carefully, Charlie. Obviously, Rosewood has somehow failed to convince her of your position."

"This is exactly what I am talking about Bud. I think we just need a nudge from the right people, to help get this thing rolling. We are planning an appeal. We are requesting a change of venue to the Eastside, and a change of Examiners. A nudge from you could be just what is needed. I am asking for a little help here. I will owe you a big one, Bud."

Charlie's vascular system was getting hotter.

"Charlie, if I could help, you know you could count on me. But my hands are absolutely tied in judicial matters." Bud thought to himself, I am not touching this one with a ten-foot pole. My constituents would have my ass if they thought I was sucking up to those rich, conservatives at Rosewood.

At times like this, Charlie wondered why he had spent four years of his life fighting for his country. Apparently so he could sit and listen to a mealy-mouthed politician whine about how little influence he had. He sure didn't remember seeing Bud Adams, over in the Vietnam jungle, right underneath the DMZ, risking life and limb every night out on jungle patrol.

"I think this is bullshit," Charlie said to him, deciding to get a little tougher. See if a little pressure might help the situation. "We have worked together on too many issues for you to ignore something like this. You are coming up for reelection next year. Would a sizeable donation help? Should we be talking about money here?"

"I know we go back quite a way, Charlie, but are you trying to influence the Office of the Mayor of Vancouver, Washington? Are you offering me a bribe?" Bud said half-jokingly to Charlie.

"I'm just trying to help some kids. I thought you might want to support your community a little more directly. I wouldn't call it a bribe, but my group is willing to be there for you, when reelection comes around. We are prepared to do whatever you might deem appropriate, or not."

Yeah, and grab some PR for yourself on that one, Bud thought. Also, most of the kids he wants to help, are their own little rich kids. This guy will be running for Mayor next.

"Charlie, once again, my hands are tied. I think this conversation is over. Good day sir."

Bud Adams stood, and offered Charlie his hand. Charlie shook it grudgingly, and left to walk back to his car. What else could he do, he still had to work with the guy on the damn Fuel Depot project?

Bud picked up his phone, and thought to himself. That stupid man, he doesn't realize that buying elections are gone, over and done. For every Rosewood voter, I've got a thousand people on the street, who want their own programs, and I am in direct communication with all of them. His secretary picked up his extension, and Bud asked her to connect him with Spence Simpson in the East Side Hearing Examiner's Office.

"Yes Sir," she said. The phone rang three times.

"Spencer Simpson, eastside Land Use, can I help you?"

"Hey Spence, how are you doing, this is Bud Adams." Bud spoke in his best-oiled politician's voice. "We need to talk for a few minutes. I've got to give you a heads up on an issue you need to avoid at all costs."

Charlie left in a huff. He was fuming, and still had to walk what seemed like a mile back to his Jag.

That jerk, Charlie thought. He didn't hesitate a minute to call when city hall needed a forty-foot Christmas tree delivered for the town square. Or when they need some extra storage space for their snow equipment every winter, did he?

Charlie decided to head over to Rosewood, he needed a drink.

The lounge was pretty quiet, Charlie sat down at the bar and ordered a Manhattan with Maker's Mark Bourbon.

Dane Knutson was sitting at the other end of the small, six seat bar. He was talking to his warehouse manager on his cell phone.

"Hey, this is Dane. I need to order some wine for an event this weekend. No, it's a special order. I'll pick up and deliver it myself." Dane went through Bob Kudlach's order with his guy.

"Ah, the good stuff. Can I go to the party?"

"Hell no. You stay in the warehouse and work. I'm not even invited."

Charlie couldn't help but overhear Dane's conversation.

"Who's partying?" Charlie asked Dane, more to pass the time than anything.

"Actually, it's for Bob Kudlach. I think he is having some people over on Saturday night."

Charlie's blood began to boil. A little celebration party eh?

"You are actually selling wine to that asshole?" Charlie asked in astonishment. "After all of the bullshit he has put this club through?"

"It's just business," Dane replied, somewhat put aback. "I'm not going to his party. He just called me for some wine. If I don't sell it to him, someone else will."

"Whatever. I wouldn't sell that guy a pile of dog crap!" Charlie knocked back his drink, and left the bar. Well, we will see how much longer that jerk is partying it up, he mumbled to himself. Christ, I can't even sit down at the damn club and enjoy a damn drink anymore.

CHAPTER NINETEEN

Wednesday dawned bright and sunny, but cool. Charlie was at his office early, and instinctively knew today was going to be a better day than yesterday.

He called Tricia at ten to check on the details.

"Everything set?"

"All set, boss."

"If I don't get a chance to talk to you today, can you pick me up at home at nine tomorrow morning?"

"Sure, no problem"

"Thanks. I want my ride in that hot car of yours."

"Anytime, Charlie."

"Plus, we will have a little time to discuss Halloween."

Charlie was sitting in the Heathman Hotel's ornate lobby at quarter to two pm. The Asians came down about five minutes later, and Charlie greeted them warmly. He was wearing a pin striped business suit, which was unusual for him. But this was a big day, and he knew his clients would be in business suits as well.

Mr. Chang slipped one surprise in on Charlie, who was not expecting a woman in the group. But Mr. Chang had brought his wife, who was apparently very involved in the operation. There was also a Mr. Thieu, and another gentleman, who looked to be Mr. Thieu's assistant.

After bowing and exchanging cordialities, everyone went out to board the limo. It was waiting sleekly at the curb of the four-star hotel. Charlie slipped the Bellman twenty bucks for opening doors, and being generally obsequious.

They made small talk for the twenty-minute drive north, which was expanded to forty minutes, because of mid-day traffic on the I-5 freeway corridor.

When they arrived at the Port of Vancouver offices, Ben Harris and Rick Ferin were, of course, there to meet them. Tricia and Rebecca were peeking out of the second-floor office window to get a look at the visiting dignitaries. Tricia even took a couple of quick photos with her cell phone. But she had to hurry back downstairs, as Ben had told her to dress it up for the day, and look a little special. She was also helping with the hospitality needs, i.e. coffee, petite fours, etc.

Charlie, Ben and Rick began the tour. They wanted to show their guests the working areas, storage capacities of the yard, and their state of the art cranes and loading equipment. When they got through with this phase, Charlie and Ben were excited to show off the Security Room and the Armory. This should impress the Asians with how well their product would safeguarded.

The group walked the yard, which took the better part of an hour. The Asians had many questions about all of the logistics they were seeing.

After the tour, they all proceeded into the warehouse. Of special interest to the group, was the small, dedicated space in which their personal cargo might be held.

"This is our most secure area," Charlie announced to the group. The seven people were standing in front of two adjacent, steel containers. The commercial sized eight by eight by ten-foot, steel doors were standing open.

Charlie and Ben swung the doors closed, and Ben clasped them locked with precision, inset dead bolts. The best locks money could buy. Next, Charlie slid an iron bar of three-inch diameter through four eye holders, that had been welded symmetrically into place, on front of the steel containers. Once the steel bar passed through the eyes, the far end fit into a foot-deep concrete column, with an eyelet positioned perfectly to receive the steel bar. A steel vault then hydraulically moved forward into position. This caused the steel bar to snap into place, through another steel eye holder, on the other end. Once the vault was in place, and securing the steel bar, the six-inch-thick vault door was closed, and locked with a built in 14-bolt locking system and combination lock.

After all of the doors were secured, the group stepped back a few paces to inspect their handiwork. It would take some serious explosives to manage an unauthorized entry through those doors.

"Now look up," Charlie instructed them. Directly overhead about twenty feet, were four spray-nozzle heads. Much like you would see in a public building, for use in a fire suppression system.

"These nozzles contain concentrated hydrochloric acid,'" Charlie explained. "Should any unauthorized person somehow gain entrance into this triple secured area, and attempt to tamper with the locked containers, this system would be activated from our control room, completely deterring any deluded attempts at unlawful entry of any kind."

Mr. Chang's group seemed duly impressed. They were not flashy or demonstrable people, but were very attentive, and seemed to be mentally recording any and all details. They even stopped to record some images on their cellular phone's cameras.

Charlie suggested they proceed to the Admin building, where they could have a look at the security room.

The ILWU offices in the Port of Vancouver, were nothing special, although they did have a nice view, and were situated close to the river's edge. They were a couple hundred yards north of the main loading docks. Once inside, they were monotoned, and basically similar to any industrial type office space.

Several support staff were working at their desks, and they looked up and greeted the visitors with smiles. But what Charlie really wanted to show off, was the Security bunker, and his armory.

At the back of the office complex, was a glassed-in room about thirty by thirty feet. It had a bank of computers across the back wall, facing the water. Meaning anyone viewing the screens, would be facing away from the water view. The computer system covered every square inch of the Port property.

The main gate was on the first screen, followed by the container storage area from two elevated angles, so the whole area was visible. Then the docking and load/unload areas. The office, parking lot, the security office itself, and finally the warehouse. Again, the warehouse was monitored from a higher angle, so that the entire space was viewable with only two monitoring cameras.

There was a security guard on duty in the bunker, who was introduced to the group. Charlie explained how the ten pm to six am shift, employed two guards on duty at all times. This was designed to safeguard against any possible human lapses or indiscretions. The film from the previous shifts, was reviewed immediately by the next shift. And there had never been any problems of a serious nature at their Port site. "Things work much different here, then in the inner-city Ports like San Francisco, Oakland or Los Angeles. We are serious about managing and preventing any theft on these premises," he told them.

"I'd like you to see our final deterrent," Charlie told the visitors. He nodded to the Security Guard, and led the group over to the west side of the room, where an automated wall was sliding open.

Against the back wall of the secret, concealed compartment, was a small arsenal, that would have made a terrorist cell proud. There were half a dozen Uzi sub-machine guns, several Barrett sniper rifles, bullet proof vests, and camo gear. Half a dozen hand grenades were attached to an Army ammunition belt. They hung ominously from a large brass hook. There were four German Luger pistols, four Glocks, ammo clips, etc.

"I am showing these precautions to you, just to emphasize how seriously we take security around here," Charlie said. "And let me assure you of one more thing. Our security personnel, are trained and retrained on a regular basis. They know how to use these weapons, in case of any issues."

Charlie offered the group an opportunity to go to the practice range, and test fire the Uzis. Mr. Thieu looked at Mr. Chang. He was definitely interested, but Mrs. Chang expressed no interest at all.

"Thank you for your generous offer, Mr. Strong. But I don't think this will be necessary."

"Well then, why don't we proceed to the conference room, and we can finish up our business."

Tricia had refreshed the facilities from their earlier visit, and was busy setting out some bottles of Perrier, and various flavored waters. She was just finished fine-tuning a nicely appointed fruit and cheese platter, with baguettes, when the tour group arrived. She looked very stylish and professional in a radiant blue, one-piece business ensemble, with padded shoulders and mid-elevation matching pumps. Charlie noticed her tanned and toned legs, which looked spectacular.

"Thank you, Tricia, everything looks great."

"Sit down everyone, and make yourselves at home," Charlie invited the group.

The Asians all sat on one side of the table, looking conservative. Inscrutable really. Quiet, observant, and circumspect. They were the epitome of international people, doing business on someone else's turf.

Mr. Chang began the conversation. "Thank you for most delightful tour. This is our first visit to your area. The reason for our visit, is to increase our shipments to twice per month."

"That should be no problem," Ben Harris replied. For once, Charlie let him talk. "We are equipped to handle your freight, as long as it keeps moving through, on a timely basis."

"Yes, Mr. Thieu will call Mr. Ferin with shipping information, when product is to arrive. Shipment will arrive in commercial crate, marked sensitive material. Then, Mr. Thieu's people will arrive next day to receive shipment. Payment in cash, made at that time of transfer."

"I have a suggestion," said Rick Ferin. "Maybe you need to pack your shipment in a regular container, and then Mr. Thieu can let me know the container number, when he calls. If we are to receive shipments on a regular basis, our goal is to turn around the shipment as quickly as possible. The quicker the product is in and out, the less opportunity the Maritime Commission or anyone else might be able to cause problems."

"Yes, we agree completely. We don't want any undue attention called here at all. How often does the Maritime Commission drop by?"

"Not that often. When they do come, they don't stay very long. They are more interested in proper documentation than anything. However, the last time they were here, they did bring some drug dogs with them."

"I can assure you our product is packaged with the utmost care. It is vacuum sealed three times, under the most sterile conditions, and then the drums themselves are sealed with paraffin. We agree completely that the safest path going forward, is to remove the product at the earliest possible time after its arrival."

"As you can see," Rick said "we are stacked six high in the yard with containers. Maybe we would be better off leaving the containers top loaded, until Mr. Thieu arrives. Then, we bring down his container, load him up, and he is out of here. That might be even better than the steel security containers, because that would be the only product in the container at that time. If we were visited, that isolated location could be a problem. I believe the key is Mr. Thieu. He notifies us of your ETA, then you come get the product out of our yard as soon as is possible. We can't be too careful on your behalf."

"I agree, if we are going to increase our frequency, then we need to increase our efficiency."

Mrs. Chang said, "We can monitor the progress of the shipment, but we should not draw extra attention to an individual container. That would-be a, how you say, red flag for both the shipping company, and also your dockworkers."

Everyone agreed with Mrs. Chang, and by now Charlie was beginning to see some of the dangers involved in what they were doing. Which of course meant that dollar signs were starting to flash before his eyes. Not only would they be able to double their cash, but the Port would also be gaining more business from an extra shipment per month. And in his opinion, the majority of the onus was on the Chang's. After all, they were the primary shippers, and if all of Charlie's people just played dumb, then what was their real risk?

"What exactly is your relationship with Tan Say Shipping, Mr. Chang?"

"My wife and I are connected to the Board of Directors and operations. My half-brother is President of Tan Say Shipping. We will take care of our end."

"Very good sir, but under the circumstances, and the additional risk and frequency of the shipments that will be coming through, we are going to have to increase our handling fees to $40,000. per."

"This is a significant increase in your fees," said Mr. Chang.

"Yes sir, it is. However, the frequency could create many problems. If we don't handle things correctly, there could be serious difficulties, and I mean serious. And there will be more people to take care of on our end." Rick added. "We need to discuss documentation on the shipments. We can still process your shipments on a fragile/sensitive basis, and that would allow us to expedite your product to Mr. Thieu. However, there should be some official paper work."

"Good call, Rick," Charlie interjected. "It probably wouldn't hurt any to have Mr. Thieu set up some type of shell company. A shipping and receiving outfit of some kind. An import/export company maybe?"

"Good idea, gentlemen," Mr. Chang replied. "Mr. Thieu, will you please see to those details?"

"Yes Sir."

"Then we will agree to your terms. Do you have any more business to discuss?"

"Yes, I do," said Charlie. "This business needs to be strictly confidential between us. Those of us who are gathered in this immediate room. If San Francisco should become aware of our arrangements, we would have to cease business dealings with your group immediately. Do you understand me? Our arrangements would stop on a dime. There can be no misunderstandings here."

"Yes. We understand the extreme sensitivity of our dealings. I think we have covered everything, and we are most aware of unpleasant consequences. It seems to me the key is Mr. Thieu and Mr. Ferin working very closely together. That will it make it safer for everyone. Also, I wish to reassure you all, how much we wish to continue on with the relationship that Mr. Harold Edmonds and I created some years ago. We will do everything possible to preserve matters of confidentiality, and continue on with our business opportunities."

"We agree," Charlie said.

"I have just one more thing," said Mr. Chang. "Is it possible for Ms. Tricia to join us for dinner? Mrs. Chang likes to have another female to chat with."

"Fine with me," Charlie replied. "Are we through here?"

CHAPTER TWENTY

Being tactful of a woman's age, one would say that she might be in her forties, but it looked more like she was in her thirties. Whatever her age, Madame Chang had matured into an exquisite and stunning woman.

She had grown up in Chaing Mai, which is in the mountains of the Golden Triangle area of Southeast Asia. Her parents were farmers/poppy growers, and she had worked in the processing labs for a while. But she was smart, and she was beautiful. Too smart and gorgeous to stay in the mountains where rural poverty was brutal. So, she and her father decided it was best if she got out.

Her family worked dawn to dark, six days a week, and barely had food on the table. Let alone running water, sanitary facilities, or educational opportunities. The Over Lords came and bought their poppy bulbs, this is true. And growing heroin was twenty times more profitable than any other agricultural product they could raise. But Mrs. Chang's father had been out of the mountains several times, and he felt sure his bright, talented daughter could somehow escape their impoverished life style, and help her family in the bargain. If she could start selling their product directly to the market, then they had a small sliver of a chance to make a life for themselves.

Her father warned her to be very careful. They would plan carefully for her departure. "You must find work in a busy bar or restaurant. Don't be flashy, just be careful. And whatever you do, don't ever take any of our own product." He gave her 200 Baht, and four pounds of finished product. Pure China White uncut heroin. This was most of his life's savings.

Her mother had sewn the two two-pound packages into the lining of her inner coat. It was going to be winter soon, and she somehow had to make it down out of the mountains, and over to the west coast of Thailand. She had rice balls and some tofu to eat. Enough for about four days of travel. Her father suggested she take his small dagger with her. She could conceal it on her person in case of emergency. He showed her how to use it.

And so, she took off one morning before dawn. She was sixteen years old, and was terrified of what lay before her. But she was also deeply honored her family would entrust her with such a huge responsibility. She was determined to make a success of her harrowing trek for all of them.

She walked for three days, ate sparingly, and made do at nights. She would put together some kind of lean-to, and sleep fitfully, trying her best to stay warm, and clutching the small dagger her father had given her.

On the fourth day of her journey, a Land Rover SUV pulled over on the road in front of her. She had seen few cars in her life, but this one had apparently passed her going up to Chaing Mai, and then had seen her again on their trip back down. They were a United Nations team doing a survey of hydro-resources in the area. "Would you like a ride?" Fortunately, they had an interpreter with them, because she spoke nothing but her mountain dialect of the Thai language. She gratefully accepted.

They traveled for about six hours, and finally arrived in Trang, Thailand. The first thing she did was rent a cheap room, and learn how to use an indoor toilet. Then she learned how to take a shower with hot and cold running water.

She rented the room for a week, which took half of her two hundred Baht. She walked the streets for the better part of the week. Her father had told her, to look for work in a restaurant. So, every restaurant she saw, she went in and asked if they needed any help.

One of the restaurants she applied to, sent her to a nearby hotel, which was looking for maids. This was at the very bottom of the local totem pole of employment opportunities, but she was elated to have found work. And it was the perfect job for her. It allowed her to learn the urban culture, study up on languages, keep a roof over her head, and even fed her one meal a day.

She worked as a chamber maid for six months, and learned through the grapevine that the hotel bar, needed a cocktail waitress. She applied immediately, put on some make up, put on her best ao dai (an ao dai is the traditional dress of southeast Asian women), and spoke with the bar manager. He liked her looks, was willing to train her, and off she went.

She worked in the bar for a year, and it was another life line for her. She kept to herself, although she had many opportunities to stray, or go out and have fun. But this entailed spending money. She saved her money. All of it.

She learned many things in the bar. Who to trust, who not to trust. She learned pidgin English, the better to flirt with the Americans who frequented her establishment. She learned who some of the unsavorys were. She looked and listened. But she needed to understand which of these guys she needed to deal with, if she ever wanted to get rid of the stuff her father had given her. She also gained information about Vietnam being the place to be in southeast Asia at that point in time.

She finally settled on one of the unsavorys, who seemed less unsavory than the others. She gave him a taste of her product, and he liked it. It was rare to get something so pure, something that wasn't stepped down four or five times. They arranged a meeting place in the light of day, and she took a couple of her bartenders with her for safety's sake. She made the equivalent of ten thousand dollars, on her first transaction.

She immediately paid her bartenders for their services. And went to four different banks, and bought four $2000. packets of traveler's checks.

She rented a guide with a Land Rover, and made arrangements to go visit her family. She brought gifts, and some extra bahts for her father. She had a wonderful visit on her homecoming. Her mother, father, and two sisters were very proud to see her again. Her brother wanted to come back with her. She told him to wait, she would send for him.

Her father had saved another four pounds of heroin for her. She told him not to sell to the Drug Lords anymore, that she would give him a better price. He said that he had to sell them something, or they would come and burn all of his crops down. She understood, and told him to do what he needed to do, but to talk to the other farmers, and secure as much product for her as he could. "But be very, very careful father. This is bad business."

She went back to Trang, worked a little longer, and got a visitor's visa to Vietnam. She landed in Saigon, and began establishing herself there. She met Mr. Chang on, of all things, a passenger train. They were both going to Cam Ranh Bay, a beautiful seaside resort on the east coast of South Vietnam. Mr. Chang was taking a vacation, the future Mrs. Chang to see her first resort as a guest. They hit it off, and managed to spend most of the weekend together.

Mr. Chang was Chinese, but was part of a large contingent of his people in Vietnam. He was a young businessman in a warzone. There was money to be made if one was prudent.

After they had dated for a couple of months, they married in a simple civil ceremony. She had told him of her opportunities on the supply side of the drug trade. Mr. Chang had connections on the demand side. It was a partnership made in heaven. Their business flourished, in large part, because of the purity of their product. Mr. Chang wanted to cut it before they sold it, but she would have none of that.

"The reason people will buy from us, is because our product is the best. They know they will always get the best from us." Hell, it was her product, who was he to argue.

They lived in Saigon, Vietnam for three years, leaving soon after the United States pulled out of the war. They had done well for themselves. The American G.I.s had proven to be very good customers. She was able to enhance her families' mountain lives. Her father continued to be her best connection and supplier. In Saigon, Mrs. Chang was known as Madame Chang. This was a very respectful title for one who was so young, but Sui Chang was up to the task. She could be stern if need be, but she was also well liked and respected. She treated people kindly, because she never forgot her early life with the mountain people of the Golden Triangle, and the arduous road to success she had courageously traveled in order to become Madame Chang.

Using Mr. Chang's family ties, they moved to Taipei, Taiwan. Of course, they wished to continue on in their lucrative export business. It took some time, but eventually Han Say shipping was born, and they were now respected Drug Lords who bought pure heroin from the Golder Triangle Highlanders.

Charlie Strong's dinner arrangements turned out to be a great success. They enjoyed the crisp, effervescence of the Dom Perignon champagne on the ride back to town. As they were a little early for their dinner reservation, he had the driver give them a mini tour of Portland.

Arriving at Ruth Chris Steakhouse, Charlie and group were ushered in with no small amount of fanfare. Charlie was a favorite at the high-end steak house, and was known as a prodigious tipper. Especially, after he had a cocktail or three.

The Local #40 guys were a little concerned about bringing Tricia into the inner circle too quickly, but it turned out that Madame Chang wanted little from Tricia. Nothing more serious than to pick her brain for shopping tips in Portland. Seems that she loved western fashion, especially smaller, boutique shops which had more exotic lines than Nordstrom. When she heard Tricia was driving Charlie back to the City in the morning, she invited her to come by and go out shopping. Tricia was excited to join her, and couldn't wait for tomorrow morning.

Charlie asked Mr. Chang to order wine, and to pick any bottle from the list, other than Northwest wine. Mr. Chang selected a nicely aged bottle of Chateau Margaux, the benchmark of the French Bordeaux region. Charlie ordered a bottle of Leonetti, Cabernet Sauvignon. Everyone weighed in on the merits of the wines throughout their meal. Without insulting Mr. Chang's choice of wines, it was decided that the Leonetti was the match of the Margaux, and at one third the price.

While the ladies were talking shopping and fashion, Charlie and Mr. Chang got to talking about Vietnam. This kept them occupied for most of the evening, and as the wine started to take hold, Charlie even managed to work in a few war stories. Mr. Chang was also able to tell some stories about his fine art collection, and their export company.

Apparently living in Saigon, with the French influence on that cuisine, had instituted an affection for western cuisine, and the Changs were in heaven when traveling to Europe or the United States.

They finished their meal of the finest prime aged beef, with a fluffy, light Chocolate Mousse, and it was time to file back to the Limo.

"Thank you for most honorable dinner," Mr. Chang said, bowing to all of the Americans.

Charlie bowed back, and invited Mr. and Mrs. Chang to stay on longer with them.

After dropping his party off at the Heathman Hotel, Charlie cracked another bottle of Dom for the ride home. He seemed to be in high spirits.

"That went very well" he said. Rick and Ben agreed.

"The key to this whole deal is to get this stuff in and out pronto." Now the alcohol was starting to kick in. Charlie was talking a little too much, and Rick looked sideways at Ben, while motioning his head in Tricia's direction.

"How about those Trailblazers," Ben said, as the limo drove past the Portland Coliseum. "This could be our year."

Rick picked up on the conversation immediately. "As long as we can stay healthy, etc. etc."

It didn't really matter, as Charlie was falling asleep on the back seat of the limo anyway.

Tricia smiled to herself, and wondered why it was so important to get a shipment of rare, Asian art out so pronto? Asian Art, my ass, she thought.

CHAPTER TWENTY-ONE

The next morning Tricia picked Charlie up at his condo, and headed back to Portland to drop him off, and then meet up with Madame Chang.

Although he was hung over, Charlie was in high spirits. Apparently, his meetings yesterday had left him in an optimum mood.

"You look better in the morning than I even remember," Charlie said to her.

"Thank you." She pulled out of his complex, and headed for the freeway. She was a little hung over this morning herself.

Charlie, feeling expansive, reached over and cupped Tricia's right breast, and thumbed her nipple.

Tricia knocked his hand and arm away, and gave him the look. "What am I a piece of meat, Charlie? Don't you want this to be something a little special for us?"

Her reaction brought Charlie back down to earth.

"Sorry about that."

"Let it go. What's going on for Halloween?"

"Oh yeah."

Charlie reached into his briefcase, and brought out five thousand dollars. It was in one hundred-dollar bills. Fifty of them. Brand new crisp, starchy, and all strapped together like they were fresh from the mint.

"What is that?"

"It's a down payment, I thought you might need some cash for shopping today."

"How thoughtful, Charlie. Put it in the glove compartment, will you? So just what am I supposed to do for you?"

"Next Friday night, Halloween night, you need to pick me up in the Rosewood parking lot right around 8:30. If you want to use your car, we will need to change out the plates. If you would prefer, I will get you a rental. Call my cell when you arrive in the lot. I will be having dinner in the bar. I'll be there early, and my car will be parked in the front row. Don't park in a stall, but just idle behind my Jag. As soon as you call, I'll excuse myself, and be right out. There will be a small satchel in the trunk of my car. I will need to get it. But don't hang up your phone, because that is part of our alibi. Just put it in the glove compartment, and I'll do the same when I get in the car." Charlie took a breath.

"Then we to drive over to Magnolia Street. It should only take about a minute. You'll need to be in some kind of a fairy princess costume for Halloween, and make sure it comes down to your knees. Have a mask on that will cover your face. I'll have my mask in the satchel. When we get to Magnolia Street, we need to turn around at the end of the cul-de-sac, no lights on, and park in front of the target. I put on my mask on, and we go trick-or-treating. You ring the bell, and then get down on your knees like you are a kid. I will be standing behind you like I am the dad. As soon as the door opens, you peel away, low and fast, and to your left. You head back to the car. I will pop the guy a couple of times, and be right behind you. Then we beat it back to the club. Grab our phones, and I go back inside. I was just outside talking to my girlfriend on the phone for a few minutes. It's as simple as that."

"Afterwards, you should go somewhere and have a drink. You will need to calm your nerves. Then we can meet back at my house, and settle up. What do you think, easy enough, eh?"

"Sounds like a plan, Charlie, unless there are a bunch of other kids around."

"I don't think they will be there so late. They all want to get their shit earlier. If there are some stragglers, I will fire a couple of rounds in the air to scare them off. They will hit the deck, and we are out of there. We will be in costume anyway, don't forget."

"Okay."

"Any more questions?"

"Well, I think we should run through it once next week, just to make sure I know what I am doing."

"Good idea. Maybe next Tuesday or Wednesday night after dark."

"Excellent."

By now they were at Charlie's Port Offices. "Thanks for the ride. See you next week, I'm going down to Pebble Beach for a Teamsters golf tournament tomorrow. You want to come with me?"

"Gee Charlie, give a girl a little more notice next time."

Damn, she always seems to be busy or something, Charlie thought. Oh well, I should have called her sooner. "Okay. But you are missing out on a great time. Let's do next Wednesday night for the trial run. Go out to dinner, and then cruise the neighborhood."

"Sounds good. Thanks for the heads up."

Charlie got in his office, and called Rick Ferin. "Can you come down for lunch today? I want to go over next week's details with you, before I leave."

"Where are you going?"

"I'm flying down to Monterrey, and doing a Teamster's two-day golf tournament at Pebble Beach."

"Where do you want to meet?'

"Meet me at that new Peruvian Restaurant in the Pearl district. Twelve o'clock."

"See you there."

Charlie got to the restaurant at a quarter to twelve. He was always early, and hated people who dared to be late. It was a sickness in his mind.

He was settled in a corner table in the bar, when Rick rolled in.

"I ordered us a couple of Mojito cocktails," Charlie said, as the waiter sidled up. "Got any specials today?"

"As a matter of fact, yes sir, I do. There is a beautiful Pescado, that is rock fish, which is deep fried and served whole, with arroz and black beans. It is crunchy, and decilioso, and also comes with a guajillo chili aioli sauce. The second selection is a broiled Carne Asada beef steak. Served with grilled legumbres, and a salsa butter sauce."

"What the hell are legumbres?" Charlie snorted.

"Sorry sir, those are grilled vegetables."

"I think I will try the bone out short ribs," Charlie ordered first.

"That seafood special sounds pretty good to me," Rick said.

"Great job yesterday, Rick. The Chinks seemed pretty happy. You did well on your end. And I think we got all we could have wanted from them. Up the ante, up the security, and basically cover our ass."

"We did fine. Mr. Thieu is easy to work with. He gets it, and understands what's at stake here."

"Make sure he has his Import/Export company up and running, and also has paperwork on each and every shipment."

"Mr. Thieu told me they already have one more container in route, which will get here before he gets his paperwork done. So, we will have to move it out. We can't let it sit around. Or do you want me to refuse shipment?"

"No, don't do that. Just get in touch with him, and tell him 40K for anything, from now on."

"Great minds work alike. I knew that's what you would want to do."

"I wanted to talk to you about Halloween."

"I sure wish you would let me get one of the guys for this. I don't feel good about you going in there yourself."

"It's not a problem, trust me. It's a clean hit. It will take about six minutes. I know the area better than anyone, especially an outsider. It will be done, and done right in a heartbeat. Especially with you having my back."

"What do you want me to do?"

"Call Bruce Cranston, and arrange for him to meet us for dinner at the club Halloween night at seven o'clock. Tell him we need to strategize over the driving range appeal. Just the three of us. Kind of like an informal Exec Committee meeting. He eats that kind of shit up."

"OK," Rick said.

"Tricia is all set up. She is going to call me at exactly eight thirty. I will answer my phone, and say it is from my girlfriend. I have to go outside to take the call. Tricia will be waiting outside with a car. She will be in costume. I grab a tote bag out of my trunk, put my mask on. We drive over to Magnolia. We idle the car outside of Kudlach's, and go trick-or-treating. She rings the bell, and when Kudlach answers, pop, pop. Silenced, Sig Sauer 226. We are back in the car, and back at the club in four minutes. I am back in the bar, and sitting down in five. You just need to distract Bruce a bit, so he doesn't pay any attention to me being gone."

"I have an idea." Rick was thinking ahead. "I should get him back into the kitchen to look at the new pizza oven. I will stall him for ten minutes or so, and you can already be back at the table when we return."

"Good call. I'll phone Larry Easton, and tell him I am coming in for dinner with a couple of board members. We want to try the new oven out, so make sure the chef is on it. Then you are set up."

"Yeah, just make sure we order pizza for an appetizer." Rick was starting to feel better about Charlie's plan. Pop, pop, and done.

"This should certainly slow them down when we appeal. No more Kudlach," Rick said.

"Yeah. They will probably postpone the whole thing, pending an investigation. And we can just proceed to plan B, giving it an appropriate amount of time for things to settle down."

"Maybe in the future, they won't be so judgmental, and we can all be friends again. They certainly won't be so quick to want to protest every little thing we do."

Lunch came, and Charlie ordered another round of drinks. They both dug into their meals. Charlie was a little hungover, and was starving to death. Rick's seafood presentation sat up impressively on an oversized platter. It looked as if it was still swimming in the ocean. Albeit, it had morphed from the sea's silvery sleekness to the golden brown of the deep fryer.

"We've got to bring the girls back here for dinner some time. This place is great."

Rick laughed. "You don't have a girl, Charlie."

"Shut up. You know I want to hang with Tricia. But she seems a little more distant, now that Harold hooked her up for life."

"Be nice to her. Treat her with some respect. She is still a nice girl, and she just wants a little romance. Man handle her, and it will never fly. Don't forget, she is a widow, and from what I have heard, her old man over dosed."

"I hear you." Charlie could pretty much testify to the fact of how man handling was not the right approach with Tricia.

On the other hand, Charlie had nicely invited her to spend the weekend with him at Pebble Beach, and that didn't seem to work either. Even though it was on short notice, he knew a lot of girls who would drop everything to go there and hang with the stars, whatever kind of notice. As a matter of fact, he would call a few of them this afternoon. He already had two plane tickets reserved.

CHAPTER TWENTY-TWO

Tricia picked Madame Chang up at ten, and off they went. Portland, Oregon is no Rodeo Drive, but it has some nice little tucked away specialty shopping salons. Especially downtown, and by the riverside waterfront.

They had a great time poking around, and Tricia knew how and where to shop. Especially when she was with someone who seemed to be of unlimited resources, and who wanted to show Tricia her gratitude for all of Charlie's generosity yesterday.

Tricia was overcome with Madame Chang's innate beauty. Yesterday for the business meeting, she had worn a dark business suit. Hair up in a bun, no makeup, eye glasses, etc. Today however, she looked simply exquisite. She wore silver walking pumps, with black, silk, flared slacks. She sported an elegant lavender silk blouse, and was wrapped against the chilly October weather, in a crimson Cashmere shawl that was as soft to the touch as a glowing sunset. Her mid length hair was down, and was lustrous. Her high Eurasian cheekbones were lightly blushed. While yesterday she wore no jewelry other than a plain gold wedding band, today, she was decked out. She showed a five-carat rock on her right hand, a sparkling tennis bracelet, and a beautiful large, leather designer belt, wrapped around her waist. She was head turning gorgeous, and Tricia although, dressed in her finest, and looking hot, felt visibly underdressed next to Madame.

M. Chang obviously loved fine jewelry, and by the look of it, fine silk also. Of course, Tiffany and Co. was a must stop. There were also numerous custom jewelry stores with a northwest flavor in town. Madame purchased a handsome fire opal piece, set in gold with a half carat diamond inset on a gold chain. She also selected a fine, if conservative gold chain for her husband.

She then offered to buy Tricia a beautiful driftwood pendant with a smaller, but still impressive, diamond inset. It too was set in gold, and Tricia tried to refuse Madame's generosity.

"Really, Mrs. Chang, it is lovely, but I am just here because I enjoy your company so much."

"Oh no," Madame responded. "It would be grave insult to refuse kind gesture of honorable gift in Asian culture."

So, what could she do? They left the store, and Tricia put her arm through Madame Chang's as they walked down the sidewalk. She just seemed so international, so mature, and oh so refined and elegant.

"Do you have children?" Tricia asked.

"No, not of my own, but many nieces and nephews. I like it better that way."

The girls went to Paloma and Adorn Boutiques, which are some of Portland's coolest, dearest, and priciest. Of course, they had to make an obligatory stop at Nordstrom's downtown mega store.

They found lots to look at. Madame seemed particularly interested in the top of the line American lingerie. They browsed, and Madame found several items she wanted to try on.

She kept looking, and found a couple more for Tricia.

"Please, come to room with me," she said. "Tell me how I am looking."

Madame Chang took Tricia's hand, and led her into the dressing room. They entered the farthest stall.

Madame stepped out of her pumps, removed her belt and shawl. She took off her slacks, and carefully folded them, and set them on the bench. Tricia was a bit taken aback, as she assumed they would be in their own cubicles, so she hesitated. Madame's silk blouse came off, she folded it, set it on top of the slacks and turned to Tricia.

"Don't be afraid. Here I can help you." As Tricia began to unbutton her blouse, Madame released her belt, and undid her waist button. With her zipper down, Tricia's slacks slid smoothly over her hips. Madame bade her to step out of them, and folder them neatly, and sat them on top of her pile of clothes. Tricia hung her blouse up on one of the hooks.

"Can you unhook me?" Madame turned her back to Tricia and pulled her shoulders forward. Tricia undid the bra clasp, and Madame turned slowly to her, and said, "Let me get yours."

Tricia started to turn, but Madame caught her elbow, and said "That okay. Stand still."

She stood facing Trish, and reached around her with both arms. She took her time undoing the bra, and when she was finally finished, they were standing in each other's arms in only the sheerest of panties. Madame was actually wearing a black, lacy thong.

She pulled Tricia to her, and stepped Tricia backwards until they were against the back wall of the dressing room. She caressed Tricia's face for a moment, and then pressed her lips against Tricia's and kissed her sweetly on the mouth.

Tricia was frozen in time. She had never been with another woman, had never even thought of being with another woman. As a matter of fact, had not been with anyone since before her husband Dean had died almost four years ago.

But this just felt so good, and Madame was so gentle, and her fragrance was so alluring. She smelled just like what Tricia imagined a lotus blossom might smell.

Madame's kisses became more urgent, and Tricia began to relax and enjoy the moment. She stroked Madame's back, from the nape of her neck, and then on down to her lovely, golden derierre. She held both of Madame's firm cheeks in her hands, squeezed tightly, closed her eyes, and let time stop. No wonder Madame was so fond of silk, her skin felt absolutely like satin.

How long did they embrace? Tricia did not know, but she was as aroused as she had ever been. It felt like a school of butterflies were mating in her pelvis. She gently pulled away.

"Oh my. We had better try something on, hadn't we?"

"Yes, yes."

As classy as Madame was, Tricia knew that sex in a Nordstrom's changing room wasn't her style. And she was right.

Madame helped Trish into a sheer teddy. She turned her around, cupped her breasts from behind, and fondled her. She straightened up the teddy, and admired Tricia's body. "You are so beautiful," she said. She seemed enthralled by the blond hair, that was bleached from the past summer in the sun.

Gosh, my boobs are sure popular today, Tricia thought to herself.

"How is everything fitting, ladies?" The sales woman knocked lightly on the outer door.

"Just fine thank you," Tricia replied. "We will be out in a moment."

They took off the teddy, and Madame reached into her Gucci handbag, and came out with a small jar of passion fruit body cream. She undid the lid, and took a dab in her hands. She rubbed them together, and began to massage Tricia's breasts. Tricia closed her eyes, and let her head lean backward.

Her nipples were very hard.

Then they tried a bustier on her. Madame thought they both looked great.

Tricia sat down on the bench next to the clothes, and pulled Madame to her. She buried her face in Madame's perfect, uplifted pear-shaped breasts and swollen nipples, and they had a very clingy moment.

Finally, Madame tried on her own teddy. It seemed as if the women were having a contest of endurance with each other. Indulge, restrain. Indulge, restrain. They were both very aroused. It was getting steamy in the little room, but they took their time and redressed. Tickling and caressing each other playfully as they went.

When they were put back together, and presentable, just before Madame Chang led the way back out to the cashier's station, she took her phone out, and asked Tricia for her email address. Tricia was only too happy to give it to her. She asked for Madame's address in return. Madame gave it to her, and said "You call me Sui when we alone together."

Tricia smiled and nodded to her. Sui Chang kissed her lightly on the nose, and they gathered up their stuff. The women headed out, and Sui Chang had her credit card out by the time they had reached their cashier.

"How did we do in there," the sales girl asked cheerfully, in the Nordstrom's manner.

"Everything was just fine. I will take it all. Please gift wrap these two together, and these two together. I want a two-thousand-dollar gift certificate for this gift box, please."

"Certainly ma'am. That will take a moment. How do you wish to pay for you purchase?"

Madame gave the young woman her Amex Platinum card. "Would you like to apply for a Nordstrom's card today. It comes with a fifteen percent discount."

"No thank you," said Madame Chang.

The young woman stepped away, and Tricia gave Madame the look of, what are you doing? This isn't necessary.

"You are so beautiful," Madame said to her. "Always stay so beautiful for me." Tricia's dimples beamed, and she blushed.

They collected their packages, and left Nordstrom's. Tricia was still a little woozy, and feeling weak. Her blood had certainly not gotten back to her head yet. But the crisp, autumn air had a bracing effect, and she felt her equilibrium returning. She reached over and took Madame Chang's hand, and they marched off down the sidewalk.

"Where are we going?" Tricia asked. "I am getting hungry."

"We are meeting Mr. Chang, and Mr. Thieu for lunch at Chef Roy Yamaguchi's new restaurant in the Westin Hotel lobby."

"Fun."

It was a little after one, so the crunch of the lunch rush was just leaving. Madame Chang kissed her husband on the cheek, and they all exchanged greetings.

"How was shopping?" Mr. Chang asked, when they were seated in their tall, wraparound, padded booth.

"We didn't spend nearly as much moneys as we should have. But I bought you a present." Madame pulled out the gold chain and gave him the box."

"Thank you." Mr. C opened the box, and dangled the chain on his finger. 'I will put it on later," he announced.

"Have you eaten at Roy's before?" Mr. C. asked Tricia.

" No, I have not. It's very new to Portland."

"He serves the finest Sable fish in the world. If ever we are in a city that has a Roy's Restaurant, I insist on going."

"Well then, let's try the Rex Hill Chardonnay to go with" Tricia said. "I hear it is one of our best white wines."

The luncheon was memorable. The Black Cod (aka Sable Fish) was fish butter, and was perfectly complimented by the oaky Chardonnay.

Tricia steered the conversation over lunch to Oriental art. Did she have any background, Mr. Chang wanted to know? Not really, but she had some money to invest, and putting it into something substantial like art or commodities seemed so much safer than the stock market. She conversed appropriately with Mr. Chang at the luncheon table, confident that he was very knowledgeable. And diversified too. He seemed to be very well informed. But she still was not convinced he was the connoisseur he posed himself to be.

As lunch was ending, Tricia asked their waiter to take a picture of the table on her phone. Madame nodded her approval, but the gentlemen immediately declined to have their picture taken.

Outside of the restaurant, they said their goodbyes. Tricia bowed deeply, and thanked her hosts for such a wonderful day. She and Madame kissed on both cheeks, and she floated back to her car. She had completely overlooked the fact she was supposed to be back at work by one pm.

Oh well, what would Ben do? Fire her? I don't think so.

CHAPTER TWENTY-THREE

While a private club is advanced beyond the basic physiological and safety needs of Professor Maslow's early Hierarchy, it does correspond to the secondary needs of Love/ Belonging and Esteem.

Historically, early castles were fulfillment centers of survival and safety needs in Western Civilization. A Private Club may be analogical to those institutions on a more superficial, first world level. Much like an early castle would protect and nourish you, then provide you with some festive activities, depending on your social and economic status, a Private Club will nourish you bodily, quench your thirst, but also seeks to meet your social and entertainment needs. While it does not need to provide for your personal security, it absolutely can and should gratify your needs of belonging, acceptance and self-esteem. Also, it offers the ability to bond with people of a similar social status.

Introduce an activity such as golf, and a culture has evolved. It is a complex culture that incorporates the above social needs, but also includes the elements of golf and related physical activities, such as tennis, swimming, and physical conditioning. It has evolved into an organization which has something to offer so many people.

The early Castles had their governing bodies, so do clubs. The early castles had their social activities, functions and intrigues, so do clubs. Those castles had their contests of athleticism and bravery, we call them golf tournaments. The early castles had their taxations and fees. We subject ourselves to dues and assessments. There are so many similarities.

The primary difference of course, is that our ancestors converged for survival, often from brutal usurpers, for their and their families very lives. We are so much more fortunate, in that we are seeking mere self-actualization, and personal fulfillment. First world issues indeed.

The modern club has activities for everyone: seniors, families, singles, kids-both adolescent and prepubescent, parents, aunts, uncles, retired people, titans of industry, housewives, golfers-to include all levels of talent and expertise, social members, dining members, wine connoisseurs, winos, dancers, fancy dancers, party people, teetotalers, doctors, and lawyers. The possibilities and opportunities are endless.

Much as at a medieval castle, where your identity and status were well known, a club is no different. And like your Castle was your place of refuge, your club is a haven for you and your family.

You go to your club for enjoyment. You play an ancient, vastly challenging game that is a contest for any age. You play with your peers. You relax at the pool in the summertime, with a cool beverage. You spend significant family occasions-birthdays, anniversaries, graduations, etc. You share the comradery and friendship of the holiday parties and festivities with your fellow members. You can build lifelong relationships at your club. Just conduct yourself appropriately, and prove to be a decent golfer. Everyone will love you.

Your club is a fraternity, that is as close to a family as you can get, but it is not quite blood family.

While we at Rosewood, are related to the game of golf, there are also of course, tennis, swimming, gun/shooting, polo, social/business, etc. clubs.

As a golf club, we love our game. Both the men's and women's club are very active. In the summer months, tee times are booked solid, and when the pros aren't booking tee times, or giving lessons, they are conducting kid's seminars.

So much has been written about the Royal and Ancient game, I couldn't probably add much commentary to its history. Nothing fresh and new, except to confirm the allure of being able to play a game which has its roots in ancient Scotland. A game that is renowned worldwide, boasts incredible characters, venues and history. It has produced larger than life figures such as Walter Hagan, Ben Hogan, Arnold Palmer, Jack Nicklaus, Tiger Woods, Babe Zaharius, Nancy Lopez and Annika Sorenstam, to name just a few.

A game that through its national and internationally televised tournaments, not only provides weekly drama on a national scale. But drama on a personal level as well. Anytime you decide to tee it up, you are a part of something. Something bigger than yourself. Something more universal than just another round of golf. You are a part of the history of the game.

Modern Golf Clubs endeavor to continue championing the game, and to extend and support the life style that has developed around the game. But they are encountering numerous obstacles toward achieving those goals.

The millennial generation has not yet become enamored with the country club lifestyle. Maslow's goal of achieving self-esteem, on the way to self-actualization, hasn't yet been adopted by them. The Millennials don't necessarily like hanging out with older generations. It is not so much a path to self-actualization as, to them, it is a just too expensive and time consuming.

A problem for us, is that we often lose sight of true actualization, and things become egotistical side trips. Sometimes those side trips become around the world voyages. We are more concerned with who has the fattest wallet, the most expensive automobile, or the biggest body part. Whether that body part is medically enhanced or not. Rather than just a normal, healthy adaptation to life. Rather than acting our ages.

The natural demographic of golf clubs is advancing rapidly. With whom will we replace all of our members, that are literally dying off?

And then consider often aging facilities, and the larger economy. When it falters like it did in 2008, that imposes another challenge. An otherwise happy, committed member may lose their job, their stocks may take a plunge. Maybe they are otherwise affected adversely by the external financial climate, and have to put their membership on the sell list. Or at worst, you are required to buy your membership out. Because remember, you bought into a Lobster trap when you signed up, and nobody can just walk away without leaving some small pound of flesh behind.

Into this challenging and time-honored environment, Charlie Strong, our dauntless President continued to sail fearlessly. Although it was now 2010, and the national economy was starting to come out of the doldrums, Charlie was deeply fixated on bringing his driving range project to fruition. Through a land use appeal, or otherwise. Past that immediate preoccupation, no one was quite sure of how he would spend his time as President. Except we were all pretty sure he would still be the head Good Old Boy.

In the meantime, we also knew that he would play as much golf as he could, and that our bar revenues would stay healthy. As in Charlie liked to drink like a fish after his round.

Getting ready to leave for Pebble Beach, Charlie called Rick Ferin on Thursday evening. "Hey, I'm going down to Pebble for the Annual Cargo Shipper's International Golf Tournament. I'll be back on Monday."

"Okay. Have fun. Who you going with?"

"One of the casual girls."

"You need a ride?"

"Nah. We're only going to be gone for four days. I'll just park it at the airport."

Charlie was looking forward to getting away. He had been busy, and wanted to take a break. He knew the coming week was going to be eventful, so he wanted to get his head cleared out. Pebble Beach was just the spot. He loved the place, who wouldn't?

The venerated history, the spectacular views, the fact that the weather didn't actually turn decent until the fall, so it was perfect timing for this trip. Plus, a nice-looking lady with on his arm, even if it wasn't Tricia. So what, he thought. It was her loss.

He and his new friend Nikki were standing on the veranda of the main clubhouse, enjoying the setting sun, with a couple of Absolut Vodka Martinis in hand. "Not bad, eh?" Charlie asked her.

"Gee, this is gorgeous, Charlie. Thanks for inviting me." There is something uniquely special about lounging on the Veranda at Pebble Beach. Certainly not somewhere a casual girl from Vancouver, Washington had spent a lot of time.

"We are going to have some fun this weekend. The pairings are coming up, then dinner. We can retire early tonight. I bought you a disposable credit card, and you can go shopping tomorrow while I'm playing golf."

"Thanks Charles. I'll buy something special for your pleasure." Nikki squeezed his arm, and wondered how much he had put on the card.

This was a big tournament, rotating over three courses-Pebble, Spyglass, and Poppy Hills, with two hundred sixteen players. There were shippers from all over the world there. And, there were some great trips for prizes, all at destination resorts, and Charlie was going to win one of them.

The pairings were done by handicaps, and computer picks, with a little oversight from the competition committee.

The Chair of the Competition Committee was now at the podium, and was welcoming everyone and their partners to the Tournament. He thanked all of the sponsors, etc., finally announced that the pairings had been posted, and the shrouds would be removed from the pairing boards momentarily. He thanked the staff in the Pro Shop for their hard work in assembling the handicaps, pairing the field as evenly as possible, and wishing all of the players' good luck in this scramble format event. He announced that there would be activities for all of the wives and partners who had accompanied the players if they were interested. Please check this evening's program for details.

"Gentlemen, we are about to reveal the teams for the weekend. Please take the time to get to know your group this evening, as you will be spending the next two days together. You will be seated at the same dinner table. Please check your tee times carefully. If you miss your scheduled time, you could be disqualified. Finally, all pairings are final, so don't even think about asking to switch out. If you didn't get paired up on the same team as your buddy, we are sorry. Thank you, and good luck."

Everyone clapped, and the shrouds came down. Charlie scanned the boards, and finally found his name. He was starting on the thirteenth hole at Poppy Hills Golf Course tomorrow in the shotgun start. He was playing with a couple of British guys, who looked to have a high and a low handicap. Charlie played to a fourteen, so he was a middle handicapper. As he looked he had to stop and read their fourth player's name again. It was Neil Horn. Neil Fucking Horn, Carol Horn's husband? From Magnolia Street at Rosewood? It said he was with Hamner Shipping, Portland, Ore.

"Holy Shit," Charlie muttered.

"What's wrong, baby?" Nikki wanted to know

"This is the worst pairing I could possibly could get. It is the pairing from Hell."

"Don't worry baby, I'll make it up to you." Nikki didn't know a thing about golf, but she was committed to making sure Charlie had a good time on this trip. And she wasn't about to let some stupid pairing, whatever that was, get in their way.

Charlie grunted, and headed for the bar.

They found their dinner table, and sat down. Fortunately for Charlie, Neil hadn't brought his wife. He was sitting across the table, between the Brits, who were also singles.

Introductions followed. Neil rose and offered Charlie his hand. He winked at Charlie, and said, "Small world, eh?"

Charlie ignored him, and sat down. Gone was his relaxing get away, it was now going to be a super, annoying weekend from start to finish. Charlie just knew it.

That wasn't too far from the truth. Charlie was a straight-line, A type personality, who seemed incapable of manipulating an uncontrollable situation. Rather than reflect on the revenge he was taking next weekend on Neil Horn's close friend and neighbor, he allowed Neil's mere presence to be a constant irritant.

Neil seemed to sense this, and went out of his way to be as annoying as he possibly could be. Whether it was at dinner or on the golf course. He was not a good golfer, and was there at the behest of his CEO, who was also not a player. His handicap was at twenty, but he managed to play like it was at forty. If his team needed him for a shot, he would flub it. It seemed to be a given.

The next day, Neil struggled, and the worse he played, the harder Charlie tried, and consequently, Charlie played nowhere near his skill level. He began a slow burn on Saturday morning, which continued throughout the day. In spite of his luxurious surroundings, in spite of his comely companion, his will to win had been detoured.

Of course, as many observers of the game of golf will confirm, golf can be quixotic this way. The disappearance of one's game, in your own mind, is anyone and everyone's fault but your own. Today, it was Neil's fault. Once your game goes away, it is usually gone, and the ultimate conundrum and peculiarity of the game golf, is that the harder you try to get it back, the more it stays away. The harder you swing, the worse you play. The worse you play, the madder you get, and the harder you swing. And you pay good money to do this to yourself, a person with average intelligence, might ask. Such was Charlie's lot for the day.

Of the two Brit's, the lower handicap tried to calm everyone down, but it was too late. Therefore, the team had one low handicapper that played well, and three hackers.

Neil could have cared less, and whenever he could needle Charlie a bit, he didn't miss the opportunity. He was elated beyond words, at the irony of fate pairing them together. And gloat he did. A chance to remind Charlie of the Hearing Examiner? He grabbed it. He truly didn't understand how close he was to personal danger. Because if Charlie had had his Sig Sauer with him, someone would probably have found Neil face down in one of the sand traps on the back nine.

By the end of the round on Saturday, Charlie had finally regained his composure. As Neil overplayed his hand, Charlie ultimately realized that he held the better cards. This was simply an opportunity to allow Neil his little moment, but not to let it ruin his weekend.

Each day of the tournament was scored separately as well as cumulatively, so the team still had a shot to win something prize wise tomorrow. At last he got his head out of his ass, and started to play golf.

After the round, he returned to the room, and found Nikki in the bubble bath, happily singing along with the FM station.

That evening, they went into Carmel and had a California Cuisine kind of a night at the beautiful Highland Inn's Pacific Edge Restaurant. Replete with a bottle of Veuve Clicquot champagne, followed by a nice selection of Cabernet Sauvignon by the sommelier, and a table on the twenty-foot-high plate glass windows. The happy couple overlooked the Pacific Ocean and thoroughly enjoyed the last of the lingering sunset, from the Highland Inn's high bank western view.

Nikki looked gorgeous, and had had fun shopping all day. She was disappointed Charlie was in such a bad mood when he came in from golfing. This guy is going to be a lot of work she thought, and this golfing thing is a little weird, if you ask me. This is such a beautiful place, and he has been in a foul mood ever since that stupid pairings thing yesterday.

"What an amazingly cute little town Carmel is," she told Charlie as they settled in for dinner.

"You bought some stuff?"

"Yeah, I bought some girly stuff, and I got you a present."

"What is it?"

"You'll have to wait until we get back to the Lodge. It's for me actually, but it's for you, too."

"Can't wait. In the meantime, this is going to be a great meal. We are seated at one of the finest restaurants in all of Northern California." And if that son of a bitch Neil Horn should show up in this restaurant for dinner tonight, I will kill him, Charlie thought.

The sommelier arrived, and poured their Champagne. Charlie ordered some Foie Gras as a starter course. He took a deep breath, raised his glass to Nikki's for a toast. They had a sip. He decompressed a little, and looked at her. It was hard not to appreciate how very attractive she had gotten herself for him tonight. He leaned over and kissed her on the neck. She smiled.

Everything was going to end well today after all.

Nikki and Charlie had a fabulous evening, and went back to the Pebble Beach Lodge, and had even more fun. Unfortunately, all of the good times didn't translate back to the golf course. But by this time, Charlie could have cared less. He played poorly, and was almost glad, because if he had shot well, they might have won something, which included Neil Horn, and that would have blown big time.

So, he went through the motions on Sunday, and he and Nikki went out again on Sunday night in Carmel, and had another fabulous time.

On Monday morning, they went to the Monterrey Aquarium, before they had to go back to the airport for their return flight.

They arrived in Portland without any problems.

"Oh Charlie, how much fun." Nikki hugged him, and said, "Call me."

"Sure. I will." Charlie reached in his pocket, and pulled out a tidy wad of one hundred-dollar bills. He took half of the money, and handed it to Nikki.

She gave it back to him. "I don't want that," she said, and looked at him disapprovingly. "Just call me."

Charlie took the money, and looked at Nikki's hazel green eyes. "I will," he said. He stared at her for another second, as if really seeing her for the first time all weekend.

CHAPTER TWENTY-FOUR

After Tricia's husband died, she went into shocked hibernation. Her mom was there for support, and Dean's parents did all they could for her and little Dean Junior. But she wouldn't take any outside calls from friends, she didn't go out, and basically stayed at home with her kid. If she did go out, it was to go to the gym early in the morning.

Fortunately, Dean's father had a proactive profit sharing program set up for their business, and through Dean Jr.'s earning over the years he had worked for his dad, he had accumulated a fairly good chunk of cash. So, she had some assets to tide her over for a while.

After about six months of seclusion, she began to emerge from her self-inflicted cocoon, and started to mingle some. She had absolutely no conjugal aspirations of any kind.

She didn't hate men, but certainly felt abandoned, betrayed and isolated by not only her late husband's terrible choices in life, but her father's poor performance long before Dean had come along. Still, she was starting to get bored, and felt like she was wasting time at home by herself, now that Junior was getting older.

After twenty-five years of working for the City of Vancouver, Tricia's mom knew everyone and then some. One morning Tricia asked her mom, who by this time was living with her, if she could set her up with an appointment with the Chief of Police.

"Certainly, Hon. What's up?"

"I want to go to Police Academy," she told her mom. "I want to work in vice, or undercover, and see if I can help get any of these drug dealers off of the streets."

"Wow," said mom. "Now there is a goal! That could be dangerous you know."

"I know, and I would be very careful for your and Junior's sake. But I just feel like I have to do something to help out."

"I can get you an appointment this week, unless Chief Farley is out of town."

When she came home that night, she was excited to tell Trish that the Chief would be happy to see her, and for her to call him and schedule an appointment. He would be around all week.

Tricia called the next morning and set up a meeting.

"Hello, Tricia," Ray Farley's booming voice welcomed her into his office. "You look wonderful, so sorry for your loss."

"Thank you Chief." Tricia knew Ray in passing, as he had been Vancouver's Chief of Police for twelve years now. They had seen each other at the annual city employee's picnic, etc. Ray had a daughter, who was also into athletics, but was four years older than Tricia.

"Your mom tells me you are interested in the force."

"Yes Sir, I am. I would like to get involved with undercover work, some narcotics prevention type thing."

"You know that can be a nasty business, Tricia?"

"Yes sir, I imagine it can be. But if I could help prevent anyone else from ending up like my Dean did, it would be worth it."

"Would you want to come to work for our department here in Vancouver?"

"Yes sir, I would. This is my home, and this is the community I care about."

"Well, we certainly welcome qualified candidates with open arms. You would have to pass your entrance exams, and then if you were still interested, I would be happy to propose you to the Academy and sponsor you for our jurisdiction. Once you get there, you have to work your way into your desired area of service.

"What are the entrance requirements, and where would I go for training?"

"They are just a battery of aptitude and psychological tests, a physical fitness test, and a check of your records. I'm sure your record is fine, all you need is a high school diploma. You look like you have kept yourself in pretty good shape, so the fitness requirements shouldn't be a problem. They would then evaluate your nonphysical testing, and during the oral portion of the testing, you might have to convince them that you are not still carrying any baggage from your husband's passage. They can be pretty rough. Their job is to identify any possible problem areas before someone gets accepted, and then can't make it through training. Even with the through screening, the drop rate can be as high as thirty to forty percent. The State of Washington's Police Academy Training Center is located in Tacoma."

" Don't worry about me Chief, I am committed to this."

"Okay Tricia. That's what I wanted to hear. Drop by tomorrow, and I will have my secretary get the paperwork started for you."

Tricia was accepted into the academy, and began her training with sixty-two other recruits. Six months later, she graduated with honors, ranked number three in her class. Due to her good work, and outstanding performance, she had offers to work for all of the larger PD's in the state. But Ray Farley held her job for her, and she was happy to be moving back home again.

She had had a hard decision to make about what do with her son while she was gone. But she really couldn't take him with her, even if she wanted to, so she contented herself with calling him every night, and leaving him in the able care of her mom.

That was six years ago now, and Tricia had worked undercover for the VPD ever since. She hung around the bars, learned how to score, and basically kept her ears open. She was a scout in terms of the Narcotics Team. Meaning that she pointed the Team at the appropriate targets, and let them do the heavy lifting, while she kept her identity clean.

One thing Ray Farley had suggested upon her joining the force, was that she try and work her way into the ILWU structure at the Port. He figured if there was anything amiss going on at or thru their Port, it would be good to have someone working there on the inside for him. That was over four years ago.

Ray was elated with Tricia's rise into the ILWU organization. She seemed to have the ability to be in the right place at the right time. She made friends easily, was liked equally by both women and men. She met Kelly, who had started to work as a causal the same time as she had, and they became friends. They happened to meet Charlie's predecessor as Chief Agent one night in a waterfront tavern, and he suggested some side work to them. He was always looking for pretty girls to work as escorts for fishing, golfing, and gambling trips. To augment their casual work, the girls could make some good side money doing hostess type work. How much good side money the girls wanted to earn, depended entirely on them.

As luck would have it, she and Kelly's first trip, was to Alaska with Harold Edmonds and the boys. And she was suddenly on the fast track to being a vested union member.

While Ray was unaware of any details of Tricia's dramatic trip up to Alaska, he was impressed by the fact that in addition to her success in the union, Tricia donated any money she made from the union hall. All of it went to Drug Prevention efforts in the City of Vancouver, and Vancouver's Clark County. She was getting her Police Department salary and benefits, and wanted her extracurricular monies to go to something useful.

If Ray Farley was elated with her rapid rise up the ranks, and into ILWU Local #40, he almost fell out of his chair later on that day, when she called his office, and told him that she needed to meet him at their safe house immediately. He arrived twenty minutes later, and she began to relate her tall tale of possible premeditated murder, her role as accomplice, and on top of that, suspected international illicit dealings of some kind or another, probably drug trafficking, in their own Port facility.

Tricia spun out Charlie's murder plot to Ray. Then described the visit by the Asians, and the extravagant money that was being thrown around. She gave him the Five grand in crisp one hundred dollar bills that Charlie had given her yesterday, telling him it was the down payment on a twenty-five-thousand-dollar contract she had agreed to with Charlie.

"If they knew I was talking to you right now," she said, "I would be dead. Most probably my mom and kid, would go in the bargain."

Ray gathered himself, but was still stunned. This was a lot to digest at 4:00 o'clock on a Friday afternoon. "Let me think about this overnight," he told her. "We might need to bring someone in on this one. I think we could be crossing state lines here, not to mention the international possibilities."

"FBI?"

"Yeah."

"Call me first thing in the morning."

"You got it. Go home and get a good night's sleep, you look tired."

If you knew the half of it, Tricia thought to herself.

Ray called her at ten the next morning.

"Steve Rodriguez is the Special Agent in Charge of the Portland branch of the FBI, and he would like to meet with us at noon today. He has a call in to Barbara Estes, who is the Special Agent in Charge of the Drug Enforcement Agency, Portland."

"That was quick work, Ray."

"Well, these are quick times I guess. We might as well bring these people in early on, as I think there are plenty of issues to discuss, especially on the alleged drug trafficking side."

"See you in a couple of hours, boss." Tricia got up and jumped in the shower. She had spent a quiet evening with her mom and son, playing board games. Then hit the sack around ten, and slept like a baby, except for a little restlessness and some dreams about exotic jewels and women wearing veils.

After a nice pancake breakfast with the fam, Tricia got to the safe house early, and watched Ray make some coffee. Ray's number two guy, Larry Larson, Head Detective for the Vancouver PD was there. Soon, everyone arrived including Barbara Estes, and introductions were made all around. Steve Rodriguez was over six feet tall, about thirty-five clean cut years old, and sat straight as a ramrod. His assistant, Tony Patmos, was with him. Barbara Estes was a career civil servant, who was back with the DEA, after having been loaned out to help start up the TSA program on the west coast. She was a tall, handsome woman with dark features. She looked alert and attentive. She had brought her number two guy, Jim Hanson with her. They were both dressed casually, in slacks and sport shirts. They all flashed their badges, and Tricia assumed their casual dress had to do with the impromptu style meeting on a Saturday morning.

She, being undercover, wore pretty much whatever she wanted. This morning, it was a dark green Adidas warm up suit, that set her hair off perfectly. She was going to the gym later on that afternoon.

"Pleased to meet you Tricia, I have heard good things about your work, and Ray says you have a story to tell us," Steve opened the conversation.

"Yes sir, I do," and with this intro, Tricia launched into Charlie's murder plot.

"Do we know who is the intended victim?" asked Steve.

Ray Farley spoke up. "I did some leg work last night, and it appears to a Robert Kudlach. He lives near Rosewood Golf Club, and has apparently been active in opposing some expansion plans Rosewood has proposed to the Vancouver Planning Commission. Charlie Strong is the President of Rosewood Golf Club, and Charlie is seemingly upset enough to take measures into his own hands."

"And your role was driver and accomplice? For twenty-five grand cash, Tricia, of which you have received five thousand dollars. Is that correct?"

"Yes sir."

"Call me Steve. Do you know where this money came from? Is it from Rosewood Golf Club, is it from private funds, could the funds have come from the ILWU?"

"I have no idea where the money came from. However, common sense, and knowing Mr. Strong, would indicate to me that the money probably came from sources other than Rosewood. I mean, why would a private country club want to get involved with a murder plot? Plus, Charlie Strong loves to throw money around like confetti. He is very impulsive, and this just seems like something he would concoct on his own."

"Tony, could you pull an evidence form, and we can get this five K signed in with Chief Farley and Ms. Watson's cooperation. We can start a trace, and look for prints when we get back to the office. This seems like your jurisdiction Chief Farley, but we would be happy to be of support in any way possible. Intelligence, surveillance, lab work, those types of things. "Tricia do you know what is the weapon of choice here?"

"No, but there are maybe two. As he told me that the murder weapon was silenced, and then he said that if any kids needed to get scared off, he would fire a couple of shots in the air to scare everyone. Then we could scram out of there."

"And why are we here," asked Barbara Estes.

"Oh, there is more," replied Chief Farley.

He looked at Tricia, and she began to tell the story about the visit by the Asians. The rumors of something not right going around the yard. The extravagant party which seemed to be more about private shipments, than general business between the ILWU and Han Say Shipping. The secrecy, the objection to any photographs, etc."

"Do you have any positive identification at all of these people?" Barbara asked.

"I couldn't get any photographs at our luncheon, but I was able to snap some shots from the Port Offices, when they arrived. Also, I was able to save a gift jewelry box, that Madame Chang gave Mr. Chang, at lunch. It might have some prints on it."

"Well, that is a start."

"It seems like we have two separate issues here," analyzed Steve Rodriguez. "The local Vancouver agency should handle the potential assault. DEA and VPD should work together to follow up on the alleged drug violations. If you would like to put together a task force, we would be happy to support it in any way possible. Such as entering Mr. Thieu in our National Database. Seems like he is the stateside guy."

"Have you seen Mr. Thieu around the Port property at all?" Barbara asked Tricia.

"No, not personally. From what I can gather, it is unusual for a special arrangement like he has with our personnel. This cargo all comes in in containers. It is hauled out by truckers, that are going all over the West Coast. To receive a small shipment under special arrangements is quite unusual."

"Have the Customs people been around?"

"They come around periodically, but we are a smaller Port, and I am sure that they have bigger fish to fry for the most part."

Barbara continued, "Steve, if you could run Ms. Martin's photos and possible prints from both the currency and the gift box through your data base, I will start an investigation into Han Say Shipping, and we will see what we can find out about them. It would seem like Ms. Martin's continued presence on the inside of our investigation would certainly be essential."

"Thank you all for coming today," Chief Farley said in closing. "We definitely have some work to do this week, and we will keep you both in the loop."

The Federal Agents left, and Ray Farley, Larry Larson, and Tricia remained behind for some planning time.

"Email your facial photo to Steve Rodriquez, and then take the rest of the weekend off," Chief Farley advised. "And I want to set up daily conference calls at noon for next week. Think about some options, and we can have our agenda set by Wednesday. Tricia, you keep us up to date on anything and everything. If the slightest details change, we need to know what is going on."

They left. Tricia headed for her son's soccer game. Ray and Larry were excited to be on the front side of a significant case, involving some pretty high-profile characters.

CHAPTER TWENTY-FIVE

Tuesday morning, bright and early, George Richardson dialed Charlie in his office. "Sorry to call your office, Charlie, but it doesn't seem like the Hearing Examiner's office wants to grant us a Change of Venue for our appeal. Did you talk to the Mayor?"

"Yes, I did, and this is pretty annoying. I'll have to call another special meeting of the Board."

"I hate to say it, Charlie, but to go up in front of the same court jurisdiction that has already ruled against us twice, seems like a waste of time. What was discussed with the Mayor?"

"We just spoke in generalities. I thought he understood our needs, but apparently not. I'll have to call a Board meeting for this week, and we will see what they want to do going forward. If nothing else, we would be harassing the neighbors to make them go to court one more time."

"Maybe it's time to stop fighting with our neighbors, and try to get along with them a little better."

"What does that mean? Because we want to use our own property to help some kids, and help our members improve their golf games, that makes us bad neighbors? Maybe we hire an attorney who can win a case for once."

"Maybe you should, Charlie."

"Great George. I think I will. You're fired."

"Okay Charlie, thanks for the opportunity. I'll have my secretary send you my final invoice."

"I am sure you will. Good bye."

Charlie slammed his phone down, and took a deep breath. He buzzed his secretary, and asked her to get Larry Easton, from Rosewood, on the phone.

"Hi Charlie, what's up?"

"Can you send out an email to the Board? We need to have another special meeting. Maybe this Friday afternoon."

"Sure Charlie. Is this about the Driving Range?"

"Yeah. Richardson called this morning. He says we can't get a Change of Venue, and because of that, we might be wasting our time. He says under the circumstances, that appealing might not be a good idea. I told him I thought we might need a new attorney."

"You fired him?"

"No, he resigned. Too bad, he was a good man."

"I'll get the email right out. It usually takes about a day for everyone to get back to me."

"Okay, try for three o'clock in the afternoon."

"Got it."

Charlie reached over and called Rick Ferin on his cell phone.

"Hey boss, how are you? How was the tournament?"

"It sucked. You won't friggin' believe who was on my team."

"I don't know, who?"

"Neil Horn, from Magnolia Street."

"You're kidding me. How did he get in the Tournament?"

"I guess he works for a shipping firm out of Portland."

"Can he play?"

"Hell no, he sucks big time."

"And you didn't off him. Good man Charlie."

They laughed. "No, I've got bigger fish to fry. But I thought about it. He went out of his way to be a dick all weekend. I finally just shut him out of my mind, and went about my business. I had a great time with Nikki, that new casual girl though."

"Yeah, I've seen her around. She's a cutie."

"Did you talk to Bruce about dinner on Friday night?"

"Yeah, we're all set."

"I need you to rent a car for Friday night also. Nothing flashy. Dark in color, but something that can get around good. Maybe a black Mustang. That would be drivable for her. Have it at my place by Wednesday afternoon, with some phony plates on it."

"You got it."

Next Charlie dialed his Vancouver office.

"Good morning, ILWU offices, how may I help you?"

"You can have dinner with me on Wednesday night. Then go for a little drive."

"Oh, hi Charlie. How was your weekend?"

"It was great, thank you for asking. How about dinner?"

"If you don't mind, can we just do the driving thing. I am a little iffy about the other part, and I'm afraid I wouldn't be very much fun."

"Don't overthink this thing."

"I'm not, it just makes me a little nervous is all."

"Okay, then I'll meet you at the Jackson Street Steakhouse Bar at eight. We can have a drink, and go for a drive. Rick is getting a car for you."

"Okay."

Tricia called Ray Farley on his private line. "Meeting still on for tonight?"

"Yeah, safe house at six."

"See you there."

Tricia got to the safe house at six, and everyone was already there. Everyone being Ray Farley, Larry Larson, Steve Rodriguez of the FBI, and now Tricia. They chatted for twenty minutes about Friday night. Finally, Steve spoke to Tricia. "You need to get Charlie's cellular phone number, and call him as often as possible. We have a request before a Federal Judge in Portland for a lawful intercept, and anything you guys talk about will be irrefutable secondary evidence. The search warrant should be in place by this afternoon."

"Shouldn't be a problem," Tricia replied. "I can get that tonight. You should also request a tap on Rick Ferin's cell. Those two guys are very tight. They talk all the time. You will pick up some good stuff there."

"Good. I'll make that happen, and we should be all set then. You guys have the ball, but my people will be in place for support and surveillance."

"I can't thank you enough for your help and expertise, Steve," Ray said in parting. "I think we are as ready as we will ever be."

"I do too. Good luck. Be safe."

"Oh, and we have IDed your Mr. Thieu. He is Bao Thieu, and he is a confirmed Tong member from the San Francisco docks. He has a jacket a mile long from his misspent youth. We have him under twenty-four-hour surveillance. He is a known hard drug trafficker, and we are definitely going to keep an eye on him."

Chief Farley looked at Tricia and detective Larson, "Anything else?"

"Nope, I'll call you Thursday morning after my meeting with Charlie on Wednesday night."

They filed out into the chilly night.

Charlie and Tricia met at the Jackson Street Bar at eight, and Charlie ordered a Stoli on the rocks for himself. Tricia ordered a glass of white wine.

"I brought your car tonight," he told her. "You can practice driving it."

"What kind of car is it?"

"It is a black Mustang. Automatic transmission."

"That should work."

"I need to get your cell phone number Charlie."

"What for?"

"Just in case something comes up, don't you think it would be a good idea if I needed to get in touch with you?"

"Okay." He gave her the number, and she entered it into her phone.

They made small talk and slowly finished their drinks.

"Let's go in your car," Charlie said.

"I thought you wanted you me to drive the Mustang."

"I do. I just don't want to drive the Mustang on Magnolia street yet. Let's go in your car, and we can come back here, and you can take a test drive. Then I am going to take it home and put it in the garage until Friday. Let's go to the Rosewood parking lot first"

"How am I going to get the car?"

"Rick and I will drive it over to the club on Friday. You can drive your car over and park it, and pick up the Mustang."

They got in Tricia's car. "There's one more thing," Charlie said.

"What's that?"

"Unbutton your blouse."

"Why, Charlie?"

"I need to check you for a wire."

"A what?"

"A wire. Sorry, but it's standard procedure. I can't be taking any chances."

"Why would I be wearing a wire, Charlie?"

"I'm sure you're not, but I have to check." By now Charlie was getting over Tricia, and didn't care if he upset her or not. She mattered little to him now.

Tricia slowly unbuttoned her blouse, and Charlie of course, felt her breasts, and ran his hand down her stomach.

"Lift your butt up," he told her. She did, and he continued to run his hand down inside her jeans, and over her panties.

"Satisfied?" she asked him.

"Sorry. I had to check."

Tricia was fuming, but she started up her car and backed out. Charlie had a smirk on his face. He knew she couldn't see him in the dark.

They drove over to Rosewood, and pulled into the parking lot, close to the backside of the clubhouse.

"I'll be parked right here," Charlie told her. "The Mustang will be in the row right behind us. The keys will be in the ignition. Park your car, and pick up the Mustang. When you pick it up, drive right here behind my Jag, and call me. I'll come out of the side door of the bar, and we are gone. Remember to keep your cell phone on."

"Okay."

"Pull up over there, and we can time ourselves."

Tricia angled her car around, and they took off for Magnolia Street. It took them all of a minute to get there, run to the end of the Cul-de-sac, turn around, and head back. "There is the house," Charlie told her.

She slowed. "We will just pull over to the curb, and leave it idling. Run up and trick or treat, and we are out of here. Got it?"

"I got it."

They drove back to Rosewood. "Should take five minutes max. Easiest money you will ever make."

They drove back to the Jackson Street' parking lot, and Tricia asked Charlie when she would get the rest of her money.

"Why don't you come over to my house after you drop me off at Rosewood. I will be there in half an hour or so, and I will pay you off."

"How will I get in?"

"I'll leave a key for you under the doormat. You've got your costume all set, right?"

"Yep, I am ready to go. You said a princess outfit, right?"

"Yes. Any more questions?"

"No."

"Okay, just be on time. Why don't you call me tomorrow, and we can go over everything one more time?"

"Okay, Charlie. Talk to you tomorrow."

CHAPTER TWENTY-SIX

Friday morning dawned cloudy and cool, but it wasn't scheduled to rain until later on. Charlie got up early, made coffee and turned on Good Morning America. He had plenty of time to check out his gear, including his Sig Sauer and his Glock 9mm, and thought he might as well go golfing at ten thirty with the boys.

At nine he called Larry Weston. "Did we get that meeting of the Board scheduled for today?"

"No, half the members can't make it today. I gave them a backup of tomorrow at ten, and that seems to be the popular choice."

"Okay, we'll go tomorrow at ten then. Let everyone know."

"Will do."

"By the way, I'm having dinner with Rick Ferin and Bruce Cranston tonight. We want to try the Chef's new Pizza oven. Is it up and running?

"Yes, and Chef is excited about it. He says it is going to make a huge difference, especially in the summer for all of the junior golfers, and the pool folks."

"Good, then tell him to give us his best shot tonight. We're excited to try it out." They talked about a few more details, nothing critical, revenues for the month, house subcommittees for the holiday activities. "See you tonight Larry."

"What time are you coming? I'll make a reservation for you."

"There will be three of us at seven, corner table in the bar, please."

"Got it. I probably won't see you then, I'm gone at six but Jimmy will be MOD. I will tell him to be sure, and take care of you."

Thanks. I'll probably see you anyway, I'm going to play with the ten thirty guys."

Next, Charlie called Tricia. "Hey, how you doin?"

"Gee, Charlie, I'm freaking out. How are you doing?"

"What are you freaking out about?"

"Can I call you back on my break? There are people all over this place this morning."

"Why don't you take the afternoon off, and just chill out a little. I'll call Ben and tell him you are going to be working for me this afternoon. Then call my cell about three thirty. Okay?"

"Okay. Thanks Charlie, I'm just a little nervous, that's all."

Charlie checked his gear one more time: Sig Sauer with silencer attached, Sig magazine full, except for the two rounds, he had fired two days ago on a test run. Back up Glock, cleaned and ready, latex gloves, George Bush Mask, black slacks and Eddie Bauer black fleece, hand towel. A roll of duct tape, just in case. Check. He was ready to go.

He took the satchel out and put it in the trunk of his Jag. Went in and took a shower, and got ready to go hit some balls.

While Charlie drove over to Rosewood, he thought about Tricia. Women! All she had to was say trick or treat, and she would make twenty-five grand in about half an hour. Why was that so tough? He was not in the least bit jittery. Actually, he was looking forward to tonight. He felt like he was back in the war zone, and the feeling of anticipation, of the upcoming hunt, was a feeling he hadn't known in years. Bring it on, he thought. Charlie's old rallying cry. The fucking creep. What a pissant. He's got it coming, and I'm the one to give it to him. Damn, it feels good!

As it was October the thirty first and not very busy on the course, he was able to park front and center outside the club. Charlie checked in at the Pro Shop, and shot the breeze with the boys for a few minutes. A couple of the younger guys had masks, and it felt like it was going to be a festive day around the club. By this time, the cart boy had his clubs brought up, and Charlie headed out to warm up

The range was still scruffy and hadn't grown back in from all of the summer's use, before the cool weather set in. This made Charlie cranky right off the bat. If they had more room to spread people out, the place wouldn't get so beat up every summer. Well, he was working on a fix, wasn't he?

Charlie's group turned out to be a five some, and they played their usual game of Wolf, Goat, Pig. WGP is a complicated game of betting that rotates the Wolf role, which is the person who calls the bets. The wolf changes every hole, you can partner up or not, double up or down on the bets, call in the Aardvark which again doubles the bet. It is a somewhat goofy game that a lot of the guys don't like to play, because it focuses more on keeping track of the game, than the actual game of golf. But Charlie's guys played it so much, that all of the scoring, and record keeping, was second nature to them.

Plus, it takes longer to figure out in the bar after the game, which means there is more time for drinks. So, the Club says, play all of the WGP you want to.

The rain continued to hold off, and the group got finished in a little over the regulation four hours round. They drank for an hour, and argued over who hit the best shots, how the Seahawks were going to do this weekend, etc.

Charlie's cell rang at three thirty. "Gotta take this, boys."

Charlie took the call, and went outside the bar. "Hi Tricia. You calmed down?"

"Well, I'm still freaking a little bit. What if we get caught?"

"Don't worry, these things are over so fast no one even knows what happened."

"You've done this before?"

"Yeah a couple of times. It's been a while, but this is a bad dude. He deserves what's coming. But you don't have to worry about any of this anyway. All you know is I hired you to drive me to go and play a trick on a friend of mine. How can anyone say any different?"

"Okay, Charlie. I've got my kid you know, and I don't want any bad news in my life. If anything should happen, you will take care of me, right?"

"Like what?"

"Like if I ever need a lawyer or anything?"

"If you just relax, nothing is going to happen. All you have to do is drive, and say trick-or-treat. I will take care of everything else. You just relax, girlfriend."

"I'll try Charlie."

"I know you will. See you tonight. Everything's going to go just as planned."

Shit, I wish she would just relax, Charlie thought, she's starting to make me nervous.

Tricia called Ray Farley. "Okay, we are all set. I just had an interesting conversation with Charlie on his cell. Apparently, this is nothing new to him."

"I'm sure they got it on tape. You be careful tonight, eh?"

"Yeah, I will. I'm more worried about having to go over to Charlie's to get the rest of the money tonight. That guy is getting pretty free with his hands. I may have to kick his ass before this thing is done with. You get anything back about the 5K yet?"

"Oh yes. Some very interesting stuff. FBI identified Mr. Thieu from your photographs with their Facial Analysis and Comparison Technology. But he has been clean for the last ten years or so. Apparently, he made his bones, and has moved into management. Seems like he has someone to do his dirty work now. The bureau has been following him, and has been making a lot of trips up to Reno. The Oriental Casino. Steve thinks there might be a connection to them and the drug trafficking. Maybe some money laundering going on. The FBI picked up some of his prints off of the money, which would mean the money is coming from ILWU and Han Say shipping. The money is in non-sequential bills, but they think it is coming out of the Federal Reserve Bank in San Francisco. So, it looks like a west coast operation. They are checking into Han Say Shipping right now. Looks like this could get real interesting. We definitely need to keep you safe. These are some bad people."

"That's awesome info, Chief. Don't worry about me. I'm ready to go, and being careful. I will be strapped with my backup pistol under my Halloween costume. You just have my back in case anything weird happens."

"Don't worry about a thing."

"I won't. Well, maybe I worry about Charlie just a bit."

"Don't bother."

Charlie went back in and collected his winnings for the day, to hoots and protestations from the boys.

"Sorry fellas, I gotta go."

"Hey, you are the big winner, you owe us a drink."

"I gotta go," but he signaled to Leon the barman to buy a round for the boys. Charlie didn't want to sit and drink all afternoon, and take a chance on getting sloppy. He had a few errands to run, which included picking up Rick and dropping the Mustang off at the club. Then he would go back to his house, take a shower, and dress for dinner.

Charlie got to the bar about a quarter of seven, and was headed for the corner table, which had been reserved for him by Larry Easton. As he was walking through the room, he passed Dane Knutson and his family who were having dinner.

He was still annoyed with Dane for his friendship with Bob Kudlach, and was going to walk on by the table, but noticed Dane was having dinner with his grandkids, who were dressed in costumes.

What the hell are those kids doing in the bar? He thought to himself. But as he got closer to the table, he realized that they weren't kids at all. It was Larin, Dane's little person daughter, and her Greek little person husband, Mylos. As annoyed as he was with Dane, everyone at the club loved the little people, and so Charlie stopped to say hello.

"What are some nice kids like you, doing out with this old reprobate?" he asked, jokingly, nodding at Dane.

"We are going Trick-or-Treating." They told him. "You want to come."

"No thanks, a little dinner will be fine for me tonight. How was your pizza?"

"It was great," the table chorused back at him.

"Nice watch," Mylos said to Charlie, admiring his diamond crusted gold Rolex Oyster.

"Thanks, kid. You have good taste."

"You play golf today, Dane?"

"No, we have the kids in town for a few days, and we've just been hanging out."

"Well, have a nice dinner. Happy Halloween." Charlie bowed to the table, and went and sat down.

CHAPTER TWENTY-SEVEN

Charlie sat, and ordered a glass of chardonnay. He was looking forward to this night, and was happy to have a few minutes to sit and visualize his upcoming mission. A normal person might have had misgivings about interrupting their dinner to go off and kill someone. But Charlie viewed it more as a challenge or an inconvenience, than an interruption, a capital crime, or a mortal sin.

He was no Philosopher King, he had never sat down and written an essay on moral standards, or the Judaic Code. He was a man of action. And while he had some guidelines in his life, i.e.- be nice to old people and kids, don't hit women, etc., his main mantra had always been, "don't get caught."

People were neither here nor there to him. As long as they didn't confront him, they were okay. He had been highly trained in the military to protect himself, and he was put into a situation, by his country, to kill or be killed. And for what? A debatable philosophical war over a bunch of rice paddies. It cost billions of dollars, killed 58,000 Americans, and proved twenty years later to be an inconsequential political hiccup.

No, Charlie thought, I'm back in the jungle for a night. I will survive like I always do. Get in, bang-bang, get out. Go back to basecamp. Get back to life as it should be. The right way, my way.

Charlie thought of several of the soldiers he'd lost in Vietnam. They had been honorable young men, trusted friends of his. More than friends, battle tested blood brothers, and they had been killed in fire fights. Cut down in the prime of their lives. The living hell of hot zone, fire fights. Where you are in a ditch on the ground eating dirt, firing at will, calling in air support, and praying for your life and that you don't run out of ammo. Ostensibly, so a piece of shit like Bob Kudlach could play around back here. Could nuzzle up to the Hearing Examiner and stretch the rules of fair play, and get away with it. Well, not this time.

This time would be different. And he was ready. The cars were in place, his team was in place, he would do his job, and be done with it. Consequences? Don't get caught, and there are no consequences. He felt like he was twenty-two years old again. Just for a day or two maybe.

Rick and Bruce came in at seven and found Charlie at the corner table. It would have been a quiet night at the club, had it been a weeknight, but it was a Friday night, and people were coming and going. The club was having a haunted house Halloween party for the younger kids in the club's dining room, and many of the Moms and Dads were slipping in and out of the bar for a quick one. Then there were the older folks, who just didn't want to deal with trick-or-treaters. Some of them lived far enough out in the country that they didn't get any kids knocking on their doors, and who were just eating out for the night. This suited

Charlie to a tee. It was busy enough, so no one would notice the minutiae of anyone's comings and goings.

"Howdy boys," Charlie greeted his dinner companions and his evening's alibis.

Dinner was very good, if uneventful. The pizza was a delicious thin crust style pie, and the guys had it as an appetizer. They took their time and had a nice bottle of Washington red blended wine. The rib eye steaks were great. There was much to talk about, with the special session of the board meeting the next morning.

Bruce thought an appeal within the same system was a waste of time and money. "What's the point?" he would ask repeatedly throughout their conversation.

Charlie had done some research, and felt like Rosewood could prevail in a court of law. His digging had suggested the Examiner would probably approve their appeal, but pound them with so many restrictions and qualifiers on her final decision, that they would be handcuffed. Rick of course, agreed with Charlie on most of the issues they discussed.

"When we get the approval, and screen the neighbors off from the club grounds, we should be able to proceed," Charlie said.

"But what if we get shot down for the third time?" Bruce asked.

"I don't think we will. Especially, if we come in with a new attorney, who has a more compatible style in the Examiner's eyes. We need to go in there showing some concern for the safety and issues of our neighbors. They will be getting tired of dealing with this for the third time, and if we handle things correctly, I think we can come out okay."

"It's still a crapshoot."

"Yes, it is, and I certainly respect your opinion. But what do we have to lose? Even if the bitch rules against us again, we just wait a while, and do what we want to anyway. If we go in showing the proper contrition, why would she kill us for the third time? She has shown us who is boss, now we just have to grab our ankles, and do whatever she thinks we should." The more they talked about it, the madder it made Charlie. Imagine, having to crawl before some low-level damn bureaucrat, a woman yet, just to do what you wanted to do. Something completely legal, on your own property, on which you paid taxes. And plenty of taxes at that.

It was important however to Charlie to convince Bruce, to at least be willing to give the appeal a shot. There was no point in going into the Board meeting in the morning, and have dissension in his own ranks. He didn't want to have more of a hassle than he already had, and so their conversation continued.

At exactly eight thirty, Charlie's cell phone rang. "Hey sweetie," he answered cheerfully. He covered his mouthpiece, and said "I've got to take this, she's got a problem, I'll be right back." He got up, and headed for the side exit of the bar, while continuing to talk on the cell phone.

Once outside, although Charlie had put on a few pounds, and was now what you would call a good-sized man, he moved quickly and efficiently to the parking lot. Not unlike a large, agile cat. Tricia was parked right behind his Jag in the rented Mustang, and he was there in seconds. He popped the Jag's trunk lid, grabbed his satchel, and jumped in the passenger's seat. He took both of their cell phones, and put them in the glove compartment.

"Hit it," he said.

Tricia accelerated out of the parking lot, not too fast, but with efficiency. "You look just like a fairy princess," he told her, taking a quick look at her costume.

"Thanks. You want me to pull over so you can check me for a wire?" You asshole, she thought to herself.

"Sorry, no time."

Charlie slipped his mask on. Then the latex gloves. He had bought the medical version, which seemed stronger than the household kind. He certainly didn't need anything breaking apart at this juncture. He pulled out the pistols, and clicked off the safety latch on the Sig Sauer. He put both the guns on the floor board of the car, and pulled on his black fleece coat. He was ready.

I just hope Kudlach's old lady doesn't come to the door. In which case, he had decided to just shoot the place up, and freak everyone out. He couldn't see how offing an unarmed woman would be a wise decision.

Tricia turned right onto Magnolia Street, and killed the headlights. She drove through the short block to the end of the cul-de-sac. She wheeled around, just as they had planned, and headed back past the street light, and down two houses to Kudlach's place, which, conveniently, was on the right side of the street. There seemed to be a fair number of cars around, and some bigger kids milling about down the way.

"Let's go." Charlie picked up the guns, and stuck the Glock in his belt as he got out of the car. He shut his door, Tricia left the car idling, and was already out, walking toward the house. Charlie held the Sig Sauer in his right hand, which was extended down at his right side. The Sig was a formidable looking weapon with the silencer attached. It measured over a foot long.

They walked up to the porch, and Charlie said, "ring the bell, and get down on your knees, I'm right behind you." Tricia rang the doorbell, and kneeled. She was four feet in front of the impressive wood and glass door and entryway, but the variegated asphalt porch surface was killing her knees. She fluffed out her taffeta skirt, and waited for what seemed like a century. She could see okay, but her mask restricted her vision some. "Hurry up," she whispered.

Don't be the old lady, Charlie growled to himself.

They could see movement behind the door, through the shoulder high window valences. The door began to open.

"Trick or treat," said a man's hearty voice, as the door opened. But it was strange, the man was dressed from head to toe in a big, black Gorilla costume. Apparently, Bob Kudlach was in the Halloween spirit himself.

The door continued to open, and Charlie hissed at Tricia, "Go."

She peeled off to the left, and when the door was about three quarters open, Charlie raised the Sig Sauer, and fired three rounds into the big, ugly gorilla's left chest area. The bullets ripped into the gorilla costume.

Bam, bam, bam!

Kudlach staggered, and pitched forward. As he went down, the door slammed shut, and Charlie heard a scream from inside the house.

He turned for the car, and pulled the Glock from his belt with his left hand. There were several kids across the street. They were staring at Charlie as he ran back to the Mustang. Charlie raised the Glock over his head. He fired half a dozen rounds from the semi-automatic weapon into the air. The sound was deafening in the quiet suburban neighborhood, and the kids instinctively hit the ground. He jumped into the car. Tricia accelerated hard. She made the end of the street, and turned the lights back on, as she turned left and headed the two blocks back to Rosewood.

Charlie stripped off his mask, and put it back in the satchel. He put the safeties on the handguns, and put them in the satchel.

Next the latex gloves skinned off of his large hands, and he put the last of the gear in his bag. He grabbed their cell phones, turned them off, and put his in his pocket. He dropped her phone in Tricia's lap, zipped up the bag, and turned to Tricia.

"You did good," he said. "The house key is in the ashtray. Go back to my place, and wait for me. I'll be there in an hour, max. Use the garage door opener, and put the car inside. I left some treats out for you."

"Okay. I need a fucking treat right now."

"Relax, you were great. Wasn't that easy? Just like I told you."

Charlie was pumped as Tricia pulled back into the Rosewood parking lot. His plan had gone off flawlessly. Even better, no one was around. He jumped out, hit his trunk fob, and dumped the satchel. He stripped off the black fleece, and tucked his shirt in. He smoothed his hair with his fingers, and took several deep breaths to lower his heart rate.

He checked his Rolex, eight thirty-eight. As he walked back to the bar, he could hear sirens off in the distance. He went back in, and sat down at his corner table. Rick and Bruce weren't there.

CHAPTER TWENTY-EIGHT

Charlie was looking over the after-dinner menu when the guys came back from the pizza oven tour.

"You want some dessert, or a cordial? How is the new oven?"

"It looks great. I think it is going to heat up the kitchen some in the summertime, but otherwise, it's okay."

"Yeah, let's have some dessert," Rick said.

"I want some of the Tiramisu, and a double shot of VSOP," Charlie said to Leon.

"At least one of you should try the Pumpkin Soufflé, with Grand Marnier," Leon advised. "It is awesome."

"I want it," said Rick.

"Me too," chimed Bruce.

Rick looked across the table at Charlie, and discreetly raised one of his eyebrows. Charlie smiled like a Cheshire Cat, and gave him a half nod. As in done deal, partner.

Over at Bob Kudlach's house, the mood was equally optimistic. Ray Farley and a couple of his people were peeling the gorilla suit, and the Kevlar Damascus upper body armor off of Willy Davis. Willy was a seven-year Vancouver PD veteran who had volunteered to stand in for Bob.

"Great job, Willy."

"Thanks, Ray, that was a pretty good jolt."

"Yeah, you had better take the rest of the weekend off to recover." Ray Farley winked at him.

Acting as Commanding Officer of the Crime Scene, Ray had had Bob's wife scream for effect after the assault. He had then called in several squad cars, as well as an aid car. They all came in with sirens blazing, creating the proper effect.

Steve Rodriguez and his FBI team had set up security cameras, to cover the front of the Kudlach house and the street in front of the house. Charlie was going to be a real item for them tonight.

The brain trust was ready for him, but they also had the major goal of keeping Tricia under cover. She was going to be vital in the ongoing investigation into the Chang's and what was shaping up to be a major smuggling operation.

For now, they were happy to announce an attempted homicide. The angle was that Bob's gorilla suit had deflected the bullets away from his vital organs. He had been very lucky to survive this vicious attack, and although he would definitely be laid up for a while, a through police investigation was being launched. Anyone from the private sector, with any pertinent information, was encouraged to step forward immediately, etc., etc., etc. This should light the switchboard up, Ray thought to himself.

Charlie, Rick and Bruce finished their desserts, and Charlie bid his adieus, saying he had to get home to mama. Apparently, he was having some kind of woman troubles.

They all left after agreeing to sleep on the options for the board meeting the next morning. At this point, Charlie didn't much care, because he left the dinner table intrinsically knowing there would probably never be an appeal. Not after tonight's little bit of side business.

Bruce left the table feeling very happy to be included in the inner working of the movers and shakers at the club. He had no clue that he had been played like an Italian violin. Charlie and Rick said goodnight to Bruce, and continued to chat in the parking lot. "We need to get the rental car out of your house, and back to the agency," Rick said. "Why don't I come for the car early in the morning. We can get it back before the board meeting?"

Charlie was feeling pretty expansive after his double Cognac and the table wine with dinner. He was also very pleased with himself and his efforts of the night. Plus, he knew Tricia was waiting for him, and knew he would not want to get up at the crack of dawn tomorrow morning.

"No, that would draw too much attention, bringing the car back that early on a Saturday morning. Let's just wait until Sunday or Monday. The car is safely locked up in my garage for the time being." Charlie had no reason to feel suspicious at all.

"Okay then, I'll see you in the morning at the board meeting. I'm glad everything went well tonight."

"Good call. See you tomorrow morning."

Little did Rick know or suspect he would also play a starring role in the FBI's upcoming feature film. No matter when they decided to take the car back.

Tricia was waiting in the well-appointed, but bachelor decorated condo when Charlie finally returned home. He had left her a note inviting her to make herself at home. There were several bottles of Roederer Cristal Champagne in the refrigerator, and a saucer full of cocaine powder on the coffee table. Charlie had thoughtfully left a couple of snorting spoons for her convenience. She hadn't used them.

Tricia had stopped off at the safe house, to check in with the task team, and let them get some still shots of the Mustang. She was sitting on the couch drinking a glass of water when Charlie arrived home. Several close-up pictures of Charlie's coke stash were sitting comfortably in her cell phone.

"Hey, there's champagne in the refrigerator. Let's party a little bit."

"Sorry Charlie. I'm just not in the mood. Tonight, kind of shook me up."

"Yeah, whatever. The guy was a fucking snake. He deserved it."

"Well, I didn't even know him, and now he is dead and gone. Did you hear all of those sirens? It sounded like a cop convention over there."

"I tell you the guy was a slime ball. Have a toot. You'll feel better."

"I better go Charlie. Can I just get my money and go?"

"Don't you want to party? I thought we were going to have some fun after this was all over." Charlie went over to the wet bar, and began to pour himself another Remy Martin.

"I just want my money, and to go home. You can check me for another wire if you want to."

"Fuck a stupid wire. I just want to have some fun is all. You are turning into a bummer, you know that?'

"Why don't you call Nikki? She wants you to call her."

"Maybe I will." Charlie snapped at her, as he went upstairs to get the twenty grand from his wall safe. He had half a mind to keep the money, and tell her to go fuck herself. Why bother, he thought, she would be sure to do something weird, as strangely as she had been acting of late.

"Here you go," he said, slinging the four banded packets of one hundred-dollar bills at Tricia. "Next time, I'll work with someone who isn't so goddamn sensitive."

Yeah, well there won't be any next time for you buddy, Tricia thought to herself.

"Charlie, I'm fucking sorry okay? I guess I'm just not very good at helping murder someone, and then go snort coke and drink champagne all night."

"Boo-hoo. I see you are not too upset to take the money with you."

"I've got a kid Charlie. Can I just have a ride home now?"

"Call a fucking cab," Charlie said to her, and scooped up a spoonful of coke to calm his nerves.

"Really, call a cab? You think it would be real bright to have a cab pick me up at your house in my fucking princess costume, Charlie? Think about it."

Charlie held up his hand to quiet her, he was already on the phone. "Hey, Nikki. What are you doing?"

"Not much, hanging out."

"You want to go out and have some fun?"

"Sure Charlie. Just give me half an hour to get ready."

"No problem. I've got to drop a friend off, and I will be over."

"I'll leave the door open."

"You're right. No cabs. Let's go, I've got a date."

"Can I please have a bag or a box or something to put this money in?"

CHAPTER TWENTY-NINE

Charlie picked Nikki up, and they had a great time of it. She looked hot, and was elated that Charlie had called. He had brought along a vial of toot, and they stopped at the Vortex Lounge, Vancouver's one and only glam nightclub. After a couple of snorts in the Jag, they headed into to the club. There was a line out the door of people with their Halloween costumes on, but a couple of c-notes from Charlie's wad for the doormen took care of any waiting in line problems. "Yes sir, Mister Strong. I have your reservation right here." In they went, adjusted their eyes to the darkness, and ordered a couple of drinks at the bar. Charlie was starting to feel really good, but he reminded himself not to get too crazy tonight, as he had a damn meeting at ten in the morning. The bar was rocking, with everyone dancing and cavorting in their costumes. Nothing like a costume party to loosen everyone up, Charlie thought to himself. Nikki was hanging all over Charlie.

Back at Bob Kudlach's house, Ray Farley had complete control of the crime scene. Made easier by the fact that, it was in reality, a pseudo crime scene. But it was his job to convince people otherwise.

Charlie Strong's attack on Bob was very real, and involved any number of felony charges. But with Tricia's brilliant undercover work, his life had been saved, and an anti-plot had been defined, developed and executed.

Vancouver PD was the first to arrive on the scene, and they immediately set about cordoning off the area with police tape, and perimeter control.

The EMT's rolled in next, lights and sirens blazing. They evaluated Bob for the correct amount of time in the house, bandaged him appropriately, and wheeled him out to the ambulance on their mobile gurney. Lillian Kudlach was allowed to ride in the back of their unit with Bob. And as the dutiful wife, she held his right hand throughout his transition to the aid car. Steadfast Carol Horn assured her that she would secure their home for them.

By now, the press was there, and Commander Farley went out to meet with them. Give them an update. He performed his role impeccably.

"Tonight, we had a brutal, seemingly premeditated assault on a home owner. A home invasion type of crime, that was thwarted by the actions of the homeowner, and the Vancouver Police Department has initiated a thorough investigation. We have some rudimentary evidence to evaluate before we can make any definitive statements. However, the homeowner did survive the attack, and although in critical condition, is being rushed to the hospital as we speak. The motive for this heinous crime is now under investigation. And if there is any information from the public, or the neighborhood related to this case, or any information on any of the participating parties, we would appreciate your contacting our TIPS hotline immediately. It is manned 24/7.

This is still our safe haven of Vancouver, Washington," Ray spoke earnestly into the bank of cameras in front of him. "We don't want our citizenry to be alarmed for their personal safety.

We feel like this was an isolated event, definitely not a serial type of situation. Again, we will do everything in our power to bring justice, swiftly and surely to the perpetrators of this murderous attack. Thank you, this is all the information I have at this time."

Vancouver's three local television stations ran with Commander Farley's interview, and as much pertinent footage of the Crime Scene as they could shoot. Armed assaults in country club neighborhoods were rare in our placid little town, so the networks were frantic to get to the air first, and break the news. Actually, armed assaults were somewhat rare in most neighborhoods, let alone country club neighborhoods, so the urgency to break the news was doubly intense for our working press. This was the biggest thing to hit Vancouver in a while. It was live news in our own backyard, and we were on it. Heck, the affiliates from Portland were even calling.

On Magnolia Street, the neighborhood was in chaos. Neighbors were milling around in the street, which was as close to the house as they were going to get. People were visibly upset, and were speculating in hushed tones among themselves. Distraught women were crying, some of the older trick or treaters were still hanging around, which gave the scene an eerie, macabre feel. The men were pissed off in general, as Bob Kudlach was certainly a pillar of their community. It was as if the attacker had gone after them personally.

Carol Horn was interviewed by several of the onsite reporters.

"We are horrified as a neighborhood that something like this has happened. Bob is our friend and a brilliant and dedicated member of our community. We are appalled, but are so thankful he is alive, and he will most assuredly be in all of our prayers tonight. We will support the police department's efforts in any way we possibly can."

Hugh and Bunny were there to console Carol and Neil, as well as Bjorn and Tammy, along with the rest of the neighbors. Eventually everyone repaired next door to the Horn's house. Indignation and speculation were running rampant among the community. Hugh was agitating that this could be related to the recent courtroom proceedings, and was threatening dire repercussions against Rosewood, if in fact there was any kind of connection.

Calmer heads were fortunately prevailing, and everyone, while still in shock, seemed willing to let the police proceed with their investigation. They were mostly there to be with other people, and try to calm their nerves. The neighborhood children were milling around, kind of in a daze, not fully understanding what was happening. Was this some kind of Video Game thing?

Commander Farley was sorry to put the neighbors through so much angst, put the whole City of Vancouver through this kind of emotional hysteria actually, but there were factors here which could not be disclosed at this time. It was unfortunate.

My wife and I walked over from our adjacent street, we weren't the only ones, to see what was going on. But the police had things all blocked off at the entrance to the Magnolia cul-de-sac. Their barricade caused another klatch of people, outside of the immediate neighbors, who had congregated, and were milling about at the intersection. Again, speculation was running wild. Was it a medical situation? Several people had seen the aid car go in and out. There was talk of some type of assault or Capital Crime. Domestic violence? No one knew what was going on, and the police weren't talking. Actually, they were telling us all to disperse, and go home to wait for the ten o'clock news. I didn't have a clue as to what was going on.

Ray Farley and his people were into their crime scene investigation, and his job was now to calm the situation. The EMT's who had been prepped by the FBI and the Vancouver PD for what to expect at the scene, had been sworn to silence in the matter. Actually, the presence of the FBI introduced a level of gravity. This fact alone, made true believers out of the medical technicians.

Bob was in transport to Portland to be stabilized, and in the morning, he was purported, as a retired military officer, to be transferred for comprehensive care to the Walter Reed Military Medical Center in Bethesda, Maryland. Although some of the press had followed the ambulance carrying him, the Peace Medical Center in Portland was a big place, and they swallowed Bob into their facility with ease. The information officer assured the press of their commitment to releasing an update as soon as there was anything of substance to report.

It was starting to get late in the neighborhood, and the gathering at the Horn's was beginning to disperse. Everyone had watched the breaking news, and it was a curious phenomenon, that actually seeing the event on television, seemed to make it even more real than what they had just seen in real life. The shock syndrome was beginning to set in all over again, but basically, everyone was just glad Bob was still alive, and was going to, hopefully, pull through.

While it was getting to be midnight on Magnolia Street, things were just starting to crank up at the Vortex Lounge. The music was thumping, and people were having a great time dancing and drinking. One of the bartenders had gotten a couple of lone ranger type eye masks for Charlie and Nikki. Now they wouldn't feel so out of place as one of the few couples without a costume. They were dancing up a storm, and partying hearty. The drugs and alcohol had kicked in big time for Charlie. He loved to dance, was extremely light-footed as a matter of fact, and was having the time of his life. Nikki was Charlie's equal on the dance floor. Maybe even smoother, because she was fifteen years younger than him.

Unfortunately, the TV's in the bar were tuned to MTV, which not surprisingly, didn't carry the live time news feeds of this Halloween night's nefarious activities on Magnolia Street. Nikki was of course oblivious to the situation, and Charlie seemed to be totally in denial of the circumstances he had created. He had rationalized the justifications in his mind for his behavior sufficiently enough, that he was apparently prepared to face the consequences of his actions. Better yet, there would be no consequences, because he felt entitled to do what he had done, and wasn't going to get caught anyway. Everything had transpired exactly according to his plan. He was in the clear, with an iron clad alibi. In his mind, it was kind of like calling the exterminator to your home for a rodent problem. It was a nuisance, but just something which had to be done from time to time.

The night wore on, and pretty soon it was closing time. Wisely, Charlie decided not to stay for the afterhours party, and Nikki convinced him to take a cab back to his place. She would absolutely not let him drive in his condition.

"We can make out in the cab all the way home," she promised.

Charlie was too wrecked to care much by this time.

The cabbie just didn't want anyone to puke in his cab.

Rick Ferin was not out partying, and was fully aware of the local news coverage. He and his wife were watching television, and Emma Ferin was aghast that something like this could happen, and right here in Vancouver. Rick was quiet, but his stomach was starting to turn a little acidic. Before going to bed, he tried to call Charlie's cell phone, but there was no answer.

"Hey pal," he said onto the answering machine. "You created quite a stir this evening. Be careful out there."

CHAPTER THIRTY

Rosewood's finest, -our august Board of Directors or Trustees, whichever pleases you-were front and center in the clubhouse meeting room well before their scheduled kick off time of 10:00. There were no absentees today, which was a statement in itself. There were always three or four board members who usually found something more important on their personal agendas, than a board meeting. Especially, an extraordinary meeting such as this, called for 10:00 on a Saturday morning. But not this morning. The room was buzzing with animated conversation.

Well, actually, there was one AWOL. Unfortunately, it was the guy who had called the meeting, and it seemed Charlie was on his way, but was running a bit late. There was actually a pretty funny scene at Charlie's Townhouse that morning.

Charlie awoke to his alarm clock with bleary eyes, and a splitting headache from last night's debauchery. "Oh shit, is it nine thirty? I've got a meeting at the club in half an hour."

He jumped out of bed, lost his balance, and promptly fell back on the bed, landing on Nikki, bruising her leg pretty good with the point of his elbow.

"Ouch," she yelled at him.

"Sorry, sorry. Go make some coffee while I jump in the shower, will you?"

Nikki, who was not in much better shape than Charlie, got up and stumbled for the kitchen in her panties. Where is the coffee maker, the coffee, etc. she thought?

The doorbell rang, which startled her. She ran for the door, but then realized that she had no clothes on. She peeked out of the side window, and saw three little girl scouts out and about, selling cookies.

"Who's at the goddamn door," Charlie shouted, and when the little girls heard voices inside the house, they kept ringing the doorbell.

"It's the girl scouts. They are selling cookies."

"Tell'em to get lost, damn it."

"Charlie, I can't answer the door, I don't have any clothes on." The doorbell kept ringing.

"Is the coffee ready, I'm dying here?"

"I can't find the filters, where are they?"

The doorbell rang again. Charlie came downstairs wrapped in a towel from the waist down, and partially opened the door. He threw a hundred-dollar bill out of the door onto the front porch, and slammed it closed behind him. The little girls, probably scarred for life, grabbed the money and ran to their mom, who was waiting in the car at the street.

"The filters are in the drawer," he said. And headed back upstairs, still stinking of cigarettes and stale booze.

He got back down stairs at ten, shaved and showered, and smelling like the Old Spice man. Grabbing his coffee cup, he kissed Nikki on the mouth, and told her he would be back in about an hour. Then the doorbell rang again.

"What in freakin' tarnation," he said to Nikki. "No one ever comes to this house."

He swung the door open, and found a rundown looking woman standing on his doorstep. "Whatta you want, lady?" Oops, all of a sudden it was Nikki's turn to scamper from the living room back to the kitchen, looking for something to cover herself with.

The lady was of medium height and medium figure, but her hair was stringy and her clothes were everyday marginal, thrift store type stuff. Her gray eyes and face looked tired, but tenacious. Charlie looked past her outside, and saw the three little girl scouts all looking at him from a beat up old Toyota sedan. This must be the mother, the troop freakin' leader, whatever they call them, he thought.

"How dare you expose yourself to my children, and then throw money at them, as if they were some kind of riffraff? We are Girl Scouts here, and those little girls take a lot of pride in what they do."

"Holy shit, lady. I wasn't exposed. "There was a towel wrapped around me."

"Don't swear at me, and that towel was flying around everywhere. You really scared my babies. I should call the police right now. Nobody opens the door to three little girls, with nothing but a little towel around them."

"Look lady. This is ridiculous. What do you want? I didn't know there were three kids out here. I was covered up anyway."

"Well, there were three of them, and you only made one donation."

Charlie was no stranger to a shakedown. Hell, he was a union executive, a negotiator. But under the circumstances, since he had a murder getaway car parked in his garage, and was late to a critical meeting, what could he do?

"Okay, I'll send the Girl Scouts of America a nice, big fat check this year," he said.

The stubborn woman didn't budge. "There were three of them," she said. She was also feeling Charlie's annoyance and impatience. She told him, "and now you got me all involved. Can I please borrow your phone to call 911?"

"No, you can't borrow my phone, you fucking crack head." Charlie was now spitting mad, which made his head throb even worse, and he was getting later and later for his meeting. He reached into his pocket, and pulled out his money clip. He peeled off a couple more Benjamins and handed them to the woman. She took the money, and stood there and stared back at him.

"What?" he said.

She held out her hand, and said "one more please."

Charlie stripped off another bill, and shoved it at her. "Fuck you. Get out of here." Charlie's blood pressure was now through the roof. What a miserable day this is going to be he thought. The mother of the scouts turned, and skipped off back down to her little troop of waiting girls.

Charlie slammed the door, went back to the coffee table, and picked up his coffee mug. He kissed Nikki again, and scrambled out to the driveway and his car.

A minute later he was back in the townhouse, "Someone stole my Jaguar," he shouted at a foggy, and now thoroughly startled Nikki. "Call the cops."

"Charlie," Nikki thought fast, "your Jag is at the club. Remember? We took a cab home last night."

"Shit. I am due at Rosewood, and I am already way late." Charlie called Rick again to tell him he was still having car problems, and was waiting for a cab. "No problem," Rick said, although car problems were the last thing he wanted to hear from Charlie this morning. "We have plenty to talk about here." He wanted to ask Charlie if he had seen the news yet, but didn't want to make things seem any worse than they were in front of the other board members.

By the time he got to the club, it was eleven o'clock. Charlie who prided himself on punctuality, was perspiring, breathing heavily and his head was emulating last night's speakers at the Vortex. It was throbbing. His hands were shaking so badly, that he had spilled coffee on his shirt during the cab ride. In short, his eyes were bloodshot and he still smelled of booze. And his timing couldn't have been worse.

The other eleven members of the board, and General Manager Easton, were seated at the conference table, and were staring at him skeptically.

"I apologize for being late" Charlie said to them. "Car trouble. I call this special meeting to order."

Charlie's mouth was suddenly dry as a box of sawdust. He was looking around for the coffee break table, and a glass of water. He was smacking his lips incessantly. His nose was runny, and he kept rubbing the back of his hand across it.

While Charlie was preoccupied with his arid palate, and generally distracted, the rest of the board just sat there staring at him. Car trouble? With a brand-new Jaguar? Several Board members just didn't seem to be buying it.

Finally, Rick Ferin opened the meeting. "Looks like we have quite an issue to discuss."

Charlie stared at him dumbly, not really aware of all of the press coverage, and the overwhelming maelstrom that was sweeping the town of Vancouver, the neighborhoods of Rosewood, Magnolia Street, and the Rosewood Board of Directors.

The Board of Directors continued to stare at Charlie.

"Finally," Charlie blurted out to no one in particular, "What are you talking about?"

Toni Duncan, who was a sharp cookie, a Municipal Judge, and an avid golfer, finally spoke up. "Charlie," she asked, "are you completely unaware of what is going on?" She was completing her third term on the local bench, and while dealing with traffic and misdemeanor issues for the City of Vancouver, she had had her share of miscreants in front of her bench. Her training included identifying a person who was still under the influence of drugs and alcohol from the night before.

"Yeah, what's going on?" Charlie asked her.

Toni looked at Charlie incredulously. "Bob Kudlach was assaulted last night. Someone shot him right in the front doorway of his own home. It has been all over the news, since nine o'clock last night, and all morning long. Local, and Portland. There are even rumors that Rosewood might somehow be implicated or involved in the whole thing. This is a freaking disaster, Charlie. How could you not have heard about it?"

"Oh shit. Sorry. I had dinner at Rosewood last night, and met up with an old friend. We hit a few nightclubs, then went home and crashed. I have not listened to the news. My phone was turned off." This was no surprise to Rick Ferin, as he had tried to call Charlie numerous times.

Rick watched Charlie's feigned surprise, and thought, nice try buddy.

Matt Mitchell, a retired auto parts executive, and another sharp pencil on our Board spoke up. He was an astute, service oriented businessman, very successful, and suggested to the Board, "We need to forget about any appeal of the driving range, and immediately get our condolences out to the Kudlach family, and the Magnolia neighborhood."

The heads of the Board members nodded in complete concurrence and unity. One of the few times we were all in concurrence on something.

"What funeral home is he at?" Charlie asked. "We should send flowers there, and also to the house."

Again, the Board stared collectively at Charlie.

"He's not dead," said Marta Koenig. Marta is a retired businesswoman from the East coast. She is a Villanova University graduate, along with having earned an MBA from Duke. She started up her own national company, sold it, and proceeded to involve herself in non-profit political and community activity organizations. She sits on half a dozen national Boards, including several prominent retail companies. She travels a good deal (always first class), with all of her executive commitments, but when she is at a Board meeting, and she has something to say, people listen. Her son had moved to Portland, with Nike Corporation, and wanting to stay close to their grandkids, Marta and her husband, who had been a prominent Washington DC Consultant in his day, moved out to the west coast. They found us, and we were very happy to have them.

That fucker isn't dead? Charlie thought. He almost fell off of his chair. His face was one of puzzlement. People began to notice, and Rick Ferin began to squirm.

"But, Toni said someone shot him."

"I didn't say he was dead, Charlie."

"Well, then we will send the flowers to the hospital, instead of the Funeral Home." Charlie tried to recover himself.

Joe Goldman suggested the feasibility of hitting pause. "Someone should give Charlie a complete summary, and get him up to speed on the press coverage. Everyone else has been inundated for the last twelve hours, Charlie." Joe was a retired Retail Estate Broker, and a local man, who had grown up in Vancouver. He was a bright guy, and a real numbers man. Why he hadn't taken over as Treasurer I wasn't sure, since he had been on the board a year longer than myself. Whatever. I guess he was committed to enjoying his retirement.

With that, John Timmons, a retired Air Force Bird Colonel, launched into a lengthy narrative of what had been burning up the news wires. John was the most loquacious of all our Board members, and we knew we would be here for quite some time with him leading the overview. John detailed the initial assault in the greatest of minutiae. A gunman, masquerading as a Halloweener, had shot Mr. Kudlach three times. Mr. Kudlach, in the spirit of the holiday had appeared at the door, himself garbed in a bulky gorilla costume, apparently, he loved children, was John's assumption, and his costume had diverted the assailant's bullets. It had saved his live. He was reportedly in stable, but critical condition, although the immediate whereabouts of his location were unknown.

John continued to report on eyewitnesses who had observed the gunman fire shots from a handgun into the air to apparently intimidate several stragglers on the streets. This came after the attack, and from the Kudlach's front yard. The Police had launched a comprehensive investigation, but were not divulging much at this time. As yet, there were no known motives for the attack. Mr. Kudlach was a very well-liked, and well educated, professional. A commercial airline pilot. Although it was fairly common knowledge of his involvement in a bitter land use dispute with the Rosewood Golf and Country Club. Apparently, the press had had a few words with Carol Horn, who was interviewed by the TV reporters last night. Mrs. Horn has been on the news almost non-stop since. She appears to have a knack for telling the press some tidbit, but always seems to have something else for them. Some major break in the case, that she could reveal, if they would just stay in touch with her. They are only too happy to oblige, as everyone wants any possible scoop that might be available. Especially since she seemed to enjoy welcoming them into her home, and feeding them ham sandwiches and cold drinks. John droned on, and our President was too hung over to realize that he need to call the meeting back to order.

But, Charlie listened very carefully. He was privately, and understandably astonished at how any man could stand there, and take three Sig Sauer rounds in his chest, at point blank range, and survive. With this news, Charlie's beleaguered adrenaline kicked in, and he began to collect himself. "Wow, some stuff we've got here."

"I suggest we get the biggest spray, from the best florist in town, and have Larry Easton take it over to the Kudlach's this afternoon. As a matter of fact, I am willing to run out to Hallmark right now, and get a sympathy card, so that the entire Board can sign it," Sonny Brown, a financial guy, and a two year board member spoke up. "We need to be proactive here."

No one disagreed, and Sonny got up and left the meeting immediately.

"If the Kudlachs are not at home, I move that Larry take the flowers next door to Carol and Neil Horn's home. This way we can still show our condolences, which could especially be effective if any of the reporters are around," interjected John Timmons.

Bruce Cranston inquired if anyone had yet spoken to Pete Collins, our attorney. No one apparently had, although if Charlie had been in better shape, it might have been a wise decision to have had him present at this gathering.

"I'm not sure this is necessary as yet," Charlie observed. "There is no intent or compunction here. We are merely innocent bystanders of a horrible situation. We didn't foster or create any of these problems."

The discussion continued. Soon Sonny returned with a large sympathy card. He turned in confusion, and gave the receipt to Mort Perry, our wonder kid ex-Treasurer. A few people looked at him. Under the circumstances, it seemed to be a rather shallow gesture to want to be compensated for a four-dollar sympathy card. Which was his own idea anyway.

The card was passed around, and signed with heartfelt commiserations from everyone. We all wished him a speedy recovery, and much encouragement.

The Board's discussion turned to going forward, and it was decided for Charlie to send out an email to the membership. It would detail the Board's abhorrence of such violence, and the confirmation of our sympathies to one of our very own neighbors. We voted unanimously, to spend up to five hundred dollars on a floral arrangement. But rather than have Larry get involved, it was decided he would deliver our sympathy card to the florist, and they could take it over to Magnolia Street along with the flower delivery.

A motion was proposed to waive Mr. and Mrs. Kudlach's social membership dues, by Sara Richards our House Committee Chair. An immediate discussion was opened on this proposal. Sara was an attractive woman, approaching middle age, but successfully staving off that process for the near future. She was an HR benefits specialist, and worked as a consultant with several large corporations in Portland

"This seems to be a little over the top," opined Matt Mitchell. Charlie agreed.

"It would certainly be a demonstrable show of support from the Club," Toni Duncan countered.

"This is excessive," said Mort Perry. "I mean members die, and their estate or their surviving spouses still have to service their dues until the membership is sold, or bought out." Mort was very protective of the club's revenue stream. "Hopefully, we are not dealing with a matter of life or death here."

"Yes, but these are exceptional circumstances. This would be a personal, as well as a public relations coup for the club. And in my opinion, we may very well need the PR." Again, Toni Duncan weighed in.

"Listen, why don't we consider proposing a reward for the capture of the perp," I threw out. "Say ten thousand dollars for anyone with any information leading to the arrest and conviction of a viable suspect."

"This is a great idea. It could take years to pan out, and we could schedule payout on our own time line," Sonny, the financial guy interjected, took the ball, and began to run with it. "We could call a press conference, have the executive committee there, and make the announcement. This would be excellent press for us, but would also counteract some of the damage that Carol Horn and the Magnolians are doing to us. We had nothing to do with this thing. Why is she over there pointing fingers at us?" Sonny Brown was excited now.

And his suggestion seemed well received by the Board. I mean, it was our sworn duty to send flowers, but what kind of exposure would we get from that? This way, we could show our support publicly, erase any kind of negative innuendo, and get some air time. Bob Kudlach was family around here. Sure, every family has their little disagreements, but we are all sickened by what transpired last night. And it was right in our own neighborhood. We needed to do something positive, and quickly.

This argument was compelling, particularly as it would cost us very little on the front end, and a motion was forwarded to dismiss the dues relief motion and move to offer a reward instead. It just seemed like the right thing to do.

Before the motion was passed, Marta Koenig informed the assembled Board members, that a reward was a unilateral contract, and we needed to be very careful in drawing it up.

It was decided that Pete Collins should write up the contract/reward, and should be present at the press conference, if at all possible.

Charlie interrupted the proceeding momentarily, and asked Larry Easton to get him a glass of water, with ice in it.

With all of the discussion being taken into consideration, the Board passed the reward motion unanimously, with the inclusion of the provisions concerning Pete Collins. Both Charlie and Rick Ferin were happy with a proposal which would move any possible shred of suspicion away from Rosewood.

"I will call Pete as soon as our meeting is adjourned," Charlie assured everyone. "As well as getting an email out to our membership. I'll outline the extent of our sympathies to the Kudlachs, and detail the offer of the reward."

"Is there any other business this morning?" Charlie asked. His water arrived via Larry, and Charlie downed half of the glass in one gulp.

Bruce Cranston spoke up. "I think we should consider the content of this special meeting highly confidential, and I would caution the Board not to speculate publicly with our members. Or for that matter, should the situation ever arise, with the press. The party line should basically be how we are all devastated by this senseless violence here in our own backyard. We will do everything possible to aid in the apprehension of the ruthless criminals who have violated all of our sanctity and peace of mind." Etc. No one disagreed.

By now the meeting was over, and the Board was tired. Due to the late start, things had carried on for well over two hours and a half hour, and everyone was ready to go.

Our Secretary, Roger Taylor, moved to adjourn. Motion seconded, and unanimously approved.

Everyone departed rather quickly, except Bruce, Rick and Charlie.

"Way to go dude," Rick poked some fun at Charlie. "Way to stick your head up your ass."

"Hell, I didn't know," Charlie replied. "I heard the sirens last night, but I thought they were aid cars. They go by here all of the time."

"Well, now that you know what is going on, watch the news once in a while." Bruce contributed, while he perambulated on out of the conference room.

That left Rick, Charlie and Larry Easton. "Larry, get an email out to the membership today for me, will you?"

"Sure Charlie. Want me to call Pete Collins too?"

"Yeah, that would be great. If you get him, tell him I will call him later on. Give him a rundown of the meeting, and the reward. Leave me a message on my phone."

"Sure, Charlie."

Charlie and Rick walked out the side door to the parking lot.

"Can you give me ride?"

"Where is your car?"

"I left it at the Vortex last night."

"You were there with Tricia?"

"No Nikki. Tricia didn't want to go out."

Well, she is a lot smarter than you, Rick thought to himself.

"I am starting to get nervous about the car, Charlie. We need to get that thing out of here. The car ties me to the whole deal, and you gotta know I can't get involved in any of this. Plus, the car is hot as hell. Some of the trick or treaters IDed the goddamn thing when you were shooting your pistol up in the air, and the cops are all looking for a black Mustang."

"Don't worry, we had phony plates on it. It was a legitimate lease, for a legitimate business trip. You wanna take it back tonight, or wait a few days, and let it cool off?"

"I want that damn thing out of here as soon as possible."

"Okay, let's wait until it turns dark tonight. I will follow you in my car the back way to the I-5 highway. Then we can cut over to the 205 Spur, and down to the airport. There's a lot less traffic on that route. I will be right behind you. Don't worry, Bro." But Charlie could see Rick's discomfort. Rick was none too happy.

"Why don't you drive the car, and I'll follow you?"

"Because it would look totally suspicious if we were to get stopped. You leased the car, you need to be the driver. Don't worry. With me behind you, no one will see you from the back. If they spot us coming the other way, we will be long gone."

Although Rick showed no emotion, he was getting more concerned by the minute, and cursed himself for getting involved with Charlie's cockeyed scheme.

"Listen, take me to get my car at the Vortex, will you. I will go home and get rid of Nikki, and get some rest. Then we can move the car. Shit, Nikki is a firecracker. Damn girl wore me out last night." Charlie smirked at Rick. Give me a fucking break, Rick thought to himself, could you possibly be more inappropriate right now?

"You left Nikki at your house with the Mustang in the fucking garage, and the APB all over the fucking news with the description of the car? Are you crazy?"

"Hey, calm down, goddamn it. You are getting paranoid. She doesn't know any more about this news thing than I did this morning. She's probably sleeping it off right now, and she is too dumb to know one car from the next. Plus, there are hundreds of black Mustangs on the road, this one is rented and licensed legit. You leased it for me for a business meeting, because I was having trouble with my car, remember? So, no problem. Even if there was any suspicion, the plates were changed out, and we both have solid alibis. Just stay calm, and be at my house at five."

"Okay. Whatever."

"Let's go then, I want to pick up my car."

They drove over to the Vortex, in a strained silence.

"Thanks for the ride, Ricky Boy. Don't be paranoid."

"I will just be glad when the car is out of here. I would have one of the guys drive the car back, but you don't seem to want to do anything like that."

"That is stupid at this point in time. Stop worrying, man. We don't have a problem here."

As with most Boards, what happens after the meeting, is just as, if not more important, than what happens during the session.

Toni, Marta and Sara walked out of the meeting, and to their cars together.

"WTF was going on in there?" Toni asked.

"That was pretty weird," agreed Marta.

"I mean the guy was obviously strung out, and seemed more shocked that Kudlach was still alive, than he was over the whole attempted murder thing."

Sara agreed. "He showed absolutely no emotion at all."

Toni lived on the law enforcement side of life, and this made her more suspicious than a normal person might be. Her training and experienced intuition were raising red flags all over the place. "How can we depend on him to communicate on behalf of the Board and the membership, with the press, the cops, even our members, with the kind of shape he was in this morning?"

"Well, he really wouldn't need to communicate with anyone, because he would probably be an hour late to the meeting," joked Sara.

The ladies, by natural instinct, tended to stick very closely together on the Board. This was also vital to their survival in a male dominated environment, but these were three very savvy, battle tested women.

And since Charlie Strong was in a lot of ways, and in their opinions, a poster boy for everything that was wrong with our society, he was far from a favorite of theirs anyway.

Matt Mitchell and I were leaving together, when we overheard the ladies talking, and stopped next to them for a minute.

"Crazy meeting, eh?" Matt said.

"We were just talking about that. What in the heck is up with Charlie?"

"Well, he certainly looked like he had a pretty good time last night, whatever he was up to."

Matt continued his remarks, "I saw him in the bar last night, and he was very much in control."

"What time was that?"

"About seven thirty."

"We were just mentioning that we were very concerned with his conduct going forward."

"I think everyone is."

"Do you feel like we should do anything about it?"

I interjected, "Gee, it's not like we could have him drug tested. I think we should just wait it out for a few days, and keep an eye on him."

"He is out of control, and his performance this morning was pathetic."

We all agreed, and it was pretty evident Charlie's credibility had taken a nose dive. We left the ladies standing there. They were still talking.

"You know it certainly isn't very far from the club to Magnolia Street," Toni said. "I hope Charlie has all of his time accounted for last night."

This was a jump in logic, and was not taken lightly by the other two ladies.

"Are you saying you think Charlie is involved in this thing?"

"I don't know, Sara. What a tragedy it would be for us if he was."

After Charlie left, Nikki saw the saucer of coke sitting on the coffee table, and helped herself to a couple of healthy sniffs. After a nice hot shower, she got dressed, and decided to clean Charlie's place up for him while she was waiting. She came back downstairs, and had a couple more whiffs to help clear her head. Glad I didn't have any meetings this morning, she thought to herself.

Actually, the morning after munchies were starting to come on a little bit, and she wished there were a box of those Girl Scout Samoa cookies around right now.

She straightened up, vacuumed, and cleaned up the kitchen. Not that Charlie ate there at home much, from the look of what was in the refrigerator. But there were plenty of empty bottles and takeout food containers around. She had a sack to go out to the trash can, which must be in the garage, she thought.

"Wow," Nikki said out loud to herself. I wonder what this car is doing here? She loved Mustangs, as her dad had bought her a used one when she graduated high school. And this was a nice new one. Why wouldn't Charlie just take this car to his meeting she thought.

Oh well. Nikki went back in the house, and finished cleaning up. She sat down on the couch, turned on the TV, was feeling much better, and almost immediately faded into a light doze with a happy smile on her face. When Charlie finally got home from his meeting, he found her sleeping contentedly on his couch.

Charlie immediately turned off the TV.

CHAPTER THIRTY-ONE

While the Rosewood Board of Trustees meeting was going on, the Task Force was having a meeting of their own. Ray Farley, Detective Larson, and Tricia from the Vancouver PD, and Clark County Prosecuting Attorney Steven Golding were there. Along with Steve Rodriguez and his assistant Tony Patmos, Barbara Estes was there along with her guy, Jim Hanson.

Chief Farley opened the meeting. "Good job everyone. Our mission came off flawlessly last night. Special thanks to the FBI for their surveillance, and to Tricia Watson for her undercover work. Not only did we execute to perfection, we also amassed a ton of incriminating, primary evidence. Additionally, I have already conducted a very interesting interview this morning with eye witnesses, civilians, who can possibly identify Mr. Strong at the crime site."

"Who is that?' inquired Steven Golding.

"A couple of trick or treaters who had previously spoken to Mr. Strong at the Rosewood Country Club during their dinner there earlier in the evening. They observed the clothing he was wearing, and also a very distinctive wristwatch they had previously seen on him. They thought he resembled the assailant very closely. Interesting part is that they are little people, midgets. Seems like they enjoy dressing up like kids and going out on Halloween, even though they are in their late twenties. They were out on Magnolia Street, right across the street from Mr. Kudlach's home. It is the damnedest thing. They would make outstanding witnesses."

"It's not like we will even need their testimony," Steven Golding stated. "We have Tricia who was physically on the scene, we have the entire episode on film, thanks to the FBI. We have the suspect under 24/7 surveillance. The getaway car is still in Mr. Strong's garage. Tricia was careful to leave several obvious prints for us when she adjusted the mirror and radio. We have recorded numerous phone conversations, mainly between Mr. Strong and Mr. Ferin. We could pinch him right now for premediated attempted murder one, illegal possession of firearms, illegal transportation of said firearms, and possession of a controlled substance if we wanted to. I would have a virtually air tight case. We could arrest both of them actually, as Mr. Ferin has incriminated himself on numerous cell phone calls to Mr. Strong. He was also a proven accomplice from square one, in that he supplied the getaway car." Mr. Golding was obviously all over this one.

"Not to change the subject, but I would like it on the record that Officer Watson turned over twenty thousand dollars in one hundred-dollar bills to me this morning. I will deposit it into evidence as soon as I get back to the station. If any of your agencies would like to have access to the money, for analysis, just let me know." Ray Farley was visibly proud of the work that Tricia had done.

Barbara Estes continued on with their conversation, pausing briefly to compliment the younger woman. "Good job, Watson. Anyway, we could have picked him up last night, but we need to decide this morning, what is best for the secondary element of this case, which is the drug smuggling operation out of the Port of Vancouver."

"We are well aware of those considerations," FBI Agent Rodriguez concurred.

"If we arrest them now," Ray Farley observed. "Charlie Strong has rights, and as soon as he contacts his attorney, word is out, and Bao Thieu and the Asians are gone. Which is why, of course, that Charlie Strong is still out on the street."

"Can we pick him up and stash him?" Tricia inquired. "You know, bring him downtown, throw his complaints at him, and tell him we will be willing to put him in rehab for a month, and then reduce his charges if he plays ball with us? I mean, go Manuel Noriega on him. We prevented any real damage from occurring, and Charlie still doesn't know anything about my cover anyway."

"No need," said Ray Farley. "We just leave him out on the street until the next drug shipment comes in, and then we pick up both of them up, as well as Bao Thieu, and the drugs. I am convinced Charlie would get some kind of word to Rick Ferin if we brought him in, and this would kill our whole deal. I am also hoping against hope that somehow, we can lure the Changs back to the states. It would save us a costly and time consuming international extradition proceeding with Taiwan. Get the whole damn lot of them."

"We need to leave him on the street," said Steve Rodriguez. "If he doesn't suspect he is in the weeds, then he is no flight risk anyway. We will cut our surveillance back on him after they return the car, so as not to create any suspicions."

"What about the attempted murder weapon?" DA. Golding wanted to know.

"We are convinced that the murder weapon is still in Charlie's possession. It could still be in the Jaguar. He drove it home from

Rosewood. He drove it to the Vortex Lounge, and he will probably pick it up this morning after his meeting at Rosewood. He was heavily under the influence last night, and there is so much coming down on him right now, he seems to have put the gun on the back burner. What he does with the weapon once the car is back at his house, we can't say. But it would still be on his premises. If he does anything unusual, like going out into the country or to the coast, we will be watching him. The only odd thing we have observed so far, is some sort of altercation this morning with some Girl Scouts and their mom."

"If the weapon is still on his premises, we will find it when we arrest him and search his house," contributed agent Patmos.

"Hopefully, the next load of drugs is coming in soon enough. We can nail that down, get to the bunch of them, and Charlie still has not yet destroyed the attempted murder weapon."

"I think the murder weapon came in the mail to Charlie from Oakland, California," Tricia said. "Charlie asked me to watch for a personal package for him, which he wanted to pick up asap. He never does that. I apologize, I should have had the package x-rayed, before I turned it over to him."

"That would have been fantastic, but even without the actual weapon we have a preponderance of evidence on both Mr. Strong and Mr. Ferin."

"You understand don't you, that because the drug phase of this investigation involves both interstate and international suspects, Mr. Golding, that we are going to have to bring in the Federal District Attorney for the Western Region here?"

"Yes, that is completely appropriate."

"What about the Mustang?" asked Ray Farley. "Should we pull it over on the return trip to the airport, just to further connect it to Mr. Ferin?"

"I don't think so," said Agent Rodriguez. "Let them think they are bullet proof. Rick is getting paranoid, but if they can take the car back without any problems, they will be more at ease. This will increase the tendency of more chatter on their cell phones. We will have the whole trip on camera anyway."

"Agreed."

Barbara Estes wanted to talk about the drug shipments. When do they come in? How often? Etc.

Tricia replied that the shipments originate with Han Say, but don't appear to occur with every single shipment. "The best thing to do, is stay on Rick Ferin's cell phone. From what I know, everything is coordinated through him. He is Charlie Strong's righthand man. I am up in the office, and I don't know intimately, what goes on down in the yard. But, Rick Ferin certainly does, and he is the one you need to stay up on. I'm sure there is cash changing hands, too. And Ben Harris would be the contact on the money side."

"Yes, we have already intercepted several interesting conversations between him and Charlie. We will watch him too."

"Where is Mr. Kudlach as we speak," Golding wanted to know.

"We took him to Peace Memorial in Portland last night. Of course, they knew we were coming, and processed Bob into their system without incident. His condition is, sic, guarded, and he is in serious but stable condition. He is currently unavailable to meet with anyone. There is a possibility he could need further attention, most probably surgery, blah, blah, and Peace will continue to keep him buried for us. In reality, he exited the building early this morning, in route to the Hawaiian Islands, and a much-deserved break from his busy life. We are in communication with him and his wife. They will be resting comfortably for the next couple of weeks. He will then come back with his arm in a sling until we wrap up our business. I have never worked with a more co-operative asset. There must have been some considerable animosity over there between Kudlach and Rosewood, is all I can say."

"And there is no chance he could be identified there in the islands, by anyone we know?'

"Well, never say never, but he has agreed to wear his sling on his left arm whenever he goes out to avoid blowing his cover."

"Does anyone have any more questions, or input?" asked Chief Farley. "We are agreed then, to allow Mr. Strong and Mr. Ferin to continue to operate. They go forward under the illusion that they were successful in their scheme, and we hopefully are able to monitor and intercept the next shipment coming in from Han Say. Special Agent Rodriguez?"

"Yes, at which time the investigation will shift to the Port and Han Say. The FBI and the DEA will assume authority over operations, with the Vancouver PD then serving as our support arm. Agent Watson, I would ask you to be hyper alert for the next couple of weeks. You are the onsite eyes and ears of this operation, and if you observe anything of interest, anything at all, I encourage you to call me 24/7. Here is my cell phone number."

"Yes sir, Agent Rodriguez."

"Please call me Steve. Special Agent Estes, you are continuing your surveillance of Mr. Bao?"

"Yes, Steve. And please call me Barbara. We have identified the cargo van that is being used as the transport vehicle. It is kept in a garage in Richmond, California, close to the waterfront there. Mr. Thieu's offices are in San Francisco, and he is not involved as a primary anymore. He has been promoted, and spends most of his time in his office. He also takes a trip to Reno at least once a week. We have had his whole pod under surveillance for some time, on related matters. We think they may be laundering drug money through the Oriental Casino, which is on the strip in downtown Reno. At any rate, the arrangements for pickup, will most probably still be made by Mr. Thieu through Mr. Ferin, even though there is another set of drivers. The Oriental Casino is a major operation in the heart of downtown Reno. Justice is looking at their charters, and we should know more about them in the near future."

"We are set then. I suggest that we continue our meeting to next Wednesday afternoon, here, at three pm. Tricia can then update us on any shipping specifics, and we can adjust our agenda accordingly."

"See you all next week." The special agents and their people filed out, and Ray Farley took the time to thank agent Watson on a job well done, before the Vancouver people left. "Between the FBI's surveillance, and the logistics we have recovered at the crime scene, this guy is hamburger meat."

"And he doesn't even know it. Ha."

"Steve is going to notify me when the Mustang starts to move on its return trip, and once it has been turned back in, we are going to impound it to sweep it for prints. Another nail in his coffin."

"Great Ray. I am going to take the rest of the weekend off."

"Good idea. Call me if anything jumps up."

"Will do."

Rick called Charlie at four thirty in the afternoon. "You ready to go?"

"Yeah, I'm ready. You don't mind if Nikki comes with us do you?"

"Jesus Charlie, don't mess with me right now. I'm not in the mood."

"Just kidding, buddy, relax. See you in half an hour."

"Okay."

"Can you believe that sucker is still alive? I mean I drained three rounds right into his fucking chest, and he is still kicking? It's incredible."

"Yeah, well I saw them take him out of the house last night on a stretcher, on prime-time TV. They don't take dead people out on a stretcher, unless they have a sheet over them.

Charlie and Nikki had Saturday afternoon sex when he got back to the Townhouse. He had a toot and a beer when he walked in, and was starting to feel like himself again. A little hangover sex and a nap, a snap, and he would be back to his normal self. Jesus, what a pain in the ass this morning had been, with the meeting and then those goofy girl scouts. He and Nikki went back to bed. When they woke up, he told her he had to drop her off, go run an errand, and would pick her up later.

"Let's go out to dinner."

"Where? What do you want me to dress for?"

"Something nice. Let's go uptown. Go to Portland. I feel like getting out of this berg tonight."

"Whose Mustang is that in the garage?" Nikki asked on her way home.

Charlie was surprised at her interest, and looked at her out of the corner of his eye. She seemed like it was an innocent enough question.

"It belongs to a friend of mine. He needed a place to store it, until he sold his other car. As a matter of fact, I think he is coming to pick it up tonight or tomorrow."

"It is a cherry car, very clean. I wish it was mine."

"I didn't know you were into cars."

"Oh, not so much. I just like Mustangs is all."

Jesus thought Charlie, what are the chances?

Charlie pulled up at Nikki's apartment, and they kissed goodbye.

"Pick you up about seven thirty or eight."

"Okay, love you."

Oh shit, Charlie thought. She loves me already?

Rick showed up at Charlie's right on time. Due to the late fall time of year, the November sun was already going down, and shadows were deepening.

"How you doin', my man?'

"Fine Charlie, you ready to go?"

"Sure. I'm ready. You want a hit before we go?" Charlie jerked his chin at the coffee table.

"No thanks, maybe later."

They went into the garage and changed the plates back on the Mustang. "Okay, let's do this."

Charlie opened the garage, and Rick started the car. Charlie's Jag was in the driveway, so he backed out of Rick's way, and closed the garage door behind Rick with his remote. Rick backed out, and they were off. Rick was very stiff and erect in the sports car. Charlie wished he would just relax.

As soon as the garage door opened, the FBI observers called Steve Rodriguez, who in turn called Ray Farley. Ray dispatched two of his troopers to the Portland Airport, with the search warrant for the Mustang. They went the more traveled route, and were at the airport well before Rick and Charlie got there.

Charlie's little convoy hit the freeway in next to no time, and was cruising toward the 205 cut off, with Rick doing the speed limit and Charlie right on his tail.

Boom, here is the cut off, thought Charlie. Boom, here is the airport, thought Charlie. No problem.

Which is exactly what happened. Charlie peeled off in front of the Hertz Rental agency, as Rick pulled the car into the processing lane. The rental agent cleared them quickly, and Rick hopped into Charlie's Jag, and they headed out. Neither of them seemed to notice the two uniformed policemen, who were standing around outside of the rental agency office.

"Told you man! Easy as pie."

"Yeah, well, I just don't like to take chances is all."

"Whatever. You know what they say, never up, never in."

"In what, Charlie? We didn't gain anything here. This seems like more of a personal thing between you and Kudlach."

"Yeah, well the guy was an asshole, and I did it for all of us. I don't think he will be messing with us too much more, even if he isn't dead."

"You plugged him three times? For real?"

Charlie pulled off the road, and into the Skyway Tavern's seedy parking lot. "Here, have a toot, and I'll buy you a beer." He said while he handed his vial to Rick.

"No thanks. Once I start on that stuff, I don't want to quit."

"Well, take the vial with you. I've got plenty more at my place."

Rick put the vial in his levi's pocket, and opened the door to get out. I don't want the goddamn vial he thought. He just wanted to have a beer, and get home. He didn't want to see Charlie again for a few days. Charlie had endangered them for personal reasons, and then had made an ass out of himself at the Board meeting this morning. They all had too good of a thing going to be taking stupid chances like this, and Rick was not happy to suffer this fool gladly. For the first time since he had gone to work for Charlie, Rick was beginning to question what direction his life was going in.

They went in, sat down at the bar and ordered a couple of beers.

"Want to play some pool?"

"Nope."

"Jesus, snap out of it, will ya? The car is gone, the coast is clear. We are good to go."

"Yeah, well I just don't like tempting fate like this. We already have the other deal going on. Why screw up something paying us solid cash money, for something stupid like this?"

"Stupid? You saying I'm stupid, Rick?"

"I didn't say that at all. It was obviously a brilliant plan, because it worked to perfection. As I have said a hundred times, I just don't like taking chances is all. Rick pulled out twenty bucks, and nodded to the frowsy bartender.

She came over. "Let me get your change, honey."

"No worries. Keep it." Rick drained his beer, and got up. Charlie wasn't ready to go, but he was starting to want to be as rid of Rick, as vice-versa. They walked back to the Jag, and drove back to Charlie's in silence.

"Sorry to bum you out man. This is all on me anyway. And its why I didn't want any of our guys involved with it."

"You don't bum me out. You are my man, and I just don't want to see anything bad happen here. You get me?"

"Sure man. I appreciate your concern, even if I think it is unfounded."

Charlie dropped Rick, pulled the Jag into the garage, and popped the trunk lid. As the garage door was coming down, the FBI agents could see the Jag's trunk lid going up. Rick had no idea the weapons were still in the car. That would have absolutely freaked him out. Charlie took his satchel out of the trunk, and took it over to the work table. He disassembled both weapons, and gave them a thorough cleaning. He threw the mask in the trash, wrapped the weapons back up in the now empty bag, and went over and locked them in his tool box. Fucking Ferin is going soft on me, Charlie thought to himself.

He was finally starting to relax, and began to think of where to make a reservation for dinner. French or Italian, he thought to himself. Something nice and quiet, for sure. No more of that night club shit. He was getting a little old for that stuff.

His phone rang, it was Pete Collins.

"Hi Pete" Charlie said. "Thanks for calling back. Some shit huh?"

"Yeah, this is about as crazy as it gets."

"Are you available for a press conference tomorrow or Monday?"

"Yeah, I could probably do it in the morning."

"Have you written up the reward yet?"

"Yes, and I must say, I have not spent a lot of time in my illustrious career writing reward posters."

"I'll bet you haven't. I will call Larry, and have him schedule with the TV guys and get back to you. I am thinking that sooner is better than later. Maybe if we can go tomorrow midday, it won't have to bother your work schedule."

What about my Sunday? Pete thought. But he had been a member at Rosewood for eighteen years, and was nothing, if not a good soldier for the cause.

"Well, it shouldn't be a problem to schedule with the network reporters. They will meet anywhere, anytime if they think they are going to get a scoop."

Charlie called Larry's cell phone. "Say Larry, I spoke with Pete, and he is ready to go. Can you contact the stations, and get us a meeting for noon tomorrow?"

"Will do. I will call back and confirm with you."

"Great. Just you me and Pete should be good enough. Don't you think?"

"At this late date, for sure."

"I am going out to dinner with a friend tonight. Call me on my cell, and if I don't pick up, just leave a message."

"Will do. Don't be late."

"Ha, ha. Fuck you." Charlie hung up and went inside to get ready for his date. He called for the Italian reservation. He wanted some comfort food.

Larry was ready to leave the club, as it had been a long day. But thanks to Charlie, he had been tasked one more time. Larry was starting to feel like someone's personal gofer, and he was too close to retirement for too much more of this.

CHAPTER THIRTY-TWO

Fall in the Northwest is a quieter time in our regional golf clubs. While Palm Desert, Scottsdale and the Southeastern courses are just starting to gear up for their seasons, our busy summer calendar is winding down. We play year around at Rosewood, because our coastal climate stays fairly temperate, but the bulk of our tee times are vastly reduced. The hardcore golfers will still tee it up, however, unless there is snow or frost on the ground.

Strangely enough, this is the time of year that golf clubs have more solid P & L statements than in the busy summer months. How so? Well, the summer months are so busy with member supported events, a lot of which are break even functions, that in the quieter winter months, there are less activities to manage, the staffing is drastically cut back, but the monthly member dues keep rolling in. To that extent, the bottom line is greatly enhanced.

During the season, there are wine tasting dinners; break even. There are family movie and pizza nights, pool parties, member guest and numerous other tournaments for both the men's and women's clubs. If not for beverage sales, they would be complete losers. The club opens and staffs the pool, the tennis courts; these events are the opposite of cash cows. More like cash enemas, but they are a vital amenity to a golf club, and largely draw in social members, who are our life blood. There is more staffing in every department, F&B, maintenance, the pro shop, recreation, supplies, R & M, office/admin, etc., and just the opposite in the winter.

The membership also quiets down. The major tournaments are over. The club champion, summer better ball, and member guest winners have been crowned. The nominally ardent floggers are seen less and less, except when they come for lunch or dinner to help use up their food minimum charges. Yes, the fall and winter social calendar stays strong in the clubhouse, and the holidays, are around the corner, which comes with a busy burst of activity. But then, after the holidays, the snowbirds begin their exit for the dessert, and depending on the severity of the winter season, the club gets really quiet for three or four months.

But this fall, and with the events that took place on Halloween night, the Rosewood Golf and Country Club was an uncharacteristically busy place.

Charlie was whistling an old Bee Gee's tune-Stayin Alive- when he picked Nikki up. Larry had called back, and he was scheduled to meet with all three local network affiliates tomorrow at noon at the club, as planned. Which would hopefully wrap things up on the Rosewood side for a while anyway.

"You're in a good mood tonight," she said. Nikki wanted to take credit for that, and was hopeful that Charlie's jovialness, was related to having a date with her, and also to having an insatiable craving for her body.

"Yep. Life is good. Got some unpleasant business out of the way this weekend, and everything went very well. Now, I am taking my girl out for a nice evening. Antonio's sound good for some Italian food?"

"Never been there Charlie, but if you pick it, I'm sure it is a great place." Nikki was wearing a cute little burgundy frock, and some tan pumps. She hiked her skirt up high enough, almost to her lap, to give Charlie a little thrill.

He noticed. "You look great tonight," he said. He was so looking forward to a quiet peaceful night. He planned to stay in control of himself, and atone for his crappy showing this morning at tomorrow's press conference.

But, one little toot probably wouldn't hurt anything. He pulled his backup vial and spoon out of his leather jacket pocket, and handed them to Nikki.

"Care for a hit?"

Rick made it home, and was resting up. Domestic time for him. In spite of the fact that he was a very taciturn man, he cared a lot about his family, and didn't want to have the same relationship with them as he had had with his siblings. He was sitting on the couch, watching a college football game, and his little guys were crawling all over him.

"What's for din din, hon?" He asked the wife.

Tricia was also in family mode, and was sitting at the dinner table with her mom and son, eating the spaghetti dinner she had prepared.

Dean Jr. finished first, and asked to be excused.

"You may, but take your plates to the sink, and then go brush your teeth," Tricia told him.

Tricia's mom was happy to have DJ excuse himself, because she wanted to talk about last night's attack, but didn't want to talk in front of him.

"Can you believe what happened at Rosewood?" She knew Tricia was in undercover work and couldn't say anything about any working cases, she didn't even know if this was one of them, but she still, like everyone else, was freaked out about it.

"Yeah, and right here in our own little Vancouver."

"I wonder who did it?"

"Who knows."

"Well, it had to be either a home invasion, a personal thing, or some kind of crazy random or gang thing. I doubt if it was a home invasion, because they didn't invade the house. It said on the TV that there were only two suspects, and one of them was a girl. That doesn't sound like any home invaders to me."

"No, I guess it doesn't."

"And gang members don't go into neighborhoods and shoot residents, do they?"

"No, they have more conflict with other gang members, or if they are doing initiations, they will select more random targets. Drive by shootings."

"Well, from the news coverage, this seemed like a pretty premeditated act. Like someone didn't seem to care much for Mr. Kudlach. How's he doing anyway?"

"From what I hear, it seems like he will recover."

"Well, I certainly hope so. How brutal to attack a man in his own home, and shoot him in cold blood, in front of his own wife. I know you can't talk too much about your work honey, but if you are involved at all in this thing, you be careful, will you?"

"Sure mom, no problem. Don't worry, I'm okay."

While Charlie was having a pleasant afternoon and evening with Nikki, the Rosewood phone lines were buzzing. The rumor mill had kicked in, and if Charlie had any idea of most of those conversations, his ears would have been burning.

It started with the lady Board members, whose phones went off as soon as they got home from their meeting, with their friends wanting to know what went on. Then those conversations started to spread like a prairie fire within the club, with the usual distortions and inaccuracies that inevitably occur from conversations of speculation.

Considering the diminutive size of our Rosewood Bar, and how much Charlie enjoyed holding court there, much like Charlie and our earlier table had been exposed to the ladies' conversation about the woman with the asymmetrical breasts, the reverse had often been the case. Wherein the club ladies who inadvertently found themselves in the lounge, had been subjected to Charlie's macho rants, often vulgar stories, and all of the above, combined with his usually offensive language. He was not a popular figure with the Ladies of Rosewood, and not understanding club politics very well, they couldn't comprehend how he had become the President and spokesperson for their club.

Charlie was no misogynist, and he did his best to be nice to the Rosewood ladies. As a matter of fact, he loved the ladies, especially young, attractive ladies. It was just more of his limited male perspective, that the bar was a male domain, no matter who was in there. And if they didn't appreciate his humor and narratives, well then, stay out of the bar.

Trouble and Charlie stayed apart on Saturday night, and he and Nikki had a memorable meal. He was ever the bon vivant, and knew just what to order and suggest for their dining pleasure. The seafood pasta with pesto sauce, was particularly to Nikki's liking. But Charlie behaved himself at all costs. He wanted to be in good shape for Sunday, and atone for Saturday morning's faux pas.

Pete, Larry and Charlie met with a dozen reporters in the Rosewood conference room at the appointed hour. Charlie wanted to wrap up the meeting as soon as possible, as the Seahawks/49ers game was on at 1:15.

"Thanks for organizing this on such short notice, Larry."

"No problem, Charlie." Larry was amazed that Charlie was considerate enough to recognize his considerable efforts, and felt some of his animosity slipping away.

"Your car working alright?"

The press was mostly on time, and were of course, interested in any new information. Charlie offered them coffee or juice or cookies from the coffee break table. They had arrived early enough to set up their microphones and cameras, and the presentation was ready to proceed.

"Thank you for coming today. I am Charles Strong, President of the Rosewood Golf Club's Board of Directors. This is Pete Collins, our Attorney, and Larry Easton, our General Manager. We want you to know, that on behalf of the Board of Directors, and the entire membership, that our Rosewood family, is shocked and appalled by the recent attack in our neighborhood. Bob Kudlach was not only an immediate neighbor, he was a friend and social member of our club." And although it has been some time since Charlie had said any prayers to anyone, he assured the reporters that the Rosewood community at large was praying and hoping that Bob was going to recover rapidly, and survive this vicious attack.

"In this regard, we would like you to know that the Board of Directors of Rosewood Golf and Country Club is officially offering a reward of ten thousand dollars, which we sincerely hope will help lead to any information that would produce an arrest and conviction in this case. Do you have any questions?"

The effect of Charlie's announcement didn't seem to have quite the impact he had hoped for, judging from the dead pan expression on most of his audience's faces. But a young woman from KAYU, Fox news, raised her hand.

"Yes, ma'am?"

"Is it true that there was recently a very hostile set of hearings over a land use proposal by Rosewood, that was an extreme intrusion on the Magnolia Street neighborhood?"

Charlie was taken aback by the question, and seemed to stiffen noticeably. Pete Collins sensed this, and immediately responded to her probing query.

"Yes ma'am, we have recently completed some hearings. However, it is our position at Rosewood, that the proposed project was well within the concept of a working golf club from a land use standpoint.

We felt that this proposal would have been very beneficial not only to the golfing members of our club, but would have also been a huge benefit to the youth of this community, and consequently to the greater community at large. The Practice Range was designed to be an expanded part of our ongoing support program for youth athletics, not only for our own member's families. But also, for our work with the Vancouver School System, and their golf agendas. This includes both the boy's and girl's athletic programs of that organization.

While the proposal was denied, we are disappointed we could not convince our neighbors of the attractiveness of the project. It essentially was a win win for all of us. We offered to mitigate the expansion of our facilities, in any way the Magnolia Street neighbors felt would be acceptable to them. Unfortunately, we were unsuccessful in those endeavors. But to suggest that there is ongoing rancor on our part, is diametrically opposite of the realities of the situation.

All families may have disagreements, which is a reality in life. But in the end, we are still family, and this is where we find ourselves at present. We essentially have agreed to disagree." As always, Pete spoke eloquently on our behalves.

Another reporter, this one from the ABC affiliate was recognized by Pete. "Isn't part of the problem, and an underlying reason for the ongoing animosity between Rosewood and the Magnolia Street neighborhood, over the manner in which Rosewood operates this club? I am especially referring to the maintenance of the golf course. I have with me copies of numerous noise complaints, which have been filed with the City of Vancouver, and the Vancouver PD. This includes information that the Vancouver PD has been out to this club on several occasions to investigate these complaints. And these complaints have been largely ignored by Rosewood. You continue to operate as you please, in total disregard of both the law, and your neighbors around the course?"

Now all three men on the dais were beginning to feel some discomfort, and a perception of hostility from the reporters.

"I am not sure where you are getting your information, sir" Pete responded. "But this Club has been a viable part of this community since the 1920's. This is a golfing community. It has always been a golfing community. It was a golfing community when Magnolia Street was permitted for development. All of the neighborhoods surrounding Rosewood Golf and Country Club benefit from the amenity of living on a golf course. Their real estate values reflect the same benefit. To expect somehow that we should be unable to maintain our course in a reasonable manner is preposterous."

"Do you call mowers and blowers and other equipment operating full blast on the course, at six am in the morning reasonable? And now you want to construct a full-on driving range right next to them? Is this what you call reasonable sir?" It was as if Carol Horn and Hugh and Bunny had somehow infected these people.

"Allow me to explain if I may," Larry Easton interjected. "We have club tournaments, that require course preparation. We have made every effort to perform our course prep in a manner which minimizes any intrusion our work may cause the neighbors. We have absolutely no complaints from anyone other than Magnolia Street. Therefore, we do the areas and holes that abut Magnolia St. last, in order to, minimize any impact on their community."

Yet another reporter stood. "Mr. Collins, is it not true that most of this course prep as you refer to it, occurs regularly on Saturday and Sunday mornings? Which is when normal people, and quiet neighborhoods are sleeping and attempting to recoup after their busy weeks? But instead, they are assaulted at the break of dawn by the obnoxious noise decibels of your heavy equipment. And in contradiction to Mr. Easton's statement that Rosewood has not received any other complaints, isn't it true that Mr. Murray, who lives over on Carnation St., on the other side of the Rosewood Golf Course, has also voiced numerous noise complaints. And has also filed those complaints with the appropriate City departments? I have a copy of several of those complaints, if you would care to refresh your memory."

Pete gave Larry a sideways look, and readily understood that this meeting deteriorating rapidly.

"Ladies and Gentlemen, we are not here to debate the logistics of operating this club. We are here to empathize with, and show our support for the Kudlachs, at their time of need. We will do anything and everything in our power to help apprehend the perpetrators of this atrocity. We hope that our efforts will help bring some closure to this case, and again, all of our thoughts and prayers are with the Kudlach family at this time. Thank you for coming today. There will be no more questions at this time."

The reporters filed out. Several of them stopped by the coffee table, and grabbed a handful of cookies on the way.

"Well, those assholes," Charlie snapped. "Did you see that last jerk walk off with half of our freaking cookies?"

"Charlie, you are personalizing this situation, which is understandable. However, I am emphatically suggesting to all of us to stay positive. We do not want to develop an antagonistic relationship with the press at this time."

"I get it Pete, but they seemed to be pretty well prejudiced against Rosewood, before they even got in here."

"Which is out of our control, Charlie. We can only continue to be supportive, and hope this thing sorts itself out as quickly as possible. God help us, if somehow Rosewood would ever be implicated adversely in this thing."

"That is not possible, Pete. I will send out an email to the Board and membership summarizing our meeting this morning. Hopefully, we can try to waylay some of their concerns, without sounding negative, and I will also relay your party line to them."

"Thanks Charlie."

Jeez, does the drama around this place ever stop, Pete thought as he prepared to leave? It also occurred to him to check with the insurance company as to indemnification of the Board members.

"You want me to get that email out?" Larry inquired of Charlie, almost by force of habit now.

"Sure, Larry."

The Seahawks lost, which was not surprising, considering the way their season was going. But the loss still did nothing to lift Charlie's spirits. Nor did the six o'clock news.

Charlie turned on the TV, and waited for the coverage on Rosewood's generous offer. He did not need or expect any face time on TV for himself, but just wanted as much favorable PR for

Rosewood as possible. Nikki was readily aware of his bad mood, and started to think that this golf thing was a pretty big bummer all around.

I mean we were in Pebble Beach, of all places, and Charlie gets bummed over some stupid pairings thing, she thought to herself. Then we are having such a fun weekend, especially last night's cozy, romantic dinner. And now Charlie is in another snit after coming back from his stupid club. He sure can be moody, she thought.

The news droned on, and finally after the third weather report, and just before sports, the station ran a segment on the Halloween Night attempted murder on Magnolia Street.

The news anchor outlined the case. He updated his audience about the latest information available to them from the Vancouver PD. Who were still processing things, and were now waiting for the result of the ballistics tests which were being run in the FBI laboratories.

"There seems to be so much support from the communities of our city for Mr. Kudlach. Flowers are arriving by the minute, and a make shift shrine has been erected in the front yard of the Kudlach residence. It is a very touching and poignant scene, to see our city respond so supportively to this tragedy, and this neighborhood," he intoned. "Although they are just a group of friends and neighbors, seemingly very close knit I might add, Magnolia Street is fighting for the survival of their life styles and wellbeing in the Rosewood Community at large. And now the sudden and vicious attack on one of their very own. To this end, the Magnolia Street Homeowner's Association is offering to match any and all efforts to create a reward fund, as an incentive to the capture of Mr. Kudlach's assailants. Isn't this inspiring? And as we speak, the fund is now over twenty thousand dollars, and climbing."

That was it? They were attempting to match any reward monies donated to date? No mention at all of Rosewood's generous offer? Am I on another planet here, Charlie thought to himself?

"What do you want to do for dinner?" Nikki asked. She was getting hungry, and there was nothing but junk food at Charlie's. And not too much of that left around.

"I don't know. Where do you want to go?"

"Why don't we stay at home, and order in. I don't really feel like going out again." Charlie said.

"I guess it's pizza then."

"That's okay with me."

"How about some Chinese. We just had Italian last night?"

"Whatever." Charlie had lost his appetite.

His phone rang. It was Marta Koenig. "Hi Charlie. I got your email about the press conference today, but I didn't see anything on the news tonight about it."

Charlie had been so wound up by the closeness of the Seahawk's game, that he had forgotten to check his email. Larry gave the members a brief summary of the noon hour meeting, but had neglected to report the antagonism of the press toward Rosewood, and had given everything a positive spin.

"Well, it was touch and go. The press wanted to talk more about our relationship with the Magnolia Street neighbors, and I think they are trying to create a conflict between us. I guess that would help their ratings."

"I don't know what happened at the press conference, but all I heard was Magnolia this and Magnolia that. There was nothing about Rosewood's offer. It certainly seems as if a bias is developing."

"Well the hell with those people. Pete is suggesting we just lay low, be supportive, and let this thing blow over. But I can tell you, I do not feel like letting these jerk-offs roll over us. We don't deserve this."

"No, we don't Charlie. But I have to agree with Pete. We absolutely cannot get into a conflict with our local press at this time." Marta rolled her eyes to no one in particular at Charlie's coarseness.

"Whatever."

"Well, yes, whatever, Charlie. But as a friend, I must caution you to stay clear of this thing. Again, as a friend, I have to tell you that there is no small amount of concern within the club about your presidency."

"What the hell does that mean?"

"Charlie, I am the messenger here, please don't get mad at me. Your performance at Saturday morning's board meeting for one thing, raised a lot of eyebrows. Plus, your abrasive style has some people worried. They are saying you might not be the right person to lead at the present time."

Charlie was stunned by her comments. "I'm surprised by your message, and if your lady friends are uncomfortable with my leadership, well too bad. I have done nothing but donate my time and energy, endlessly I may add, to do what is best for Rosewood. If my efforts are not appreciated, well, I guess I just can't really please all of the people all of the time, can I?"

"I get it Charlie. And we all appreciate what you have done for the club. I am just hoping, as a friend, that you will walk softly for the short term. I can tell you there are rumors flying around like a flock of mallards."

"Whatever. I have to go."

I will walk softly, Charlie thought as he clicked off. And my boys will have my back for sure.

"Who was that?" Nikki asked.

"Just some damn club business."

Oh shit, here he goes into another one of his moods she thought. "You want to go to a movie after I order pizza?"

"I thought you wanted to stay in tonight."

"Well not if you are going to be bummed out all night. Let's go see a happy movie." A love story she thought to herself.

"Whatever."

"What kind of pizza do you like?"

"Whatever."

"Jesus, Charlie. Do you just want me to go home?"

Charlie realized that he was being a jerk. "No, no. It's not you. It's just some problems I am dealing with, that are most annoying."

"I'm sorry. Is there anything I can do to help?"

"Not really. Just you being here is great."

Nikki pulled him down on the couch, and began to tickle and bite him. Charlie started to love wrestle with her, and his mood brightened a bit.

"I like sausage and mushrooms," he whispered in her ear.

"Oh Charlie. You are my big sausage man!"

They continued to tumble around together. The next thing he knew, they were on the floor, and breathing hard.

CHAPTER THIRTY-THREE

Charlie's email, via Larry, had been received by the club's membership, with no small amount of interest. Everyone was dying to know about what was going on. They wanted inside information, and were happy to help with reward money, if that might assist with the case. But, they were also confused by the seemingly innocuous informational feedback. The greater reality didn't seem to correspond with Rosewood's reality. Not with Charlie Strong's emails anyway.

For example, Rosewood held a Sunday press conference, which was reported to have gone very well. And offered a substantial reward, yet on the evening's news reports, there was no mention of Rosewood or their efforts. And what the heck does the Magnolia neighbors, fighting for their very survival in the greater Rosewood Community mean? What is being unsaid here?

Monday dawned, and everyone went back to their respective careers and livelihoods. Excepting most country club women don't necessarily need to help provide for their personal or families' livelihoods. Unless they so choose. So then, a lot more of their time was spent on the phones, and a lot more questions were voiced and discussed.

One of Toni Duncan's press contacts called her at work to inquire about the relationship between Rosewood and Magnolia Street, and Toni was taken aback by her attitude. Toni quoted the party line, and mourned the injury to Mr. Kudlach. Nevertheless, the questions were asked, and in more detail and with more venom than had been voiced at the press conference. It almost made Toni feel guilty about her membership at the club. She was well aware of her public personae.

When Toni shared her conversation and some of her concerns with a few friends, this initiated another round of speculation. Who would do this? Was anyone from Rosewood involved?

Well, even Dane Knutson's little people thought they had seen something, and people were talking.

If anyone from Rosewood was involved, I think we all have a pretty good idea of who it might be. What did the Police know that they weren't saying? Etc., etc. This thing was spreading like warm butter over hot toast.

By the time Monday evening came, Charlie Strong was being portrayed as a drug crazed, psychotic killer in some circles. He was to be avoided at any cost. Most of the Rosewood ladies, if not outright afraid of him, were certainly intimidated by him. It should be a pretty interesting ladies golf day on Tuesday, Marta thought.

Tuesday mid-morning, Tricia was typing a couple of letters for Ben Harris, when her cell phone dinged with a new, incoming message. Tricia picked up the phone and was delighted to be receiving an email from Sui Chang.

"Hiya, how you are? Hello from Taipei, Taiwan. Was thinking of you today, and missing to touch you.

I had so much fun going to shopping. Mr. Chang has bought a condominium in Honolulu. It is very beautiful, and we are going to spend more time there. Maybe you can come visit me some time. XoX, Sui."

Tricia wrote right back. "Would love to come visit, and soon. XoX, T."

This was the text Tricia had been waiting for. Hopefully, a very timely break.

Charlie worked his normal six-hour day on Monday and Tuesday, which usually included a two hour/three drink luncheon somewhere. Unless there was a new contract to negotiate, or a rare labor issue of some kind to mediate, he was on a pretty flexible schedule. He also had to prepare for his upcoming annual meeting in San Francisco. It was scheduled for a week and a half out. But his business was in order, and his regions were current and performing up to San Francisco's projected budgets. Charlie expected little, if any problems at his annual review.

It would be a time of catching up and renewing old acquaintances, a little golf. A lot of cocktails and social functions. The ILWU National Convention was being held at the Hyatt Regency/ Embarcadero hotel in San Francisco. It was one of his favorite spots, and he was looking forward to seeing the Corporate Executive team. It was the time of year for annual bonuses, and the renewing of his employment contract for the coming year.

Charlie was feeling pretty secure. Expansive even. Between his legitimate earnings with the ILWU, and his side money from the nefarious shipping operations, he was knocking down some pretty nice cash. And with lifetime benefits accruing. Easy reasons for which to feel expansive. Especially, as he didn't have a family to support, most of his income was expendable in nature.

Since Rick and Ben and their wives would be coming down with him, I guess his biggest decision was whether or not to take Nikki along. He had better make up his mind, because she would surely need time to get set up. Namely, some major Nordstrom's floor time. All in all, Charlie was very happy with his life, except for the small to middling annoyances that kept popping up at Rosewood every time he turned around. He ought to just get the hell out of there, and let them deal with their own damn problems. Things were a lot simpler for him before he had agreed to become their president.

Carol Horn was busy as well. Not just her practice, but in Bob Kudlach's absence she had become the de facto voice and brains of the Magnolia neighborhood. She missed Bob, but was very happy with the way their propaganda war was going, and felt like it was a stroke of genius to align with the press as quickly as they had. After all, they had a much more compelling story to tell, than a bunch of stuffy jerks at Rosewood, and she was very proud of the way they had turned the Rosewood reward press conference into a nonevent. It was her conviction, beyond a shadow of a doubt, that it was Rosewood who was responsible for the attack on Bob. And she would continue to do everything possible to keep this concept before her new buddies in the media. Even though she appreciated their support, Carol found it interesting how easily small-town media allowed themselves to be manipulated.

Bunny and Hugh had invited her and Neil to dinner on Monday night. It was a welcome relief to get out of the house, not have to cook, and continue to hone the master plan with her two old friends and trusted allies.

They all sat down for a glass of wine, and Hugh immediately said, "I feel positive it is that Charlie Strong dude who is behind all of this. Who else would it be? I know he's a macho dickhead, from seeing him around the bar all these years. I wonder who he brought in on this little job of his?"

"Didn't have to bring anyone in very far, probably just used one of his union goons. He wouldn't be stupid enough to get involved himself, would he?" Carol thought out loud.

"I doubt it. I just hope the cops got enough evidence from the scene to pin him to the wall."

"I am very busy at work, as is Neil," Carol said. "So, you two have to be our eyes and ears, since you are around here full time. I would even go up to the club from time to time, Hugh. Just hang out in the bar, and stay alert to what is going on."

"Have you heard anything from Bob yet?"

"Not a word. But I called Chief Farley today, to try and get an update. He assured me Bob is doing well, and past any serious problems. I think they must be keeping Bob under wraps, to prevent further attacks. But I am sure he will get in touch with us, and let us know he is alright."

"What a relief for us, when his call comes in. Be sure and let us know, won't you," asked Bunny.

"You will be the first, trust me."

"Wasn't it great on TV last night? Not a word about Rosewood, and all their big hoopla, reward build up. I thought our people did a great job on them." This development seemed to appeal to Hugh a great deal.

"Yes, I think one of our gals kept after them today. The press is really on this thing. This is a huge story, and they really want to break it," Carol acknowledged.

"So do we," said Hugh and Bunny simultaneously.

"What's for dinner?" Neil asked. "We've got to get back to the kids."

"One more thing," Hugh asked Carol. "Shouldn't we ask for a meeting with the Rosewood Board? Have a neighborhood style meeting, inquire about their future intentions. Take some of the press with us. See if we can get them talking about a land use hearing appeal over the driving range. That would make them look pretty bad, pretty callous. Especially if the press came away with some coverage, that they were going to pursue their issues, in spite of everything that has happened."

"This would be another nail in their coffin. But it might take some time to set something like that up," Carol said.

"Just something to think about," Hugh concluded.

Charlie was done working about two o'clock on Tuesday afternoon, and decided to stop off at the club for a drink on his way home. Tuesday is usually Ladies day at most golf clubs, so none of the guys could play until after one in the afternoon. But, since the weather had turned into a nasty rain around noon, there would probably be more guys hanging in the bar, than there were playing golf.

It was also the first Tuesday of the month, so the ladies club was scheduled for their monthly business luncheon.

The girls were indeed having their business luncheon, and were busy organizing their month, the holiday calendar, officer nominations for the upcoming year, etc. But the undertone of the luncheon was humming with curiosity and rumors about Magnolia Street.

The ladies were proceeding in their structured style. If for example, there was a conflict about a date for a future event, the women's club Captain would have minutes of the exact meeting when the dates were released from the golf committee, etc., so that there would be no controversy. But today, it was hard for the Captain and the Assistant Captain to keep the assembled meeting in order. All the women wanted to talk about was the attempted murder, and it had occurred only a stone's throw from where they were now seated. Their collective voices made a large clacking sound in the big, main dining room.

Charlie found some drinking buddies in the bar, sat down and ordered himself a cocktail. He was getting thirsty, and was starting to lose his buzz from lunch.

"Hey Leon, how about a gin and tonic?"

"Sapphire?"

"Of course."

"Double?"

"Of course."

The guys started chatting about the Seahawks game on Sunday, and after they wore that sore topic out, one of them asked Charlie who he had been banging lately. This was always a lively topic. And Charlie loved to share and discus his exploits with the boys. There was little doubt of the vicarious nature a lot of the guys shared with Charlie.

"Oh, my God. You should see this girl. She has hazel blue/green eyes, and jet-black hair. She is long and lean with double d's. Her ass could stop traffic on I-5. So, the game is over on Sunday afternoon, and she comes in and sits down straddling my lap. She thinks I am down over the game, and she has a bowl of something in her hand. I ask her what she's got there?"

So, she takes one of these things, and breaks it in half longways. It is pear shaped, but smaller, and juice is spilling all over the place. It is all deep pink and juicy, and looks just like a you know what. And she bends forward and licks the juice that squeezed out, off of my chin. Then she says to me, "It's a fig Charlie, it is my favorite fruit. It is sweet, and juicy and luscious. And the texture is just so smooth and creamy. It melts in your mouth, and it even looks sexy. Here, you wanna try some?'

"Well, hell yes I want to try some. This thing does look luscious." Charlie's voice was rising as he began to get into his story.

"So, she leans forward, and starts to feed me some of this fig. She squeezes it so that all of the fruit starts to bunch up and pooch out of the skin, and she is hanging all over me, with those double d's. So, then she says, "they are kind of messy, aren't they?", and starts unbuttoning my shirt. And the damn fig juice is dripping everywhere, and she is licking it off of my chest. So, she gets another one, and starts in again, but this time she undoes my belt buckle, and drops my fly. By now her fingers are all sticky and gooey.

And I tell her, hey, we better unbutton you too. And I grab one of the damn things and start to squeeze it down her top." Charlie is full on into it now, and his naturally strong voice is carrying nicely.

The only problem, is the ladies club luncheon, which is right in the next room, our dining room. The dining room is adjacent to the bar, with no partition, and no sound barrier. Charlie signals Leon for another drink, but Leon is looking back and forth between the bar and the dining room. The closest women to the bar, are also starting to look back and forth at each other, and Leon. Charlie doesn't get the message.

"After we go through a half dozen of the damn figs, the wacky broad wants to know if I would like to taste the real thing? Yeah, hell yeah," I said, "and so..."

Melinda Burke spun out of her chair, and stomped into the bar. Melinda is a big girl. Not unpleasantly large, just physically big. Like a women's collegiate softball pitcher. As a matter of fact, she is the current women's golfing champion at our club. As a single gal, she is a most pleasant person, is adored by the ladies, and is friends with everyone. She is a very serious golfer, works at her game, and also works out regularly in our fitness center.

"Why don't you take your smut out of here, Charlie? We don't want to hear any more about it. We are having a Ladies Club meeting, in case you couldn't figure that out."

"Well EXCUSE me, Melinda, but why don't you mind your own damn business?" Charlie was taken aback, and said the first thing that came to his mind.

"We are minding our business, and you are annoying us to the max. So just stop it." By now, there were a dozen women standing behind Melinda, looking seriously at Charlie, and nodding their heads.

Charlie was not one to be shushed, especially after three or four cocktails, and in front of his boys. Unfortunately, he was into his fifth stiff drink of the day, and the liquor was kicking in. Who gives a damn anyway, he thought, I'm the president of this place. "Yeah well, maybe if you would go out and get a little once in a while, you wouldn't be so interested in other people's conversations." Leon picked up the phone, and called Larry's office. No one answered.

Charlie waved his hand dismissively at the women. "Go back and sit down, Melinda. You are embarrassing yourself." His attitude of course, infuriated the women even more.

"Charlie, you are drunk and disporting yourself in public. In your own Club, of which you are the president at that. Why don't you grow up and act like a gentleman, if you have a clue how to do that?"

Charlie got up, and put a mean glare on the women.

One of the women back in the dining room, picked up her phone and dialed 911.

"911, can I help you?" said the operator.

"Yes, there is a domestic violence episode starting here in the bar at Rosewood Golf Club. Please come quickly."

"Is anyone injured?"

"No, but there are some drunk men, and there is a very serious confrontation going on."

"Yes Ma'am, we well be right there."

"The address is..."

"Yes Ma'am, we know where you are."

Charlie walked around his side of the table, and was now standing directly in front of Melinda. "Listen, you stupid bitch. We are just sitting here in the bar, minding our own business, and you come in here, and start some shit. Just leave us the fuck alone, and go back to your stupid meeting." Charlie's blood pressure was way up, his face was beet red, and they were standing so close to each other Melinda could smell the alcohol on his breath. But she was not backing down an inch.

Marta Koenig who had been in the restroom, heard the ruckus as she was returning to her seat, and came running for the bar.

"What's going on Charlie?" she wanted to know.

"Nothing, nothing at all. Just tell these crazy bitches to get out of the bar." He said, shaking his finger in Melinda's face.

"Can we just calm down," Marta ordered. "Please."

"Don't you fucking touch me, you pig," Melinda screamed at Charlie, and slapped his hand out of her face.

Marta tried to step between the two of them, but she was no match in size for either of them. She looked at the men standing stupidly behind Charlie, as if to say, can't you get him out of here? Apparently, they were still fantasizing about figs and female nakedness, because they just all stood around in mute silence, rooted to their spots.

By now the bar was crowded with ladies pushing into the smaller room from the dining room, and with the mass force of some forty women, they surged forward and pushed Melinda and Marta forward into Charlie, who stumbled backward over a chair. He went down and Melinda fell right on top of him.

Melinda struggled to get up, and her elbow inadvertently struck Charlie in the mouth. Semper Fi. No one elbows an ex-marine in the mouth and gets away with it. So, Charlie with his back to the floor for leverage, got his hands-on Melissa's chest area, and gave a tremendous shove. He was apparently in closer contact with her breasts than she considered appropriate.

And then Melinda began screaming in Charlie's face. "Get your fucking hands off of me, you fucking pig. Don't you ever touch me there, etc."

Marta Koenig was right down there in the middle of it, knocked down, and now rolling around on the floor with Charlie and Melinda. Although because of the chaos, she couldn't or wouldn't, verify the breast groping allegations.

And who walked in the side door of the bar, but officer Willy Davis, of the Vancouver Police Department. There had been so much excitement in the bar, that no one had even heard the sirens.

CHAPTER THIRTY-FOUR

Officer Davis stood and calmly assessed the situation. It was not a pleasant sight, with people down on the floor, and much cursing and hysterical screaming from the women's club going on. Finally, he pulled out his traffic whistle, and gave it a shrill blast. This froze everyone in the room, like deer in the headlights.

Well, almost everyone. Hugh Schmidt, was doing his bidding from Carol, and had been seated at the far end of the bar, nearest the door. He had been quietly drinking a beer, throughout the entire fracas. He had his phone in hand, and had recorded a couple of videos of the incident.

Of course, every time a police unit is dispatched, someone from the press is listening on a scanner. And although a little late to the party, a young female reporter had just entered the bar from the same side door Willy Davis had come in through.

Larry Easton, who had finally gotten through with his tour of the back nine with Frank Davis, had come into the bar just as Charlie's confrontation was winding down. He was trying to make peace, but like everyone else, had been immobilized by Willy's whistle blast.

But he saw the young woman, saw the Fox logo over the left breast of her windbreaker, and he immediately headed over to her. "This is a private club. You need to leave now."

Hugh also made an immediate move, and reached out for the young woman's hand. He pulled her close to him, put his arm around her, and told Larry, "This is a friend of mine. She is my guest here."

"She has to go," Larry told him.

"Listen asshole, you want another serious scene on your hands?"

"No, I don't Hugh, and we will talk about this later." Turning to the woman, Larry snapped, "Absolutely no pictures."

Larry turned away. Hugh was now in rare Hugh form. "Not to worry, honey. I've got video of the whole thing. What's your name, can I buy you a drink?"

"Thanks, I might need one. My name is Suzie."

Officer Davis' presence had put a damper on the hostilities. Between Larry, Leon, Marta and Willy himself, they managed to disentangle Melinda and Charlie. Both were now standing, glaring at each other. The bar was still crowded with women, who were trying to comfort Melinda. Charlie's posse was standing protectively behind him.

"What going on here?" Officer Davis asked no one in particular.

"Nothing officer," answered Marta Koenig. A smart woman, Marta wanted to diffuse the situation, and although she was as disheveled as she had ever been in a public place, she wanted to get Willy Davis out of there as soon as possible. "Just a small misunderstanding that got a little out of control, Officer."

Willy Davis was staring at Charlie Strong. He was feeling an eerie sense of deja vu. It was only five days ago actually, since he had been standing a similar distance from Charlie, and received three Sig Sauer slugs in the chest for his trouble.

"I want an official statement from you, you, you, and you." He said, pointing to Charlie, Melinda, Larry and Marta.

By now backup had arrived, and four more cops were on the scene.

Hugh snapped a couple more stills of the bar scene. Larry gave him a dirty look. Many of the women were shouting that Charlie had started all of the trouble, and were suggesting to the cops to haul him away.

Hugh was filling the reporter in on the details of what had happened.

Sargent Davis was gradually taking control of the scene. "Quiet everyone. I want you women to move back into the other room. We are going to take statements from the principals. If you have something to add to our information, stick around, and we will get to you after we take our statements."

Willy motioned for the other cops to help guide the ladies back into the dining room. And poof, just as quickly as it had flared up, the whole episode was over. The bar was eerily quiet, but the dining room was buzzing with chatter. Willy told Charlie's posse to sit down over in the corner, and they could also comment later if they had anything to say. He kept them in the bar, as the last thing he wanted to do was put them in the dining room with the distraught women.

Recognizing the Vancouver PD's strategic interest in Charlie and his activities, Willy was very tactical in his handling of the situation. He personally sat down with Charlie to take his statement. He would have to run this one by Chief Farley.

Marta and Melinda sat down with two other cops, and the last two cops stood around and kept the fragile peace. Marta looked over at Charlie as he sat down with Officer Davis, pursed her lips and ran her thumb and forefinger over them. It was the classic zip it gesture to Charlie. He was looking rather the worse for wear, as his shirt was torn, his hair was rumpled and he had a fat lip. His lip was bruising, and swelling rapidly where Melinda's elbow had caught him.

Melinda sat down with her cop, and still had fire in her eyes. Marta, a most proper, circumspect southern gentlewoman, was still discomposed and frowsy looking. She hadn't had time to straighten herself out as she sat down, and she still looked like she had been caught out in a hurricane. Her hair was a wild mess. Somehow her blouse had been torn open, and she had to clutch it together at the neck, to keep from revealing herself. Her hip was sore, and her pride was severely damaged

Willy told Larry to close the club, and lock the doors. He looked questioningly at Hugh and the reporter. Hugh smiled pleasantly at Officer Davis. "I am a member of this club, I was here the whole time, and would like to make a statement, if I may." Hugh was calm as a cucumber. He absolutely loved being in the eye of the storm, and cherished the opportunity to do as much damage to Rosewood as he possibly could. He could scarcely believe that Carol had been so prescient as to suggest his hanging out at the bar in the first place.

"Who is she?"

"She is a friend of mine, and my guest here at the club."

This guy is out of here Larry thought to himself. Charlie had his back turned to Hugh, or would probably have started another melee, had he realized what had been said.

The statements didn't take long. Marta and Charlie maintained their positions that this was merely a verbal altercation that had gotten out of control. Charlie actually claimed his assailant had charged him, knocking him over a chair, and then had tumbled down on top of him. It was all inadvertent, because of the crunch of the crowd, and as far as he was concerned, the confrontation was already forgotten.

"What instigated the disagreement," Willy asked.

"I'm not sure. My friends and I were sitting in the bar, and apparently, our conversation intruded on their business meeting next door. We tried to apologize after they confronted us, but obviously, to no avail."

Marta's statement pretty much echoed Charlie's. She wasn't sure what had started the confrontation, and was sure that the physical portion of it, that Officer Davis had personally witnessed, had been totally inadvertent. "This is a private matter that will be handled internally. You can rest assured there will be no reoccurrences of this type of situation."

Melinda, was more understandably animated and verbal about what had happened. Charlie Strong was in the bar carousing with his friends. Their conversation got raunchy, and the women, Melinda in particular, took issue with it. One thing led to another, and here we are. Melinda did agree that the physical portion of their disagreement was inadvertent. She didn't want to press any charges at this time.

The statements were duly recorded, and Officer Davis asked if anyone else had any further statements to make. Several of the women immediately volunteered. Charlie's buddies agreed with Charlie's version of the incident. Willy Davis looked at Hugh, and he just shook his shoulders. He wasn't really interested in giving a statement to the cops. He wanted to go prime time, and was saving himself for a full disclosure to his friend Suzie, from Fox, as soon as they could get out of there.

Suzie had already called her station for a lighting tech and a camera crew.

Willy wanted a statement from Leon, who had seen it all. For that matter, Willy had seen plenty of bar brawls in his day. He knew well enough to start his investigation with the bartender's version of the fun.

Everyone began to disperse, even some members who had dropped by the club for various other reasons. The cop's cars were of course a magnet, and anyone who happened to be in the area wanted to see what was going on.

Officer Davis had released Melinda, Marta and Charlie as persons of interest, and told them they would be contacted by the department for possible further processing of the case. This would include formal affidavits administered by an officer of the court. "Don't leave town," he told them.

Melinda was embarrassed how things had gotten so far out of control, but was happy she had stood up to Charlie. She was also thrilled with the way the girls had backed her up.

Marta was mortified that she was involved in this thing from a defendant's position. She was a peacemaker here, and it was simply bad timing on the cop's part about when they had walked into the bar. As far as her getting tangled up between Charlie and Melinda, how embarrassing. She would be calling her attorney as soon as she got home. She advised Melinda to do the same. As far as Charlie was concerned, he could do whatever he wanted. She had tried to warn him to lay low, and now she was done with him. He was done anyway, he did it to himself, she thought.

Marta did hang around and help Larry and Leon try and put the bar back together.

Since she had been in the restroom, and had missed the start of the action, she asked Leon, "What in the world happened?"

"Charlie was entertaining the boys, and things started getting a little off color. I tried to signal him to keep it down, but he kept on talking. Finally, Melinda came in the bar, and told him to shut up. Things just went to hell from there."

Charlie was starting to feel hungover. He was pissed off, and couldn't believe that he was involved in yet more Rosewood drama. This one was worse even, than the fiasco of the Hearing Examiner's trial. As distracted as he was, he was also unaware of the extent of prime media coverage he was helping create. He was duly released by the cops, was getting hungry and thirsty, and he called Nikki. "Meet me at Jackson Street for dinner, can you?" he asked. "I've had a tough day."

"Sure Charlie. What happened?"

"We can talk when you get there."

"You okay?"

"Hell yes, I'm okay."

"I love you."

"Me too."

Nikki was thrilled.

Charlie tried to help straighten up the bar, but felt nothing but bad vibes from the club. So, he went his way.

Hugh and Suzie left the bar, and Hugh invited her over to the house for a glass of wine. To calm your nerves, he told her. "Or should we do an interview here in front of the club?" he asked.

She felt like the interview would have a lot more impact, if they filmed it in front of the club. Plus, she kind of felt like Hugh was coming on to her. Since he had a wedding ring on his finger, and was about twice her age, she thought it was probably wiser if they stayed in a public venue. If she had to go to his house to get his statement, she certainly would have, because this was undoubtedly, the biggest scoop of her young career. But better to err on the side of caution, she thought.

"Well, why don't we do this. Let's go over to my house, it's just around the corner and have a glass of wine. Kill an hour, and come back and do the interview. I think it would be better to let everyone clear out of here, before they see us doing an interview."

"No. Not that I wouldn't be delighted to visit your home, but the crew is already here, and I am getting close to deadline. If we are going to get this on the six o'clock news, we had better do it right away. It is pretty quiet out here now, and this will only take about five minutes."

"Well, okay."

"Good evening, this is Suzie Davis, reporting live from Rosewood Golf and Country Club. I am here with Mr. Hugh Schmidt, who, is a resident of the now famous Magnolia Street here in the Rosewood neighborhood. Mr. Schmidt is also a member of Rosewood Golf and Country Club. Mr. Schmidt, can you tell us in your own words about the bizarre scenario here at the Rosewood Clubhouse this afternoon? Both of us personally witnessed an incident in which the police had to be summoned by Rosewood's own membership to break up a full-on brawl in the Rosewood bar between the president of the club, a Mr. Charlie Strong, and virtually the entire women's club. A group of Ladies were having their monthly business meeting adjacent to the Rosewood bar, and Mr. Schmidt…"

"Thank you, Suzie. Yes, today is women's day at the club, which means the guys can't play golf until the afternoon hours. I came up to the club to play a late nine holes, but then the rains came. So, I went into the lounge to have a soft drink, thinking maybe the weather would break later on. Mr. Strong was sitting in the bar with four or five other male members, and he began a totally inappropriate and rather vulgar account of a young woman he had spent some time with this weekend. Mr. Strong has a rather loud voice, and he appeared to be inebriated at a rather early hour, I might add. The Women's Golfing Club were having their monthly business meeting right next door, from where Mr. Strong was located. I was sitting at the bar, conversing with the barman, and Mr. Strong just seemed to be getting louder and louder, and more and more crude and offensive. He was talking about dribbling fig juice and fig pulp over his lady friend's private areas, and proceeding to remove them from her private areas in a most carnal manner.

"Finally, one of the ladies came into the lounge, and politely asked Mr. Strong, who again is the President of this club, if he wouldn't please tone it down some. Well, Mr. Strong began to swear at her, which continued to upset the ladies all the more. They began to crowd into the bar, and there was now a major verbal confrontation going on between the ladies and Mr. Strong. By this time, Mr. Strong was out of his chair, and was jaw to jaw with the original woman who had come into the lounge to ask him to quiet down.

"I don't quite know what happened next. It seemed like there was some pushing that got started, or the surge of women pushed their member into Charlie. The next thing I know, there are three of four people, all of whom are women, except Charlie, and that includes another one of our board members, rolling around on the floor swearing at each other. Fortunately, someone had the presence of mind to have called 911, and all of a sudden Officer Davis of the Vancouver police Department, was in the bar. He then had a very difficult time restoring any semblance of order.

"It was the most embarrassing behavior I have ever seen at a private Country Club, and I have been a member of this particular club for over ten years. Especially, in light of the tragic events that occurred just last Friday evening. I am referring to the vicious attack on our dear friend and Magnolia Street neighbor, Mr. Bob Kudlach.

"We on Magnolia Street are still in mourning and in shock over the brutal, senseless attack on our neighborhood. And to think that the President of our own Club, Rosewood Golf and Country Club, is falling down drunk in the middle of the day, and absolutely brawling with the fair members of our own Ladies Club is beyond embarrassing. It is a travesty and an open affront to the very character of not only our club, our membership, and our community. But the City of Vancouver at large as well."

Hugh was laying it on as thick as he dared. Suzie was starting to feel like his statement was veering strongly to the subjective side of his report, and smoothly cut into Hugh's commentary, guiding it back to the factual, credible side of his narrative.

But he was an eye witness, and he definitely told it like it was, she thought. Off of the record, he was, in her mind, absolutely right. She had been at Rosewood's press conference just last Sunday, where Charlie had convened over the meeting, and had tried to be so remorseful. So phony, and here he was two days later, drunk as a skunk, and rolling around on the floor in his own bar, Indian wrestling with the very wives and daughters of his own Club members.

Well, this was going to hit the six o'clock news like a bullet train. And she was going to make sure there was a nice, life-sized file photo of Charlie and Rosewood, as a backdrop for the whole headlining news story. She would personally post it just before she ran Hugh's homemade videos on the air.

"Thanks again, Hugh. You are a good man." Suzie put her arms around Hugh's neck, stood on her tip toes, and gave him her best hug. "Here is my business card. Call me, if anything comes up, or if you want to do lunch sometime."

"Will do, Suzie. Thanks for being here."

"Where have you been? And what's going on up at the club, I heard sirens again. Another EMT call?"

"Holy shit, Bunny. Wait until you hear this one. I was up in the bar, and a freaking brawl broke out between the women's club, and Charlie Strong. The cops came, and then the press. I was there for the whole thing. This girl, Suzie, from Fox, interviewed me for the six o'clock news. I killed it Babe. Wait until you see the news. I absolutely, slayed it. Rosewood is going down hard. I got it all on video"

Willy Davis rolled back into the station, and headed straight for Chief Farley's office. "Chief, you've got another situation on your hands. I'm surprised that the press isn't here after you already."

"Yeah, I heard you got called out to Rosewood this afternoon. What happened?"

Willy gave him the details. "I didn't arrest anyone, because I didn't know what you would want me to do with Charlie Strong. I can tell you that it was pretty weird standing about the same distance from him as I was last Friday night, before he tried to drill me."

"You did good, Willie. I don't know what is the matter with this knucklehead. You think he would have the good sense to cool his jets a little, after going for capital one just a few days ago."

"I hear that, boss."

"Well, we have a task force meeting tomorrow morning. Let me see what the powers that be want to do. You warned everyone that they were under investigation, didn't you?"

"Absolutely."

"Good. I think I will let you have the collar on this jerk when we arrest him. You deserve it."

"I tell you, boss, it was bizarre today. Here is this guy, and he is the CEO of the ILWU, and also President of the Golf Club, and he is rolling around on the floor of his own bar. Like a pig in shit. He is a crazy man."

"Thanks again, Willy. Good job today."

Charlie got to the Jackson Street bar about five thirty, and was there ten minutes before Nikki came through the door. She looked stunning as usual, in designer jeans, a pull over ski cap, and a lavender fiber parka, that looked very warm. Charlie hadn't been home to change. He had his wind breaker on, and it was zipped up to the top to cover up his torn shirt.

"Hi," kiss. "What happened to your lip? You've got a fat lip Charlie."

"Oh, I bumped it today."

The bar was half full. Happy hour was over at six, so not many new bar patrons were still coming in for the early part of the evening. The national news was on both TVs, but no one was paying much attention.

"May I offer you a beverage?"

"What are you having, Charlie?"

"Sapphire and tonic."

"I think I would just like a glass of chardonnay, please. Can you please order us some nachos? I am starving."

"Sure," Charlie said. "Large or small?"

"Large."

"Carnitas or smoked chicken?"

"Smoked Chicken."

The national news droned on, the economy was in terrible shape. The coming holiday sales were going to be a barometer of the retail activity for the coming year. Senator John Edwards, D-NC admits sexual affair, Sarah Palin ready for vice presidency, etc. Charlie ordered a medium rare rib eye steak, but Nikki just wanted a Caesar salad. They munched on their nachos.

At six o'clock, the news shifted back to local coverage, and as luck would have it, the bar's TV was tuned to the Fox Channel.

Our lead story tonight, is a strange tale of public domestic violence, battery, disturbing the peace, lewd and lascivious conduct, at of all places, Vancouver's own Rosewood Golf and Country Club. The news anchor began to outline the events of the day, and all of a sudden, all eyes in the room were on the television. "Hey, turn that thing up will you, Sean?" someone shouted from the back of the bar.

True to her word, when the news anchor turned to Suzie Davis for an onsite comprehensive report, she had pulled Charlie and Rosewood's file photos from her computer, and Charlie's picture split the screen big as life. No one but Nikki and the barman realized Charlie was right there in the bar, but Nikki's eyes got big as saucers, and Charlie face turned ashen pale.

Suzie went on to report on the day's fracas in more vivid detail, showed some clips from Hugh's videos of everyone rolling around on the floor, and then played Hugh's sound bite in its entirety.

"Thank you, Suzie for another comprehensive report. Remember folks, you heard this breaking news story here on Fox Channel 13. We will be sure to keep you informed of any further updates involving this story at ten PM."

"What the fucking fuck, Charlie? You are at that stupid club, and now you are on fucking television talking our personal stuff around your buddies, like I am some cheap, skid row, junkie ass hooker? You fucking asshole!"

"Listen baby, it wasn't like that at all. This stuff is all made up, because for some stupid reason, there is a damn conspiracy at that damn club, which is out to get me. I don't know why, maybe it's not even me, maybe it is just that they hate the club so much, and are out for me just because I am the President." Charlie was backpedaling as fast as he could. He could readily see he was about to have his second major bar brawl with a woman, in the same afternoon. And he was sure that somehow, someway, Suzie fucking Davis, from the Fox fucking Network, would be in the room to cover this one too.

Nikki was crying hysterically, and people were starting to stare. "You were rolling around on the floor of your club, fighting with a bunch of women? What kind of a man are you anyway?"

Charlie signaled Sean. He came over. "Have them make that order to-go will you Pal? I've got to get her out of here."

"Sure Charlie."

Charlie gave him a credit card, and a hundred-dollar bill for a cash tip.

"It's going to be about ten minutes or so."

"Well, here's another hundred, tell them to step on it."

"Sure Charlie."

The bartender went into the kitchen, and told the cook to just box it up, ready or not. He passed on one of the hundred-dollar bills, which made the cook ecstatic. When Sean came out of the kitchen, Charlie had finished his drink, and was waiting. Nikki was just storming out of the women's room, and they needed to go. Now.

"Let's go over to my house, and talk about this, can we?"

"I don't want to go over to your stupid house. I don't ever want to see your sorry ass again."

"That's not fair, Nikki. This is a bunch of lies, and you shouldn't believe a word of it."

"It doesn't matter a damn, Charlie. All of my friends know that I am in love with you. My co-workers, my family. My mother for Christ's sake, Charlie. My mother, who watches Fox damn news every night of her life. They all know that we were together all weekend, and now you make me look like a complete tramp, and all over the TV, and everything." Nikki was crying uncontrollably. Charlie tried to take her in his arms and comfort her, but she was having none of that.

"Get away from me. You are the worst man I have ever known. You are a Pig. I never want to see you again." Nikki was fumbling for the keys to her car.

"Nikki, I am so sorry. I love you. I would never do anything to hurt you. This is a conspiracy I tell you, don't let them turn you against me."

"I have to go, Charlie. Please get out of my way."

"Baby."

"Go fuck yourself Charlie."

Nikki drove away. She was young, smart enough, beautiful, and very confident. For a local girl, she had been around the block, but this was more than she had bargained for. Maybe she had been blinded by the bright lights. Pebble Beach, San Francisco, private jets, nuzzling at the best restaurants in Portland. If this is what it cost for the good life, the big time, Nikki didn't want any part of it. She wanted someone fun, someone as smart as she was. Someone who could provide a good home for herself and the family she wanted to have someday. Not some asshole that wanted to start a reality show of her in his bedroom, on live television. She was over him before she even got out of the Jackson Street parking lot.

Charlie got into his Jag. Well, the hell with her, if that is the way she wants to be. I am a tough guy. I will get by this. And, I'll tell you something else, Hugh Schmidt, and old Bunny girl, are toast at Rosewood. By force of habit, Charlie was still calling the shots, but surely it would dawn on him pretty soon. His shot calling days at Rosewood were all but over.

CHAPTER THIRTY-FIVE

The Task Force meeting was scheduled for ten o'clock the next morning. This time Steve Rodriguez had invited everyone to his Portland FBI offices. They were on the third floor of the downtown, federal building on Madison Avenue. "Just tell the parking attendant in the basement garage that you are with the FBI, and all is good."

Ray Farley volunteered to drive down. He, Tricia and Larry Larson met at the safe house, and left Vancouver around nine fifteen. As Tricia expected, their meeting room looked out over the Columbia River, and was beautifully appointed.

Steve offered everyone coffee, and called the meeting to order. The Vancouver PD team all appreciated his hospitality, but also realized that this was a subtle nudge to remind them, how he was the bigger fish in the local pond now.

"Let's get started. I heard that you had a little more drama up there yesterday afternoon."

"Yeah," said Ray. "I hope this guy can stay in one piece, long enough for us to put him away. He is turning into a real train wreck."

"I think we need to minimize this last incident. The less bad publicity Charlie has the better. We want him to stay in place, and stay running the ILWU for the short term anyway. All we need to do is start tracking the incoming shipments, and hope against hope that we can ever get the Chang's back in the country after we have done our homework. We also need to make sure that we don't have any possible leaks from any of our people. The press is obsessed with this case, and the last thing we need, is for someone to spill the beans, and ruin our cover."

No one could disagree with this.

"Well, I have some good news," Tricia announced. I got an email from Sui Chang yesterday. She told me she and her husband have just bought an apparently very nice condo on Oahu, and they are planning on spending plenty of time there."

"Wow, that is some great news. Another fantastic job, Tricia."

"I would assume they believe they are far enough removed from day to day operations, that they feel safe exposing themselves like this," observed Ray Farley.

"Now all we have to do is keep an eye on things, and wait for the stuff to come in. We track it, and hopefully when the Changs are in country. Then we can grab the whole operation. I know we don't have very much on the Changs. They are executive level here. But once we have them, and pinch Charlie and Rick, I'm sure those two will start singing like canaries. They just had a very strategic meeting in our area. Surely, that will be enough to put the Changs on the hot seat." Barbara Estes was starting to warm to the task.

"Any word on a shipment coming in, Tricia."

"This is not my area. You need to monitor Rick's phone. And I think it would be a great idea if you let me know when something is going to go down. I will have a heads up, and I can keep my eyes open. Also, I might be able to lure Sui Chang into the country at the same time."

"Good to go," said Steve. "We have profiled the whole operational channel of the ring. We have analyzed the last twenty thousand dollars Charlie gave to Tricia. We are certain the money is coming through Vancouver, via Chinatown or the Oriental Casino in Reno. The serial numbers are very close to the bills the Fed has being issuing, and are circulating down there. We have the Fed Bank recording carefully what their traffic pattern is. Bao Thieu should be just about ready for some more product if you ask me. We believe he is distributing heroin from San Diego to Seattle, and inland from Spokane to Albuquerque. This will be an international bust of significant size and impact, ladies and gentlemen.'

"In the meantime, Tricia, please keep Mr. Strong out of trouble." Barbara Estes again, always ready with an appropriate suggestion.

"If you mean I should take him as my own, until this thing is over, forget about it. Did you see what just happened to his current girlfriend?"

"No, what is that?"

"Well, it's a long story, with a lot of local twists and turns, but basically he was busted yakking publicly about his personal love life. Half of the eyewitness report, last night on TV, was about the fiasco at Rosewood, and the start of it seemed to be about him telling some juicy stories about going popsicle stick with his girlfriend all weekend. His monologue is what started the bar brawl. The whole thing got videoed, and headlined on the six o'clock news."

"Oops, that's not good."

"No, it's not. But I 'll talk to him anyway, and try to calm him down. Just another news flash here, but he has an annual union meeting in San Francisco next weekend. Please make sure he is cleared to travel, and not on any restricted lists. It would not be good for him to mess up this meeting."

"Agreed. We want everything functioning normally. Things need to keep going status quo. I am sure that Rosewood is going to discipline him, but that is no big deal. It's a private club, and their goings on are none of our affair."

Ray Farley ended the meeting with the following summary: "We will wait for you to contact us when the next shipment is coming in. We will co-ordinate our activities, as far as the shipment, according to your needs and your leadership. We will keep an eye on Charlie and Rick, as will you. We will down play the Rosewood bar incident, in order to keep Charlie propped up. We will also let Bob Kudlach have some contact with his friends and neighbors, and will allow him to re-enter his old life in a couple more weeks. He has been fully cooperative, and knows there is something bigger than meets the eye going on. Anything else?"

Barbara Estes weighed in one more time. "Time is definitely an element. We don't want to hurry or jeopardize our efforts here, but I firmly believe we have our ducks in a row, and the longer we wait to move in, the more heroin is flooding the streets."

"Right Barbara, but if we can just wait until we apprehend a shipment, and are lucky enough to catch the Changs in the states, then we hit a homerun. But it has to be a very closely synchronized bust. The shipment arrives, we grab it and the traffickers. The Changs are in Hawaii. We grab them before they can get word there is a problem. Then we grab Chinatown. Then you finally get to bag Charlie. Bam, Bam, Bam, Bam."

Tricia agreed with Steve. She told him, "I have an opportunity to start a relationship with Sui Chang. I can monitor her end. I believe I will be able to anticipate their travel in and out of the country. I will let you know when they are arriving. If a shipment coincides with their schedule, then we are in business.

It could be in two weeks, it could be in two months. It will just depend on how much patience you have."

"Right on Tricia. For now, we wait." He wondered to himself what "start a relationship with Sui Chang" might mean, but he continued on. "One more thing, Ray. Give Tricia a big bonus for Christmas, or I will steal her away from you. I would put her to work for the FBI when this case is closes in a New York minute. Good day everyone, thank you for coming."

Marta was up and on the phone, first thing Wednesday morning. First, she called her local attorney, and explained yesterday's situation. "I have never been so embarrassed in all of my life. I was trying to calm the situation, and the next thing I know, I am rolling around on the floor like a biker chic. I twisted my knee, hurt my hip, tore my blouse, and then here it is on the evening news, that I was a Board member, and right in the middle of the melee. To see myself on television in those circumstances was mortifying. If any of my clients saw that video clip, it would be a disaster, etc."

The attorney was more than happy to check into things. "I want to be removed from any culpability at all. You understand me?" Marta told her.

"Absolutely," she said. "I know Chief of Police Ray Farley very well, and I think I can say with some certainty, that Charlie Strong is the perpetrator here, not you. I am sure that Chief Farley is not out to villainize any of the Rosewood Women's Club."

"Thank you for taking care of this, Nancy."

Next, she called Larry Easton at Rosewood. "Larry, Toni Duncan and I are calling a special meeting for tomorrow night at seven pm. Charlie can come if he wants to, but we have got to relieve him of his duties as President. We need to deal with this situation now, before it gets any worse than it already is. We are about to completely lose control of this club."

"I am so glad to hear of your plan."

"And listen Larry, I am sorry for what this guy has put you through for the last few months. He has been out of it."

"Well, I won't miss him much, if that is what you mean. But then again, it never gets too boring with him around here."

Then Toni Duncan's phone rang. She was off of her bench duties on Wednesdays, and was waiting for Marta to call.

"I just spoke to Larry, and he is going to get the special meeting email out."

"Good. I recorded last night's late news broadcast, and have the tape, if we need it. Actually, I may keep it, and use it to blackmail you."

"Just shut up."

"But you looked so cute there rolling around on the floor, with that surprised look on your face. And the hair. I loved the punked out hair, all messed up. Spikey and everything. You should do it like that all of the time."

"Are you done with me, you little biach? I have never been so humiliated, and you should be ashamed of yourself, yanking my chain like this. We have some serious business to tend to here."

"So sorry, I just couldn't resist. Yes, let's get serious. What are you suggesting? Obviously, he can't be President any more. Does he even stay on the Board? Do we suspend him from the club for a specific period, or kick him out entirely? And what about Melinda? She wasn't the perpetrator, but she was involved to some extent. She was right down there on the floor with you guys."

"That is a good question. I hadn't thought about Melinda all that much. But she was definitely involved. I think it depends on the mindset of the Board, after reviewing the facts. We should ask Larry to make Leon available to the meeting. He was right there the whole time also. While I was in the restroom, and missed the first part of the confrontation. Leon saw the whole thing. I mean, he will know how crude Charlie was, and how loud Charlie was, and did the women overact, or was their response provoked by the guys in the bar?"

"My guess would be a split Board on the issues. Rick and Bruce will of course support Charlie, and Mort, Sonny, and Joe will probably go with them. You, I and Sara, are good. Then we can probably count on Brad and Matt. That leaves John as the deciding vote, and he seems like a reasonable person for the most part."

"Charlie should definitely recuse himself from the meeting. If he wants to come and make a statement, and support his point of view, that would be allowed. Then he should recuse himself."

"I agree. When he leaves, we will then have an odd number of Board members, and will be able to reach a decision without getting deadlocked."

"Now that calmer heads are prevailing, I would bet you he resigns, under pressure of course, and we put him on some kind of probationary period. It wouldn't hurt if he and Melinda had a meeting, apologized, and kissed and made up. Charlie should apologize to all of the women. But I don't know if he would ever be willing to do something so tasteful."

"Oh, he will probably issue some kind of generic statement. Something about detesting violence in any form, that he has and will always continue to combat it at every opportunity. This type of thing."

"If Charlie is allowed to make a statement to the Board, shouldn't we invite Melinda, to also make her statement?"

"Absolutely. They were the two antagonists, and both should be heard from."

"Then there is the issue of Hugh Schmidt. That guy certainly didn't do any favors for Rosewood. According to Larry, he invited the reporter into the bar as his guest, then gave her his video clips of the event. Both of those actions are grave offenses, and a direct violation of our bylaws. Rosewood can clearly expel any member with due process for unbecoming conduct, or anything which is prejudicial to the best interests of the club. His conduct yesterday, was absolutely not in the best interests of our club."

"I think the Board would want to start expulsion proceedings against him. For whatever my personal opinion is worth."

"Well, it should be an interesting meeting. Can you call Melinda, and ask her if she wants to make a statement? I will call Bruce, and request him to have Charlie recuse himself, with the exception of making his statement."

"Great, see you tomorrow night."

"Ciao."

Charlie was up at the crack of dawn, and after a long hot shower and a couple of Aleve's, he was off to his office. He took an overnight case, and planned to get lost in Portland for a couple of days. Anything to get out of Vancouver, and away from Rosewood. He had tried to call Nikki later on last night, but she wasn't picking up. It was too early to call her this morning.

He stopped for some sausage and eggs at his favorite dive diner on the way into town. The girls at the diner were always happy to see Charlie, and of course he left them a hundred-dollar tip. At least someone loved him. Then he got into his office, and puttered around for an hour. At ten o'clock, he called RFD and ordered a couple dozen long stemmed, red roses for Nikki. Even if she didn't want him back, he still didn't want to be the jerk that Hugh Schmidt had made him out to be. Heck, he was just slinging some bull with the guys anyway. Nikki had never attacked him with a basket of figs.

"I love you too much," he wrote to her on the card.

Right after he ordered the flowers, he called Rick Ferin.

"Hey, how's it going?"

"How's it going with me? How's it going with you, bro. You are quite the local celebrity."

"Yeah, well that is all a bunch of crap. It's a conspiracy, I hope you know that."

"I saw Hugh Schmidt on TV last night. He was laying it on pretty thick, that was for sure."

"We were just sitting in the bar, when Melinda Burke came in and started yelling at me. She wouldn't quit, and I finally got up to try and talk some sense into her. All of the women kept pushing into the bar, and finally Melinda bumped into me, I tried to back off, and she kept coming, and pushed me back over my chair. Next thing I know, I am down and that Amazon motherfucker is right on top of me. She actually popped me in the mouth with her elbow, gave me a fat lip. Then, one of those crazy broads called 911, and next thing I know there are cops all over the place. And that Hugh Schmidt piece of crap, is sitting there and taking videos on his phone of the whole thing. Then he gives them to that little twink of a reporter from Fox news. I will get that jerk."

"Calm down, Charlie. Don't get all worked up again."

"I'm not getting worked up, but I'm pissed off at the whole circus over there right now. And the real bummer, is Nikki is super mad at me. She won't even talk to me."

"Do you blame her?"

"No, but it was just guy talk. It wasn't even real stuff I was talking about. It wasn't even about her. I tried to tell her that, but it just looks bad. I know how it looks."

"Well, if I see her, I will tell her you are sorry, and it was all a big mistake."

"Please do that, and give her some work too, will you? Keep her busy. Maybe she will forgive me."

"I will do my best."

"Yeah, I sent her roses this morning. Damn, I was just getting to like that girl, too."

"Charlie, listen to me. As a friend, I am telling you, you have got to lay low for a while. You are taking on too much exposure here. What if you got arrested over something stupid like this, and the cops came and searched your place and accidently found something? Have you gotten rid of the thing yet?"

"Not yet, but it is secure. Don't worry about it."

"Well, I do worry about it, dammit. You are my boss, and my best friend, and you need to be more careful."

"Yep, I agree with you. You are talking to a new man here. No more trouble."

"Did you get an email from Larry this morning? I guess Marta and Toni have called a special board meeting for tomorrow night."

"No, I didn't get an email. They probably don't want me at the meeting. Maybe they want to dump me off of the board. That would be a pleasant relief. I've just about had it with old Rosewood."

"Well, maybe you should send a few roses to Melinda and the Lady's Club Captain. See if you could mend those fences."

"Did you hear what I just said? The hell with the Women's Club and the hell with Rosewood. I think I am out of there. I just might move myself down to Portland. Join a real golf club."

"Don't talk crazy Charlie."

"I'm not. Say have you heard anything from our man? When can we expect another package to come in?"

"I am expecting a call from him any day now. Our client has a large shipment scheduled in soon, but I'm not sure if there is a package on it. He never calls me until the last minute. Say, does your phone ever act weird? I feel like there is a cracking sound on my phone line sometimes. It sounds like something I don't remember hearing a month or two ago."

"I haven't heard anything. Probably just bad reception. Did you pay your phone bill on time?"

"Yes, you jerk, I did. Now try to behave yourself, eh?"

"Will do. Give Nikki my love."

"Okay."

CHAPTER THIRTY-SIX

Ray Farley got out Willy Davis' report of the incident at Rosewood when he returned to his office. He called Larry Easton at the club, and they had a decent conversation. Ray was an amateur golfer at best. Not that we all aren't amateurs, but Ray was the kind of guy who played in three or four charity tournaments a year, whether he liked it or not. He had met Larry a few times at Rosewood, and they knew each other on a very casual, professional basis.

"Hi Larry, this is Chief Farley down at the station. I hear you had a little dust up over there yesterday afternoon."

"Hello Chief. How are you?"

"Good, thank you."

"Yeah, we had a little disagreement in the bar. Seems like tensions are running kind of high these days, after last Friday night's assault and all. Everyone still seems to be a little on edge." Everyone except Charlie, he thought to himself. "Any leads in the case?"

"Yeah, we are making some progress, although I am not at liberty to discuss anything at this time. We believe we should have something concrete pretty soon here."

"If I can be of any help, don't hesitate to call."

"Much appreciated, believe me. However, I called to chat about yesterday. My report doesn't seem to indicate any injuries, is that true?"

"Yes sir, it is. As a matter of fact, the only reason there was even physical contact of any kind, was just the crunch of the crowd, who were pushing into the room. They caused our President to fall backward over a chair, then one of the lady golfers was nudged on top of him. While they were trying to extricate themselves, your officer Davis came in, and was very helpful in restoring order. It looked a heck of a lot worse than it actually was."

"That's pretty much what officer Davis told me. I also have the statements from the three main parties in the case, and it seems like it was pretty much of an internal misunderstanding. If you feel like you can deal with the situation on your end, I think we can file this one for now. That is as long as we aren't being called out there every week to break up fights between your members."

"Well, Chief, I can assure you this situation was indeed a one of a kind, and we can and we will deal with it. We have a special meeting of the Board of Directors scheduled for tomorrow night as a matter of fact, for just that very purpose."

"Yes, I think we have all been through enough over at Rosewood of late, to let a minor situation like this one cause any more problems. I know the press loves to sensationalize everything, but so long as no one was physically injured, I see no reason to press charges."

"Thank you so much Chief, for taking a common-sense approach. Like I said, we have a meeting scheduled for tomorrow night to deal with this thing."

"Okay then. Just behave yourselves over there."

"Will do, Chief."

"I'll call my Information Officer, and have her notify the papers that there will be no further consideration of any disturbances at Rosewood, and there will be no charges of any kind filed. Why don't we just leave the TV stations out of this one."

"You are a good man, Chief. Thank you so much. Please let me know if you ever need a favor or a donation,"

"Not to worry, Larry. Take care."

Larry expelled a sigh of relief. This was the first good news he had heard in a while. I better call Bruce and Marta he thought.

"Hello, Bruce?"

"Yep, this is."

"Hey, this is Larry Easton. I have some good news for you."

"Oh yeah? What is it?"

"I just got off of the phone with Police Chief Farley, and he is not going to file any charges on anything from yesterday."

"That is certainly welcome news."

"What's not to like, eh?"

"Why the soft touch?"

"He just felt since there were no injuries, and with all of the other trauma being suffered lately, that we should just let this one go away. He doesn't want any more trouble from us though."

"I bet he doesn't."

"I also just got off of the phone with Marta Koenig. She and Toni are requesting that Charlie recuse himself from the meeting tomorrow night. Charlie is welcome to make a statement, or have one of us make one for him. Melinda is coming, and has also been invited to make a statement. But I think the lack of any charges in yesterday's incident, will work to calm everyone down a bit."

"Shouldn't hurt any."

"Okay. See you tomorrow night. And, can you please call Marta and give her this update?"

"Will do."

"See you tomorrow then."

Marta took Bruce's call, and while happy for Rosewood that there would hopefully be no more bad publicity, she was quite surprised the police had acted so quickly on the matter. Usually it took an act of God and then a couple of years to get any action from them. Not this time apparently. After chatting with Bruce for a few minutes, she called Toni Duncan.

Toni was equally surprised. "This is highly unusual," she said to Marta. "There is something funny going on around here. Chief Farley is a very conservative man, and for him to respond to something this sensitive so quickly, is quite unusual." She, too, was happy from the publicity standpoint, which for once seemed to favor Rosewood. But also, hopeful that the quick response from Chief Farley wouldn't minimize Charlie's boorish behavior in the eyes of the board.

Bruce called Charlie, who was elated, felt vindicated, and also felt like someone had finally cut him a well-deserved break. Hell, he hadn't had one in how long? Now if the Chief would just call and apologize to Nikki. But he knew that that would never happen.

"The women want you to recuse yourself from the meeting tomorrow night, except to come and make a statement."

"That's fine with me."

"Okay. The meeting convenes at seven o'clock. Come at seven fifteen, and I will see that you are first on the agenda. If you don't want to come to the meeting, fax me a statement, and I will read it for you."

"Yeah, let me decide what I want to do. I will get in touch with you tomorrow morning."

"Good enough. Talk to you."

The press release went out late Wednesday afternoon, and was given discretely to the Vancouver Guardian, our morning paper. The news broke on Thursday am, it was lower first page copy.

The TV stations were not at all happy about being left out of the loop by Chief Farley. Especially Fox news, and Thursday night's televised updates pounded Chief Farley's decision. Both to downgrade the incident, and also to grouse about being excluded on a story they had worked so hard to break. There was much acrimony on the dropping of charges, because no charges, means no news. The visual media also seemed solidly in the corner of the Magnolia St. neighbors, and therefore, wanted almost as much carnage for our club as the Magnolia neighbors did themselves. It was a David and Goliath thing for them. Screw the rich bastards! As if we were all millionaires or something!

Thursday evening's local TV news pounded the Chief some more, but the die was already cast, and there was little more they could do about it. Give it to me, Chief Farley thought to himself. I will make it up to you when this whole thing finally breaks.

Our Rosewood membership community seemed rightfully relieved, and wanted little more than to stay out of the limelight for a while. Although, the rumor mill was still swirling, especially among the ladies, with the who, what, when's of the situation. i.e.-who the hell made Charlie president, what the hell was he thinking, when the hell is the board going to get rid of him?

Thursday's night's special meeting was well attended. It was another full house, and started right on time at the stroke of seven. Charlie decided to fax his statement to Bruce. He didn't much care at this point what the Board decided to do. He was holed up in the penthouse of the Portland Marriott, preparing for his annual meeting with the ILWU brass. He didn't care enough to bother driving back up to Vancouver.

Bruce, as Vice-President, called the meeting to order. "This is a special meeting of the Board which was called by Marta Koenig, and Toni Duncan. We are here to deal with the unfortunate events of Tuesday afternoon. "Marta or Toni, do you have anything else to add to this?"

"Yes, Bruce we do." Marta was speaking for the two of them. "We are, of course, very concerned with Charlie Strong's ability to continue to lead this club. We have invited Melinda Burke to make a statement concerning last Tuesday's fiasco, and we also feel like the behavior and actions of one of our members, Mr. Hugh Schmidt, should be reviewed."

"Very well, if Melinda is here, why don't we let her proceed. I have a printed copy of Mr. Strong's statement. We can present this at any time, and therefore we can spare Ms. Burke the task of waiting around.

"Thank you, Mr. Chair, very thoughtful of you."

Melinda made her statement. She was not apologetic or contrite by any means, but her hostility had visibly calmed. She was sorry for the raucous confrontation in the bar, and felt the whole scene was rather inadvertent, and had been mostly caused by the crunch of the crowd. She was also sorry for the ugly publicity Rosewood had gotten, but she was adamant Charlie Strong had been the instigator of the situation.

"His behavior was provocative beyond reason," she said. "And when I went into the bar to attempt to quiet him, I was met with hostility, contempt, and derision. I would hope the Board would not tolerate this type of behavior around here, especially from such a leading light as the very President of our organization. I would also request that the Board look into some kind of sound barrier, between the bar and the dining room, so this type of situation would not and could not possibly happen again. I am just happy no one was physically injured, and implore the Board to take steps to ensure Rosewood is a safe and secure place for all of its members. Especially its women members. Thank you."

The Board thanked Melinda for taking the time to come to the special meeting, and assured her they would weigh her comments very carefully.

Next, Bruce announced the reading of Charlie's statement. This would be followed by an eyewitness account from Leon the bartender. Leon's presence throughout the events of Tuesday afternoon were duly recognized.

Charlie's statement was well prepared and well presented. He apologized profusely for the bad publicity that Rosewood had received, and was also adamant that the physical nature of the altercation was inadvertent, and was caused by the diminutive size of the bar, and the aggressive nature of the crowd. He was especially apologetic to Marta Koenig, who he felt was there as a conciliator, and became entangled in the chaos. He apologized for his conversation with his friends, if that was enough to cause any discomfort. This was certainly not his intention. He was merely there as a member, who was stopping by to relax after work, and have a drink with some fraternal company.

He related his pleasure concerning the Vancouver Police, who had responded in such a prompt manner, and had exonerated all of the primary participants without charges of any kind. The swift action by the police, who had been first hand observers of the activity, indicated to him that they were confident there was no malice or intent involved. He therefore felt like this was, in their opinion, a minor incident which should be looked at, learned from, and left behind by us all.

He was careful to apologize for tarnishing the office of the President of Rosewood, and declared his immediate compliance, should the Board see fit to make a command decision, and request his resignation.

After that, Leon was asked to give his view of the events he had witnessed on Tuesday afternoon. He was predictably non-committal on a lot of the issues. Yes, Charlie had been rather loud, and rather coarse. But no more so than he had heard on many occasions in the same bar, from many different members. He had been more titillating than vulgar, and Leon related how he had heard no real "f" bombs, or terms relating to the female anatomy that could offend anyone. It was more of just a clash between the two groups, due to the closeness of quarters, and a lack of sensitivity by Charlie to what was going on around him. Once the confrontation started, things got out of hand so quickly, it was hard to say who was at fault, if anyone.

The Board thanked him for his time, and also thanked him for the steady job he always did behind the bar for the members of Rosewood. One of the Board members asked if Leon felt like Charlie was unduly under the influence of alcohol. "I do not believe that to be the case. Charlie had just ordered a second drink, after approximately one hours' time had passed, and this is his usual procedure. The one drink per hour rule, is also a standard operating procedure of most reputable bars. It is certainly ongoing policy here at Rosewood."

Leon neglected to mention that Charlie always ordered a double going on a triple, which is a very stiff drink, and that he had probably had had two or three or those prior to arriving at the club.

Everyone had their impressions of the three statements, and we were all seemingly inclined to seek a solution to the situation, which would, as much as possible, be a win-win for everyone. There was much discussion, and no small amount of it was directed at the inadequateness of our current facilities. I was quick to jump in there, and tried to impress on the Board how a club that can't even conduct a meeting and a lounge gathering simultaneously, was in much need of a serious review and a consequent visit with an architectural firm. And the sooner the better.

It was decided that Melinda had conducted herself most properly, and was inadvertently involved in the physical portion of the disagreement. She was completely exonerated.

It was also decided Charlie was inadvertently involved in the physical side of things, and had no guilt or malfeasance in that altercation. It was, however, recognized that he had demonstrated poor judgement in his behavior prior to the confrontation, and had been known to do so in the past as well. This was particularly distasteful to the Board for a President to act in such a manner. Especially in this incident, as there was so much bad exposure for the club which resulted from it. Therefore, it was motioned, seconded, and brought to a vote that Charlie's offer to resign as President should be accepted. He would be allowed to remain as a Board member at large because of his contributions to the Board and our membership in the past. Also, because of his noticeable contrition for his recent actions, and Chief Farley's decision to forgo any further punitive action.

He would be asked to write a formal letter of apology to the women's club, and also Melinda Burke, in order to resume his continuance on the board. He would also be placed on probation for one year, which would allow the Board to closely monitor his behavior. Any more issues, and or complaints about him, and he would be immediately relieved from his duties on the board. He would also be suspended from active membership pending an investigation. The measure passed with only several Board members in opposition, and the overwhelming sentiment of the Board was one of relief concerning this situation, and it now being behind us.

Chief Farley's position on avoiding any further conflict, and his neglect in filing any charges on our behalves, had seemingly created a paradigmatic shift in the mood of the Board. Everyone felt like a new, positive direction had emerged in our collective auspices of governance, and we all embraced and welcomed this approach. We were all so ready to move forward from all the negativity engulfing us of late.

There were several matters of no small gravity remaining to be decided, however. Namely, the election of someone to take Charlie's place as President, and the issue that Marta Koenig had raised about Hugh Schmidt, and his participation in Tuesday's episode.

Rick Ferin nominated Bruce Cranston to be our new President, and in a related motion, I was nominated by Matt Mitchell, to assume the office of Vice-President, which Bruce would be vacating. Both Bruce and I accepted our nominations, and were unanimously voted in as the new ongoing Rosewood Officers. In becoming Vice -President, I was obliged to resign as Treasurer, and Joe Goldman agreed to undertake this position until the end of the current term of officers.

Hugh Schmidt's fate was yet to be decided, but the bulk of the opinion concerning his conduct was not very favorable.

Larry Easton related how Hugh had insisted the Fox reporter who had wandered into the bar, was his guest, and thereby, had aided and abetted her presence during our unfortunate conflict.

Not only had he facilitated her presence in the bar, and after Larry Easton had specifically forbidden the reporter from taking any pictures, Hugh had given her his videos of the skirmish between Charlie and Melinda. This was in the board view, a cardinal sin. It was what had aired on prime-time news, and was tremendously injurious to the club.

It was noted that he had been a prime mover in the opposition to the Practice Facility project, and that certainly wasn't very well received by anyone either.

I related the earlier incident involving Edgar Cordoba in the bar. The time when Hugh had rudely bitten Edgar's head off at the waist, for no reason, other than personal avarice and venality. This was absolutely frowned upon. Larry related how there had been other situations where Hugh had conducted himself either questionably, or with open hostility and an abusive demeanor, toward staff and or management. He also seemed to hang just around the edge of prurient propriety with the line staff. He was always talking inappropriately, and was probably a sexual harassment lawsuit just waiting to happen.

It was pointed out that our bylaws specifically emphasize that any member of Rosewood should avoid conduct which was unbecoming to a member, or prejudicial to the best interests of the club. Hugh Schmidt had certainly violated those basis tenets of membership by his actions on Tuesday afternoon, let alone his other conduct issues which the club had either tactfully ignored, or that the Board of Directors had been unaware of.

A motion was brought to the floor, for an expulsion action to proceed, and be initiated against Hugh Schmidt immediately. This motion was seconded and passed unanimously by the board. The process required notifying Hugh of the Board's decision. He then had ten days in which to accept said decision, and resign from the club, or file an appeal. If he filed an appeal, he would be entitled to a hearing before the entire Board within ten calendar business days of his file date. He would be without benefit of legal representation (this was not a court of law), and then a three fourths majority vote of the Board would be required to complete the expulsion. At the appropriate time, the club would assume his proprietary stock, settle any outstanding dues or debts against his membership, and the Schmidt's relationship with Rosewood would end. Larry would compose a letter indicating the position of the Board, their proposed action, Bruce would sign it, and it would be sent to Hugh and Bunny Schmidt by registered mail tomorrow morning.

The Special meeting was moved and seconded to adjournment. Everyone seemed happy. The women were happy, because Charlie had been reprimanded, and stripped of his office. Charlie's guys were happy, because he had survived a major ordeal, and retained a seat on the Board. Larry was happy to be rid of Charlie as President. Leon was happy, because Charlie would still be around to slip him C notes now and then. Charlie was happy in absentia, because although he had been deposed as President, at least Hugh Schmidt had been given the boot out of Rosewood. I was happy, because now maybe some attention could be focused on our inadequate clubhouse facilities. Bruce was happy and honored to be President. Although, he would probably end up doing Charlie's bidding a lot of the time anyway.

We were a big, happy group. We left feeling accomplished, and all of us entered optimistically into the night, and the future.

Ignorance is bliss, they say.

CHAPTER THIRTY-SEVEN

"Hi baby, how are you?"

"Oh hi, mom. I'm good thanks."

"You've been a busy girl this week."

"Yeah. I think Charlie is trying to suck up to me, and is making sure I get lots of work," Nikki said.

"Well, at least he is good for something."

"Oh yeah, he's been calling every day, and even sending flowers. He wanted me to go to San Francisco with him this weekend, for some big union meeting. But I told him I wasn't ready for anything like that just yet."

"What kind of work do they have you doing?"

"I'm doing computer postings. Tracking freight. It has to be entered, then catalogued as received, then reassigned for surface shipment, then scheduled, and tracked some more. Just bookkeeping. Best of all, there is no container lashing or bilge cleanout type stuff."

"Well this has to be good for your seniority as a causal, too, as far as qualifying for permanent status."

"Yes, it definitely is. I am up to about four hundred hours now. Another eleven hundred, and I should be in good shape. It takes forever, but it is worth working for."

"I am so proud of you."

"Mom, not so much to be proud of yet."

"Well, don't be too hard on Charlie. He is a pretty connected guy. I know he is intense, and a bull in a china shop. But still..."

"We'll see what happens."

Charlie, Rick and Emma Ferin, Ben Harris and his wife, and one of Charlie golfing ringers, were scheduled to fly out of Portland for San Francisco at eight am on Friday morning. They were ETAed into SF International around ten. By the time they got to their hotel, checked in and freshened up, they should be ready to attend the meeting launch, which was a luncheon for staff and wives in the Embarcadero Hyatt Hotel's mini ballroom.

The luncheon would be accompanied by an address from ILWU International President Malcolm McElfresh. After the opening luncheon and welcoming speech from President McElfresh, the ladies would be invited next door for a champagne tasting and a fashion show. The remaining management staff, would breakout in the rear of the ballroom, and would start their annual reviews with the HR and Executive staffs. President McElfresh would meet with the local west coast Port Presidents. ILWU International Vice President Robert Sinclair, would meet with the local VP's, and HR would meet with the smaller Chapter Officers. There were pool tables and adult beverages available to help pass the afternoon, until your appointed meeting time arrived.

However, it was very wise to imbibe carefully, before going in to sit with your superiors. Nothing worse for your career, than appearing tipsy at your annual review. However, it frequently happened every year with some nincompoop, usually a lesser light from one of the smaller jurisdictions, who would stub his toe and his career.

In their absence of Charlie, Rick and Ben from the North-West offices, Charlie had appointed Mike Wenchak, Portland's Harbor Master, and Barry Smith, his Vancouver counterpart, in charge of operations in their respective Ports of Call. Tricia and Rebecca would man the office in Vancouver, and Charlie had appointed his executive secretary, Betty Brown, as PIC, in the Portland office. The boys would only miss a couple of official work days, and the weekend period of Saturday and Sunday should be a nonevent.

The only problem for Rick and the Vancouver office, was that the Han Say freight was coming in on Friday afternoon, and it included another special shipment.

Rick had communicated with Bao Thieu, and told him of their important meeting in San Francisco, and how he wouldn't be available on the Port property on this particular day. It was the only time on the annual calendar that he wouldn't be hands on available, but after conferring with Charlie Strong, they had arranged for the normal delivery.

Rick's regular crew would receive the fragile shipment. It would be left in the assigned container, as usual. It was agreed that Boa Thieu's personnel should pick up the shipment on Saturday, when there were less people around. Then the transfer could be downloaded and moved more inconspicuously. They should come for the pickup at ten am on Saturday. Boa's drivers were registered for entry at the front security gate. Boa Thieu should have the forty-thousand-dollar payment, packaged in an official Han Say parcel, and should give it to the ILWU loading crew. They in turn would release it to Tricia in the office. She would put it in Ben Harris' safe, and go home. Done deal.

Bao Thieu communicated to Rick of future shipments coming in every two weeks from now on. The FBI was very happy to hear this update.

It was actually killing the FBI to have to do little more than monitor the drug dealing process. Steve Rodriguez and his guys wanted to grab the goods in the worst way, and impound anyone and everything in sight. But, they were being patient, and would wait to grab the whole body of the crab. Rather than just plucking off one or two of his legs, however fat and juicy said leg might be. In the meantime, the more they could learn about the operation the better.

They went so far as to borrow a road maintenance truck from the City of Vancouver. They took a couple of weighing devices which resembled rubber mats, and after conferring with the Security Staff at the main gate entrance, placed the mats outside the entry to the Port of Vancouver property. The rationalization given to the security personnel, was that they wanted to monitor traffic in and out of the Port. It was part of an ongoing WSDOT study, related to maintenance and future planning. In reality, they would now know exactly how much dope was passing through those gates as of late Saturday morning.

Steve Rodriguez had checked with the US Attorney for the North-West region, and also the District Attorney from the City of Vancouver. They were both on board, and up to speed. They were documenting their upcoming cases as evidence and communication came in from the FBI. The one thing that the DA from the City wanted, for a completely airtight case, was the attempted murder weapon. This was a priority, Steve Rodriguez assured him, but as of yet, they weren't ready to move in. Steve was relatively positive from his surveillance, of the weapon's location inside Charlie's house, but they had yet to request a search warrant. In lieu of all of the other recorded evidence they had, as well as Tricia Watson's undercover presence, Steve was confident the recovery of the weapon would be the frosting on the cake. And recover it they would. All in good time.

Steve and Ray Farley were in close communication. Steve informed Ray it appeared from intercepted communications between Rick Ferin and Bao Thieu, that shipments were going to be coming in on a regular basis from now on. "If there is anything that Tricia can ascertain from Sui Chang, this seems to be just what we are waiting for."

"She is working on it," replied Ray Farley.

Charlie's first major brain fart occurred Thursday night when he returned home to pack for his big business trip. He had checked out of his penthouse suite, and after a late lunch with Rick and a couple of his usual cocktails, Charlie had stopped off at the Portland Athletic Club for a massage. He and Rick had discussed the importance of their impending meetings, and Charlie had forewarned Rick about his comportment at the meetings and especially with the execs. "You don't want to drink too much. It would be a reflection on all of us." Rick found it rather odd to find Charlie warning him about behavioral issues, but didn't say anything. He absorbed the advice in the spirit that Charlie was his mentor and cared about his career with the ILWU.

After a two-hour deep tissue massage, and another glass of wine in the PAC bar, Charlie left for home in the Jag. He was as mellow as a well-fed mountain lion lying in the warm spring sun. Apparently, he was so mellow, his defense mechanisms were already on vacation. Or maybe he had been getting so much negative feedback lately, he subconsciously wanted to be the good guy again. Nothing sounded better to him than returning home to his condo, having a snack, another glass of wine, getting packed, and bedding down for an early night. He would be totally prepared for his trip tomorrow, and he would be taking care of his old friend JoJo in the bargain. Rick was picking him up at seven am, and he was excited to be getting out of town.

Ben and his wife were coming on their own, and bringing Bobby Mixon. Bobby was a crane operator with the Kelso/ Longview, Washington Port. But he had been a collegiate golfer at Washington State University, and Charlie was hoping to slip him in with a seven or eight handicap as the fourth for their Portland District golf team. Bobby played to a three handicap, and Charlie's plan was fairly crafty. Bobby, along with himself, Rick and Ben if they played well, could do some damage at Saturday's eighteen-hole annual ILWU Tournament. Especially with Bobby's inflated handicap.

He got some drive through fast food on the way home, chowed down, and went upstairs to pack. He had two Armani suits, one for the Friday luncheon and one for the Saturday night gala ball. He needed a golf outfit for Saturday's tournament, slacks and a blazer for the sendoff brunch on Sunday mid-morning, and some casual clothes for in between. Although Nikki wouldn't be going with him, there was always lots of women around the annual meeting. And who knows who he might get lucky and run into.

He packed his sundries and necessities and remembered that he needed to take some hard cash to square up with Jojo, for the supply of the Sig Sauer. He was happy to pay Jojo for the job he had done, but why didn't he also just take the weapon back to Jojo? That would kill two birds with one stone. I.e.- give Jojo the opportunity to resell the gun, and also get the damn thing off of his hands. Hell, he was pretty sure that Jojo could find a way to move it again, and would be happy with those arrangements.

So, he emptied the candy out of a box of Whitman Sampler chocolates he had bought for Nikki, went down to his tool box in the garage, and retrieved the Sig Sauer. He wrapped it up in tissues and paper towels and packed it up in the chocolate box. Shit he thought, everything had gone so smoothly with his plan, there was absolutely nothing left to worry about. Although Kudlach had somehow, some lucky way avoided going down, there had not been even a shred of suspicion directed his way. So maybe this was an unorthodox move to carry the gun with him, but the bag would be checked anyway, and away from security. He was sure Jojo would appreciate his gesture. Pump Room, here I come, he thought to himself.

He finished packing, and rolled into bed. After watching a little of the Portland Trailblazer's game, he drifted off to a deservedly, satisfying sleep. He was through with Rosewood, let somebody else worry about the place. The Cops had dismissed their case against him and everyone else as proof that it was all a stupid misunderstanding. And that asshole Hugh Schmidt had gotten busted, and was getting kicked out of Rosewood. He was in the process of making up with Nikki, and now all he had to do was go down to San Francisco, and see how much money Malcolm Mac was going to give him for the coming year. Life was good, and sleep came easily and effortlessly to him.

Tricia was not too excited about working on a Saturday morning, but being the good cop that she was, and also having Steve Rodriguez call and inform her that she was going to be receiving another payoff in the amount of thousands of dollars from the Chang syndicate, made it a lot easier. The package she was supposed to put in Ben Harris' safe, needed to be handled very carefully. Steve had asked her to make sure and photograph it from all angles prior to stowing it in the safe. Also, please make sure her fingerprints got all over the package, just in case it was ever to come into the FBI's possession. Also, to keep her eyes and ears open, and make a special note of who it was that delivered the package to her in the office.

She was going to spend some time today and tomorrow morning, trying to get in touch with Mrs. Chang via the internet. Maybe it was time to take a little trip to Hawaii. While she was anxious to go to the islands, especially to entertain a chance to get out of the northwest's dreary fall weather, she was also a bit apprehensive of another encounter with Sui Chang.

What would be the expectations of her? She knew she could set up the encounter with Sui, to her specifications with the FBI anyway. But what about Sui Chang? She had been so self-assured and decisive, when they had been on their shopping trip together. Did she feel attracted to Sui Chang? She didn't think she was a gay woman, by any stretch of the imagination. But the elegant aggressiveness of the woman, her exotic Asian beauty, her incredibly exquisite touch, taste and delicate sensibilities, created some problems. Her tough as nails worldliness, made Tricia slightly shiver with pleasure, and feel a receptive warmth spread throughout herself. She smiled, and tightly pressed her young legs together.

On the other hand, the woman was a heroin dealer, and deserved to get what was coming to her. What a waste of talent, Tricia thought, as she pulled herself back from her erotic reveries, and focused on her job at hand. A truly magnificent woman, who had evolved from an illiterate mountain peasant girl into the most sophisticated of women, but who had misdirected and totally misused her plethora of talents. Tricia knew she might find herself in a compromised position with Sui Chang, and she might be required to bide some time, or forestall until the opportunity was right. How would she handle that? Would she be alone with Sui again? If so, she was very sure that Sui Chang would come at her. That was the whole purpose of her impending visit to Hawaii.

At any rate, Tricia was ready for the weekend to come. She was happy to handle her Saturday responsibilities. It would also be nice to have Ben and Rick out of the office, and not have Charlie calling all the time. Even though she had been instructed to call Rick once the transaction was completed, she felt like all of the cats were definitely away, and the mice could relax a little bit.

CHAPTER THIRTY-EIGHT

Tricia rolled into her office at seven thirty in the morning. She needed to get a few emails out before the day's activities cranked up. All Ports are 24/7 operations, and Vancouver was no different, albeit it was definitely a little slower on the weekends. About half speed, in reality.

Rick had told Barry Smith that Tricia would be the supervisor on duty Saturday morning, and to take his morning time off. He could swing by Saturday afternoon to check on his personnel and operational status. It was going to be a collaborative effort for the weekend to cover the absence of the brass. It didn't affect them so much anyway, as the regular Longshoremen rarely saw Charlie or Ben in the yard. And Rick had seen to it that everyone was organized and knew what their duties were for the next four days.

The first problem occurred when the switchboard lit up almost as soon as Tricia arrived. Donny Harper, who was one of Rick's two man loading crew for his special projects, called in sick. There had been an automobile accident the night before, and he was laid up. He was home, but gotten banged up pretty good, had not slept much, and was on some pretty heavy pain meds. "Better he stays at home," Tricia told his wife. I can fill in for him, she thought to herself. She had actually spent plenty of time on the loading docks, during her casual days. Rather than bother Rick, and try to bring someone else in, she would just plug herself into the hole. She was supposed to collect the money anyway, so she could save everyone a trip up to the office.

After calling the other loading specialist, who was already on property, via his short-wave radio, Tricia told him about Donny Harper. "Is Donny okay? How is he doing?"

"Sounds like he got knocked around pretty good, but he didn't break anything, and just needs a day or two to recover." Donny's partner was fine with Tricia filling in. He knew her already from the docks, and told her "It's a smaller load, and the fork lift will take care of everything. I'll get the warehouse prepped, and ready to go. That is where they always pick up."

"When do you need me down there?"

"Oh, quarter to ten or so."

Tricia then emailed Sui Chang. When was she going to be in Honolulu? Tricia was available in a couple of weeks for some vacation time, and would be very excited to see her again. This would be an ideal time, if Sui was available, because the week after was the American Thanksgiving holiday, and then the year-end Christmas holidays would make things too busy to get away. Tricia was glad that she was in early, because Taiwan was fifteen hours ahead of her west coast time, which put Sui's time around midnight, so she was unsure if she would hear back before tomorrow.

But Tricia was excited to get an almost instantaneous post back from Asia. Yes, Mr. Chang wanted to make another trip to Hawaii before the year end, and that timing would work out well. All Tricia had to do was get to the islands, and everything else would be taken care of. They would have a long weekend together, as Mr. Chang had some business meetings, and would be in and out. Sui Chang said she would email Tricia tomorrow concerning flight times and their itinerary.

Tricia was excited, and called Steve Rodriguez immediately.

"Hi Steve, how are you?"

"Good Tricia, how is it with you?"

"Well, a couple of things here. I am confirming that the special shipment is being picked up at ten as planned. Also, I just got an email from Sui Chang, and she is offering to meet me in Honolulu in two weeks, for a long weekend. This should coincide perfectly with the next special shipment."

"Yes, it should. Did she say anything about their location? "

"No. She just said for me to get there, and everything would be taken care of for the weekend."

"We can't seem to pick up anything at all concerning a property purchase or transfer of any kind on the island of Oahu, under the name of Chang."

"Well, we should find out in a couple of weeks."

"Try to learn anything you can about their location. It makes it so much easier for us to do our mobilization, the more information we have."

"I'm sure it does. I will try and get whatever I can for you."

"Thanks, I know you will. We will track the flights from Taipei to Honolulu for sure, but I am a little nervous about the residence. Maybe they are traveling under altered passports, and doing business in the US under assumed names, or some kind of an umbrella."

"She likes me, so maybe I can get something out of her."

"So, we should have a task force meeting early next week. Can you call Ray, and give him an update, and see what his schedule is?"

"Sure."

"And another good job, Tricia. Maybe we should go out and have a drink to celebrate one of these nights."

Tricia's antennae immediately went up. She found Steve to be attractive, intelligent and a successful professional in her own work-related field. How could he still be, not only available, but interested in her as well? "Gee, Steve, anytime really. I would enjoy that."

"How about tonight?"

"Sure. Where would you like to meet?"

"How about Toro Bravo in the Pearl District? It's a Spanish place, and has great Sangria. Seven o'clock? Great. I am in Oakland as we speak, but I will be back this afternoon. I also have some good news for you."

"Awesome. See you soon. I'll call Ray in the meantime."

Tricia called Ray, and gave him his update. He was excited to have their project coming to fruition, and in such a timely manner. "Great work Tricia. I'll call Steve and arrange a meeting. How about Tuesday evening at the safe house, six o'clock?"

"Perfect, Ray. Have a nice weekend."

At nine forty-five, Tricia went down to the warehouse. As she was the only person in the office on a Saturday morning, she locked up, took her phone and went to look for Harlan and the forklift. It should be pretty close to the entrance of the warehouse.

Harlan was ready for her. There were two metal grey, fifty-five-gallon steel drums loaded on a pallet. They were set length wise on a special linear pallet, and the forklift was engaged from the rear, and just waiting for the white, Econoline cargo van to arrive.

The Asians arrived promptly at ten. They were passed in at the gate, drove to the warehouse, and backed their van in through the double wide, vertical lift loading doors.

Harlan greeted them with a nod of his head, and immediately jumped up into the caged, bucket seat of the idling fork lift. One of the Asians pulled the last shipment's pallet out of the van, and stowed it to the side. Apparently, the crews rotated the two specially designed pallets every trip. Once they were out of the way, Harlan inched the forklift forward. He was only about ten feet behind the van, but due to the linearity of the load, and the shortness of the tines on the fork lift, his cargo was canted forward at about a fifteen-degree angle.

As luck would have it, Donny Harper was the usual fork lift driver, and sure enough, when Harlan began his approach, his foot slipped a bit on the clutch petal of the lift. The machine gave a small jerk, and due to the downward angle of the load the first barrel lurched, and bucked forward. It slammed onto the ground, and rolled toward the loading van. It crashed into the rear bumper of the Econoline van, and the steel lid popped directly off, and clattered onto the ground.

The Asians reacted immediately. They pounced on the lid, and began trying to put it back in place on the barrel.

One of them cursed at Harlan, and the other Asian snarled, "Where's Donny and Rick?" Harlan, idled the fork lift again and jumped down to help right, and reload the barrel.

"Donny was in an accident last night, and can't be here today," Tricia said.

She immediately pulled out her phone, and began taking pictures, of the incident.

"What the fuck are you doing?" snapped the head Asian. "Who the are you anyway?"

"I'm Tricia Watson, supervisor in charge here. Rick also is unavailable today. I'm just taking some pictures to document that your freight is okay, and not damaged."

"Freight is okay, stop taking pictures."

Between Harlan and the Asians, they got the drum back upright. It was heavy. They resealed and reloaded it onto its original place on the special pallet. With the help of the Asians, who steadied the load, Harlan got the drums into the van. The Asians were not happy, and were seriously scowling at Tricia, when they handed her the package to finish the deal. But hand it over they did, and they left her and Harlan still muttering to themselves, as they secured their load, locked the van's rear doors, and pulled out of the warehouse.

Tricia hadn't seen anything except a lot of bubble wrap inside the steel drum, but she had managed to get half a dozen pictures, and several of them included the drivers. Steve would like to see those tonight. She grabbed the package, and tried to console Harlan, who was pretty embarrassed.

"Don't worry about it, man," she told him. "There was no damage. Those guys are just jerks. No harm no foul.

She went back to the office, and took another dozen pictures of the package.

CHAPTER THIRTY-NINE

Charlie's team rendezvoused at the Portland International Airport, and everyone was in good spirits. And why not, heading down to San Francisco for a weekend of wining/dining/golf and cocktails. They checked in, passed through security, and headed for their gate. Portland is a smaller airport, and processing security is a relative joy compared to bigger airports such as LAX or O'Hare.

The FBI was monitoring their movement closely, and had developed a system, where they passed off their surveillance vehicles and personnel while under route from time to time, thereby doing their best at avoiding suspicion. Rick was busy chatting with Charlie and his wife, and was not paying that close of attention anyway.

Steve Rodriguez was in one of the interrogation rooms at the airport, and was working with TSA supervisors, helping insure all of the checked bags of the group were hand searched in his presence. He had a warrant. Tony Patmos was with him.

Rick and Ben's bags were transferred, and searched. Nothing. Charlie who had checked in last, was the final bag to go. And

Bingo! There sat the Sig Sauer. It was like a cute, cuddly new puppy, just sitting in a box under the tree. Waiting patiently for the kids to come down the stairs on Christmas morning.

Steve Rodriguez couldn't believe his good fortune. He and Tony photographed everything carefully. The travel bag, the candy box, the weapon. Closeups of the weapon. Closeups of the filed off serial number sequence. They were ecstatic, but had to put everything back in the bag, just as they had found it. They were still maintaining Tricia's cover at all costs, but would now monitor Charlie closer than ever once he got to San Francisco. Maybe he would pass off the weapon, and then they could surely grab whoever that might be on some pretext.

The two-hour flight went very smoothly. Charlie, who remembered his temperance advice to Rick, confined himself to a single Bloody Mary on the trip. But he did buy their party a round as well. Never drink alone, was his philosophy. Bobby Mixon was seat mates with Charlie, and he was only too happy to support Charlie's efforts at morale building. Heck, he didn't have to go to any annual reviews in the afternoon.

The Portland crew picked their limo up outside SFI's baggage claim gate, and headed for the Embarcadero district. They used express check in, and were soon on their way to their rooms, riding up the glassed-in elevator, while gazing out at the beautiful atrium lobby of the thirty story Hyatt Regency Hotel. The plan was to relax in their rooms for an hour, and then meet in the ballroom before the luncheon started. Bobby was on his own, as he wouldn't be needed until the next day.

The luncheon was a marvel. San Francisco, famous for seafood, and haute cuisine, put her finest foot forward, and the chefs of the Regency property did the grand old city proud. Mediterranean Mussels in saffron broth, arugula greens tossed in a shallot vinaigrette, with smoked sturgeon. The boneless, grilled squab for an entrée was an inspired choice, as it was perfectly crispy, and flavorful to the max, but not overly filling for a noon day meal. Napa Valley supplied some Rombauer Chardonnay for the initial courses, and the quail was served with a delightful bottle of Cab Franc from Newton Vineyard.

President Malcolm McElfresh made a passionate speech about the function and the future of the ILWU. His sentiment and message was, that the role of unions in America, especially the vision and direction of the ILWU, was not only to continue their historic battle for the protection and rights of the working person, but now, as well as the basic needs and job security of their membership, the ILWU was focused on enhancing the quality of each and every one of its member's lives. Whether it be education, scholarships, health care, family planning and counseling, financial support through their network of credit unions, political representation, etc., their union was there to help its members achieve a firm foothold in the American dream. It was happening, and a good deal of the credit was due to the managers and leaders that were seated in this very room. Thank you all for coming to this year's special gathering.

After the delicious and stylish luncheon, the ladies were escorted into the adjoining section of the ballroom for a fashion show and a glass(es) of champagne. When the day's activities were wrapped up, Friday night was free time in San Francisco for everyone. Tomorrow's golf tournament and the Gala Dinner Dance took care of Saturday, and then the weekend culminated with Sunday's sendoff brunch. Everyone was excited about the Dinner Dance. Tony Bennett, Mr. San Francisco himself, was rumored to be the evening's keynote entertainer.

As the ladies went next door, the gentlemen repaired to the rear of the ballroom for some billiards and a glass or two. As ILWU Union tradition had annual reviews for all of the different

Port managers beginning right after lunch, the process started with the managers of the biggest Port operations. The larger your Port volume, the earlier you were called in for your review. And the lineup descended down from the big dogs to the smaller ranks and units. Of course, the Ports of Los Angeles, Long Beach, Oakland, San Diego, Seattle, etc. were bigger than Portland, so Charlie and crew chalked up their pool cues, and bided their time.

There was a team of a dozen or more HR execs from headquarters doing the reviews, and things moved along pretty smoothly. Of course, the pecking order of which managers were processed first was pretty evident, and it was also noted who was had the broadest smiles on their faces when exiting their interview room. The first boys up, were definitely the big, swinging dicks, and were to be watched and emulated as much as possible. Like the NFL draft when the Commissioner of the League personally handles the first-round draft pick selections, President McElfresh stuck around and accommodated the biggest tuna fish in his fleet. He was as happy to congratulate them on their performances, and outline their upcoming bonus structures, as they were to strut out of their meetings and into a large room filled with their peers. Nothing like a private sit down with the El Presidente himself.

Just after the bigger fish had been fileted, and President McElfresh was to depart, Charlie was pleased and surprised to be called in for his review with the man himself. While Charlie knew Malcolm on a passing basis, he had never had his review with him, and was proud and honored to be called out in such a prominent manner.

"Hello Charlie, how are you?"

"Very good sir, thank you for asking."

"How are things up in the great northwest?"

"Very well, sir. Our volume is good, we have enhanced some of our key accounts this year, and we are working hard with the

City and the Port of Vancouver to expand our facilities. Once we get past all of the legal hurdles and technicalities of getting the refinery processing and shipping dock approved there, we will be starting construction, and eventually should be able to increase our freight volume by thirty to thirty five percent. Thank you for your support with that project."

"Good work there Charlie. That dock should be a definite asset to us. I believe that the refinery installation up in Anacortes Washington, is the biggest outfit in your region, is it not?"

"Yes sir, it is. But they are an independent group, and not under our jurisdiction. Once we get approved in Vancouver, it will be strictly ILWU Longshoremen manning those jobs."

"That is very exciting, Charlie. As National President, I can only commend you on your efforts. Increasing not only revenues, but also membership growth is very well received around here. However, Charlie, in order to achieve these goals, we need a man up there in Portland, who is squeaky clean. Who clearly understands and supports the vision of the ILWU, and can represent our management team and our members with unparalleled integrity in this, your community."

Charlie felt a stirring of uneasiness in his stomach, but replied, "Yes of course, sir. Anything else would be below our standards." He was fishing for words, but wanted to respond in kind to the President's observation.

"Charlie, to put it bluntly, there is no small amount of concern on the Executive Committee about your recent behavior, and the incident at your Golf Club. Can you explain that kind of a situation to me, please?"

"Yes sir, I can. As you may have heard, there was an armed assault in the club's neighborhood a couple of weeks ago. Ever since then, there has been the closest scrutiny of our golf club by the press and media. Apparently, there was some bad blood between the club's management and some of the neighbors, to the point that the media got involved. Now, every chance they get to make a mountain out of a molehill, they jump on it." As a pathological personality, Charlie was able to discuss serious matters such as this, as glibly as if he were talking about the weekend's weather.

"But aren't you the president of that club, Charlie? Why wouldn't you take it upon yourself to mitigate any differences between your organization and your neighbors."

"Well sir, there seems to be some fairly longstanding, entrenched differences and opinions, and sometimes you just can't seem to please all of the people, you know what I mean? Another problem, is the limited nature of the facilities of the club, which produced some friction between a couple of events that were going on simultaneously, and in my opinion, caused the disturbance. This disturbance was reported, and was investigated by the local police. They responded by dismissing the issue as very minor, and were willing to completely ignore it going forward. Since then, I have resigned as president of the club. I am very sorry to have inadvertently gotten myself in the middle of that situation, and am beginning to distance myself from it."

"Charlie, did you hear me use the term, squeaky clean, earlier in our conversation? Squeaky clean does not include the head of one of our premier districts rolling around on the floor of a barroom, and being accused on regional television of assaulting fellow women club members."

"No sir it does not." Charlie replied, and hung his head.

"It has been decided by the Executive Committee to place you on the strictest of probationary status. Instead of getting involved in barroom brawls, you need to get out of the bar, and involve yourself in your community. Go join the Chamber of Commerce, the Rotary or Kiwanis Clubs. Join a health club, go to church if you want to. Because of your long standing and faithful service to the ILWU, you are being spared demotion or termination at this time, but please understand my message to you today. Another mishap of any kind up there, and you will be working on a dock somewhere. Do you get me? DUI? You're gone. Bad press? You are relieved of your duties. Domestic Disturbance? You are out.

"I must also remind you that as a part of our management team, you are held to a higher standard than our line members. If you should be removed from your position for disciplinary reasons, you will forfeit any union supplementation or augmentation to your employment or retirement contracts. Do you understand that?"

"Yes sir."

"Furthermore, you will not receive any performance bonus for this year."

"Yes sir."

"Go on about your business now, Charlie. You come back into this room, and you sit down with me at this time next year, with your head held high, and your priorities straightened out. Can you do that, not only for me, but for yourself, your fellow union members, and your own future?"

"Yes sir, I can and I will do that."

"Thank you, Charlie, that is all."

Fuck that pompous asshole, Charlie thought to himself as he exited the enclosed, portable cubicle. My condo is paid off, my Jag is paid for. I have plenty of cash sitting around. Don't give me too much crap buddy.

He managed to get just enough of his mojo back as he left his review, so as not to be conspicuous, but Rick and Ben could see that he was not a happy man. More like a whipped dog. Rick could surmise what might have happened in there, and only hoped that he and Ben were not going down along with Charlie.

"How'd it go, Chas?" Rick asked when they eased outside and got a little privacy.

"Not so good."

"How so?"

"Well, somehow McElfresh got wind of Rosewood this week. He was all over me."

"That isn't good."

"No. He put me on probation. No more incidents, or I'm out. I don't think it will affect you guys though. It was all about me and Rosewood. Fuck Kudlach. I should have shot Schmidt. What an asshole. He's the one that caused all of this shit." Charlie volatile temper was getting the best of him again.

"Shut the fuck up Charlie. Lower your voice. Are you crazy?"

"No, I'm not crazy, and I don't think I'm going to going to be going to dinner tonight, either." Charlie had made a reservation at Aqua restaurant for everyone, but now he wasn't in the mood for it. Screw it, he said to himself. I'll just go see Jojo, and have a few drinks.

"Whatever," Rick told him. "You should come to dinner though, it is a great restaurant."

"I'll see you tomorrow for the golf tournament. Good luck with your review."

Charlie went up to his suite, and kicked back on his king-sized bed. He felt drained, and before he knew it, he had dozed off. An hour later he stirred, and got up and took a shower.

He relaxed, dressed in casual slacks and his black leather jacket, and retrieved the box of chocolates that held the Sig Sauer. He took some Benjamins out of his money belt from the hotel room's safe. Five thousand dollars' worth, as a matter of fact, and put three thousand bucks into the box. What more casual cover, he thought, than to exit the hotel with a box of nice chocolates under his arm.

The hotel room door closed smartly behind him. He was down the elevator, and across the busy, modern décor lobby in no time. He was more interested in the atrium architecture than anything. He didn't even notice the four FBI agents lurking around. They couldn't care less about the atrium lobby, but were very interested not only in where Charlie was headed, but what was in the candy box he had under his arm.

He caught a cab, and headed for Oakland. It was almost six o'clock, and the night shift should be on by the time he got to the Pump Room.

CHAPTER FORTY

Instead of going straight to Oakland, Charlie had the cabbie drop him in San Francisco's North Beach/Little Italy district. He wanted a bowl of good pasta, and Sotto Mare was the best around. But also, he could kill two birds with one stone, and wouldn't have to start drinking with Jojo on an empty stomach. Keep it squeaky clean, he thought to himself. I am now a squeaky-clean guy.

Charlie arrived at Sotto Mare, generously tipped the doorman a Bengy, and got a nice small table for two, off to the side of the dining room. Perfect for watching people, and having a relaxed meal. Charlie put the candy box on the chair seat opposite him, and sat down and unfolded his napkin.

Whenever you tip the doorman a c-note in a family style restaurant, you are guaranteed to have the best service the house is able to provide. This was certainly true tonight as Charlie's server was on him like ham on eggs.

The waiter was an old pro, having worked Little Italy for over forty years. Probably came directly from Sicily, probably owned a piece of the place. He was five foot eight inches tall, greying hair, black eyes, and olive colored skin. But he had that regal bearing of the Southern Mediterranean, that could have been royalty, had he been born to better circumstances. He would work at Sotto Mare until his legs and feet gave out, which in all probability, was not too far in the future.

"I would like a plate of Carpaccio as an appetizer, and seafood pasta for my entrée." Charlie was a connoisseur of seafood pasta.

"Si, Si Signore. What you drink tonight?"

"Just a glass of Pinot Grigio to start. Grazie."

The glass of Pinot was chilled perfectly, and was an ample serving. Nothing worse in Charlie's opinion, than a big flashy bowl of a wine glass, with a thimble full of wine in the bottom of it. And for eighteen bucks at that. This wine was not stiffly refrigerated, but just on the side of being refreshingly chilled and tart. The tall white wine glass was still frosty. When you tip the Maitre'd one hundred bucks, you get a frosted wine glass.

Life was good. Charlie was very happy with his decision to go solo for the night. Aqua was a superb restaurant, and he really should have been with his troops. But he also knew it was important for him to get away. Take a break, before he said something stupid at dinner about Sir Malcolm. How did the old man get full footage on him from Vancouver or Portland television anyway? Who in the hell can you really trust out there anymore, Charlie thought to himself?

Dinner was superb. The carpaccio melted in his mouth, and his pasta was excellente. He ordered one more glass of Pinot Gris halfway through his dinner. He loved the atmosphere of Little Italy. The old-world feeling was palpable. There was a brotherhood of substance here, that you could cut with a knife.

If I ever leave ILWU, he thought, I should go to work for the Cosa Nostra. At least they have each other's back. And I could join the Sons of Italy or Ireland, instead of a service club.

He settled up, and asked Luigi to call a cab for him. Of course, he left Luigi a hundred-dollar tip.

Charlie grabbed his cab, and headed for the Bay Bridge and Oakland. The Pump Room was down towards Alameda. It was not an upscale neighborhood, by any stretch of the imagination, but these people knew how to party on a Friday night, and Jojo always took good care of him.

The Pump Room was primarily a black bar. A working-class bar. They served a decent soul food menu, and had a full array of drinks on their beverage card. You could order a bottle of Dom, if you were styling. Or you could sit at the bar and drink Ten High bourbon and coke for three bucks a glass. Just behave yourself, was the one rule of the house. Jojo kept a double barrel shotgun stashed under the bar, in case anyone forgot the primary house rule. Things stayed pretty much under control. The black community knew how to police themselves, and nobody wanted the cops around. This was for sure. Oakland is a very edgy, quasi militant, black community. They are the home of the founding fathers of the Black Panther Party after all. But still the neighborhood enjoyed a good watering hole, and therefore they collectively kept order in the Pump Room. There were a few white people around together, and some Asians, working people. The local Hispanics all drank in their own bars.

Jojo for his part, ran a clean business, and poured an honest drink. He kept the drug dealing down to a dull roar, and if there was trouble, it was going to come from these damn, young gangsters. They didn't seem to get the status quo, and were apt to come around with their guns blazing, more often than not.

Charlie got dropped off in front of the Pump, and it was still early enough for him to grab a seat at the end of the bar. Happy hour was over, and the late crowd was just starting to file in. Jojo was happy to see him, and Charlie gave him the candy box. "Here is something for the little lady," he said.

Jojo was shocked to receive his shipment back, and he gave Charlie a quizzical look. "Is that what I think it is?"

"Yeah. Your juice is in the box. I just thought you could recycle it again, make some more ching."

"Yeah well, that's thoughtful of you. As long as the item is clean."

"Clean as a whistle. Just trash it if you are assed out about it."

"What you drinkin' man?"

"Sapphire and Tonic."

Jojo poured his drink, and stashed the candy box under the bar. This is very weird he thought.

The Pump Room's FBI guests, two black undercover agents, filed into the bar and grabbed a couple of stools down the line from Charlie. They ordered tap beers, and began to drink very slowly. Without being too obvious, nothing escaped their attention.

After inspecting Charlie's bag, and finding what they found, Steve Rodriguez thought it was important enough to head down to the Bay Area for the day. He alerted his counterpart in the SF FBI, who met his afternoon shuttle flight at the airport. He actually ended up, because of the late notice, of flying into Oakland, which turned out to be perfect. That's where all of their action was going to be for the night anyway.

"Nice of you to come down Steve, although we've got things under control pretty well."

"I know you do. I just thought if we can wrap this up, I can get this piece of critical evidence and get out of your hair."

"It looks like it is going to be a waiting game. We have tracked this guy Jojo down to the Pump Room, a bar on the far south end of Oakland. If Strong heads over there to drop off today, I have my people on him. But we won't be able to grab Jojo, until he is on his way home. Which will probably be late."

"That's cool. I can wait. Oakland police have been notified, and I have a couple of agents, who can follow him into the bar, and keep an inconspicuous eye on him."

"You are all over it. Why don't you let me buy you an early dinner?"

"Where are you staying?"

"I've got a room reserved at the Radisson, by the Oakland airport."

"Okay, let's get a bite, then you might as well go back to your room, kill some time and get some rest. It's going to go late tonight."

"Sure. Can we go back into the city, someplace around Ghirardelli Square? I want to get some chocolates for a friend."

"Yeah. Let's just go get the chocolates, then get out of town before the traffic gets bad. We can eat on this side."

Charlie was on his second Sapphire and Tonic, and some of the older, crustier clientele, seated along the bar were eye balling him. Not menacingly, but not with welcome home smiles either. Charlie didn't care. He loved black people. He had loved black people ever since Vietnam, where he had been ass deep, through thick and thin in the jungle with them.

Charlie knew exactly what to do. "Jojo, will you buy the bar a round for me?"

"Sure Charlie. Good call."

The tension eased noticeably. A, Charlie was buying drinks, and B, Charlie seemed to be tight with Jojo. He was going to be okay with them. Charlie was more concerned with the young ladies who were beginning to filter into the circular booths around the dance floor. It was early, and the DJ was playing some Marvin Gaye. Something Charlie could relate to.

A huge black man was dancing with a beautiful mulatto woman. The dance floor was still largely empty, and the couple were putting on a public display of their moves. Sexy, agile, smooth on his feet for a big man, spins, dips, rolls. You name it, and his woman was following him perfectly. Charlie loved to dance, and for his age, he was very fluid and graceful. He wished Nikki was there with him right now.

Charlie picked up his drink. "Save my spot," he asked Jojo, and he moved down to a barstool next to the DJ and the dance floor. He began to stare intently at the black man.

After a few minutes of this, the black silver foot and the rest of the crowd began to notice. Hell, Charlie was the only white guy in the room, and he stuck out like a sore thumb anyway.

The black dude stared back at Charlie, and gave him a head waggle. Charlie stared back, and began to dip his left shoulder rhythmically. They continued to stare at each other. It was a damn stare down.

Charlie grabbed the hand of the girl nearest to him, and hit the floor. He started slow, working the shoulder dip, suddenly he did a 360 spin, dropped into a split, bounced out of it, and started to seriously shake it. All while staring the black man down.

I don't know how many bars you've been to in Oakland, but it is unusual to say the least, for a white boy to go into one, and start a dance off. You can get yourself shot pretty easy doing something like that. The Black dude was still staring, and was working his stuff overtime, but Charlie was also dancing his ass off. The crowd was now into it, and were cheering the competitors. The black dude would take the floor. Charlie would stand aside, and keep his shoulder dip working. Charlie's young lady partner apparently had no fear of crazy white men, and was also enjoying the attention. She was hanging all over Charlie, and grinding on him to the music.

Charlie's turn now, and he spun out onto the middle of the floor and started a series of rapid but smooth, jiggy/disco moves, with some colorful twirls, that brought the house down. He had worked up a sweat, and was ready for a drink. So, he did one more split, bounce up, and then bowed to his competitor. They hugged. The crowd cheered for all four dancers, and Charlie signaled to Jojo to bring drinks all around.

The Pump Room adopted Charlie as a blue eyed black man that night, and he was the toast of South Oakland. He headed back to his bar stool, and his dance partner followed close behind.

"You've still got it Chaz," laughed Jojo. All of the old bar flies nodded at him, and he bought them all another drink.

It was getting a little late, and Charlie didn't want to get crazy, as he still had his golf tournament tomorrow. So, he closed out his tab, and got ready to leave. His new date, wanted him to stay. But Charlie apologized for having to go, and asked Jojo to call him a cab.

"Sheeit, man, you usually stay and close the place down."

Charlie wanted nothing more than to do that, and wanted nothing more than to take his new friend back to the Hyatt Regency with him. But even Charlie knew that would be a bad move. Squeaky clean, eh? From now on. Charlie kissed her good bye, gave her firm, brown ass a lustful squeeze. He bought her a bottle of Dom, and told her he'd be back. He didn't say when, so it was no lie there. While Charlie waited for his cab, the girl pouted.

"Why you dance me all up, get me all wet, then want to go, and leave me here alone on a Friday night?" she whispered in his ear.

"Sorry baby. I have to go is all. I will come back and make it up to you."

"When?"

"The next time I am in town."

"When is that going to be?"

I don't know. Here," Charlie handed her a couple of big bills. "Here is some cab fare home." Charlie had his wad of cash on him, but he was being careful not to flash it around. Not in Oakland.

She took the money. "You should stay, we could have lots of fun." She had her hands in Charlie's lap. He was beginning to firm up.

"Hey, sorry, but I have to go." He got up, and pushed away from the bar rail.

"It was good to see you Charlie."

"Back at you Jojo. Thanks for taking care of me."

"Always, my man."

Charlie settled his tab, which was now a thousand bucks, slipped Jojo five hundred as a cash tip, and headed out. Not bad for a couple hours work he thought. He put the drinks on his personal credit card. I'm sure they will be monitoring my expenses like crazy now, he thought. No reason to give anyone any ideas. Hey, he was a team player.

"Your cab is here, Charlie. Let me walk you out."

"Thanks, Jojo."

The black FBI agents killed their beers, and got ready to move. The outside FBI agents picked Charlie back up, and followed his cab. No candy box now, they noticed.

After Charlie left, the black girl asked Jojo to take the Dom Perignon back, and give her the money. A sale is a sale, he thought to himself, but then, Charlie had been more than generous to him tonight. He took the bottle back, and gave the girl a hundred bucks.

"Go dance some more," he told her.

Jojo stayed until midnight, and let his partner close up. He had had a busy night, and was ready to head home. Maybe one stop off, he wasn't sure. But he wanted to get the Sig Sauer out of his bar. Nothing worse than a hot weapon sitting around for the wrong person to find. What was Charlie thinking anyway, bringing the damn thing back to him.

Jojo took off. He put the Sig under the front seat of his Escalade, and headed for the Silver Dollar Saloon. He wanted to see a friend on some business. The FBI was watching. They saw the candy box go into the SUV. They were following at a respectful distance. It was actually to their liking that he stop off on his way home. Especially, if it was at a bar. That way they would have probable cause to pull him over.

Jojo was in the bar until closing time. He didn't make it a mile toward home, before red lights were blazing in his rear-view mirror.

By this time, Charlie was back in his room in San Francisco, and sound asleep.

The Oakland Police pulled Jojo out of his car, and gave him a sobriety test. He passed the test, but they still had reason to believe there was criminal evidence in the car. They retrieved the box, and brought Jojo downtown. It was late enough, so they threw him in a cell, and told him they would talk to him tomorrow. He wanted to make a phone call. Tomorrow, they told him.

At nine am the next morning, Jojo was in one of the interrogation rooms. Where did he get the weapon? "On the street." Why do you carry it in your car? "For protection. This is Oakland man." Why were the serial numbers filed off? "I don't know man. I didn't really notice. I just bought the gun from a guy who came in my bar, and needed some cash." Why is there a silencer in the box?" "Fuck, I don't know. It came with the gun I guess." "Has the weapon ever been used in a crime? "I don't know man. Certainly not by me." Are you a gun dealer? "Fuck no man. I own a damn bar. I work my ass off. I pay taxes. Why you hassling me? I passed my test last night, I want to call my lawyer."

The detective left the IR, and went next door to see his Shift Captain, and the FBI agents.

"He is straight. He is really no trouble. We are going to have to charge him, or let him go. If I charge him, I will need to keep the weapon for evidence, because he passed his sobriety test."

"The hell with it. Just let him go. We need the weapon as evidence in a much bigger case than this." Steve Rodriguez and the SF FBI guy looked at each other and nodded.

"Fine with us. This guy is small potatoes. He actually is a good guy. Anytime we have a business owner here who pays taxes, this is a big bonus. We have a lot worse trouble to deal with."

The law enforcement officers all shook hands, and the FBI side of the room thanked the Oakland City PD for their help. "We owe you one," said the SF FBI chief agent.

The detective went back into the IR. "You are free to go," he told Jojo. "But we are keeping the weapon. It is not registered in your name, and it has been altered. Don't do this shit again, or it will be some big trouble for you."

"Whatever." At least I had enough brains to leave the three grand in the safe at the office, the damn pigs would have kept that too. He walked out of the central precinct, and hit the bricks. What the fuck was Charlie thinking about anyway? It wasn't like him to do something stupid like that. Jojo was not a happy man. He spit on the ground, and started walking. It was a full mile to the impound yard. He thought he should probably call Charlie, and tell him what had happened. So, he dialed Chas up on his cell. No answer. How could he know Charlie was already four holes into his golf tournament?

Fuck Charlie anyway, he thought. If that idiot hadn't brought the gun back to him, none of this would ever have happened. What a cheeseball. He didn't deserve another phone call.

CHAPTER FORTY-ONE

Charlie made it back to the hotel. He had had a great dinner, and a lot of fun. Plus, he had enjoyed himself, but still saved his best for the golf tournament tomorrow. He was sure that his guys had enjoyed their night out as well. What fun would it have been for him to be hanging out as the fifth wheel, with some married couples anyway?

He got up at the crack of dawn, shaved, showered and was sitting in the Regency coffee shop, when Rick rolled in. "Morning partner," Rick said.

"Good morning yourself. How was dinner?"

"It was fantastic. We had the tasting menu." Rick pulled a chair up. "Seven courses of fish butter. It was better than fantastic, it was phenomenal. How was your night?"

"Great. I had some top dog Italian food in Little Italy, then went and saw a friend of mine. Got back early, and saved myself for you guys today."

"Great. Ben and Bobby should be down in a few minutes."

Their waitress came over, and poured coffee. More coffee in Charlie's case. "You gentlemen ready to order?"

"I'll have the Gruyere Omelet please, with polenta and a cup of fruit. How about you Ricky Boy?"

"Just the regular old bacon and eggs. Rye toast please, with country potatoes"

Ben and Bobby came in ten minutes later, and the whole procedure was repeated.

"What time does the bus leave?" Charlie asked. "Are our clubs already loaded?"

"Yeah. I took care of that yesterday. We've got about half an hour for the bus."

"I sure would like to win this sonofabitch today," Charlie said. "First place purse of six grand. That's fifteen hundred bucks apiece."

"I don't care about the money," Ben said. "It's all about the bragging rights."

No shit thought Charlie to himself. Especially after the old man getting in my grill yesterday. Hell, when we win the damn thing, they will probably think that we play too much golf up there, and don't do enough work. Then he will have the opportunity to get on me again.

"What's the format?" Bobby asked.

"They changed it to three net balls out of four this year. But winter rules I think."

"We can do this. Just everyone get in their rhythm, and stay smooth. Don't try to kill the ball."

"Bobby, you are our man. This course should suit you just fine. It is short enough that you can do some major damage."

"I'll try, boss."

"I like our chances. Let's finish here, and get on the front of the bus, so we can get over to the practice range lickety split."

The beautiful thing about a golf tournament, is that everyone is tied for the lead when the shot gun start kicks off. Therefore, hope springs eternal for all thirty-six teams in the tournament. Twenty-nine working jurisdictions, three teams from SF headquarters, and four teams from the Port's major shipping partners. There would be two teams per hole, so it was going to be a long round. But, every one of those teams were thinking the same thing. I.e.-we can do this.

Kind of like the old joke about the guy whose friend call him up. "Hey, let's play in the charity golf tournament this weekend."

"How much does it cost?"

"It's $200. Bucks each."

"Nah, I don't think so. That's too much money."

"Come on it would be fun."

"Nah, I don't think so."

"Come on, man. I am talking about special needs people here."

Suddenly it dawned on the guy, "Hey, we could win this thing."

The tournament was being held up at the beautiful Marin Golf and Country Club. Everyone would be going over the Golden Gate Bridge and into Marin County, San Francisco's affluent neighbor to the north. It was a rolling layout, wooded hills, with scrub oaks and redwood trees. There were some water hazards, some sand hazards, but it was not nearly as challenging a course as say, the Presidio in San Francisco. That prestigious layout is situated on an outcropping point in the northwest corner of the City. It has gorgeous views of the Pacific Ocean, but is hilly and twisty and exposed to the off-shore winds like crazy. You can hardly keep a hat on your head sometimes. The Scots would love it. But it was much more comfortable to be back in the sheltered valleys of Marin County. And it even looked like the rains were going to hold off. All in all, it appeared to be a capital day ahead.

Most of the ladies were going on a bus tour of San Francisco: Nob Hill, Pier 39, the Modern Art Museum, lunch at the venerable Cliff House Restaurant, etc. Not many of the union management ladies cared about going out into the cool, grey elements and whacking a golf ball around. But a few of them were diehards, and had signed up for the bus ride and the golf tournament. There was actually a rumor going around about Headquarters requiring each foursome to be comprised of at least one woman. Charlie didn't care. He would just hire the best woman golfer he could find, give her some kind of title, and have at it. Hopefully, she would be good looking too.

They all warmed up. Charlie felt good. He was still playing to a fourteen, and was hitting the ball well. They had Bobby for their low handicapper, and Rick and Ben who both played to eighteens. If Bobby and Charlie were on, all they had to do was get one hole out of either Rick or Ben. Just play steady boys. At least they both got a stroke a hole, and Charlie had seen either one of them get hot plenty of times.

The tournament went pretty well. Charlie played steady, Bobby tore it up, and Rick and Ben ham and egged perfectly. It takes probably twelve to sixteen under par to win this type of tournament under normal conditions, but depending on how many sandbaggers the big Southern California Ports were able to sign up on their teams, these were not normal conditions. Tournament rules mandated that actual working managers were required for at least three of the team slots, which Charlie's team was right on. But it seemed like every year, there were some pretty outlandish scores for this format from certain districts. Wow, we had a career day, was always the response. Headquarters never seemed to pay much attention.

Charlie's Portland team came in at fifteen under, which was a spectacular day for them, and by far the best score they had ever shot. They doubted they had won, but hoped to be in the top three, and get either a second or third place trophy. "Guess we'll find out at dinner how we did." Someone opined. "Fuck it," Charlie said. "You guys played lights out. I'm proud to have played on your team."

Ben was jacked. He never seemed to play to his handicap when he wanted to, but today went very well, and he was feeling great. This is golf. You have to depersonalize it, because if you take it too seriously, it can be very frustrating. Ben had walked off of the course too many times, shaking his head sideways, not to appreciate how pumped he felt today. What a glorious time of it. Now, a ride back to town, over the Golden Gate Bridge, drinking fine Napa Valley wine, and then the gala dinner dance coming up. Wahoo!

Tricia had had a busy day. She got the package back to the office, and photographed it from every angle. She put it in Ben's strong box, and put that into the safe. She emailed Rick, and told him about Jimmy calling in sick. She told him about the mishap in the warehouse, and what she and Harlan had done to rectify the situation. She told him how the Asians had seemed pretty grumpy, but everything had been completed as planned, and the package was put away safely.

She emailed Steve Rodriguez the photographs she had taken of the Asian drivers, and wished him a safe trip back to Portland. She relayed the projected task force meeting time on Tuesday to him. She emailed Sui Chang, and requested her address, so she could send a house warming present. She talked to her son three times, and her mom once. Yes, Junior could stay overnight at his buddy's house. She would pick him up in the morning at eleven. She told her mom to make some fun plans of her own, because she actually had a bona fide, real date with a man. Her mom was thrilled.

Steve called her and told her about the incredible stroke of luck they had found in Charlie's luggage, which was the reason for his trip down to the Bay area. With the casings they had recovered, and the surveillance they had done, they could prove beyond a doubt that this was the assault weapon. Iron clad. He did tell her that he might be a little late for their dinner date, because of his travels, "but I do have a surprise for you."

She was elated. Now all she had to do was wait for a reply from Sui Chang.

The crowd began to gather in the Grand Ballroom around seven pm, for cocktail hour. The guys had had some time to get back and refresh after the tournament. The same was also true of the ladies' excursion around town.

The award ceremony for the tournament was scheduled for the last fifteen minutes of the cocktail hour, and always made a lively wrap up to that segment of the evening. As Charlie was a single, the registration desk ladies had set him up with a young lady escort for the evening. She was a tall, attractive brunette who was a casual from the smaller port city of Burlingame, California. Charlie was happy to have someone to spend the evening with.

President McElfresh's assistant got on the microphone, and called for everyone's attention. The awards ceremony was about to begin. This was a very festive portion of the program, as the tournament winners were traditionally showered with as much abuse as the losers could get away with in good taste. It was a lot of fun.

Of course, The Port of Los Angeles won the tournament at eighteen under. That was a totally unrealistic score, and all of the other players knew it, and gave LA some big-time grief. "And now, this year's second place trophy goes to a dark horse team from the northwest. Charlie Strong, bring your team up here for a photograph, and grab this trophy, will you?" Charlie was Mr. Proud, and was only too happy to hit the stage with his guys. They graciously accepted the trophy, and thanked headquarters for another fantastic event. They accepted the envelope with four grand in it, and headed back to the reception. Charlie held the envelope in the breast pocket of his suit coat. They got some grief of their own, on the way back down, but that was to be expected. Charlie would hold onto the envelope until tomorrow. It was never a good idea to pass out C-notes in front of the wives.

One of the shippers won third place. The Longshoremen are all smart enough to lay off their shipping brethren, their bread and butter, as far as the good-natured harassment goes.

"Ladies and Gentlemen. Thank you for your attention. On behalf of President McElfresh, and the executive team, I would like to invite you to join us in the grand ballroom, for tonight's dining and dancing pleasure. Thank you all for being Longshoremen, we hope you are enjoying yourselves."

Charlie didn't expect a very good table after his review yesterday, and therefore he was not surprised. At least he wasn't sitting on the very last row, but he was a considerable distance from the stage. The gala's attendance mirrored the Golf Tournament's pretty closely. There were thirty-six golf teams, and with wives and escorts joining them, that made thirty-six tables of eight. Plus, another dozen or so tables of staff and shippers, that came to about four hundred guests in the room. Which made for a pretty good-sized party.

Of course, everyone was dressed to the nines. Charlie had his custom-made Armani on. It fit like a glove. Ben and Rick were also looking sharp. But for someone like Bobby, who didn't own an Armani, it was cheaper to go out and rent a tuxedo for the weekend. Why buy a two-thousand-dollar suit, that you would seldom wear. So, there were any number of tuxes around also.

The ladies looked the very face of elegance. They were smartly draped in silks, pastels and jewels. Not only were their diamonds glittering, their eyes were sparkling as well. They were made up to the nines, their hair was styled, and they had probably bikini waxed too. Nothing seemed more important at this time, than to have their husbands draped all over them on the dance floor. And for the better part of the evening. It was indeed their special night.

If the rumors were true that Tony Bennett was performing tonight, then that was big. He may be a little passé in LA or San Francisco, but in the outlands, places like Vancouver, or Astoria or Bellingham, he was legendary. And these women couldn't wait to tell their friends back home, that they had spent time with this beautiful and talented man.

Everyone found their seats, and settled in. The first course was Moet Champagne, and a caviar soufflé. While this course was evolving, and everyone had been poured a crystal glass of bubbles, the lights were dimmed, which brought up the candlelight, and gave the room a warm, inviting glow.

President McElfresh took the podium. It had been moved to the side of the largish stage. He called for our attention, and cleared his throat dramatically. Yes, it was true. "Ladies and Gentlemen, it gives me the greatest pleasure to present to you this evening, fresh from an international tour of the great capitals of the world. A man who needs no introduction, a leader, a giant in the world of entertainment. Ladies and gentlemen please put your hands together for San Francisco's own, Mr. Tony Bennett."

Tony and his band/orchestra knocked everyone's socks off. We sipped French Champagne, nibbled caviar in a creamy, rich veloute custard, and listened raptly. The staff slowed service down for the performance, but kept the champagne coming. That worked for our table. A lot of couples were up on the dance floor. What a thrill, dancing under the simulated stars, to the man himself

Tony's grand finale was, of course, "I left my heart in San Francisco", and it brought the house down. Finally, dinner resumed, and was also knockout. Baby arugula and pea vine salad, Filet Mignon or planked Salmon. They served Gelato for dessert with little ILWU logos made out of caramelized sugar on top of each one. We all drank the finest white and red wines France and California could offer. With dessert, every table was presented with a bottle of VSOP Cognac, souvenir crystal snifter glasses, and a platter of Ghirardelli's best chocolate. Jesus, Mary, Joseph, Charlie thought to himself, this baby is setting us back a few bucks. No sweat. As long as we keep it squeaky clean.

After Tony, there was a combo playing Billy Joel/Elton John type stuff. Charlie got up and danced with his escort several times. He was getting into it, but she was stiff and seemed disinterested. No big, he was missing Nikki anyway. He spent some time working the room, visiting with friends. Some of his old relationships seemed a little frosty. It was like rumors were already starting to circulate of his review troubles. No one wanted to get too close. That's okay he thought, we are shipping most of Asia out of Seattle and Portland, so if you assholes want to shine me on, that's your problem. I will be back and kick all of your sorry asses again next year.

Rick and Ben and wives were hitting it off, having a grand time of it. Bobby and his cute, little escort also seemed quite compatible. By midnight Charlie was done. He bid his bored escort goodnight, released her from her subtle purgatory, and went on up to his room. He was tired, deflated, and ready to go home. Well, at least they had gotten second place in the golf tournament, and he hadn't seen Neil Asshole Horn around here anywhere.

Sunday morning's brunch was another display of opulence. Ice carvings, twenty-five feet of freshly caught shell fish available for consumption, avec sauces. An omelet station, mimosas, too many cremes and pastries to fathom, etc., etc. Charlie was fried. He came late and left early. He was ready to go back to the airport for their three o'clock flight before anyone else.

CHAPTER FORTY-TWO

The flight back to Portland International was uneventful. Everyone except Charlie was basking in the glow of a very memorable weekend, and were content to revel quietly in their own memories and reflections. Their hosts from the ILWU were most gracious, and the two couples were very happy, proud and thankful to be a part of such a successful and generous organization.

Charlie was still smarting from the dressing down he had received from President McElfresh, and was quietly contemplative on other subjects. He realized how thin the ice upon which he was skating had gotten, and knew he had enemies back home. Any one of which could cause him serious problems, if he wasn't careful. To avoid any kind of negative press was going to be hard, but he realized that it was time for him to lay lower than a gopher hole. His new and lower profile, needed a lower profile.

For example, he should phase back out of Vancouver, and spend his time in Portland. Bigger city, more anonymity. The small-town realities and politics of Vancouver were killing him.

He needed some separation there. It was time to let Ben Harris take the point on the jurisdiction, and the refinery project with the port and city people. He would assume a review and advise position only. He needed to cut back on his drinking, and take Malcolm's advice to get back in the gym on a regular basis. He could also focus on getting more cargo into Portland, and away from Seattle and Tacoma. But he definitely needed to get his act cleaned up.

Also, what about the continued special shipments into Vancouver? Maybe, just maybe, in spite of how lucrative it was proving to be, they should let someone else take on that kind of risk. He would schedule a meeting with Rick and Ben tomorrow morning. They could break down the last payout, and discuss the future of their relationship.

The guys were all waiting at the baggage carousel. "Let's get together tomorrow morning and have an organizational meeting, can we?" Charlie asked.

"Good idea," was both Rick and Ben's response.

Not collectively, but individually, both men had begun to seriously consider their options going forward. They wanted to have this planning session more than Charlie imagined.

Tricia heard back from Sui Chang on Saturday afternoon. Don't worry about a housewarming gift. We already have everything. Better a nice bottle of perfume, or something personal. She could bring that with her, and Sui would be waiting for her in a limo at the airport. They would exchange flight information.

This was a disappointing reply to her, but Tricia was beginning to see how careful the Chang's were in their movements. They probably came in on a private jet, so as to leave little if any footprints around, she thought. Yet, this chapter was going to soon be wrapped up, and she was excited not only for her date with Steve tonight, but also for the upcoming task force meeting.

Her first big case, and the end result was exactly what she had hoped for when she had joined up. Get some drugs off of the streets, and hopefully help some people. Lots of people.

Monday morning at eleven, Rick and Ben met Charlie at his executive offices in Portland.

This meeting was going to have some gravity, as Charlie could feel both of their seriousness and sense their concerns, as soon as they all sat down.

"Fun weekend, eh?" Charlie opened the conversation.

"Great weekend," both of the guys agreed.

"It was a great of a weekend, but we have some issues going forward," Ben gave his input, and looked at Rick for support.

"I agree. I am starting to love this organization. They take special care of us, and I personally don't want to do anything to screw up the good thing we have going here," said Rick.

"No one does," said Charlie.

"Well then, what are we going to do with the Asians?" This from Ben. "I know you inherited this from Harold, Charlie. And I know this business has been going on for some time, and there are a lot of fingers in the pie. But, this is some serious shit we are dealing with here."

"This is very true," Charlie agreed. "I think at the very least, that we can continue to process the shipments, as if they were part of the Chang's private art collection. We don't know what is in those containers. Just how fragile they are, and we handle them as a special service. No one can prove we know what is in those drums. We should establish an off-shore account. Maybe Switzerland, and have the money wired directly there. Then we are not handling any cash, and are clean on this end of things."

This was not what the guys wanted to hear from Charlie. "Uh, Charlie. We don't want any off-shore accounts. We both want out. With your problem at Headquarters, and your negative review, they will be watching us like chicken hawks. They have contacts with our people. It would be so easy for them to have an insider buried in our operations staff, and we wouldn't have a clue who it was. They will figure out what is going on, and we are dead meat. How do you think they knew about your TV coverage? They have spotters, either active or retired people, in every jurisdiction. They are not stupid people. They know what is going on, especially when someone elevates his profile like you did. And this is not just career damage we are talking about here, this is drugs, IRS shit, jail time. You name it."

Wow, Charlie thought, this is a more serious than I thought it was going to be. "If we are going to pull out, it is going to take a little time. They already have another shipment on the water, due into port a week from Friday. I could contact Mr. Chang or Mr. Thieu, and tell them this will be the last shipment, if you both want me to."

"This is what both of us want."

"This timing is okay with you?

"What else can we do? I will arrange with Donny and Harlan to make the transfer, but I will not personally be at the Port a week from Friday morning."

"What do you mean you won't be at the port Friday morning? Where the fuck are you going to be, Rick?"

"I have a dentist's appointment."

"Convenient. Who is going to pick up the money then?"

"Let Tricia do it again."

"She won't be here," Ben said. "She has requested vacation time next week."

"Well, then you do it, Ben."

"I am not going to do it either."

Whatever the fuck happened to the good soldier concept, Charlie wondered. "Well, I can't do it. That would look suspicious as hell. Me down on the docks, with the line staff, running errands."

"I will get some casual to be there, and get the package up to the office. I will prep him to just keep his mouth shut, and act like he knows something, and get it done. But this is the last time I have absolutely anything to with any special shipments."

"Okay, Rick. Thank you. This is the last shipment then gentlemen. I will call Mr. Thieu this afternoon. Anything else we need to discuss while we are all here?"

"Yes, there is," Ben said. "We are concerned about you, Charlie. We love you, man, and it has been a pleasure working for you, but we want you here for the long haul. If Headquarters should decide to make some changes, this would affect all of us. If someone new comes in, they will want to bring in their own people, and then we are out to sea, so to speak."

Rick said, "We like it right here, and want to stay here."

"Hey, so do I guys." Charlie came right back at them. "I thought that the police handling of the whole Rosewood situation would have more impact than it did. I thought that would mitigate the situation for everyone. But, I admit it, I fucked up. I never should have been involved in that kind of a debacle in the first place. I am committed to lowering my profile considerably, and I will be spending my time in Portland, almost exclusively. Portland is a much bigger operation, and that is where our bread and butter is. It is almost like Vancouver is a hobby to me, but I have let myself get sucked into the small-town shit that goes on there. Ben, from now on, you will have a much stronger hand in running the Port of Vancouver, and you will take over the Port/Refinery negotiations with the City. You will keep me in the loop at all times, but it is now your baby.

Rick, you will continue to manage operations here in Portland, Vancouver, and also Longview/Kelso. You won't hear a peep out of me, and I sincerely hope that my personal problems, didn't affect your annual reviews, or your futures." Charlie knew this update would be well received, especially with Ben, and would hopefully help to calm everyone's nerves a bit.

"I hoped we would hear this kind of thing today, Charlie. Thank you for your confidence in me. I have a good relationship with Mayor Adams, it is a great opportunity to pursue, and I will give it my utmost attention. Also, my annual review went very well, thank you. I received a generous bonus check, and Headquarters spoke well of us. They like what we are doing here. We are very profitable, and it would be a major mistake to let some negative, peripheral personal issues create problems for us."

"Rick?"

"Ditto Ben," Rick said. He was very happy to be out the drug trafficking business, and just wished he had been more adamant about Charlie's ludicrous decision to go after Bob Kudlach.

The three men, all got up simultaneously and shook hands to end their meeting. "I will call you as soon as I get in touch with Bao Thieu, Rick."

"Okay, Charlie."

Ben gave Charlie a fat envelope as the men went their separate ways. "I need to split up the backlog of cash in the other two safes. When would you like me to do that?"

"By the end of this week? Is that enough time?"

"Sure."

I could use the extra cash Charlie thought to himself.

CHAPTER FORTY-THREE

Steve Rodriguez got back from Oakland about five in the evening. He had been able to rest a little on his return flight, and had also had plenty of time to freshen up, and make his date on time.

For her part, Tricia had on beige slacks, a cream-colored silk blouse, a nice three-quarter length furry, a warm winter sweater, and medium high heels. Steve was about four inches taller than she, and she didn't want him to dwarf her. But she was excited to be out and about. It had been so long. She imagined she was coming out of the far side of a dark tunnel, or going out for a first date in high school with a guy she really liked. It just felt good. She was finally herself again. There were a few tingles in her stomach, the normal jitters, but maybe it was just as well she had laid low for as long as she had. Judging from the many dating horror stories she heard from her friends, that had divorced or separated, she hadn't missed much. So, it looked to be a good start back for her. She liked and respected Steve, and sensed that he felt the same way about her. So, who knew what actually might happen tonight?

She was waiting in the foyer of the restaurant, when he arrived. He was tall and clean shaven. He looked very handsome in his bomber jacket. He walked over and gave her a kiss on the cheek.

"How was your trip?" she asked.

"It was very successful. I'll tell you about it when we get seated."

They had a reservation, and Steve, who knew the restaurant well, had asked for one of the booths at the rear of the dining room. They both scooched toward the center of the booth together. Steve pulled out her present, and gave it to her. "Just a little something."

"Thank you so much. How thoughtful of you."

"It is from San Francisco."

"Should I open it?"

"Sure."

Steve ordered a Sangria, and Trish opted for a margarita. She began to open her present, and when she got to the bottom of things, she found the box of rich, dark chocolates. She was just as impressed with the chocolate, as she was with the fact that Steve had taken the time out of his busy trip, to stop and think of her in such a special way.

"These are my favs, thank you so much." She looked at him, and decided to go for it. She put her arm around his shoulder, and her hand on the back of his neck, and pulled him forward for a kiss. Their first real one, and it was sweet.

"Well, we won't have to order any dessert tonight," she said.

The rest of their evening went smoothly. They had much to talk about, and Steve was happy to tell her about all of the excitement in Oakland. "We actually found the assault weapon, and it is now in our custody." He told her of the FBI's search at the airport, then their surveillance of Charlie, and that Charlie had actually inadvertently bought a couple of drinks for his agents in the drop bar. They both had a good laugh there.

Drinks were followed by three or four small tapas courses to start, and they split an order of paella for an entrée. The food was superb, and so was the casual table talk. When they finished the business end of the conversation, they shared their personal stories, the why and how they had gotten to the Northwest.

Steve had grown up in Colorado, loved the outdoors, especially skiing. He had always wanted to follow his father's path in law enforcement, and after receiving a Bachelor's degree in Criminology from the University of Colorado, he was recruited by the FBI. He had been with them for thirteen years now. He loved his job, and loved the Northwest.

Tricia shared her story, and they seemed to be edging closer to each other in the center of the big, high booth.

"Would you care for anything else this evening?" their waiter asked. He was looking at the box of chocolates on the table, and wasn't very optimistic about a dessert sale.

"How about it?" Steve asked.

"Maybe a cup of Spanish coffee, if you will join me."

"Done. Two please."

The coffee came flaming to their table, and Tricia opened the chocolates and fed one to Steve. He playfully nipped at her fingers.

"Wow, you bite the hand that feeds you?"

"How can I make it up to you?"

"Well, I don't have to be home until eleven tomorrow morning."

Steve motioned to their waiter. "Check please," he mouthed, while air scribbling with his right hand.

They finished their coffees, and left the restaurant arm in arm.

Tricia didn't have the least bit of anxiety about seeing Steve at the task force meeting on Tuesday. They had had a very pleasant evening together, she had already developed a great deal of affection and respect for him. He had promptly called to thank her for such a nice evening, and inquire about next weekend. She actually felt warm and gushy inside when she saw him, but they were both professionals. By the time this meeting was over, no one in the room would have the slightest inkling that they had spent any meaningful time together. And all of the crew was there at the safe house, as no one was about to miss this meeting.

Ray Farley called the gathering to order. Steve Rodriguez and Tony Patmos were. Barbara Estes and Jim Hanson were there from DEA. Steve Golding, the Clark County DA, and Phillip Brown, the US Attorney from Portland sat together, along with Ray, Tricia and Larry Larson from Vancouver PD. Steve was happy to turn the Sig Sauer over to Ray. "Put this one in the evidence room," he said. The Vancouver DA was very happy to take possession of the final piece de resistance in his case against Charlie.

As Charlie's situation was all but wrapped up, Steve and the rest of the assembled wanted to proceed with the coming weekend. "We are very fortunate in that the timing of these events are such as they are," Steve said. "We intercepted a call between Charlie and Bao Thieu yesterday, and apparently Charlie and his guys are spooked. This might be the last shipment which will be processed through Vancouver. Charlie and Company are pulling out of the deal."

This information created some surprise, but everyone was happy they had this last chance to pull off the bust. Also implied, was an even more heightened awareness of the importance tonight's, and any other ensuing planning sessions in the coming week and a half might entail.

"We've got one chance to get this right, and it is a tricky proposition. One element after another has to be pulled off simultaneously, and with precision." Not a soul in the room could disagree with Steve.

"So, let's review our procedures here. We've got Charlie, Rick and Ben to deal with, and also the retired President of ILWU Local 40, Harold Edmonds, who we believe is in on the payouts. Obviously, Charlie is the big tuna. But Rick is guilty as a possible accessory in two separate felonies: The assault on Bob Kudlach, which may be a little harder to prove what he knew beforehand. But we've got him pretty solid on abetting in the distribution of controlled substances, and concealing income. Ben Harris is the money man, and so he is also an accessory to the smuggling, but also for concealing and distributing illicit money. These guys are a low flight risk, and we should deal with them separately from the primary drug smugglers. We can pick them up after the other busts have occurred.

On the drug side, things are considerably more complex. This involves a synchronized operation. If our timing isn't precise, we could alert the other factions of the operation, who could then become extreme flight risks. For example, we want to apprehend the transportation van and its operators. We estimate that each shipment they are transporting, contains from six to eight hundred to pounds of pure China White heroin. But we also want to arrest the San Francisco operators, who are located in Chinatown. They are under our surveillance. Then, we have the opportunity to grab the Changs in Hawaii, which would not only be a major international bust, but would also accomplish three vertical levels. I.E.-street, west coast, and the Asian supply side."

Ray Farley spoke up, "How can we help?"

"The first thing we need to do is detain the van and its drivers. Ray, if you pulled them over in Washington, before they reached the Columbia River Bridge, that would be a local stop, and would seem more authentic than the FBI or DEA swarming them. As soon as they see us coming with a swat team they call it in, and we are already in jeopardy of losing our element of surprise in Chinatown. If a local squad car pulls them over, we have a better chance of getting to them, and getting their cell phones shut down.

As soon as the van and the drivers are secured, we go after Bao Thieu and Chinatown. Their office is in a second story walk up building, right in the heart of the district. We can have our people all over the location, and ready to converge once the van is secured. We want Bao Thieu and his people. We have search warrants to grab their computers and anything else in the office that might be useful. We also have people in place to converge on the Oriental Casino in Reno. We will secure their hard drives and cash drops and asset records as well.

Finally, we have the Changs in Hawaii. Tricia Watson is going over to Honolulu a week from Thursday, and will be staying with the Changs. The object is to apprehend them without their being alerted to any of our stateside ops, or to have them at all aware of our presence in Honolulu. To further complicate the issue, we have been unable to track the residential whereabouts of the Changs. Officer Watson reports that they have purchased property in Honolulu, but we can find no record of any purchase in their names. There are so many property transfers in Hawaii, and so many of them by Asian buyer/sellers, that we have as yet been unable to pinpoint their location. Also, we think they may be traveling by private jet, which is another curveball. If they should slip through our fingers, they could be out of the country again in the blink of an eye. We also have Officer Watson to deal with. She will be Mrs. Chang's houseguest, and we can't do anything that would jeopardize her safety or wellbeing. The last thing we want, is a hostage situation here."

"Any suggestions?"

Barbara Estes interjected. "If Tricia is arriving on Thursday, that gives us approximately twelve hours to ascertain her location. I would be hesitant to plant any bugs or surveillance equipment on her, as the Changs might have anti-surveillance sweep systems in place. This could immediately compromise her status, and could put her in danger. Something as simple as a cell phone call to her son could be enough to allow us to track her."

"Agreed," Steve countered. "Especially as we will be following any airport pickup vehicle, we will know their approximate location. But there is the possibility there is no reception, and the use of a cell phone is not an option? Or the Changs don't allow the use of cell phones in their home?"

"We will just have to wait and see what happens. But we will get to them one way or another, and once we have an approximate location, we should be able to proceed. If they are in a secluded location, then they are more isolated, and vulnerable. If they are in an urban setting, we can isolate them. If they are in a clustered development, such as a large condominium project, we are at more of a disadvantage to identify their specific location. Assuming there is a central office in this type of a scenario, it could be a resource, as long as they are not hostiles. If they are, we must proceed with the utmost care. There is also the possibility of bodyguards or other armed personnel on their premises. We must be extremely careful here."

"Indeed". Barbara spoke again. "Maybe we could have Tricia just stay downtown at the Outrigger or somewhere, and not allow her to stay with the Changs. If she did stay with the Changs, should she carry her service revolver? This would give her some protection, but could also be a tell. I doubt if the Changs would make their guests submit to metal detectors on the way into the house, but who knows. Maybe we just pick up Mrs. Chang at the airport, and look for Mr. Chang later."

"That would cause problems. We need both Changs at one time. Only one or the other of them would be counterproductive, as well as creating a flight risk."

"I don't have a problem with Tricia carrying a piece. We will need to get her something out of evidence, that is not service connected. Just a small caliber weapon of some kind. Something a woman traveling might carry for her personal safety."

The US Attorney weighed in. "I'm no electronics specialist, but I know we have bugs with tracking devices. Maybe something Tricia could deactivate on the way in. That way she could avoid any kind of internal detection, but also give us some directional assistance."

"All these options are doable," said Steve. "Our objective here, is to isolate the Changs and Tricia together in a timely manner. If we can apprehend them anytime on Thursday, prior to Friday's stateside arrests, we can hold them incommunicado, until the appropriate time. We have already begun to work with the Hawaiian agencies and the authorities who will be involved with our ops. Tricia, what are your feelings on the subject?"

"I have a week and a half to try and get as much information out of Sui Chang as I can. I think I can get her farther down the road in that area. My only problem would be the relationship I have been trying to build might now be compromised by Charlie and his people trying to pull out of their deal. We could have a problem here. As far as carrying a weapon, it might come in useful, and I think there is a reasonable rationale for such a position."

"Steve, we need to get tech ops on this, and do our electronic due diligence. If Tricia is emailing Sui Chang, it is something we can track. If Tricia can get Sui's cell phone number, that would be a slam dunk. Then we've got her. If she is using any major system, a smart iPhone, AT@&T, Gmail, AOL, with a lap top computer, etc. we are all over her."

"Right on, Barbara. I will get Tech involved not only on the tracking, but a transmitting device. Just something helpful if we needed it. It seems like we need to focus on Thursday as the day to proceed on the Changs. If they go out for dinner Thursday night, or if they stay in, as long as they are together, we move. Again, the challenge is timing, their security, and their location."

Everyone agreed on this overview, and also agreed we they should meet again on Friday morning at ten am. Steve Rodriguez offered his Portland FBI offices.

Steve and Tricia sat in her car after the meeting, and continued to strategize.

"I am very concerned with the shipments being curtailed. What will this do to my relationship with Sui?" Tricia reiterated.

"She does not see you as a part of that process, does she?"

"Not really. Although I was a part of the last shipment. Remember when Charlie and the boys were down in San Francisco?"

"Oh, yeah."

"Well, what can I do but play it by ear? If she thinks I am in on the deal, maybe she will think I can help in some way. I think I need to let her take the lead. I will try to communicate my support for them. But, I just don't know what their thought process is going to be. Sui Chang is much more pleasant than Mr. Chang. He is kind of a dick. I hope this plays out okay."

"Well, you will do the best you can. Anything you can uncover, call me immediately. This is going to be our best shot anyway. Good luck."

"Thanks. Kiss me goodbye."

CHAPTER FORTY-FOUR

Charlie received several calls during the week from Bao Thieu. "Mr. Chang is not happy. We made a deal. If you change the deal, Mr. Chang is prepared to move all of Han Say's shipping up to Seattle."

"Let me see what I can do," Charlie replied to him. "We are getting a little heat around here on our side, and we are just trying to be careful. No reason to jeopardize anyone."

"Yes, no reason. Except now our supply lines might be interrupted, and we could have no special product to deliver to our customers. This makes Mr. Chang very nervous."

Charlie was between a rock and a hard spot. His people wouldn't handle any more of the shipments, which without saying so to Bao Thieu, was probably the right thing for them to do. But, on the other hand, he certainly didn't want to lose Han Say's business. Especially to Seattle/Tacoma.

After reflecting for a couple of days, he called Mr. Thieu. "Why don't you just continue to ship your product inside of one of your super containers, and let someone else process it as a secondary handler. I will do everything I can do to support that on this end. I know it will slow your distribution process down in the beginning, but in the long run it would also save you a lot of money."

Mr. Thieu also took a few days of conferring with Mr. Chang, but they finally agreed this was an agreeable solution to their problem. Mr. Thieu would have to work out different logistics on his side, but he would make it work. It would no longer be Charlie's problem to deal with.

Tricia continued to email with Sui Chang. She was so excited to be coming to Hawaii, she had never been, etc. When were the Changs coming in? What clothes should she bring? Would they be going out a lot, or staying in? Were they going to be at a pool or the beach? If so, what beach? She had heard all about Waikiki, would they be going there? Were they going to be close to Waikiki? What if her plane was late? Shouldn't she have Sui's cell phone number?" Could they go climb Diamond head? Can we ride horses on the beach?

Sui was distant at first. Unbeknownst to Tricia, Sui was under instructions from Mr. Chang to cancel their plans. But as the shipping details with Charlie were smoothing out, Mr. Chang calmed down, and Sui started to be herself again. She was amused by what she considered Tricia's youthful exuberance. In her own regal manner, she began to calm Tricia down.

Bring a combination of things to wear.

Like what are we doing my first night? I want to look so special for you.

Mr. Chang will decide. Just bring lots of stuff, and I will dress you every morning and evening. You need some formal wear, and lots of casual wear. I need a new cell phone. I will give you the number when you get here, etc. Yes, we are close to Waikiki and Diamond head, yes, we can go there. Wear a skirt on the plane. Sui Chang was being her usual, inscrutable self.

Tuesday's Task Force meeting was a rehash of last weeks. Ray had a handgun for Tricia, and Steve reported they had been tracking Sui and Tricia's emails. The Changs were still in Taipei, but there was a manifest for a private Lear Jet 60SE arriving on Wednesday from Taipei. Steve felt sure this was their target coming in, and he was researching the international registration of the jet. They would also be tracking any and all activity surrounding the sleek private aircraft once it hit the ground. The earlier they could establish a residential location, the better, and the FBI's vast resources were now at work. Steve would personally be in Hawaii to oversee the operation, and his counterpart in San Francisco, Special Agent in Charge Rich Stevenson would be handling the Chinatown roundup in the bay area.

Tricia was able to provide info to Steve that the Changs were located somewhere around Waikiki, but not much other personal information on Sui or her whereabouts. She would keep the email activity up as much as possible, to allow the techs to keep on tracking Sui.

Ray was on the van pickup Friday late morning, and would be working with Barbara Estes' people on this particular patrol. He was ready to proceed with Charlie Strong and amigos, when given the go signal by Steve Rodriguez. Barbara was now in San Francisco, preparing and ready to help the US Attorneys start sifting through the mountain of information they hoped to impound down there.

Tricia was excited to be finally getting under way. She stayed in Portland, and had lunch with Steve. He was leaving for Hawaii first thing in the morning, and she wouldn't leave until Thursday. Too bad they couldn't travel together, but he wanted to get there and start digging in. She thought it would be very nice if they might be able to spend some time alone together, after all their business was done. So did he, actually.

They kissed good bye. “You be careful,” Steve told her. “Do whatever you have to do to be safe. Be especially nice to Sui Chang, so that she has no suspicions. And this is an order, you call me as soon as you get off of your plane, before you exit the secured area. I will be able to give you an update on what we have uncovered to date over there.”

“You be careful too, baby.”

Back at Rosewood, we had our first Board of Trustees meeting under our new President and Vice President. I was excited to begin a new chapter with our Board, but after the meeting, it seemed like more of the same old stuff to me.

Bruce opened the meeting with the approval of the minutes. Then he launched into his first introductory remarks as our new Prez. “We are hoping for new energy on the Board, as we leave our recent problems in the past, and proceed to carry out our mission to be the finest golf course in the Northwest, etc.” He pontificated on creating some member surveys which would help set the board in the direction the collective pulse of the membership would articulate. Since the surveys were going to be done professionally, they would take some time to process. it would take a while to create them, release them to the membership, then properly assess the results, etc.

This could take months to accomplish, and by then we would be approaching summer, and the club would be too busy to do anything other than keep up with operations. So, in effect, he was giving us nothing of substance. Nothing relevant, from my standpoint, was going to happen in the coming year. “What about the barrier between the bar and the dining room which is so sorely needed?” I inquired.

“Larry is looking into some temporary dividers. We have also discussed the necessity for stricter supervision in the bar area, when there are events going on in the dining room.”

Seriously? That's it? You are going to put up some portable screens, and call that a solution? I looked at the women members of the Board. Marta Koenig was unfortunately not present, due to a prior commitment. But Toni Duncan, continued the issue. "Do you think this approach will be sufficient, considering the major problem we just encountered?"

"Yes. Yes, I do." responded Bruce Cranston. "I believe this is the most appropriate, and most fiscally responsible approach for all of us. At least until we get the results back from our member survey."

I interjected. "Larry, as a hospitality industry professional, I do not feel like this is an adequate attempt to mitigate our comprised, and conflicted clubhouse sectors. I have personally seen how an upgrade to the physical facilities, can and will be a direct stimulus to added membership and increased revenues for our club. I would like to volunteer to form an Architectural Review Committee, and really begin to look at the feasibility of doing some meaningful renovation around here."

"I volunteer for the committee," Toni Duncan said.

"That won't be necessary at this time," Bruce finalized the conversation for us. "While an approach of this kind might stimulate some new members, it would also potentially drive away many of our existing older members, who are not interested in a club assessment at this time of their membership. Maybe if our professional member surveys articulate a preference for a refurbished facility, we can pursue a reasonable objective at a later date."

Sarah Richards raised her hand, and in spite of Bruce's obvious reluctance to go there, made a motion to go ahead and form an Architectural Review Committee. Her motion was seconded by Toni Duncan. Sarah mentioned that the clubhouse was old, and in disrepair. "We have inadequate facilities that actually disrupt operations. As the House Committee Chair of this club, I am referring to the raw sewage problem in the kitchen. Raw sewage! It occurs at the worst possible times, is unsanitary, and could possibly shut us down if the health inspector should come by at the wrong time. It is also a terrible morale factor for the kitchen staff, and sends an awful message to them about our commitment to supporting their operational areas. Then there is the obvious issue of the bar/dining room separation. The downstairs locker rooms are a disgrace, the carpets and window coverings are obsolete, not to mention threadbare. The décor is mid nineteen sixties anyway." She finished her motion, with the editorial comment that, "It is time we step up to the plate and get our heads out of the sand around here."

I thought Sarah summed up the situation pretty well. It was just the tip of the iceberg in reality. And so, Bruce called for all Board members who were in favor of forming an AR Committee to raise their hands. Sarah, Toni, Matt Mitchell, and I raised our hands. All opposed? We were out voted seven to four. I looked at Toni in frustration, and shook my head. She gave me an annoyed nod in return.

"There are several more items of business, before we get to the committee reports," Bruce said. "One, is the disciplinary action against Hugh Schmidt. I can report that Mr. Schmidt has contacted Larry Easton, and would like to have his appeal hearing as soon as possible. It would be preferable if we could schedule his hearing next week before Thanksgiving. Is next Thursday evening acceptable for the Board?"

We all agreed it was doable, and thought it wise to get this last portion of unpleasant business out of the way as soon as possible.

"And the last item of business, is a minor reorganizing of our Finance Committee. In my early review of this department, both Joe Goldman and I feel that it is imperative going forward, to form a new, super committee. This committee would do a great service to the club and to the board. It will now co-ordinate all of our capital and our replacement expenditures going forward. This would take a great load off of Joe as Treasurer, would help organize and itemize our future obligations, and we have agreed on a structure for this new committee. Myself, as President, would be the Chair of the committee. The past president of the Board would sit on the committee, as well as Joe Goldman who would serve a five-year term. The Board would appoint two other past Board members to sit on the committee for five-year terms. We will have a list available, should this proposal be approved. From this list, the Board can start the selection process of the other two committee members at the next Board meeting. Any discussion?" Charlie Strong, who would be sitting on this new committee, as the past President, was quiet as a church mouse. He hadn't said much all night, but he had been heard loud and clear by his voting record. And there was no doubt which way he would vote on this issue.

What the heck, I thought to myself. They are appropriating all future spending of the club into one powerful, and biased committee? They are essentially gutting the Finance Committee of any vestige of power or input? Whose brilliant power grab, I mean idea, is this? These good old boys will have complete power and control over all future appropriations and expenditures. Any idea of some much-needed clubhouse upgrades was fading fast into sunset. Wow, I thought. These guys are brighter and more aggressive than even I expected them to be.

"Uh, this is a major exit from the guidelines of our Bylaws, ladies and gentlemen. I hope there will be an extended feasibility study of the potential fallout of this new and radical departure from our established structure." I wasn't at all happy, which people could probably read this from my comments.

Toni Duncan weighed in, as did Sarah. After some halfhearted discussion. Joe Goldman made a motion to accept the reorganizing proposal which was under discussion. It was seconded by Rick Ferin. All in favor say aye. The same seven hands that shut down the Architectural Review Committee were raised, as well as the same four hands who were in the process of losing their second major motion of the evening.

The rest of the evening went uneventfully. November was a quiet time of the year, and the committee reports were short and sweet. There being no further business, the meeting was adjourned.

What a fiasco this place getting to be. My thoughts were tumbling around like a swimmer going down for the third time. I was just about ready to walk away from it all right then. Toni Duncan left the clubhouse right behind me. "What just happened in there?" she asked me.

"Bend over, we just took it in the shorts," I replied, laughing derisively.

CHAPTER FORTY-FIVE

Steve made a seamless touchdown into Honolulu. It was pretty nice to be FBI, and not have to jump through all the security hoops civilians are forced to endure.

He was picked up by the Special Agent in Charge of the Hawaiian Islands. They connected with their units and the debriefings began. The private jet sector of the airport was under surveillance, and file photos of the Changs had been released to customs officials, and FBI personnel. The suspect Lear Jet was due in late Wednesday afternoon, and it could accommodate up to eight passengers. The flight manifest for the 60SE indicated a pilot, a co-pilot, an attendant, and four passengers, none of whom was named Chang. If in fact this was the Changs, they were already in trouble for filing false documents. Maybe Chang was a nom de guerre. Who knows?

The FBI office in Honolulu was tracking the names on the manifest, with real estate transactions in Honolulu, and hopefully a connection could be made soon. There would be an FBI agent accompanying the customs agent, upon the jet's entry inspection into US territory.

Tricia was greeted by a cold rainy Thursday morning, and was impatient to get to the airport. She hugged her son goodbye, and promised him presents. Lots of presents.

"I want a live porpoise, Mom," he told her importantly.

"I'll do my best, kid," she replied, and winked at her Mom. They hugged, and Junior was off to meet his school bus. Tricia was very psyched, and excited to get on the road. She had been waiting for this day for years.

It was an easy drive to the airport. In spite of the morning rain, Tricia got there in no time and parked in the long-term lot. She had a big roller bag to check, and also a pretty good-sized carry on. As a police officer, she could have carried her weapon onto the plane, but she didn't want to create suspicions. She just checked her bag in like any civilian, and made her way to security.

Another easy leg of the trip on Hawaiian Air. She dozed off, she read a little bit, did a crossword puzzle, and before she knew it, she was gliding down the tarmac in Honolulu. She was finally here, and especially excited talk to Steve.

"Hi, how are you? It's me."

"Aloha. You had a good flight?"

"Smooth. Seemed like I was only flying up to Seattle."

"Well, we are making good progress here. We had a positive ID yesterday evening at the airport. The Changs came in on a private Lear Jet, although their names and ID were registered differently. Maybe the other name is their real name. Anyway, we followed them to a high rise in Honolulu. It looks like they bought the penthouse condominium, which is on top of the building. Twenty fourth floor. It is very posh. Hopefully they were able to catch up on their sleep, as Taiwan is ten hours behind Hawaii. But they aren't picking you up until late afternoon today, so they should be okay."

"What is the plan?"

"Well, we figure we will just wait until the wee hours, four AM Hawaiian time, and if we have an all clear from you, we will go in. We are based right directly under your unit. There is an empty condo on the floor below you, and we commandeered it from the building manager."

"Ah, that's reassuring. Who were the other two passengers?"

"Two males. They looked like bodyguards or security personnel. I believe they are also staying at the penthouse. We have good communication with the admin office of the building, and we have full access to the property. Actually, one of our agents was issued a doorman's uniform, and is now on staff. He is working the building. This arrangement could have been a lot more complicated, so we are happy with what we've got. We will pop the front door at four. I have a floor plan from the building manager to work with, so I think we are in pretty good shape."

"Impressive work, Agent Rodriguez. How big is the condominium?"

"It is a six bedroom, with a three-hundred-and-sixty-degree panorama view."

"Should we have a code or anything?"

"Might not be a bad idea. Just put me on speed dial, and if there is a problem, call me and say 911. It also might be good if you can find out anything about Mr. Chang's schedule tomorrow. If we grab them in the morning, he may have some kind of early appointment or something. Something he could miss, which might send up a red flag."

"I will see what I can do, but getting any information out of these people is like pulling teeth."

"Just remember, if anything negative happens I am very close and will bring my posse with me.

"Again, most reassuring. Anything else we need to cover?"

"Just take care of the Changs. Keep them happy tonight. Work with them. They still don't suspect anything. Also, call me before you go to bed."

"I will, and I'll use the utmost discretion."

"Bye for now. See you tomorrow, be careful."

"I will. Love you, Bye."

Tricia grabbed her carry-ons, and headed for baggage claim.

Her bag rolled down the ramp in fifteen minutes, and Tricia was met at the terminal's exit by a chauffeur. He was holding up her name on a square, neatly lettered, homemade sign.

She acknowledged him, and he gestured her to the street. "Right this way, ma'am."

They crossed over into the commercial waiting area, and angled back to a waiting black, stretch limo.

The chauffeur opened the rear passenger door for her, and she jumped in, and fell into the waiting arms of Sui Chang. The women hugged, and Tricia plopped onto the back, rear bench style seat of the limo next to Sui.

"You like glass of champagne?"

"Sure, sure," Tricia replied. "Here, let me get it."

The bottle was already open, so Tricia poured for herself, and then refreshed Sui's glass.

"How was your flight?"

"Very smooth. It is so warm and tropical here. I like it already."

"Hawaii very nice place. We like very much. Come here, give me kiss."

Tricia was hoping that Sui wasn't going to be too aggressive, but she never knew. Sui picked up a remote, and before she closed the curtains that separated the cab from the pleasure end of the limo, she instructed the driver to tour around the island for an hour, while the girls talked. Then she closed the curtains, and pulled Tricia to her.

It was going to be tough to do too much talking, with Sui Chang's tongue in her mouth, but Tricia soldiered on. They embraced for what seemed to Trish like an hour. Sui's mini-skirt was climbing, which can happen in a limo, and Tricia could see Sui's black, mesh panties, that were becoming more and more visible.

Tricia pulled away. She looked at Sui and said, "You look tired. Come here." She put her arm around Sui, and pulled her head onto her breast, hoping against hope that Sui might want to relax for a bit. Maybe even doze off.

All that did was make Sui want to play with her breasts, and soon Tricia's skirt was also rising. Sui had her head on Tricia's left breast, and her hand between Tricia's legs. Tricia felt like she was back in High School again. Oh my God, she thought to herself, I'm in a limo with an octopus.

"Don't you want to wait until we are home?" Tricia asked.

"Yes, we wait, I am just so happy to see you."

"Me too. Does Mr. Chang know about us?"

"Oh yes. He also likes to play if I invite him, but I want to keep you for myself."

She bent down and kissed Sui on the forehead. "He will behave himself?"

"Oh, he does what I tell him, and I take good enough care of him."

The next thing Tricia knew, Sui had shifted, and was kneeling between her legs. Tricia's skirt was now up towards her waist, and she could feel Sui's hands caressing her. She began to weaken. She closed her eyes. She let her head fall back on the soft limo headrest. She let her body relax.

When their ride ended, Tricia popped out of the dark, cool limousine, and into the bright, tropical sunshine. "Please, can we go out for dinner tonight? Let me treat you and Mr. Chang, you have done so much for me," she asked Sui Chang.

"Let me check with Mr. Chang. He doesn't like to go out too much."

"Oh please. You said he would do whatever you asked him."

"Sometimes. Most of the time. But not all of the time."

"I would love to go to Buzz's Steak House in Kailua. I have several friends who have been there. They loved it so much. President and Mrs. Clinton even ate there."

"Well, he does like a good steak. I will ask him."

"Please, please. Make him say yes." Tricia was ready to call Steve right then. "We are going to Buzz's for dinner," she would tell him. "Come arrest these people now, and get me away from this aggressive woman whose hormones are like a horny teenager."

The doorman opened the glass entryway for the ladies. There were two doormen actually, and the new young man offered to help take the luggage up to the Penthouse. They rode together in silence to the twentieth fourth floor, where Sui Chang unlocked the huge mahogany doors to the unit. She showed Tricia to her guest suite and master bath. "You unpack, and I will go talk to Mr. Chang. I have pretty things for you to wear tonight. I will come and dress you." Oh God, Tricia thought.

Tricia discretely rolled her eyes at the doorman, and Sui Chang left the room. "Please put my carry-on bag in the restroom," she told him. She followed him in, and gave him an "are you who I think you are look?" He nodded ever so slightly.

"I think we are going to Buzz's Steak House in Kailua tonight," she whispered to him. "Tell Steve to run them in tonight right after dinner."

He nodded again, and left the room and the deluxe condominium.

An hour later Sui knocked softly on the door and entered Tricia's suite. Tricia was resting on her king-sized bed. Sui had a beautiful tropical print, sheath frock over her arm, and some lingerie in her hand. "Here, love, this is for you. It's a Bergdorf Goodman. Let's take a shower. We have seven o'clock reservation. We get dressed, and go to lanai and have glass of wine. Watch sunset."

"We are going to Buzz's?"

"Mr. Chang say yes, but only if he can to sleep with us tonight."

Oh my God, again, Tricia thought. Sui Chang was one thing to deal with, but the thought of Mr. Chang's filthy little hands made her skin crawl.

"Sure. That sounds like fun. At least he wants to go out tonight. What a pretty dress."

"Come. I will run the shower, and we will try it on for you."

The guest suite's shower was one of Sui Chang's pride and joys. It was earth toned, Italian marble, with a dozen shower heads. It could cascade water on a person from any and every angle. It pulsed, it misted, it had attachments, it had a bench to sit on, if you wanted to take a steam bath. There were heat lamps, you could actually tan while you were taking a shower. It was big enough for Tricia's high school basketball team's starting five.

Sui took Tricia's hand and led her into the bathroom. She raised Tricia's arms, and slipped her sun dress over her head. It dropped on the floor. She slipped out of her own dressing robe. Then she unclasped Tricia's bra, and knelt in front of her, and began to pull her panties down. She took one of Tricia's cheeks in each hand, and bent forward and kissed her mound.

She reached in and tested the water temperature. Turning back, she put her arms around Tricia in an embrace. They then had the most erotic/exotic shower Tricia had ever experienced.

Sui Chang, it seems, was a master with the loofah sponge, and Tricia was so spanking clean by the time Sui was through going over her, she didn't think she would ever have to shower again. It was ecstasy at a glacial pace for Tricia. Sui gently scrubbed her from head to toe. Then massaged her with gardenia scented coconut oil. Afterwards, they had a steam, and Sui Chang made her moan all over again.

Finally, the royal shower was over. They toweled off, and Sui led Tricia into the bedroom. She picked up the scantiest pair of thong panties, and had Tricia step into them. Next, she had a matching, mini pushup bra for the occasion. It provided some support, but was also very provocatively revealing. Tricia's nipples got hard just having Sui's fussing around over her. Teasing her, Sui hugged her before she slipped the sheath dress over her shoulders.

"You look so beautiful. We do this every day. You like?"

Tricia smiled dreamily at her, and said, "You should go put some clothes on. We will never make it to dinner."

Sui Chang went into the bathroom, and retrieved her dressing gown. She came out, and kissed Tricia on the mouth, before she left the room. Tricia picked up her cell phone as soon as Sui was out of the bedroom door, and walked back into the bathroom. She closed the door, hit Steve's contact number, and he picked up on the first ring.

"We are going to Buzz's Steak House. Reservation at seven. Please, please grab them after dinner. I can't come back here. This is bad."

"Ten four," he replied, and hung up.

Mr. Chang opened a bottle of Pouilly Fuisse, and they enjoyed the nectary atmosphere, and the brilliant Hawaiian sunset on the lanai. Soon enough, the lingering sun faded, and it was time for the twenty-minute drive to the restaurant. Mr. Chang announced that John Fong would accompany them, for security purposes. He wouldn't be eating with them, but would be nearby in case of any emergency. They arose with effort from their sunken, deeply padded chaise lounges.

By the time Mr. Chang's group set out for dinner, due to the three-hour time difference, Hugh Schmidt's disciplinary hearing was over in Rosewood's conference room. Hugh had requested his attorney be present. "Sorry, not admissible, Mr. Schmidt. This is not a court of law. It is an informal hearing only."

"Then I would request permission to record the proceedings."

"You may record whatever you please, Mr. Schmidt."

"Rosewood has assailed the wrong person," Hugh began. "I, am the victim here. I was at a meeting with a friend, who happens to be a reporter. Trouble broke out, which I did not start. As a matter of fact, I studiously sought to avoid getting involved in the fracas. Which is more than I can say for some people in this room. I have been a member here for almost ten years. Bunny and I have never had any problems of any sort at this club. We are embarrassed to be put in this position by the Board, and are trusting you will see fit to correct any misperceptions concerning our membership. We feel strongly we should be reinstated immediately. We should be issued a written apology, which would categorically absolve us of any and all culpability which occurred at this club this past November the seventh."

Bunny was just as strident in her comments. "You have falsely accused my husband of misconduct, which has been a huge embarrassment to our family. This has caused a difficult, almost unmanageable amount of stress in our lives. Our son has been teased and harassed at school. We have been affected socially, and many club members have not only snubbed us in public, but have snidely insulted our family, and spread vicious rumors about us. Neither of us are sleeping well. We are having problems operating our business, which has negatively impacted our personal income. This is a steep price to pay for stopping into our club's bar to have a beer with a friend, and being forced to watch the president of this club defile himself in front of a large portion of the membership. The same president, whose actions necessitated the Vancouver Police to be called into this clubhouse. What a disgrace he is to all of us, but who still sits on the Board of Trustees of this club. How is it possible that Charlie Strong sits in this room unscathed, and my family is being persecuted by this organization? You want to dishonor us, who did nothing but try to act as peacemakers in this disgusting fiasco, but the real problems are in this room. And they have nothing to do with us. It is you, the Board of Trustees, some of your Board members, and your questionable decisions that have caused so many problems." Bunny, never one to shy from controversy or speaking her mind, was a lot more adamant and protective of her husband, then even he had been of himself. But with her direct reference to Charlie Strong and the autocratic approach of the Board, she burst into audible sobs and effectively lost complete control of her emotions.

Bruce needed to get this discussion back on firmer footing for Rosewood, and he began his counter attack when Bunny, who was still sobbing quietly into the tape recorder, had said her piece.

"Mr. and Mrs. Schmidt, there is a considerable disparity in your stated position, and the reality of your conduct around our premises. You say that you have never had any disciplinary problems at the club, but we have it on numerous accounts, and from widely varying sources, that you, in particular Mr. Schmidt, have been difficult, dismissive, rude and abrasive to our staff and management. You also say that you were meeting a friend at the club, when the problems occurred. In reality, this so called "friend" of yours, was a random reporter who was chasing around after police cars, looking for a storyline. You egregiously extended her another such opportunity, by championing her admission into our bar at a very sensitive time. The Board of Trustees has determined that your willful act caused irreparable harm and damage to Rosewood's image and reputation. This type of behavior is strictly prohibited in our bylaws. And not only did you help perpetrate and magnify the internal problem which was transpiring, you defied our General Manager. After he specifically forbade the young woman in question from taking any pictures, you are alleged to have shared your own video footage with this reporter. Mr. Schmidt did this with the explicit knowledge it would be embarrassing and harmful to the best interests of this club. It was the same video that was publicly aired on regional television, and could only have come from you.

Finally, Mr. Schmidt, I must remind you how our own Vancouver Police handled the case. They publicly called this a very minor internal incident, and dismissed any further actions. Which is why Mr. Strong, who has served this club and this membership faithfully for many years, and who has resigned his Presidency of this club, still sits on this Board of Trustees."

Hugh spoke again. "Mr. Cranston, you have absolutely no proof, and I categorically deny releasing any video footage taken in this club house to my friend. You also have absolutely no proof, concerning any prior engagement I may or may not have made with this friend. If you would please recall, our neighborhood has been the subject of an incredible amount of press coverage, ever since the savage attack on Mr. Kudlach. We have developed many friendships through this process, and this was one of them. My friend will be happy to corroborate our arrangement to this Board of Trustees, or in a court of law if necessary.

Also, no one has ever spoken to myself or my wife about any inappropriate conduct of ours here at this club. And to me this reeks of something similar to vigilante justice, and after the fact hearsay. If we were remiss at all in our conduct, you as the managers and directors of this club, were at fault for not bringing it to our attention sooner. We might then have been able to remedy any issues. Instead, you did nothing until now. This is despicable, and I have nothing further to say."

"Do any of the Board members have any further questions of Mr. and Mrs. Schmidt? No? Thank you then, for coming in this evening to present your position. I will contact you by certified mail tomorrow morning of the decision of the Board of Directors."

The Schmidts departed. And the Board deliberated no more than fifteen minutes. Toni Duncan felt that the Schmidts had a point about the charges against them being based on conjecture. But the circumstantial nature of the evidence against Hugh Schmidt and the leaked videos, if in fact it were true, and all indications were that it was, was simply overwhelming. Larry Easton saw what he saw. And it was Hugh shooting video on his cellular phone.

"Where would she get the footage she had, if Hugh didn't give it to her? The events she reported on and aired to the public, occurred before she was even physically in our bar. It was impossible for her to witness those events without someone's assistance. And I saw no one with, or around her, besides Hugh Schmidt."

Largely based on Larry eyewitness account, and in a secret ballot, the Board voted ten to two to expel the Schmidts from Rosewood Golf and Country Club.

Just before we adjourned, Bruce Cranston gave his final instructions to our General Manager, "Larry please compose a short memo to the Schmidts detailing the Board's decision tonight. Initial it in my name, and mail it out by certified mail to the Schmidts first thing in the morning. Better yet, call one of the courier services in town, and have it hand delivered. For all of our sakes, this chapter is now closed."

The Schmidts on the other hand, didn't go straight home, but stopped off at their legal advisor, one Carol Horn, for a glass of wine.

"We nailed it," Hugh Schmidt crowed to Carol and Neil. "They even let us record the proceedings on your tape recorder. They have no plausible platform for proceeding against us. We refuted every one of their positions."

"Good job you two," Carol said. "And I have some more great news. Bob and Lillian are coming home tomorrow. They will be home for the Holidays. How's this for a special treat?"

"Hell yes, I like it. How is he doing?"

"Apparently, he is well into the healing process, and there won't be any lingering after affects. We will have to have a gathering this weekend to welcome them home. In the meantime, I would strongly suggest you speak with your friend, the reporter. Relate to her the latest developments concerning your expulsion. She might have a spot for you on the news."

"I will call her tomorrow morning. She is a good kid. She will be only too happy to cooperate with us. I can invite her to Bob's welcome home party if you think it is a good idea."

"Sure, why not. Hey, let's listen to your tape."

CHAPTER FORTY-SIX

The Chang's limousine pulled into Buzz's valet parking lane, and the driver stopped and let his four passengers out. Too bad it was dark by now, and the group was unable to enjoy the spectacular drive through the lush, tropical, botanical valleys between Kailua and Honolulu.

Mr. Chang led the way into the restaurant, and everyone followed the hostess back inside the building, as Mr. Chang had requested a table in the indoor/outdoor bar area. It was a balmy night, and the temperature was still in the mid-seventies. A light breeze was blowing, and the air was fragrant from lilacs that were blooming in the venerable restaurant gardens.

The courtyard boxed in one side of the bar, which served meals as well as a long list of tropical, hand shaken drinks. John Fong parked himself on one of the barstools that faced his employers table, and set about looking preoccupied. The service staff was on them immediately, maybe because both of the women, Sui Chang in her black silk, strapless cocktail dress, and Tricia in her expensive Bergdorf tropical sheath, looked so stunning. Probably because one just got great service at Buzz's anyway. Mr. Chang ordered a round of Mai Tais, and everyone glanced at their menus. Tricia was starving. She not only had had a long day, but an emotionally and physically taxing day as well. She hadn't eaten anything since breakfast.

Looking around the bar, she spotted at least three FBI Agents, and immediately felt better. She hoped they weren't as obvious to John Fong as they were to her. Madame and Mr. Chang were oblivious.

Dinner was fabulous as expected. Expensive, but fabulous. Mr. Chang ordered some sautéed Conch as an appetizer, and Tricia had Hawaiian lobster tail and a petite filet mignon combination. Too bad the circumstances weren't different, and she might have been able to taste some of her food. Trish sat between the Changs, and they made small talk for the most part.

Mr. Chang got a little handsy under the table, but it was nothing Tricia didn't expect, or couldn't handle. "Call me Joung," he told her. She felt like slapping his little weasel face for him.

Tricia offered to pay for dinner, but Sui Chang wouldn't have it. Mr. Chang paid the bill with his Platinum Amex card, the ladies gathered their wraps, while John Fong went to fetch the limousine. It was 9:42 PM and two happy diners, and one extremely apprehensive diner walked out of the restaurant. As soon as the stretch pulled up, it was surrounded by a dozen FBI Agents, with their weapons drawn and trained on the three surprised guests, and the two men in the limo.

The FBI went through the usual procedure. Spread eagle, pat down, Miranda rights, purses and phones confiscated, limo impounded, hand cuffs all around. Half a dozen Honolulu PD mobile units emerged onto the scene. John Fong went into the back of a squad car with Joung Chang, and Tricia was escorted to a squad car with Sui Chang. As quickly as the pinch had materialized, it disappeared, quietly and ominously, back to Honolulu's main downtown Police Precinct.

"What in God's name is going on here?' Tricia blurted, wide eyed, at Sui Chang.

Sui Chang sat in silence, looking straight ahead. She had come so very far in her lifetime, but this night was not in her master plan, and she was in no mood for conversation. She stared straight ahead, and ignored Tricia.

Back at the Precinct, the prisoners were processed, their possessions catalogued, they did their mug shots, and were then escorted back into the bowels of the big station to separate cells, in separate wings. Once out of sight, of course, Tricia was escorted out of the cell block and into the arms of Steve Rodriguez. She was trembling and crying all at once, but she was hugging Steve in a death grip. "Oh, thank you, thank you," she said to him. "It was awful. I think they were going to kidnap me for a sex slave, or something terrible."

Steve held her in his arms until she calmed down. He sent one of his agents to take Tricia to the Outrigger Hotel in Waikiki, and told her he would be there presently. "I still have to secure the Penthouse condo, collect anything of importance there, and grab the other security guy. If there is anything else of value around, we have to get it now."

The Precinct knew exactly what to do. Hold the Changs incommunicado, until noon tomorrow, and then let them make their phone calls. There would be no bail for them.

Steve's first call after the arrests, was to Ray Farley at the Vancouver Police Station. "All clear here in Paradise. Everything went as smoothly as planned. No glitches whatever. Proceed as we mapped it out on your end, and pass this conversation on to Barbara Estes."

"Will do, and congratulations. Tricia is okay?"

"She's fine, a little shook up, but fine. We're all good here. See you in a day or two."

"Please grab my stuff for me," Tricia told Steve. "I had two bags."

"I know. I will see you at the hotel as soon as I can get there. Here is the key card."

Steve headed for the Penthouse with the Hawaiian station chief. FBI agents were waiting downstairs in the empty condominium. They had a battering ram, wore Kevlar vests, led a drug canine, and plenty of agents. The plan was just to beat the door down, and secure the premises. Do a thorough scan of the unit. Impound any kind of records, receipts, laptops, drugs, flight plans, etc. Steve wasn't sure if the other security person was going to be in the Penthouse or not. Anyone who was on the premises, would be taken into custody. Once the agents were through with their search and seizure, they would leave a team of agents in the lobby and the hallway, to apprehend anyone who attempted to access the Condo. The last thing Steve needed, was for the daytime domestic maid, or some other low-level personnel to show up, see the forced entry, freak out and call someone.

The FBI team convoyed back to the condominium development. Instead of blasting their way into the penthouse, they took Mr. Chang's keys with them, and quietly slipped in the front door. The number two security guard, was sleeping peacefully. Someone kicked the bed, and before he could react, he was overwhelmed. The residence was quickly searched, and everything of value was loaded into a waiting FBI van. There were no other personnel in the residence, so Steve left the provisional FBI crew in place and wrapped up operations at that location. He grabbed Tricia's bags on the way out, and headed back to the Outrigger. He still had to touch base with FBI personnel in Reno, in order to help with the raid on the Oriental Casino. And he had to contact the Honolulu airport, and request a lockdown on the Chang's Lear Jet. He also wanted to take the Chang's laptops back to Portland with him.

For now, he just needed to get a few hours of sleep. In spite of how well this first leg of the operation had gone, it had been a long day, and he had a couple of even longer days ahead of him.

He keyed quietly into their room at the Outrigger, sure Tricia would be asleep. But she was still awake, just lying in bed and waiting for him.

"You did well today kiddo," he said to her.

"Thanks. I thought everything went very smoothly. How did it go tonight? Thank God, we wrapped it up when we did. Come to bed."

"Let me brush my teeth."

Steve rolled into bed, and Tricia put a bear hug on him that said, please don't leave me for a very long time. They kissed, and she dropped off into what would be a restless sleep in about half a minute.

Although it was three hours later on the West Coast, and getting into the wee hours, Ray had taken Steve's call, and assured him that his team was ready for phase two of the op. When the transfer vehicle, the Ford Econoline van, entered the Port of Vancouver shipping lot, FBI agents disguised as City of Vancouver maintenance workers, would check the vehicle weight of the van on the scales they had laid out earlier in the week.

When the vehicle exited, they would carefully and quickly check the exit weight. If there was a discrepancy, then the product had been transferred, and van was in, to use layman's terms, a shit storm. There would be no margin for error here, because each vehicle's ingress and egress times were recorded, and matched to the digital read out weight and times on the scales. As soon as the van's cargo was IDed, calls would be made to the Chinatown and Oriental Casino FBI and DEA units to proceed at those locations.

At nine fifty-five am, Pacific Standard Time, the white commercial van in question, pulled up to the Port of Vancouver facilities. It was promptly waved through at the entry gate security check point. At ten am, Donny and Harlan loaded the two steel drums into the cargo section of the commercial vehicle, and received the payoff package from Bao Thieu's drivers. They in turn, gave it to the casual longshoreman, who had been recruited by Rick to be the runner, and he took off for the office. The van pulled out of the security gate of the Port of Vancouver at zero ten hundred hours and twelve minutes.

As soon as the van was out of visual range, the FBI checked the scales, verified the weight differential, and radioed Ray Farley. He immediately called his best patrolman Willy Davis and his partner, and told them their target was on its way. Next, he called Steve Rodriguez in Hawaii to tell him that the Vancouver op was in progress, and all the systems were cleared to proceed in Chinatown and Reno.

Willy was parked to the side of the road, a half mile down the four-lane highway, as if he was on a routine, radar monitoring assignment for speed control. There was a police helicopter overhead, tracking the van. Willy let the vehicle pass, waited ten seconds, and pulled out. He followed the van east for about a mile, before turning on his flashers and pulling it over. Immediately, Willy's back up units were in route to his location.

The backup units really weren't necessary. By the time they got there, the drivers had been subdued, and were already in handcuffs. Their defense would surely rest on ignorance of what was in the drums, and how they were just doing their jobs. Hopefully, for their sakes, this would be plausible in a court of law. For now, they were both on their way to the Vancouver city jail, and the van was headed to the evidence depot.

A dozen agents comprised of both FBI and DEA personnel, stormed Bao Thieu's Chinatown offices, and actually arrested Bao himself, who was jumping up from behind his desk, when they entered the premises. The agents were relieved there was little, if any resistance, but the element of surprise, and planning and coordination of the agencies, had been superb. There had been no leaks, and the bureau had kept their profile low enough on the streets of Chinatown, to avoid attracting any undue attention.

Reno was another success story. Combined FBI and DEA crews, numbering two dozen strong, were in the offices of the Oriental Casino, flashing their Search Warrants, before anyone knew what was happening. They grabbed hard drives, arrested the General Manager, the CFO and the Office manager. Had the safe opened, and generally made a large nuisance of themselves.

There would be so much to sift through, after this particular leg of the mission, it could very well take months and months to sort out. The operators and money behind the Casino, could face the criminal charges of money laundering, but stood to have their day to day operations severely interrupted, and also faced the very realistic contingency of losing their valuable Gambling and Liquor licenses.

Four legs down, one to go, and it gave Ray Farley the greatest pleasure to finish the final lap in this spectacular law enforcement relay. He wanted nothing more than to wrap up his investigation into the Magnolia Street Halloween assault, and on his own terms. The community at large had been badgering him since day one for an arrest in the case, and he had never seen a situation in his dozen years as head of the Department, where both the paper and the visual media were so interested and amped up about an event. Kind of like the Lindberg baby kidnapping in an earlier era or the Patty Hearst situation in San Francisco, had generated so much interest. This particular case had truly captivated the imagination of the entire Vancouver community. Therefore, it had been extremely frustrating for him to sit on the details of the case as long as he had, when the culprit was right at hand, and was known to him from day one. Yet, because of their patience, they had reeled in a much more effective haul.

Ray had had his Chief of Detectives, Larry Larson, shadowing Charlie Strong all day. Charlie left his condominium around eight in the morning, and kept his usual routine of breakfast at the diner on his way into town. He worked until around two thirty, and left his office in Portland, apparently on his way back to Washington State. Ray wanted Charlie arrested in Vancouver if possible, and avoid having to book him into an Oregon PD facility. This was their collar, and Chief wanted the bust to come down in their jurisdiction.

Charlie obliged. He headed for Rosewood, apparently wanting to get nine holes in before dark. He had a new driver, and couldn't wait to start breaking it in. Later on, he had talked Nikki into meeting him for a bite to eat. Just friends he had told her. Let's just talk about stuff. Charlie would not make his dinner date with Nikki. On this night, or any other night.

Larry called Ray and updated him on Charlie's whereabouts. "It appears as if he is going to go out and play a few holes. He is at Rosewood, and he just went and got his clubs, got his windbreaker, and his golf cart out of the cart shed."

How convenient that the Pro Shop and the first tee, sits right next to the parking lot, Ray thought to himself. "Perfect. Let him go out and play. That will give me time to get over there, and we will pick him up in the bar after his round of golf. Don't you think this is ironic to nab him in the very bar where so much of this case has transpired?"

"It's almost surreal boss."

"What about Rick Ferin and Ben Harris?"

"Charlie is our first priority. We get him and take him downtown. I think we can call the other two from the station. Let's just tell them to come down and surrender on their own recognizance. The alternative for them is for us to come out to their homes, and arrest them in front of their families. I would prefer the former, if possible."

"Good call Chief. Still, I will put a car outside of their houses just in case."

"I will have someone drop me off down there in fifteen minutes. Don't let him leave the premises, should he decide to quit his golfing."

"I won't."

Larry Larson went back and sat in his unmarked car. He started the car, turned the heater on, and watched Charlie tee off. It was fifteen hundred hours exactly. He couldn't help thinking how similar Charlie's round of golf was to a condemned man's last meal or cigarette. Too bad Charlie was clueless, he might have enjoyed himself more had he been remotely aware of what was awaiting him.

Charlie played until four thirty, when the late fall, natural light was fading rapidly, and the outside temperature was beginning to noticeably chill down. He played quickly, as he was alone out on the course, and was very happy with his new Titleist 910 driver.

When he finished playing nine holes, Charlie stowed his gear, and headed for the bar. He wanted to have a quick one before going home and freshening up for his date with Nikki.

He took a seat at the bar. "Howdy Leon," he said.

"How ya doin' Charlie? What'll it be?"

"Gimme a shot of Laphroaig will ya. Neat, no rocks. It's cold out there."

"Comin' up."

The bar was about half to three quarters full at ten to five on a Friday evening. Mostly, a happy hour, TGIF type of crowd.

Charlie's drink was in front of him, when Ray and Larry entered the bar through the same side door Charlie had come in. He had downed a couple of sips of the premium, smoky scotch, and was just beginning to relax and warm up, when he was confronted by the two law enforcement officers. Charlie didn't even see them coming, but Leon sure did. Like any good bartender, he knew damn well who the Chief of Police is, and he turned a little pale.

"Charles Strong?"

Charlie half turned, surprised to be addressed so formally, "Yes?"

Ray Farley had drawn his police chief's badge, and was presenting it toward the back of Charlie's turned head. Larry Larson had his hand on his service weapon.

"Charles Strong, you are under arrest for attempted murder one, for the unlawful possession and transportation of a firearm, for aiding and abetting the distribution of a controlled substance, for illegal possession of a controlled substance, and for receiving and concealing undetermined amounts of illicit cash. Please stand up, and place your hands on the rail of the bar."

Charlie turned in disbelief, and stared dumbly at Ray Farley and Larry Larson. His brain went numb, and he was having trouble cognitively processing what was happening. "What the fuck?" he said.

"Please stand up and place your hands on the bar now."

As if to brace himself, Charlie turned to the bar, and knocked the rest of the Laphroaig back in one gulp. He stood up, and placed his hands on the rail of the bar. Ray Farley quickly patted him down, while Larry Larson kept his hand on his service revolver. "You have the right to remain silent, you have the right…." Ray Farley read Charlie his Miranda Rights, while he pulled Charlie's right arm behind his back, and started placing a cuff around Charlie's thick wrist.

You could have heard a pin drop in the shocked bar. Everyone was watching in rapt attention. Leon the barman, who was standing six feet away from the scene, was slack jawed. It happened so quickly, no one even thought to take out their cell phone for a picture or video. Too bad, it would probably have been worth a small fortune to someone.

As rapidly as the whole scene had developed, the officers walked Charlie out of the bar, and were gone. The bar remained quiet for a minute, and then erupted into chaos. Cell phones came out, and were lit up like a giant switchboard. Leon finally regained his wits, and called Larry Easton's office line. "You better get down here now. The cops just came in the bar, and arrested Charlie Strong for murder one."

"What?"

"Yeah, murder one. Kudlach. And a bunch of other stuff, big time stuff. Right here in the bar."

"Holy Mother of God. I'll be right there."

CHAPTER FORTY-SEVEN

Ray and Larry placed Charlie in the back seat of Ray's cruiser, and headed for the station. Ray called his information officer. "Please schedule a press conference for nineteen hundred thirty hours this evening. You, Detective Larson, and myself. Be sure and stress the importance of this meeting to the stations and the papers. They won't want to miss this one."

"You've got him, Chief?"

"Right here in the car."

"Okay. I better go. I've got a lot of calls to make."

"See ya."

Charlie cringed in the back seat of the cruiser. It was well beyond a cringe. It was more of a powerful recoil due to a compelling, life altering spasm from deep within his pancreatic diaphragm. He was busted. Big time busted. It was over for him, and he had brought it all on himself. Shit, shit, shit he thought to himself.

Ray asked Larry to dial Steve Rodriguez, and put the phone on speaker mode. "Steve, hi. Ray Farley here."

"Hello Ray, how is it going?"

"Very well, Steve. We've got Charlie Strong in custody as we speak, and are headed back to the station. I have a press conference scheduled for seven thirty tonight. Am I cleared to disclose the rest of the operation to the press?"

"I think so, Ray. The two elements are tied together so closely, it would be hard to discuss the one without the other. But keep it basic. I'll be back tomorrow, and we can schedule another press conference for Sunday at noon. That will be the time to go into more detail."

"Got it. Would you like me to go ahead and release the time to the press for you?"

"Sure, and that it will be held in the FBI offices in Portland. As far as your conversations tonight, I would just say there was a very extensive corollary operation also taking place, which was in part responsible for the delay in dealing with the Magnolia Street episode. It involved both an international, regional and local drug supply syndicate, and as soon as we have completed processing enough information, we will be disclosing more details Sunday's press release."

"That sounds good, Steve. I'll give them your teaser. I hope they don't kill us for more information tonight."

"Be strong, Ray."

"I will."

Chief Agent Rodriguez knew how much this bust meant to Ray and the Vancouver PD. He was happy to let them break their major scoop to the news agencies. He would be back there soon to finish up his report.

"Let's get Charlie checked in, and call Rick and Ben before we sit down with the press," Ray said to Larry.

"Ten-four, boss."

Charlie sank even further, both literally and figuratively, into the back seat of the patrol car.

Despite the shortness of the turnaround time, all Ray's information officer had to do, was mention to the stations, about an arrest in the Magnolia Street case. By seven, the public conference room in the police station was packed to the rafters with reporters. All of them were in a very clamorous mood, when Ray and Larry Larson entered the room a half hour later.

They took their seats on the dais, and Ray cleared his throat.

"Ladies and Gentlemen, thank you for coming tonight. I am Vancouver Chief of Police Raymond Farley. This is our Chief of Detectives Larry Larson, and this is Information Officer Jenson. I would like to announce an arrest in the assault on Mr. Bob Kudlach three weeks ago tonight. The primary suspect is currently in our custody, and has yet to be arraigned. That will happen on Monday morning. We believe we have compelling evidence against the individual, and we are hoping for a quick and speedy trial to resolve this dismal chapter in Vancouver's history. Are there any questions?"

"Yes, Chief Farley. Are you able to identify the suspect at this time?'

"Yes ma'am, I am. His name is Charles Strong, he is forty-nine years old, and he is a resident of Vancouver." A collective gasp was heard in the room.

"Chief, is this the same Charlie Strong from Rosewood Golf and Country Club?"

"Yes Sir, I believe it is."

"Chief, where did the arrest take place?"

"We apprehended the suspect, at approximately sixteen hundred forty-five hours this evening, in the Rosewood Golf Club Cocktail Lounge."

Cell phones were lighting up. All of the network teams wanted to get a scoop in before seven pm. "Chief, do you believe that the Rosewood Golf Club was at all complicit in this crime?"

"No, we don't. Although the suspect was deeply involved with that organization, to the point that he was the President of the club during the time frame of the assault. We do not believe, nor do we have any evidence, that Rosewood Golf Club was involved in, or had any prior knowledge of the assault. We have nothing that would connect them to this crime in any way."

"Chief, are there any other suspects involved this crime? It's seems rather difficult to consider someone pulling something like this off by themselves."

"There were some peripheral participants, but I am not at liberty to divulge that information at this time."

"Chief, several eyewitnesses have reported that there was a woman who assisted the suspect, as the driver of the getaway vehicle at the crime scene. Do you have any information on this person at this time?"

"I am not at liberty to discuss any other suspects at this time."

"Chief, you say you have compelling evidence implicating Mr. Strong, yet a significant amount of time has transpired between now and the date of the crime. Was there any specific reason that this suspect could not have been arrested sooner?"

"Ladies and Gentlemen, I am now able to announce that there was a very complex, parallel operation proceeding at the same time as the Magnolia Street investigation. There will be a major press conference held Sunday at noon concerning that operation, at the FBI's Portland offices."

Now the room really lit up. All hands in the room were raised.

"Chief, can you give us indication of the nature of this parallel investigation?"

"I can only say that this was an investigation that involved international suspects, and a sophisticated smuggling operation of controlled substances that involved virtually all of our western states. There have been numerous arrests throughout the related regions, and you will have that information on Sunday as well."

"Chief, Charlie Strong is the CEO of the Ports of Portland, Vancouver and Longview/Kelso. Was there contraband coming through, or involving those Ports of Call?"

"All of those details will be disclosed Sunday at the FBI press conference."

"Chief, was the Vancouver Police Department part of an undercover effort working to help solve this smuggling operation?"

"Sorry, but there will be much more information for you Sunday afternoon. Mr. Steve Rodriguez, Special FBI Agent for our Region will conduct the meeting. I am not at liberty to divulge any more information at this time, except to say I would like to thank Detective Larson here, and all of the dedicated staff members of the Vancouver PD who participated in this investigation.

I would also like to recognize the contributions of the Magnolia Street neighborhood, and thank them for their patience and perseverance during this case. We at the Vancouver PD are elated to be able to bring some resolve and closure to them, and to the entire population of our city. We hope everyone will be able to sleep a little better tonight.

With those comments, Chief Farley and his crew departed the room, and left the reporters scrambling. One of the reporters was none other than the infamous Suzie Davis, from Fox Television. She of the Rosewood bar brawl fame, and after calling in her release to the station, she put an immediate call in to Hugh Schmidt's cell phone.

"Hi Hugh, this is Suzie from Fox TV, how are you. Have you heard the news?"

Hugh and Bunny were sitting in Bob and Lillian Kudlach's living room, along with Carol and Neil Horn and several more of the Magnolia Street inner circle. They were drinking a celebratory bottle of Leonetti Merlot, and welcoming their dear friends, the Kudlachs, back home.

"What news are you talking about, Susie?"

"Holy shit Hugh. Vancouver PD just arrested Charlie Strong from Rosewood for the attempted murder of Bob Kudlach. It's all over the news as we speak."

"You are kidding me? You better get over here. I am at Bob Kudlach's house right now, and we have a scoop of our own for you."

"I'll be right there."

Marta Koenig's phone rang, it was Toni Duncan. Bruce Cranston's phone rang, it was Joe Goldman. My cell rang, it was Sara Richards. Word was spreading fast.

"Bruce, this is Joe Goldman. Did you hear the news?"

"Yeah. I better get down to the club, and see what I can do there, if anything."

"Did the letter go out to Hugh Schmidt this morning?"

"I have no reason to think it didn't. Why?"

"Why? Don't you think that is going to be a problem? We eighty-six the guy from the club for misconduct, and later that same day, our ex-president, who is still on the Board, and voted on his disciplinary case is arrested for the attempted murder of one of his best friends. Don't you think that could be a problem, with those litigious assholes?"

"Yeah, I guess it could be. Jeez, what a freaking mess this thing is turning into. What in the world was Charlie thinking?"

"Don't ask me. He is in a world of hurt now. And then this smuggling thing coming down on Sunday, he had to be involved in that as well."

"I will call Larry Easton right now, and check in with him."

"Put your damage control hat on."

"Jesus, I better wear a full-on contamination suit. Holy shit, I just thought of something else. I haven't heard anything from Rick Ferin. I hope he isn't involved in any of this. He and Charlie are thick as thieves you know."

Suzie was at the Kudlachs in fifteen minutes. Hugh introduced her around, and Lillian offered her a glass of wine.

"Thank you, but no thanks. I'm officially on the clock." And to Bob, "It is so nice to see you, welcome home. Are you okay? What an ordeal you have been through."

"Thank you, Suzie. Hugh told us about your work, and on behalf of all of us here on Magnolia Street, I would like to thank you for your support."

"Of course. This whole scene just keeps getting wackier and wackier. I can't believe Charlie Strong would do something like this. Not that he isn't capable of it, but shouldn't someone in his position be a little smarter or wiser or something? How are you anyway, you seem to have recovered well."

"Well, grab your socks here Suzie, have we got another story for you."

"I can't wait."

Bob launched into the tale of the night of the assault, and the incredible story of how the Vancouver PD and the FBI had foiled the attempted assassination. That it had actually been a member of the Vancouver PD in the gorilla suit, with a Kevlar vest on, standing in for Bob himself. "I wasn't injured at all, but have had to lay low, and have been under the supervision of the FBI the last weeks. We had to keep a quiet profile so they could continue their ongoing investigation. Apparently, this involved the international smuggling ring.

Suzie was dumbfounded. "Did you know at the time that Charlie was your attacker?" she asked Bob.

"No, I did not. All of the authorities were mum on that one."

"Do you know who else may have been involved in the attack? Or who was the mystery woman who drove the getaway car?"

"I'm sorry. But I do not have any of that information. The cops and the FBI just came in, and said I was to be targeted on Halloween night. They set up the precautions to prevent any success from the attack, but kept any further details from us."

"Once the murder attempt was dealt with, don't you think this had to involve one of the ports? And possibly even the ILWU? This thing just keeps getting bigger and bigger. I wonder if anyone else from the ports was implicated?"

"Wait Suzie, there's more," Hugh interjected.

"No way, what more could you possibly add to all of this? Charlie's brain was abducted by aliens?"

"This is more on a personal note, but last night, I was officially expelled as a member of Rosewood Golf Club, for our involvement in the bar brawl. And Charlie Strong was sitting there at the Board meeting, as a Board member, and voting on my dismissal. Then today, he is arrested for attempted murder. We have it all on tape. We were just sitting here discussing how much we are going to sue those jerks for."

"Wow, oh wowie, wow. You guys are freaking heroes." And now Suzie felt a personal involvement. As if Hugh's helping her with her earlier exclusive report had caused these annoying problems for him and Bunny.

"Not so much Suzie. Although, many of us suspected Charlie Strong all along. Bob is the man, for having to sit on all he knew. And for so much time."

"Thank you, Hugh. But Suzie, we are all just normal people, trying to live normal lives. I was sworn to secrecy by the officials, but we were actually having a great time in Hawaii on the government's dime."

Both Rick Ferin and Ben Harris had received earlier phone calls requesting their presence at the Vancouver PD. Rick immediately called his attorney, who he had actually been in contact with for the last month anyway. They made arrangements to go downtown together in an hour. Then Rick called Ben. "Did they call you?"

"Yep."

"I am going down in a few minutes with my attorney. He thinks he can get me out of there on my own recognizance. I didn't really discus the charges with them yet. I'm sure it's not going to be good."

"Well, they didn't come right out to the house and bust us, so we probably aren't in as deep as Charlie."

"No, not that deep, that's for sure. I told his sorry ass not to do what he did. But he wouldn't listen to me. He never listens to anybody."

"Well, that makes you an accessory to the crime, if you knew about it, for not reporting it to the cops."

"Shit."

"How could he fuck this thing up so bad? We all had it dicked."

"Well, we're screwed now." But less me than you guys, Ben thought to himself as he hung up the phone. "I have to go downtown for a while," Rick said to his wife. "Put a movie on for the kids, and don't let them watch any television."

After the press conference Larry Larson, Officer Jenson, and Ray Farley all went back to the Chief's office. Ray sat down at his desk, and pulled a bottle of Dewar's out of his bottom desk drawer. He poured three healthy shots into paper cups, and passed them around. "Whew. What a day. What a week, what a month. I am just so glad we were able to accomplish all we did, and without even coming close to a single casualty. Here's to you guys, Skoal."

The three veteran officers picked up a paper cup, they all repeated the traditional Scandinavian toast, and took a good nip of scotch together.

"There's one more thing Larry," Ray said when they were through with their shots. "Let's go talk to Charlie. He's probably ready for his phone call by now."

"Let's go."

Back in his holding cell, Charlie was sitting on his bunk, staring at the bars. "Hey Charlie, where are the keys to your condo?"

"What do you care."

"Well Charlie, we have a search warrant for your place, and we need to go in there tomorrow morning. If we have a key, then we won't have to beat the door down, which will piss off your neighbors. And then you will have to pay to fix it. Wouldn't it be easier to just have a key?"

"Fuck you."

"Charlie, what kind of an attitude is that? I am trying to help you here."

"I want to make my phone call." Charlie was desperate to get his attorney over to his condo, and get his wall safe cleared out.

"I'll get someone on that Charlie. There is no hurry really, because the arraignment and bail hearing can't happen until Monday morning when the Judge sits. Looks like you will have plenty of time here with us this weekend. So, do you want me to have the keys or not?"

"Fuck you."

"What about the combination to your safe?"

"Fuck you." Charlie was thinking about the significant cash distribution that had just happened earlier this week via Ben Harris, and his cleaning out the Vancouver Port safes. The last thing he was about to do at this time, was give out the combination to his safe.

"Larry, make sure the detail stays outside Charlie's house until tomorrow morning, and then we will be there for our visit about ten o'clock."

"Good night, Charlie."

"Fuck you. I want my phone call."

Ray and Larry were walking through the front office, just as Rick Ferin and his attorney walked in. "May I help you?" asked the dispatcher.

"We've got this," said Ray Farley. "Please come into my office, Rick." He held the half swinging door open for the two men.

Once in the office, Ray broke the bad news to Rick. "I am placing you under arrest as an accomplice to attempted murder. You are also charged with aiding and abetting the transfer and illegal distribution of large quantities of a controlled substance. You will also face illicit money charges, when they can be sorted out. You are hereby advised of your Miranda Rights, etc."

Rick Ferin's attorney spoke next. "Chief Farley, we would like to thank you for your sensitivity in the handling of our case here. We appreciate you allowing Rick the opportunity to come in of his own recognizance. I would like to assure you that my client appears to have colluded here, but in fact was compelled to do so by his direct supervisor. My client is a veteran of the United States Coast Guard, he is a family man, and has endeavored to do nothing more than to support his family, and labor for their well-being. He is not a principal in any of these heinous activities, but merely a victim of his employer's willful vengeance and corruption. We would like to go on the record at this time, as volunteering to assist the authorities in any way possible. We are willing to provide access to any and all information known to us, that you may deem significant in the resolve of these crimes. My client is not an accessory to murder, Chief, nor is he a drug trafficker. I believe his character will emerge as this trial unfolds."

"You need to save all that for the Judge and the District Attorney. Larry can you please take Mr. Ferin down and book him. The arraignment will occur sometime Monday morning. Is there anything else here?"

"No Sir."

"Very well, thank you for coming in."

Larry, I am going home. When Ben Harris comes in book him, but just on the money charges. Keep all three of these prisoners separate and unable to communicate with each other. Then you are free to go. I'll see you tomorrow.

"Sure Chief. Talk to you in the morning."

Nikki was at home waiting for Charlie to call. Why was he late, she thought, that's not like him? She turned on the TV to kill some time, and almost fell off of the couch. Her roommate heard her scream, and ran into the living room. "What's wrong?" she asked.

"They just busted Charlie for attempted murder, and a bunch of other stuff. Holy shit. I was supposed to go out with him to-night. I'm sitting here waiting for that sonofabitch to pick me up."

"You're kidding."

"No way. I'm wondering why he is so late calling, and the guy is probably sitting in a jail cell somewhere. Murder one. Can you believe it?"

"That is just bizarre. It's beyond bizarre."

"There is even more. I think I was out with him the night he actually shot the guy. Remember, he called here late, and we went out and partied at the Vortex on Halloween night? Then I spent the weekend with him. I thought I was in love with the guy."

"Wow. Now you are like a gun moll."

"Won't you just shut up. This is serious stuff. What a fucking creep. He asks me out the same night he tries to off some guy. I can't believe it."

"Well thank God you have been avoiding him. They would probably want to take you in, and talk to you, too. I can see the headlines now, Famous Gun Moll brought in for questioning."

"No kidding, that's all I need right now."

As Vice President, I thought it wise to head down to the club, to support the staff if nothing else. Turns out there wasn't much to support. The clubhouse was like a morgue. Apparently, Rosewood was getting so much spectacularly negative press, no one wanted to be seen anywhere near us, or the ABC Network van that was parked on the street in front of us. I parked in the maintenance area, and came in around back through the locker room entrance.

Bruce and Larry Easton were in the bar when I got there, and Leon was just leaving. They were getting ready to lockup, and close down. But we all stopped to chat for a minute. "We were just talking about you," Bruce said. "Larry and I have sent out an email to the Board for another special meeting first thing in the morning."

"What time?"

"Nine AM."

"Can you believe this?"

"Not really."

"Leon, what was the reaction in the bar, when the cops came in for Charlie?"

"Everyone was just in shock. All the members finished their drinks, and maybe ordered one more, but by and large, everybody was done. After they left, no one but a couple of Board members has come in at all."

"Not much of a surprise there. Well, see you guys in the morning."

Bruce, as a good friend of Charlie's, was in an awkward position. After all, it was he, who had railed at Hugh Schmidt just the night before, and soundly sung Charlie's praises to all of us. And in all probability, it was just beginning to dawn on him that he had been set up by Charlie and Rick Ferin as Charlie's alibi, on the night of the attempted murder.

"Do you want to talk about tomorrow's meeting at all?" I asked him.

"Not really. We will have plenty to discuss tomorrow morning. I'm going home."

"Did the expulsion letter go out to the Schmidts this morning?" I asked Larry, before Bruce left us.

"Yes, it did. It was my first order of business this morning, actually."

"Shit. They are going to sue our butts. You just watch."

"Let's talk about it in the morning."

"Okay."

Tricia called her mom at three on Saturday afternoon, noon Hawaiian time. "Hi mom, it's me."

"Oh my God. I was so worried. Are you okay? Your boss has been arrested for attempted murder, did you know that?"

"Yes, mom. We had him all along, but were just waiting to pick him up after we rounded up all of the drug traffickers."

"OMG, the drug traffickers. You be careful. I would die if anything happened to you."

"It's all right mom. Everything has already gone down. Watch the news, we are having a big press conference with the FBI and the DEA on Sunday. I am actually at the airport, and already boarded for my flight home. I will see you this evening."

"You be careful."

"Relax mom. I'm okay."

CHAPTER FORTY-EIGHT

Much like the sky is lit up with fireworks on Fourth of July, Charlie lit up the networks on Friday night. He was the lead story on ABC, CBS, NBC, and Fox news. Each of whom built up tension throughout the evening with intriguing little tastes, small bytes, of the bigger story, which was coming on the late-night news. Attempted Murder in Poshville. Country Club President runs Amok, Severe Hazard (sic) at Rosewood Golf Club, etc. The story lines were running rampant, and the reportage ran the gamut from fact to speculation to hearsay to conjecture. This was the stuff of every news editor's dreams. A community based story of such lurid content that none of the news desks could have dreamed it up. A tragic flaw in human nature, where the mighty have fallen, and fallen hard. And oh, how most of us love to see the mighty taken down a peg or two.

The stations did profiles of Rosewood Golf Club, profiles of Charlie Strong, profiles of the International Longshore and Warehouse Union and their membership. They relived the actual incident, they profiled the injured, and they theorized on various motives. They actually had all day Saturday to stir the pot.

Do some people really take golf that seriously they wondered? It was one consistent theme throughout the day.

But, no one lit up the virtual sky as brightly as Suzie Davis at Fox News. She broke the story that the whole assault was staged, that Charlie Strong was duped from the start. There was apparently a mystery undercover woman, and the resulting coverup ensued to protect the larger ongoing drug and smuggling investigation. She had live footage with Bob Kudlach, and some of the Magnolia Street neighbors, all of whom were elated to see the truth finally emerging.

She raised the question of who was the undercover person or persons who had worked to create all of this intrigue? Who was the mystery woman that drove the getaway car on Halloween night? Did the Vancouver Police Department dismiss charges that could have, should have in her opinion, been filed from the brawl at the Rosewood Bar to keep the cover up intact? How deeply was Charlie Strong and the ILWU involved in the drug and smuggling operation? She had done her homework and was able to report that there were two more arrests Friday evening after Ray Farley's press conference. Who were Rick Ferin, and Ben Harris, and what bearing did they have on this case? And there was more to come. Much more. The stations and their respective staffs now had until Sunday to sensationalize and stir the pot.

Tricia and Steve's jet took off on time, and they enjoyed a pleasant flight as they were winging across the Pacific. They were due in Portland in the early evening, and the extended airtime of the lengthy trip, gave Steve plenty of time to organize his thoughts for the coming press conference. Tricia dozed off, with her head on Steve's shoulder.

Meanwhile, back at the Rosewood Conference Room, Bruce Cranston had called Rosewood's special Board meeting to order promptly at nine am. The entire Board was in attendance save two conspicuous non-attendees. If the clubhouse seemed like a morgue the night before, the mood of the Board was certainly no livelier this morning.

"Ladies and gentlemen, this meeting is called to order, but I am basically at a loss for words. Does anyone have any suggestions?" Of all of our Board members, Marta Koenig was certainly the most experienced, and apparently, she had been through several of these crisis management situations before. She was the first to speak up.

"We as a Board need to stay the course. We must remember we are the spokespeople for our organization. Although we are in a very unfavorable position, and no matter how dark it seems right now, it is up to us to make good decisions, and begin to right the ship. I would suggest that we compose a letter to the membership at this meeting, and reassure them that we are on top of, and monitoring the situation closely. Some terrible decisions were made by a former officer, and member of this Board, but in absolutely no way do we condone those decisions and subsequent actions. Instead, we congratulate the Vancouver Police Department for their excellent work on the apprehension of these suspects, and we will do anything and everything to assist the VPD in any way possible.

We need to distance ourselves from Charlie Strong immediately, and emphasize our recent decision to demote him from his Presidency, and place him on a conduct related probationary period. We need to expel him from the club immediately. We also need to take action concerning Rick Ferin, and get as much distance as we can from him, also. Our biggest job right now is to assuage our membership, and regain their support and confidence.

"The community will probably be prejudiced in their opinions of us for some time to come, which may affect our ability to attract future members. But I believe that those type of wounds and opinions will heal with time. After all, we are a private organization, and we can basically lie low and stay out of the public spotlight as necessary.

"My biggest concern now is, and I say again, to regain the confidence of our membership. We need to emphasize that Charlie Strong for whatever unknown reasons, began of his own volition to make disastrous decisions, which have betrayed all of us. Rick Ferin was a minor player at Rosewood, who was apparently adversely influenced by Charlie Strong, and the Board apologizes for both of their behaviors, etc. We are hoping we can all pull together, to overcome this terrible adversity Charlie unjustly visited on us.

"The last thing we need right now, and I repeat this in all confidence to the assembled Board members, the very last thing we need right now, is an adverse run on memberships. This would create a financial crisis which, to be honest with you, I am not sure this club could survive."

Marta's words were like a life line to us, and we immediately began to make suggestions to Bruce Cranston concerning his composition of a letter to the membership. We also discussed some special member friendly Holiday events that would serve to bind us together, and work at rebuilding morale. It was also considered how critical our ongoing relationship with the press was, and it was motioned that Marta Koenig be appointed our media representative going forward. If anyone, she would be the person to relate to the press, and begin to bring them if not back to us, at least back to a middle of the road, and more impartial coverage of us. It was obvious that Marta would certainly do a better job than Charlie had done. And trying to inject a bit of humor into our moribund meeting, Marta assured us there were no skeletons in her closet, and that she had not tried to kill her husband, or anyone else, lately.

When the letter writing exercise was completed, I raised a question concerning the expulsion of Hugh Schmidt from the club, and in lieu of the critical events of the last twenty-four hours, if there was anything we could do to mitigate his situation. This was another thorny problem, and in my opinion, one that was going to come back and bite us later on. Maybe I just knew the Magnolia Street neighbors better than anyone else on the Board. I knew well their tenacity and the extent of their loathing of Rosewood. And also of their uncanny knack of seeming to never endingly get the breaks. To always be in the right place at the right time, to always say the right thing. To be able to manipulate the press, etc., while we forever seemed to be sitting here like dumb shits, trying to defend ourselves.

"So, what can we do at this juncture?" asked Bruce Cranston.

"Well, if we reinstate him, it will look bad," Joe Goldman opined.

"I agree," said Marta. "He earned his expulsion, let it stand. We can deal with any fallout later, if it is even necessary. He seriously injured this club, and we have bigger problems to deal with right now anyway."

"Even though two sitting Board members who voted for his expulsion, are now sitting in jail, and involved in attempting to murder his friend and neighbor? Right or wrong, this is a public relations nightmare," I replied.

Joe Goldman weighed in again. "I believe the Magnolia neighbors are so happy to have Charlie behind bars, they will let it go. This will be the end of it."

Not that I have a solution, but we have created another monster here, I thought to myself.

The discussion turned to replacing Charlie and Rick on the Board of Trustees. Tom Thompson's name was thrown into the ring, and the women wanted Mary Lou Rousseau to come on. Tommy was a long-time member, and had served for numerous years on the finance committee. He had also spent numerous years as the Men's Club Captain, and was well liked by everyone. He was within a whisker of being nominated to run for Board election this year, and we all felt sure he would be willing to step in and serve. His presence would go a long way toward providing some much-needed stability to our group.

Mary Lou Rousseau was currently the Ladies Club Captain. She was a good golfer, and was very popular and influential with the women. She had been a member for about ten years, was a retired businesswoman, lived on the course, and was very involved. These were the type of people we needed right now, mature longtime members who cared deeply about the club. Bruce Cranston agreed to call them right after our meeting, and if they were willing to serve, they were in.

We debated as we closed up our business, whether we should have another special Board meeting between now and the Thanksgiving Holiday, and it was decided that we should just lay low, and hope that today's FBI press conference would put the bigger focus on Charlie and international drug smugglers, and take some of the heat off of us.

We thereby adjourned. Happy Thanksgiving. May the Golf Gods be with us. Actually, we all felt a little better, knowing how we at least had a plan going forward. And with a few breaks here and there, we would get through this situation. We had successfully started to navigate our way through the rapids again. Albeit, this time they were some serious Class A rapids.

Just as Rosewood's Board of Trustees began their meeting, ILWU's sleek Lear jet touched down at Portland International's private traffic wing. It taxied to a halt at the terminal, and four suits got off the plane. Two of them were carrying attaché cases, and one of the other gentlemen was rolling a travel bag. They cleared the terminal quickly, picked up their waiting Lincoln Town Car, and headed for the Vancouver Police Station.

ILWU President Malcolm McElfresh, ILWU Treasurer Richard Morgan, and two of their five hundred dollar an hour attorneys, snugged up in the Town Car, and looked out at the leaden grey skies. The sky matched their collective moods. None of them had been very pleased to get up at five am on a Saturday morning, to start off for a fire extinguishing mission, and on their own weekend time.

When they arrived, the desk sergeant asked them in, offered them coffee, and ushered them into VPD's conference room. "Chief Farley will be right with you gentlemen."

"Good morning Chief," President McElfresh boomed when Ray walked into the room two minutes later. He had risen to shake the Chief's hand, and introduced the rest of his party. "Thank you for meeting with us on such short notice, and I wish to assure you, we are here on a mission of peace. We are absolutely appalled at the conduct of our CEO here in the Northwest, and are here to support you in any way possible."

"Thank you so much Mr. McElfresh. We appreciate your personal attention. Let me give you the complete details of what's been going on here." And Ray Farley launched into a twenty-minute description of the case. The lawyers were taking furious notes.

At the completion of his monologue, Malcolm McElfresh sat shaking his head. "What a mess. We are nauseated. I don't have the words."

"Would you like to speak with Mr. Strong?"

"Yes, we would. We would appreciate a few minutes alone, and then I'm sure we would need to chat again for a moment on our way out. Mr. Morgan, by the way, is our International Union Treasurer, and will be the interim CEO here in Vancouver and Portland. He will be invaluable to us in sorting out the financial details, if any, involving the ILWU, and will be in place until we are confident that the situation here is in hand. At that time, we will have a viable party identified to replace Mr. Strong permanently. Mr. Morgan is at your disposal, should you need his assistance. By the way, how has Mr. Strong's behavior been since his arrest?"

"Thank you, sir. Let me go get Mr. Strong for you. Unfortunately, I must tell you he has been anything but co-operative with us so far."

"Thank you, Chief Farley. Let me see if I can help calm him down a little for you."

"Good morning, Charlie, you've got visitors."

"Fuck you, I want my phone call, and I want it right now. I want to talk to my lawyer."

"Oh, probably not necessary Charlie. I think that there are a couple of lawyers out there to see you right now."

The Chief had his deputy handcuff Charlie, and lead him out of the holding tank and over to the conference room.

"Are the cuffs really necessary?" Charlie asked.

"Well, we don't let prisoners just roam around the hallways here."

"Fuck you. What time is it anyway?"

"Oh, I think it is party's over time for you, pal."

"Yeah? Well, fuck you again."

Chief Farley turned the hallway's corner, opened the heavy door, and ushered Charlie into the room. "Here you are gentlemen. Just signal for me, when you are done. He's got a bit of a potty mouth this morning, but there will be a deputy stationed right outside of the room. If there are any problems, just call for us."

Charlie's eyes bulged when he saw who his visitors were. He was expecting to have a conversation with his lawyer, instead he was facing the Gestapo. And he knew they were none too happy with him. Of course, after sleeping in his clothes, wearing a day's worth of whiskers, and not having combed his hair or brushed his teeth, he already looked and felt terrible. And now this.

"Sit down Charlie," said President McElfresh. "We need to have a little chat."

"Yes Sir."

"Why don't you tell us in your own words, what happened up here, Charlie. Please don't leave anything out, and please don't spin anything for us. You are already dead meat, and if you lie to us, we will proceed to cremate your dead meat for you." The two attorneys turned over new pages in their yellow, legal pads.

"Well Sir, I messed up big time. I let my emotions get away from me, and made a couple of bad decisions. Fortunately, no one was fatally injured."

"Don't spin this thing Charlie. Don't even try."

"Sorry sir."

"Explain to us how this could happen. We entrusted you to manage one of our premier properties, and you throw our name and our organization's name down in the dirt. You flaunt and degrade everything the International Longshore and Warehouse Union stands for. Then you have the audacity to sit there and say that there were no fatalities? You have debased our organization, and everything we stand for. You have endangered our whole operation. We as an organization strive to build lives, and you our leader in these parts, are out trying to kill people. By the time this fiasco is done with, you will have cost us thousands upon thousands of dollars. But there were no fatalities? Start over, you little piece of shit, and tell us in detail, exactly what happened."

"Well, Sir, I was the President of the Rosewood Golf Club. We had some plans to expand some of our facilities, but got into a conflict with some of the neighbors over our land use proposal. They won several decisions by the Hearing Examiner, and were quite obnoxious about it. For some reason, they were very hostile to our club, and I took it personally. I hatched a plan to eliminate the leader of the neighborhood opposition group. I recruited one of the casual girls who had done a lot of hostess work for us over the last few years. She had been promoted to regular status by Harold Edmonds before he retired, and I thought she would be solid to just drive for me. I set it up, and somehow, the guy was dressed up in a gorilla suit for Halloween, and that deflected the rounds. I guess I only wounded the guy."

"Oh, that's right Charlie. You were in jail last night, and didn't get to hear any of your news bytes. The girl you recruited to do your dirty work, was a Vancouver Police undercover cop. The reason you didn't kill your guy, was because it wasn't even him. It was a Vancouver cop in a Kevlar vest and a gorilla suit."

Charlie's face dropped to his navel. "What? I had no idea, sir."

"I'm sure you didn't, Charlie. How much did you pay Tricia to drive for you?"

"Twenty-five grand."

"Where did you happen to find twenty-five grand lying around, Charlie?"

Oh, shit Charlie thought to himself. "From some extra money I had sitting around."

"Just sitting around, eh? Don't piss me off any worse than I already am, Charlie, I am warning you. Where did the money come from?"

"We have been receiving some special shipments of some valuable artwork at the Port of Vancouver. Apparently, it is valuable enough to them, that they pay us extra cash to handle it for them. That's where the money came from."

"Valuable artwork? Are you kidding me? Really too bad you missed the news last night, Charlie, because all of the networks are reporting that the FBI busted a major international drug smuggling ring yesterday. Through our contacts, we have learned about a van with close to eight hundred pounds of China white heroin which was impounded right outside of your shipping yard yesterday. The FBI is prepared release the gory details at noon tomorrow. They not only busted your little connection, they busted your buddy Bao Thieu in San Francisco's Chinatown, they busted the Oriental Casino in Reno, and they busted the Changs in Hawaii. Remember your little dinner party at Ruth Chris' Steak House in Portland a month ago? The one where you wined and dined your pals on our ILWU dime? Apparently, there were a lot of details to discuss concerning their valuable art shipments? You make me sick, Charlie."

"Sorry Sir. I had no idea."

"That is a crock of shit, Charlie. You had a damn good idea of what was going on, and I guess you thought you were the man up here. Bullet proof, eh Charlie? Okay to pick up a little free-lance work."

"Sorry Sir, I said I made some bad decisions."

"Yes, you did Charlie. Do you know Chief Farley tells me that they have you on film on every step of your little adventure? And if they don't have you on film, then you are sideways with the undercover cop, running your mouth, and putting your hands all over her. Your cell phone has been tapped for the last month. That's how screwed you are Charlie. Now, what are we going to do about it?"

"Well Sir, I guess I am innocent until proven guilty, and I will just have to fight it out in court."

"Unfortunately, Charlie, that's not going to happen. If you even think in those terms, we will bury your sorry ass in so much human waste, that you will never dig yourself out. You can dig your way to China, and you will still be covered in shit. We will call out the dogs on you. We will use the formidable power of the ILWU to make your life miserable. Remember how I told you at your annual review that any more problems up here, and we would possibly freeze your assets with us? Consider them frozen Charlie. You are suspended as we speak, and therefore you have no income. We will see to it that the FBI impounds your vehicles, your illegal under the table cash, and quarantines your residence. Should any of our people attempt to come to your assistance, we will step between that."

No Charlie, the path of least resistance for you right now is to do a one eighty, and co-operate with us. We want to clear our good name up here, and you can help us do that. You need to work with the FBI and the Vancouver PD. You need to supply them with any information that will help them with their investigation. You need to release names, dates and numbers. In return, we will see that both the US Attorney and also the District Attorney offer you decent plea bargains. But you are going away for a good long while Charlie, and you are not going to take us down with you. Do you understand me?"

"I think so, but I don't see how you can crush me like this. I have been a ILWU member for over twenty years, and I have done some dirty work for you along the way as well. That has to count for something."

"That counts for nothing now, Charlie. Because you fucked up. You fucked up big time. If you don't think we can crush you like a bug, why don't you try us?"

"I don't think so, Sir. What do you want me to do?"

"You will cooperate. You will cooperate with anyone who talks to you, get it? You make good, make nice, that is your only option now."

"Yes sir. What do you think they will set my bail at?"

"Bail? Are you serious, Charlie? There will be no bail for you."

President McElfresh called for the deputy, "could we please speak to Chief Farley now?"

"Chief Farley, we have had a good meeting with Mr. Strong. We have tried to impress upon him that, although he has created some serious problems, he can start to rectify those problems by co-operating with your agency in any way possible. Isn't that correct, Mr. Strong?"

"Yes sir."

"Do you have anything else to say to Police Chief Farley, Charlie?"

"Yes sir. I apologize for my attitude this morning."

"Thank you, Mr. Strong."

"Chief Farley is here anything else we can do for you?"

"Yes, there is. We are going to search Mr. Strong's condominium in a few minutes. I suggested to Mr. Strong last night, that if he supplied a key for us, we wouldn't have to break his door down. Also, the combination to his home safe would be helpful."

"The key is in my Jaguar, which is still parked at Rosewood unless someone had it towed. The combination to the safe is ….."

"Thank you, Mr. Strong."

"Chief Farley, if we could speak to Mr. Ferin and Mr. Harris briefly before we leave, that would be appreciated. "

"Certainly, both at the same time?"

"Mr. Ferin first please."

"Mr. Ferin, please sit down. What unpleasant circumstances we meet under."

"Yes sir."

"Chief Farley tells us that you and your attorney are ready to co-operate in any way possible to help correct our little problem here."

"Yes sir."

"If you don't mind my asking, you seem like an otherwise intelligent young man. How did you get mixed up in all of this trouble?"

"I guess my loyalties got in the way, sir. Charlie Strong has been very good to me, and although I was aware he was starting to go down some wrong roads, I didn't say enough. I shouldn't have let him go ahead with the Magnolia Street thing. The other thing with the Changs, has been going on for some time. It was set up all the way back in Harold Edmonds day. I was the new guy, and just went along, for the most part. Although I did recently tell Charlie I would no longer have anything to do with the shipments. No one ever came out and directly said hard drugs to us, but I think it was fairly obvious what was going on. The money I received, is secured and I have not spent any of it. I will be happy to turn it over to whoever should have it."

"Thank you for your attitude Mr. Ferin. I personally appreciate that. We are here on behalf of the ILWU to restore and maintain our good name in the northwest. Although you were a minor accessory to Mr. Strong activities, we still need you to cooperate with the authorities in any way you can. I will see that our attorneys attempt to have a favorable influence on your bail hearing on Monday, and as a group here, we will personally meet today, to review your ongoing status with us."

"Thank you, Sir."

"Mr. Strong is no longer affiliated with the ILWU. You should disassociate yourself from him. If you should return to us after a probationary period, your loyalties can now belong strictly to the ILWU. Does that make good sense to you?"

"Yes sir. Very good sense."

"Mr. Harris, what do you have to say for yourself?"

"Mr. McElfresh, I was just following orders. Charlie Strong was calling the shots, and I did what I was told. What goes on down in the shipping yards is none of my business. If some cash comes in, Charlie tells me what to do with it, and that's pretty much it."

Mr. Harris, you are certainly aware that your employment contract stipulates that you, as a financial manager, have a fiduciary duty to protect the interests of the ILWU at all times. In my opinion, that doesn't include sitting around splitting up wads of cash between certain members of the staff, does it?"

"Probably not, Sir."

"Probably not? There is no probably not here. If there is money coming in, it rightfully belongs to the ILWU, or it is illegal money, period. If it belongs to the ILWU, then you are stealing money from your fraternal brotherhood when that money is not processed correctly. If it is illegal money, then it should be reported to headquarters immediately. Am I right?"

"I was just following orders, Sir."

"Mr. Harris, do you have anything to say about any unreported, questionable cash which might be in your possession at this time?"

"No, I don't."

"Mr. Harris, you are summarily terminated from any and all employment with the ILWU, as of this meeting. You will be given absolutely no legal assistance by our organization. You will be given no extra compensation to any retirement accounts, other than monies that you have personally contributed. You are eligible for no pension benefits. I will have your desk cleared out tomorrow morning. Your personal effects will be in a box, and we will have your effects delivered to your residence. I do not want you on any of our ILWU properties in the future, on the penalty of immediate arrest for trespassing. Do I make myself sufficiently clear?"

"Yep." Ben Harris stood up, and was escorted back to his cell.

"Some of these guys have the ethics of a cockroach," President McElfresh said disgustedly to his associates.

The ILWU team prepared to leave. On the way out, they paid their respects to Chief Farley. "Please pass my regards on to FBI Agent Rodriguez. I would like to speak with him prior to his press conference if at all possible."

"He should be in from Hawaii late this afternoon. I will be happy to give him your phone number."

"Thank you. Here is my business card. My personal cell phone number is on there. Please don't hesitate to call if may be of any assistance. Mr. Morgan will be in your area to replace Charlie Strong for the time being, so he is also at your disposal. Here is one of his cards. We are bringing attorneys in from the Portland and Seattle offices to assist in any way possible. The rest of us are leaving for the airport, and should be back in San Francisco before Agent Rodriguez arrives back here. Please have him contact me."

"Will do. I will certainly speak to him before his conference."

"Thanks, one last time, for all of your help, and please tell Mr. Rodriguez that Ms. Watson's continued employment will no longer be required at our facilities."

"No problem. And thanks for the Charlie Strong attitude adjustment."

"Any time. Please let me know if there are any further problems in that area."

"Is there anything else, sir?"

"Well, if I were you, I would certainly get another warrant, and search Ben Harris House."

"Yes sir."

There was one more meeting of any significance before the FBI's big blockbuster, and it involved the Magnolia Street neighbors. Through Carol Horn's contacts, the neighbors had already decided to go ahead and meet with a personal injury attorney.

Their meeting was setup for three o'clock that afternoon, and although it was a Saturday, most personal injury attorneys will make an exception to their active weekend schedules for an opportunity like this one. The usual core of the Magnolia Street leadership was at Bob Kudlach's house, when their new attorney arrived.

"First, we have to establish cause, and then evaluate potential damages. I am assuming that this will be a class action lawsuit?" the lawyer asked. And thus, the process began. "This will take some time to structure properly, where should we begin?"

Hugh and Bunny initiated the process, and related their emotional problems and stress to the attorney. "How could an attempted murderer possibly sit on a panel, and expel us from our own club," they wanted to know. "We are scared to death any time the doorbell rings of someone who is going to try to kill us. And if that is not enough. Now they have cut off our only real social artery to our friends and acquaintances, one that was helping us cope. And the expulsion was all hearsay anyway. The Rosewood Board had no solid evidence of any wrong doing on our parts."

"It is amazing to me that the club would, in the first place, not remove Charlie Strong from their Board, and then that they would proceed against you on the strength of the evidence that you have related to me today," the attorney told them.

Everyone in the room told of similar fears about interacting with the public after the attack on Halloween night. Particularly the Horn family, who were not only in therapy personally, but their children were as well. The kids it seems are skittish and inattentive. Their studies have suffered at school, and they frequently break out in hives.

Bob Kudlach is, in the attorney's opinion, the potential critical element in the whole process. He reported that even though the attempted assault had been staged, he is to this day wracked with anxiety and paranoia. He persistently hears Lilian's scream on the night of the attack, and is having trouble sleeping. He must be having Post Traumatic Stress Syndrome, because any time he hears a loud noise, he has heart palpitations. He finds he must stop whatever he is doing, and go to bed and rest. Although it is early in his treatment, his therapist is not sure when, if ever, he might be able to resume a normal life.

Lilian is even worse off. She is extremely nervous, and jumps at the slightest disturbance. She has a hard time being in the present, and can't seem to focus on anything anymore. She doesn't sleep well at all, and consequently, is tired and exhausted all of the time. Her quality of life has deteriorated to the point that she may be having a nervous breakdown. She could have to consider a stay at some type of convalescence home, where her medication can be monitored 24/7.

The horror stories went on for two hours. The lawyer took notes furiously. At the end of the personal revelation session, the bleed out he liked to call it, the attorney advised the neighbors that he felt that they had an extremely strong case. He would evaluate the material he had gathered today, and be in touch about how and when to proceed. He advised them all to continue with their individual therapies, and to be there for each other as best they could. Perhaps a weekly support/encounter group gathering, would also be beneficial. You could all have a relaxing glass of wine, and form a deeper bond with each other. Reinforce to each other, that there is strength in numbers, and that absolutely none of you are in this thing alone. Communicate your experiences with other.

As the legal portion of their meeting ended, the Magnolia neighbors rallied. They decided to take their attorney's advice and scheduled a group meeting for tomorrow at noon, which would coincide with the FBI's press conference. Neil Horn laid down half a dozen bottles of good wine, nice regional varietals, and anticipation began to build for the FBI show. Due to extraordinary demand, the press conference was now going to be telecast live. The neighbors, would of course, be watching Fox News.

CHAPTER FORTY-NINE

The flight from Honolulu to Portland touched down right on time, and Steve was in a hurry to head to his office. He had lots to catch up on. Tricia wanted to go home and see her family. "Take the evening off, and come on back tomorrow. But be sure and write up your report," he told her. "Your cover is probably blown, so you may as well be at the press conference with us."

"Do you think?"

"Well, I'll know in about half an hour. I'll call you."

Steve got back to his office, and got on the phone. He checked in with Hawaii, and found everything under control. There could be no arraignments until Monday, and the US Attorney was recommending no bail. The Changs were of course, a definite flight risk, even with their Lear Jet impounded.

He called Barbara Estes in San Francisco, and she was doing well. Bao Thieu was in in custody, as well as a dozen of his staff. Her team was going through his hard drives now, and would have another dozen names to put warrants to. As well as the overview of his processing, delivery and sales network, they had also impounded half a dozen vehicles, and half a million dollars in cash. This was the gift that just kept on giving.

"How's everything in Reno?"

"Great there, too. We caught them flat footed, and bagged all their hard drives. They are under review in the Reno office right now. You want to talk to them?"

"No, that's okay. You should continue to be the liaison with that office. Just keep up the good work."

Steve told her she and her team would all receive high praise in the coming press gathering. And then he called Ray Farley.

"All's well in Vancouver, Steve. I had a very interesting visit with a Malcolm McElfresh this morning. He is the President of the ILWU, and he personally flew up here on his private jet, with a team of guys to assure us we have his full and unequivocal support in pursuing justice here. He would very much like to talk with you today."

"He will help us flip Charlie Strong?"

"Especially with Charlie Strong. Charlie was acting all bad ass with an attitude, and my boy Malcolm turned him into a little pussy cat. He even calls me sir now. Mr. McElfresh really wanted to speak to you before your press conference if at all possible."

"What about?"

"I don't know, he didn't say. I would give him the courtesy of a call though. He was a very cool dude. Let me give you his cell number."

"Sure, I'll call him when I am done here. Thanks for all of your help throughout our process, Ray. It was a pleasure working with you."

"And vice versa."

"Who's coming down here with you?"

"Well myself, the District Attorney, and Larry Larson for sure. Tricia might as well come too, because they know about her. Her cover is blown. As a matter of fact, Malcolm introduced me to

Charlie's replacement, and told me it was not necessary for Tricia to come to work at the ILWU offices anymore."

"Really. How did he find out?"

"They pretty much pieced everything together. These are some pretty smart cookies. By the time they got through talking to Charlie and Rick, and by looking at the money trail, I think they just figured everything out. Or maybe they have their own inside sources, I don't know. Thank God, we don't have to go after them too, that would be tough."

"Well, we have done most of our work. It is in the hands of the attorneys now, and they still have a lot of information and paperwork to wade through. I just hope they keep bail at the max on these people. They are all fly aways if you ask me."

"Right on, so I'll see you about 11:30."

"Ten-four."

Steve had his own office load to catch up on, but most of his resources had been dedicated to the Chang caper, so he was okay there.

He checked in with the US District Attorney Phillip Brown. "Everything seems ship shape on our end, Phillip. Is there anything you need from me before the debriefing tomorrow?"

"Everything is good in all areas? Reno, SF, Honolulu, and Vancouver?" Phillip asked in response.

"Yeah, all is well. You should be busy from now on with all of your paperwork and court appearances. I think you've got about two dozen arraignments to start on."

"I've got each of the offices working on them in the different jurisdictions, as we speak. This is really a wide spread case, and a major break though on the supply side here on the west coast. Congratulations, Steve, you and your team did an excellent job."

"Thanks Phil. I have my people working on their preliminary reports now, and we should be able to get you our information by tomorrow at the latest. Barbara Estes may be a different story, as she took down a lot more people than we did."

"Thanks again. See you in the morning."

Steve called Tricia. He wanted her to be at the meeting. She did all the hard work, she should be there. This plan was okay with her, and she promised to see him about an hour before the PC started.

After his call to Tricia, Steve dialed up Malcolm McElfresh. "Hello Mr. McElfresh, this is Portland, Oregon FBI Chief Agent Steve Rodriguez, Police Chief Farley suggested I give you a call."

"Thanks so much for calling, Steve. I know how busy you must be this afternoon, so I won't take up a lot of your time. We had what I felt was a very good visit to your area this morning, and I would just like to say that we at ILWU offices are very much in support of your work. We communicated to Charlie Strong that his conduct was diametrically opposed to our core values and mission statement here at ILWU, and pledged our support in any manner possible. As a matter of fact, on our return flight to San Francisco, our team discussed sizeable donations to both the Cities of Vancouver and Portland. We want to assist all of our communities, and will show our thanks and support to some worthy charities up there. I just have one small favor to ask of you."

"Yes sir, what is that?"

"Our concern about your press conference tomorrow, is that you please do everything possible to minimize ILWU exposure in the investigation. In our take, Charlie Strong was a renegade officer of our organization and he let his power and opportunity cloud his responsibilities. He got greedy, and exercised extremely bad judgement, which unfortunately reflects on all of our membership and the organization as a whole. I am trying to do some damage control here, is all."

"I completely understand Mr. McElfresh, and I want you to know your visit this morning was very well received by Chief Farley and myself. We appreciate your help, and all of our suspects except maybe Mr. Harris, are demonstrating a willingness to cooperate with us going forward. Especially, after you had a few words with them. I will do everything possible to keep Charlie Strong in the limelight, and the ILWU on the back burner."

"Thank you so much. I hope you have a good meeting, and congratulations on a job well done up there."

"You're welcome sir, have a good evening."

All of a sudden, the office couch looked pretty inviting, as he had had about six hours of sleep in the last three days. He dozed off for an hour, and then roused himself, to get up and keep slogging forward with his paperwork. He loved the adrenalin of the hunt, but it was nice to slow back down again afterward. Maybe he and Tricia could get away next weekend for a few days, when they had their details all wrapped up.

By eleven am on Sunday morning, the FBI conference room was crawling with reporters and television crews. The transmission circuits were hard wired in the CR, so at least there weren't a lot of TV cables dragging around the floor, but the area was still very congested, with everyone jockeying for position.

Promptly at noon, Steve Rodriguez convened the regional press conference. Seated on the dais were Officer Rodriguez, Steve's Assistant Tony Patmos, Ray Farley, Larry Larson, Tricia Watson, the Clark County District Attorney Steven Golding, and Phillip Brown, the US Attorney for the Northwest Region.

Steve thanked everyone for coming out on a Sunday midday, and launched into a detailed narrative of the investigation. He covered its ongoing development, and finally detailed a description of Friday's multiple arrests in the four wide spread jurisdictions.

"Our whole chain of events was triggered by the Vancouver Police Department having a strategically placed undercover officer on the job. This led to an awareness of Charlie Strong's activities, and led us further on to the larger case of international drug smuggling and distribution." Agent in Charge Rodriguez was particular complimentary of Ray Farley and Tricia Watson's work. "You have exemplified professional law enforcement accomplishments, and your attention to detail and dedication to crime prevention duties have honored your communities."

Steve Rodriguez went on to extol his own crew and that of Barbara Estes. He was justifiably proud of the successful wrap up of this investigation, and was well aware that these were the type of cases that have an upward effect on careers. Particularly his and Barbara Estes.

But at the same time, Steve was an honest and equitable man. He believed in giving credit where credit was due, and he was the last person in the room to take all of the accolades.

After his lengthy discourse, he opened up the floor to questions. The room was immediately filled with raised hands. Would the Changs be extradited to Portland. "Yes." Were there any more details on their Asian organization and supply chain? "With the State Department, we are working on the international aspects of the case." Will the California suspects be tried there or here? "Probably there." Have any bails been set yet? "Not yet. Tomorrow is the start of the arraignment process, especially in our local cases here in Vancouver." Etc.

Finally, the questioning turned to Charlie Strong. Had the FBI and the Vancouver PD had actually known about the planned attack well before anything happened? "Yes, we did." Will Charlie Strong face drug smuggling charges as well as attempted murder charges? "Yes, he will, among other charges." Such as? "Possession of a controlled substance, aiding and abetting distribution of a controlled substance, unlawful possession and transportation of a firearm, illicit money handling and income tax issues, to name a few." Was Charlie a heroin addict? "No, there are two issues here. Charlie's possession charges stem from a considerable amount of recreational drugs we apprehended in his possession. The aiding and abetting charges are a completely different consideration." Was Tricia Watson the driver on the night of the Halloween attack? "Yes, she was." Will she continue to work in under cover? "Well, now that she has one of the most famous faces in the North West, probably not." Tricia, how did you come to be working with Charlie? "In my undercover functions, I became ingratiated with him. He trusted me to the point that he offered me a healthy sum of money to be his accomplice." And he had no suspicion at all that you were in law enforcement? "Apparently not." Where did Charlie get this large sum of money that he gave you. "You would have to ask him that." Did any of this money come from Rosewood Country Club? "Not to my knowledge." Wouldn't Rosewood have benefited by having Bob Kudlach out of their hair? Wasn't he a main adversary of theirs? "You would need to ask Rosewood about their relationship with Mr. Kudlach." Do you feel that any charges concerning the bar brawl at Rosewood several weeks ago were suppressed, in order to maintain the integrity of your investigation? Steve Rodriguez stepped in once again, "yes, that is a consideration. Our objective at the time, was to keep Mr. Strong in a viable position as far as his management duties at the Port, and to keep the drug shipments coming through. Our objective was to keep him on the job, and keep his operation flowing smoothly. Any adverse publicity could possibly have spooked his employers and also his customers, and obstructed our investigation."

Will Charlie Strong be charged in that episode now that all of the cards are on the table, and your larger investigation is complete? "I believe Mr. Strong has bigger issues to deal with, than a misdemeanor disturbing the peace charge." Do you have any opinion on what would cause such extreme animosity between Mr. Strong and the Magnolia Street neighbors? Enough animosity to cause Mr. Strong to attack Mr. Kudlach is such a violent manner? "You would have to speak to Mr. Strong about his motivation to allegedly commit this violent felony."

Do you feel the International Longshore and Warehouse Union was involved in your investigation at all? "No, I do not. As a matter of fact, Mr. Malcolm McElfresh, the President of the ILWU, personally flew up to Portland yesterday morning, and met with us. He gave us his full support in our investigation, and was adamant in his disappointment of Mr. Strong's conduct. He assured us that the ILWU stands for social responsibility, and law-abiding justice, in their longstanding advocacy of working men and women. We have his unflagging support and resources as necessary to help resolve any inkling or supposition that the ILWU was involved in any of the unlawful activities discovered by our investigation."

The questions went on for another half an hour. Finally, Steve Rodriguez signaled that the end was near, and announced that he would entertain one final question. He called on Suzie Davis from the Fox Television News team. "Agent Rodriguez, do you feel Rosewood owes the Magnolia Street Community any reparations for the considerable stress and anxiety Mr. Strong's activity has visited upon that community? Particularly Mr. and Mrs. Kudlach?" "I am sorry Ms. Davis, but those are civil issues, and this is a criminal investigation. Therefore, I am unable to answer your question."

The press conference was over. The investigation team adjourned to Steve Rodriguez office, and this time they were treated to imported scotch in cut crystal glasses. Congratulations and appropriate approbatory asides were exchanged all around. But everyone also acknowledged that the difficult, tedious work of the prosecutors, and their respective teams was just beginning. The group began to disperse, leaving Steve and Tricia as the last two people in the room.

"Great job kid, I am very proud of you."

"You too Steve. The resources of the FBI are incredible, and what an organization to work with. You must be elated at the outcome of all of our efforts."

"Yes I am. But I am also hungry enough to eat a bear. Do you have time for a bite before you head home?"

"Sure."

So, he leaned down and gave her a playful bite on the neck.

"Ha. You are a comedian. Where do you want to go?"

CHAPTER FIFTY

Paul Cranston watched the FBI's Press Conference with his wife. Had Charlie and Rick Ferin not been in jail, he would most probably have watched it with them, as they were his main allies on the Board. But he shuddered to think how close he had unwittingly been to the whole plot.

After the Conference, Paul felt that while Rosewood had been exposed, there was, of course, no indication of any involvement by the Golf Club in Charlie's escapades. Charlie had cast Rosewood in a bad light, and had put himself in dire straits. But it was his doing, and just as the ILWU had separated themselves from Charlie, this is what Rosewood needed to do.

Paul called Marta Koenig. "What do you think?"

"Whew. Who could have imagined?"

"I think it is manageable. We need to get as far away from Charlie, as quickly as we can."

"Agreed. And don't forget about Rick, he is involved in this thing, too."

"Well, the Board has officially replaced both of them, and we need to educate the membership about those changes. I will make some calls, and work with Larry. I would not only like to distance the board and Rosewood from this situation, but I would like to create some positives for the membership."

"Such as?"

"Holiday promotions, feel good stuff. That type of thing."

"Sounds good to me. Why don't you do your thing, and then send a group email out to the Board for final review and suggestions. Do you think we should send a preliminary email out to the membership, telling them that we are on top of the situation, and will be getting back to them momentarily?"

"I don't think so. I should be able to put something together by tomorrow afternoon. I will run it by you before I go public."

"Okay. Talk to you soon."

Bruce dialed Larry, and requested a Monday morning meeting. Larry's thoughts weren't much different from Marta's. Also in the difficult but manageable vein, but an opportunity, if handled correctly, to make a major dent in getting past this whole situation.

Monday morning dawned bright and early, and found Bruce busy on the phone. He was meeting with Larry at eleven, so he had some time to get going on his personal agenda. We need to get this thing turned around, make a positive impact, and do it now, he thought to himself. I am the man to get after this thing, and get it done. He loved Rosewood too much not to make the effort. Besides, this was his chance to shine, his chance to show some leadership, and save the club from Charlie's ill advised (lack of) leadership.

From his working days at the University of Oregon, he had an acquaintance from the Athletic Department, who was affiliated with the Portland Trailblazers Basketball Team. He wanted to renew that connection. He also wanted to review the Christmas programs with Larry.

Bruce's friend with the Trailblazers came through, and Larry had some good ideas for the Holidays. Those parties were always difficult to organize, because the older members liked Della Reese type entertainment, and the younger members wanted Pink and/or hip-hop type stuff. But everyone likes free, and that would be a central theme this December.

Bruce knew the coverage of the developing criminal cases would dominate the news again tonight, with all of the arraignment hearing updates, and he wanted to be able to have something substantial from Rosewood out for the membership today. The Holiday parties had all been previously budgeted by Larry and the finance committee, but all of the budgeting needed a revisit. There would be little if any monetary constraints on this season's activities. He and Larry had some serious financial and operational discussions that early afternoon.

By three, everything came together, and Bruce went to press.

Dear friends and fellow Rosewood members:

I write to you today, with a heavy heart, and sincere regrets over the recent developments in our Club and adjacent community. As you well know, several Officers of this Club, who most of us considered longtime friends and supporters of Rosewood, have taken it upon themselves to act in a manner which completely surprises and repulses all of us.

The Rosewood Board of Directors especially finds Mr. Strong's behavior to be regrettable. He was involved in a questionable incident at the club, prior to his recent arrest, and because of his other nefarious and related activities, the Vancouver Police Department, downplayed his involvement in this clubhouse conflict. Had the prior matter been considered under normal circumstances, and reasonable adjudication had occurred by the VPD, the Rosewood Board of Directors would have reacted quickly and surely to terminate any involvement by Mr. Strong with this organization.

As it was, due to an absence of knowledge by the Board, Mr. Strong was removed from his position of President of Rosewood, but allowed to remain on the Board as a member at large. Again, had we as a Board known what we know now, decidedly different decisions would have been made.

All this being said, what will the future bring for us?

First of all, let me assure, your Rosewood Board of Directors have offered our complete support and assistance to the Vancouver Police Department and the FBI prosecutors in their investigations.

Secondly, we have confirmed two new Board members Ms. Mary Lou Rousseau and Mr. Tom Thompson, two long time Club members, who are firmly committed to having the best interests of Rosewood at heart.

Thirdly, the Board will attempt to repair the estrangement with our friends and neighbors on Magnolia Street. While we have had our differences in the past over land use and maintenance issues, Rosewood sincerely regrets any inconvenience visited upon those fine folks by our former Board members. We wish to express at this time, the serious efforts we on your Rosewood Board will be making to mitigate any ongoing issues within our community's families.

Finally, and on a much more positive note, your Board wants to wish you a most happy Holiday Season. To help put the unpleasantness and controversy of the past month behind us, the Board has designed the following activities for your seasonal pleasure.

The Annual Member Holiday Cocktail Party will be held on Saturday the seventh of December, at seven PM. It will feature, as usual, a superlative heavy appetizer buffet, and your favorite beverages, as well as a DJ for dancing and your entertainment. However, this year, it will be an event that is COMPLETELY HOSTED to all active proprietary members in good standing by your club. Please call the club for a reservation to all of the following events, as response to this generous offer is sure to be very strong.

The annual dinner dance, will be scheduled for Saturday evening the twenty first of December at six thirty PM for a champagne toast prior to dinner and dancing. The dinner will be a choice of broiled Filet Mignon or roasted Chinook Salmon Hollandaise, with all of the trimmings. Tony Ramsey and his band of renown, will entertain. Again, this event will be hosted IN ITS ENTIRETY by your Club. Due to expected overwhelming response to this generous offer, we will honor the first one hundred and fifty requests for reservations.

But that's not all folks. On Sunday morning the twenty second, we will have Santa at the club for visits with all of the children who can come by with their parents. There will be a photographer, homemade egg nog and hot chocolate available. And in the afternoon, Jamaal Wilkerson of the Portland Trail Blazers, will be at the club for a meet and greet with any of the middle and high schoolers who care to drop by. Mr. Wilkerson will be here from two to four PM to chat and sign autographs. There will be non-alcoholic beverages available for the kids.

The annual New Year's Day Open House will be held at its traditional time of noon to four pm. There will be our usual fabulous COMPLIMENARY food buffet, and a hosted selection of new release wines for your tasting pleasure provided by our premier vendors. The Rose Bowl game will be televised, and we hope that this is another opportunity for you to renew old acquaintances, make some new ones and welcome the New Year in with style. As is traditional, the New Year's open house is an event that is HOSTED IN ITS ENTIRETY for your enjoyment by your club. But again, please call ahead and reserve, so that we will have an idea of how many of you will be in attendance.

As an update to the membership, I will be sending a survey out to all Proprietary and Social members as soon as possible. Your timely response will assist the Board in planning the direction of the club for the coming year.

Also, please remember that in order to facilitate all of the holiday events I have outlined above, our Rosewood staff is a primary factor in supporting your secular and holiday activities throughout the year. We recognize and appreciate their contributions to the quality of our Rosewood lives, and I would like to remind all of our members that there will be an opportunity to donate to the Employees Christmas Fund in your December statements. You will receive your statements around the first of the month, and your generosity is greatly appreciated.

In closing, I would like to wish each and every one of you the best of the coming season. Thank you for your continued membership at Rosewood Golf and Country Club, and I encourage you to participate in as many of the fabulous December events as your schedule allows.

Happy Holidays,

Bruce Cranston, PHD
President

Before the general email went out, Bruce as promised, forwarded a copy to Marta. She was around the house, and was waiting for his post, but none the less, was somewhat taken aback by the scope of the proposals for December. She called him.

"Wow," she said when Bruce picked up. "You are going all out on this one."

"Don't you feel it is necessary?"

"To some degree, yes. However, the financial considerations seem somewhat daunting. Have you run the numbers on this with Larry and Joe Goldman? Should we call an Exec Committee meeting and review this?"

"In my opinion, we don't have the time to do that. I strongly feel that we should get this offer out to the membership, and try to counteract the negativity that is killing us. This is a public relations nightmare, and it is just beginning. The media will be reviewing the arraignments and the bail hearings tonight. The trials will be going on forever. Although we are in a peripheral position, Rosewood's name will be connected, and this can't be good. We've got to reach out to our members in a big way, before it is too late."

"I agree with what you are saying, but I just don't want to jeopardize the long-term finances of the club."

"This is a supply side approach to our problems. An economically proven, scientific approach, if I may add. If we add short term benefits to our members, we will reap increased long-term benefits on the back side of the equation."

"I know what supply side economics are, Bruce."

"Marta, you said it yourself. If we start to lose members over this thing, we will have worse long-lasting problems. Potentially fatal problems. Not only could we lose members, it will be very hard to replace those members. And you know that any club survives on its monthly membership dues. Don't you think it is better to be proactive?"

"Yes, I do. But to what extent? You realize we are not only giving away considerable revenue, but we are also losing all of the employee gratuities from that revenue? That is like a double hit. And how much is Jamal Wilkerson costing us?"

"Twenty-five hundred dollars. But I have discussed the numbers with Larry, and he is comfortable going forward as proposed. I would appreciate your support, but if necessary, I will proceed on my President's prerogative."

"Bruce, there is nothing I can do to deny your President's prerogative, but I am advising you we should review this proposal as a Board before we release it."

"We don't have time to do that, something strategic needs to go out today. However, on your advice, I will run it by Joe before I go to press."

"Okay then. You are taking a big risk here, and sticking your neck out, in my opinion."

Treasurer, Joe Goldman, was a conservative man. He was concerned by the cost factors of Bruce's approach, but could also see the ramifications of an ongoing assault in the media on Rosewood by association alone. More than either of those two cognizant issues, however, he seemed impressed by the power of the Presidency, and admired the chutzpah of Bruce Cranston. "I say go for it, Bruce. We could be screwed either way, we might as well err on the side of the membership."

"Thanks for your support, Joe. I feel like an opportunity will be irretrievably lost if we don't do something significant now. I mean right now, and with some sense of urgency."

"Agreed." Also, a frugal, as well as conservative man, the thought of his December social calendar being underwritten by Rosewood, was not at all disagreeable to Joe Goldman.

As a scholar of history, Bruce Cranston, PHD was reminded of a quote by the late General George S. Patton, to wit: "A good plan violently executed now, is better than a perfect plan executed next week." His email went out that afternoon, in spite of the recent moratorium placed on unauthorized executive communications by the Rosewood Board of Directors.

CHAPTER FIFTY-ONE

The Press had their expected field day reporting on all of Monday's trial proceedings. The momentum of the coverage seemed to be drifting away from Rosewood, and onto the principle suspects themselves. But Susie Davis from Fox news, for some reason seemed to have an axe to grind with Rosewood, and never missed an opportunity to drag our name through the mud. Bruce Cranston made a mental note to contact Pete Collins, and see when he could get a letter off to Fox concerning matters of libel.

The reaction to Bruce's email was also quite dramatic. More than several of our Board members, myself included, were offended with its release prior to any official approval. Insulted might be a better term. But now, here we were again dealing with another substantial policy email that had been peremptorily sent out. And hoping it didn't blow up in our faces. This was getting a little old.

There was also a very large problem in logistics, as the club switchboard lit up like a Christmas tree with requests for the club hosted holiday events. To the extent, that it became immediately apparent as to the number of requests for reservations was going to be overwhelming. By Wednesday morning, all of the parties were booked, and members were being turned away. Rather than creating good will with the membership, the opposite effect was becoming evident. As usual, with any private club, there are politics involved. A longtime member, say, an ex-Board member type who had been out of town on Monday and didn't receive Bruce's email in a timely manner, was already shut out for any reservation. As could also be expected, email was a new enough phenomenon, that the younger members were much more adept at receiving and reacting to email. Therefore, the older members were being excluded from the activities. This made them furious.

On Wednesday afternoon, Larry called Bruce's cell phone. "Can I have a meeting with you this afternoon, or Friday morning right after Thanksgiving? I have a real mess on my hands here."

"I can be there Friday at ten, we are busy getting ready for turkey day here."

"Okay."

"What's on your mind Larry? How was your Holiday?"

"It was great Bruce, thanks. Let's grab a table here in the dining room, would you like a cup of coffee?"

"Oh, no thanks. I'm a tea drinker."

"Our problem is that the club secretary has been absolutely inundated for the last three days, with requests for reservations. And then there were one hundred messages on the answering machine for her this morning after the Thanksgiving Day break. She is manning the phones, and I am trying to keep up with the emails. We are buried. Do you want to add any more party functions? How do you want me to deal with the people who are shut out?"

"Just deal with it. You should have thought of this contingency before we sent out the email."

"Just deal with it? What does that mean? I have been dealing with it nonstop. I asked you if we shouldn't run this by the Board on Monday, and you were adamant about going public immediately. Now I am supposed to just deal with it?"

"This is an operational issue, and I clearly communicated to the membership that reservations were a must. What more could I have done?"

"That's not the point, Bruce. The point is that half of the members are booked for parties, and the other half can't get a reservation. You have created a negative instead of a positive, and a lot of people are unhappy. Pretty pissed off actually. Even worse in my opinion, is the fact that some members have reserved for all three parties, while other members do not have a single reservation."

"We have never had this kind of response to any of our promotions before."

"Well, we have never given away the house like this before."

"Given away the house? This is crisis management here, Larry. This is supply side economics at work. We are in trouble, and at least I had the balls to do something."

Yes, you did. And now we need to fix what you did."

"Fix what I did? Again, I see this as an operational issue, Larry. If you were so concerned, you should have voiced your reservations to me earlier."

"I told you that we should wait and discuss the offers with the Board."

"These are specific problems, and, I repeat myself, you did not voice them to me appropriately. You should have been more candid."

Candid? I'll give you candid, Larry thought. "I guess I thought that the potential problems were significant enough that the Board should weigh in on the whole offer in the first place. All of that being said Bruce, what do you want me to do? I have upset members calling in numbers, and that is not good. Do you want to add more events, or limit attendance to one event per member? I have got to do something, and fast, or you are going to have a revolt on your hands." This guy is not going to hang me out to dry with the Board Larry thought to himself.

Bruce responded, and the irritation in his voice was readily apparent. "We have the December Board meeting next Tuesday night. I don't think that the Board is going to want to add any more complimentary functions. We can't afford it. Just tell people we are currently overbooked, and stall them until after the Board meeting. Tell them that we are overwhelmed by the response to our offer, and we will review all of our activities on Tuesday, and we will come up with a plan for everyone then."

"I think that we should limit the membership to one Holiday function per family, so that everyone has an opportunity to attend at least one freebie. The open house will take care of itself, because it has always been a come and go/open attendance type thing. People will understand that. Plus, the Cocktail Party is scheduled for a week from tomorrow. We have got to have time to communicate with people, and let them adjust their holiday schedules. This is going to be a major ordeal to unravel." Why won't this guy listen to me, Larry thought.

"Larry, first you tell me that I should have waited to run my original decision by the Board, and now you are telling me I should make a snap decision to readjust our position?"

This is what you get when you have a retired academic with no operational experience for a President, Larry thought. "Bruce, I am just trying to communicate to you the urgency of the situation we are now in. It was your email, with your name on it. You will be barbequed by the members if we don't act fast to try and resolve this situation. Some members have reserved for all three major functions, and other people have no reservations. Is that fair? I am just trying to help resolve the situation here."

"Well, Larry, I'm afraid I disagree with you on who is going to get barbequed. You are the General Manager of this club. You are responsible for member satisfaction on an operational level. You failed to communicate with me effectively. As I said, we will give you proper direction at the Board meeting on Tuesday evening, and you can solve any difficulties on Wednesday. End of discussion." Bruce was beginning to feel empowered. In charge.

Larry Easton looked at Bruce Cranston in disbelief. I am retiring in three months anyway, he thought, what the fuck. "Well, sir, you can have someone else deal with the problem on Wednesday, because effective as of right now, I resign."

"What. You are resigning? Just like that? You can't do that."

"Watch me. I will be out of my office within the hour. Here are my keys. Thank you for all of my opportunities here at Rosewood." Larry turned, and walked out of the dining room. The waitress who was setting up for lunch, and was eavesdropping on their conversation, hurried into the kitchen. She had some hot news to share with the Chef.

Bruce continued to sit in the dining room, and stare out the windows at the grey, darkening sky. What would George S. Patton do now he thought? Fight on, that's what he would do. Or something.

Or something. Bruce sat for another five minutes, apparently waiting for Larry Easton to come back to his senses. When it was obvious that that was not going to happen, Bruce got up and trudged across the dining room to Larry's office.

Larry had stopped by the bar on the way out of his meeting, and picked up a couple of empty cardboard wine boxes. He was starting to pack when Bruce walked in.

"Listen Larry, why don't we calm down for a minute here. You don't want to end a brilliant career with a rash decision like this, do you? I apologize, I might have over-reacted out there. What can I do to get you to reconsider?" Bruce hated to grovel, but he was now in full brownnose mode, and both men knew it.

"You can stop being an asshole, and call a special meeting of the Board for tomorrow morning. We need to get this thing back on the right tract, and right now."

This was not a favorable ultimatum for Bruce. Should he comply, he would have to inconvenience the Board members with yet another special meeting, and on a holiday weekend. Then, he would have to eat crow for not consulting with them on his executive decisions in the first place. And all this while he was caving in to Larry big time. But he really had no choice.

"Done. I will schedule a meeting for ten am tomorrow. Will that work for you?"

"Sure Bruce. But no more problems, eh?"

"No more problems." The two men shook hands, and Larry put his half full wine box away.

CHAPTER FIFTY-TWO

The Special Meeting of the Rosewood Board of Trustees, was short and not very sweet. After some intense discussion and negotiation, it was decided in the first place that there would be absolutely no more fucking rogue emails sent out to the members by anyone, without full Board approval. A red-faced Bruce was properly chastised.

Secondly, the Board agreed to add one more partially hosted function for the membership. It would be communicated that due to overwhelming response to the earlier invitations, there would be another Holiday Cocktail party added on Sunday the eighth of December. Again, due to overwhelming response, all of the club hosted functions would be restricted to hosted beer and house wine events only. Any members who wished to imbibe in spirits would be doing so on their own chits.

Larry Easton pointed out to the Board that by limiting the scope of the food menus and comp liquor, they could add another function for approximately one half of the previously planned same cost, except for the labor. It was also decided to advise members of the limitation to one complimentary function per family. This would necessitate some unraveling, but should be doable under the circumstances. Crisis averted hopefully. Except for all of the additional work for Larry and the admin staff, except for a red-faced President, and except for all of the other Board members who hated special meetings, and were still largely cranky with said new President.

Before we adjourned, I asked Larry and Bruce if they had a specific amount budgeted for the complimentary parties. "We are looking at approximately fifty grand. Fifty-five tops on the high side." Bruce replied. "Fifteen thou each for the cocktail parties, and twenty for the Dinner Dance. The New Year's Day Open House is already in the operating budget. If we can buy back the confidence and support of this club's membership for that amount, it would be in my opinion, money well spent." Apparently, the rest of the Board agreed with him, because there weren't any more questions. Maybe everyone was just tired and upset, and wanted to get the heck out of there. Those figures are way too low I thought to myself, unfortunately it was after the conclusion of the meeting, while I was driving out of the parking lot.

As a special meeting had been called, and the regular Board meeting was scheduled for only three days hence, and due to the busy December schedule, there was a motion for this meeting to stand officially as the December Board meeting. Motion was seconded, and approved, and our meeting was adjourned.

President Cranston had gone from personal musings on General George Patton, to more of an experience of General George Armstrong Custer. But, at least it was only his pride that had been scalped. No real blood had been shed, and none of his staff had been massacred.

Steve Rodriguez, with Tricia's blessing, had booked a holiday trip to southern California, including a stop at Disneyland. All of the law enforcement side under Steve's jurisdiction and coordination were very happy with the way the arraignments had gone. Charlie Strong and Bao Thieu were both denied bail. The Changs were still in transit from Hawaii and hadn't been processed yet. Rick Ferin had been granted bail to the tune of 50K. But as he had already turned state's evidence, he was certainly no flight risk. His status with the ILWU was pending. Ben Harris, however, was on his own.

Tricia had taken the Thanksgiving week off, and was looking forward to not only getting out of town for a few days, but for some quality family time. Steve, with Tricia's enthusiastic approval, had thoughtfully invited Tricia's son and mother along on the getaway. Tricia's mom, Maggie, seemed as excited as her grandson to be going to Disneyland. It would be a good time for everyone to get to know each other, and for Steve and Tricia, it looked like things were getting serious.

Tricia's only request of Steve in wrapping up all of the various details of their investigation, was for him to make a call to Malcolm McElfresh for her. "Will you please ask him to vest Nikki, and let her take my old job in the ILWU offices at the Port of Vancouver?" It was a small request, but to Steve, it showed the thoughtfulness he was beginning to find so attractive in Tricia. He called Malcolm, and the request was granted post haste.

His other details in place, Steve was now free to spend some time with, and get to know better, what he hoped would soon be some special people in his life.

The Magnolia neighbors were amused, to say the least, by the Rosewood invitations to their members. There would be some lively discussion at this year's neighborhood pot luck Thanksgiving dinner about Bruce's email. The dinner was being hosted, of course, by the Kudlachs. The whole street was invited. The only caveat, was to bring a dish and a bottle. Hugh Schmidt had even invited Suzie Davis over.

Since Hugh and Bunny had been expelled from the club, there were no more Proprietary members left on Magnolia street, so no one was eligible to attend any of the Holiday Parties. The New Year's Day open house was available to the Kudlachs and the Horns, but it was still up in the air as to their attendance.

The preponderance of opinion on Magnolia Street concerning Rosewood, was that their December promotions were a move of desperation. It was pure speculation, but the heavy toll of public vituperation and bad press appeared to be showing its effects.

Bob Kudlach and Carol Horn were both in agreement on the gratuitous promotions eliciting a sign of distress from the Board at the Club, but that the email also demonstrated some culpability for past actions, and decisions made. The email had already been forwarded on to the neighbor's personal injury attorney for his input and evaluation. And in their dilettantish (except for Carol Horn) opinions, the culpability issue may not be enough to produce a sizeable up-front settlement in a civil suit. But it certainly seemed like it was damning enough, with all of the other evidence considered, to make a defense attorney or insurance company be concerned about appearances in front of a jury of one's peers.

The neighbors were still glowing over their land use victories, and the thought of winning a sizeable civil suit against the Club, to them, was like blood in the water of a shark tank. Their friend and leader had been returned to them. And the extent of the Magnolian's adverse distaste, no, hatred of Rosewood, which was curiously debatable before the attack on Bob and Lillian, had now crystalized into a cancerous malignancy. Hugh and Bunny's abrupt dismissal had helped fuel those fires. Now the neighborhood wanted total destruction of Rosewood. They would seemingly stop at nothing short of their collective goals.

It says in the Lord's prayer that He will "Forgive us our trespasses, as we forgive those who have trespassed against us." With the Magnolia Street neighbors, it was more like "We will make every attempt to avenge one hundred-fold any perceived trespass against us. Amen."

And so, in the meantime, everyone was going faithfully to see their therapists twice a week, doing their homework, and documenting the devastating toll the last month had taken on their personal lives. As far as dinner was concerned, Lillian Kudlach did a masterful job with a thirty-pound, organic bird. Bob carved almost professionally, and the oyster stuffing turned out to be moist and pungent. Willamette Valley Pinot Noir seemed to be the beverage option of the day, and a good time was had by all. A much-needed respite from the Rosewood Wars for all of them.

Watery mashed potatoes and limp turkey slices, frozen peas, and lumpy gravy with a tasteless biscuit, rounded out the menu for the incarcerated complainants in the Rodriguez Investigation, as it was now called. It seemed like this menu was a universal offering at most, if not all, stateside correctional institutions. Charlie Strong silently cursed his fate, and poked at his food. Bao Thieu couldn't give a twit about Thanksgiving, and the Changs were not even allowed to eat together. Rather than Oregon Pinot Noir, Charlie drank some unfiltered water from a plastic glass, and retired to his cell to stare at the walls some more.

As soon as the Special Board Meeting was over on Saturday morning, Larry and two of his staff manned the phones, and began to sort out the reservations snafus. First, they had to contact all of the multi-reservation people, and find out preferences for which single event they would prefer to attend. Then there was the waiting list to contact regarding the additional Cocktail Party. As many of the members were out of town for Thanksgiving, it was going to be a process to get in touch with everyone. Still, Larry preferred this personal approach, rather than sending out another email, and creating another avalanche of phone calls and electronic mail for his office personnel to deal with. Then, of course, there was the matter of operationally staffing another major back to back member function on top of the previous one.

Larry took a break and went to visit with the Chef. "How you doing man?"

"Good, you?"

"Okay. I am having some issues with the new Board, but nothing out of control."

"Yeah, I heard you were ready to walk yesterday."

"Who told you that?"

"You know the walls have ears around here."

"It got a little tense, but we kissed and made up."

"Well, just so you know, if you go, I am right behind you."

"Thanks for your support. But I've only got another three months until my retirement. You are going to have to slug it out on your own after that. One thing did change, however, at our Board meeting this morning."

"Now what?"

"The Board added another cocktail party on Sunday."

"Back to back?"

"Yeah, but we can do the same menu, and we decided to pare the buffet down to bare necessities."

"Whew. It's going to be a busy weekend."

"I know, but I've been getting some calls from some people who want to work for the Holidays, so we should have plenty of help."

"What do you want to serve."

"I will write it up this afternoon. But I think a lot of P & D Prawns, an oyster bar, lots of cheese and cold smoked salmon.

Some canapes and crudité. Throw some of your sauces at them, the usual."

"Do you want a carving station?"

"Yeah, we better do that. And a Caesar salad station. Once you get your ordering done, why don't you take a couple of days off before the month starts. It's going to be a busy."

"I can do that. Maybe I'll take the kids over to Mount Hood tomorrow, and go skiing."

"Just cover yourself on the schedule."

"Any word on the ad we posted for a sous chef?" As usual, we were always looking for good kitchen help.

"Nothing yet. Hopefully soon. We need to get someone in here."

"Well, you keep an eye on my crew for the next couple of days. We are a little light, until we hire someone."

"Will do. See ya."

Of course, the first call Larry got when he came into the club on Monday morning, was from the Chef's wife.

Clubs, restaurants, hotels, yachts, whoever is functioning in real time, have this thing called Murphy's Law. Murphy's Law states that, "anything that can go wrong, will go wrong." The service industry has extended that Law to include, "and usually at the worst possible time." For example, if you have a critical piece of equipment or a computer, a printer, a vehicle, a point of sale system, etc., that is absolutely needed for a specific task, it will break at the most inopportune time. The propane leak never occurs on Tuesday morning, when you have until Friday to get it fixed. No, it waits until five thirty pm on Friday evening to go south. Just when you need it the most, and when it is next to impossible to get anyone in to fix anything.

As Larry took his Chef's wife's call that morning, he heard Murphy giggling sadistically in the background. "Larry, I am sorry to have to tell you this, but John broke his hip skiing yesterday. We are still here at Portland General, and John is in a full body cast. He won't be home for a couple of days, and won't be able to work for two or three months at best."

"You're kidding me. What happened?"

"We were up at Mount Hood, and it was pretty rocky up there. John caught an edge, and slammed into a tree. We had to airlift him."

"Wow. This is not good news."

"Yes, I know. John feels terrible, and wanted me to tell you he will start checking around as soon as we get home. He thinks he can find someone to help out. He is still pretty woozy though."

"I am sure he is. Give him our regards, and tell him we will muddle through here." Damn it, Larry thought to himself. Does this place have a black cloud over it or what?

CHAPTER FIFTY-THREE

Larry got on the phone, and found a woman sous chef, who had worked at the Club some five years ago. She was willing to come in and help out for the short term. Of course, she hadn't worked in a few years, and was not ready for battle by any means. She helped as best she could, but two days in, her back went out, and she was done.

The rest of the crew limped through the week. At least John had done the ordering before he went down, but his back up Sous Chef was young and inexperienced. He was the guy Larry and John had wanted to replace, and now he was trying to run the show alone. Food and Beverage was definitely not Larry's forte, he actually hated dealing with it. It was nothing but problems, in his mind, always problems. All the same, he helped out as best he could.

Saturday was on the kitchen crew before they knew it. Prepping for a party of one hundred and fifty members plus spouses, was stressful enough under normal circumstances. But now with John was out, it was a frenzy of the blind leading the blind. When the wait staff arrived to start setting up, someone discovered that there was no ice in the dining room ice machine. Murphy struck again. A critical piece of broken equipment, and no ice for you. While the young sous chef was distracted by ice machine issues, the prime ribs of beef were left in the oven for too long, and over cooked. At the same time, the boiled prawns were left in the cookpot too long, and they turned into rubber.

Chef John had been unable to make sauces before his injury, and so the cocktail sauce was sour. Way too lemony. But that minor fault was disguised by the fact of the Prawns being tasteless. They chewed like rubber bands. The creamy horseradish sauce was overly thick and too spicy. Little did that matter, because the rib roasts were well done, and of shoe leather quality. The Caesar Salad dressings anchovy portion somehow got doubled, and was therefore basically inedible. You get the drift. And Sunday's efforts were as bad if not worse, as everyone was tired and sorely in need of a day off.

Leon, the barman, did his best to save the day. But refilling three hundred wine and beer glasses continually is not an easy task, no matter how much staff you put on. Larry had Leon give last call at ten thirty on Saturday night, but the usual gaggle of revelers kept at it until midnight. Even after Larry cut off the comp drinks, the members ordered from the back bar, and kept Leon busy until late. It was three in the morning before he got his restocking done for Sunday night's party. He said a silent prayer on his way home that the refer boxes didn't go down, too.

The refer boxes held up, but Sunday nights party didn't go much better.

Larry ended up closing the entire clubhouse on Monday, just to give everyone a break.

Larry and Bruce met on Tuesday morning. They talked. The weekend had been a disaster. An unmitigated disaster. But what could Larry do without a Chef?

"I've heard nothing but negative comments about this weekend," was Bruce's opening salvo.

"Thanks. We did the best we could without John here. What timing, huh?"

"Yeah, well, what about the Dinner Dance? That party is even trickier to deal with."

"I know, but hopefully we will have another professional in here before then."

"I certainly hope so. It looks like we have basically blown north of thirty grand on this weekend's parties, and all we did was proceed to look like amateurs."

"Well, hopefully they will understand the timing and personnel issues we are trying to work with."

"People don't care about timing issues, Larry. They want to be wined and dined, not fed a bunch of inedible crap, and have to fight all night to get a glass of wine."

"We did the best we could, Bruce. Under the circumstances, I am proud of our staff and their hard work."

"Listen, we have got to get better, and quick. Right now, before the Dinner Dance and New Year's party," said Bruce. "If we don't, we are dead meat. Can't you borrow a Chef from one of the Clubs in Portland?"

"The problem is the holiday season. They all have their own parties and functions to deal with right now. You know this is one of the busiest months of the year for all of us."

"What about Brad Young from Jackson Street Steak House. Maybe he can help us. He is a Board member, and he understands what we are dealing with here."

"Hopefully. I'll will be happy to talk to him."

"No, let me. Maybe as President, I can convince him that we need some help."

"We'll see. But he has his own business to run, too."

"I know that. I'll talk to him today."

My phone rang around one in the afternoon, and who but my buddy, President Bruce, was on the line.

"Hey Bradley, how're you doing? I am calling to see if you might be able to give us a hand over here at the Club. I am sure you have heard about Chef John breaking his hip. Unfortunately, this has adversely affected the quality of our weekend Cocktail Parties. I am very concerned about the upcoming annual Dinner Dance. If we drop the ball on this one, we will look like rank amateurs."

"Yeah, I heard that the kitchen really struggled this weekend. So, what can I do for you?"

"Do you know anyone who might be able to help us out, or if not, might you be able to step in, and help us out personally?"

My wheels were turning. "I might be able help you out, Bruce. But it will cost you."

"What do you mean, cost me?"

"Well, Bruce, for some time, I've been advocating for us to adjust our priorities, and start to put some resources back into the clubhouse. I will help you out if you will assure me of your rock-solid commitment to hire an architect to begin a process of remodeling and revitalization of our facilities at Rosewood."

"Brad, you know there are covert pressures against this type of thing from both the Men's Club and the Green's Committee. However, I have also felt for some time that we need to begin to refocus. And therefore, I am in agreement with you. It is time we should hire someone, and start a feasibility study. Look at a complete clubhouse remodel. Does that work for you? How about if I name you Chair of a Project Committee to work with the Board and the House Committee? I think we can get this effort started."

"You nailed it Bruce. Of course, it works for me. You will not regret this decision. In no time, you will see what a new clubhouse will bring to this organization. Not only as an amenity to the membership, but also as a revenue center for the club. As a matter of fact, we don't even need to hire anyone. Ron Atherton is one of our members, and he is a brilliant Architect. He designs hospital facilities all over the west coast. I'm sure he would help us at least get started with the process if we asked him. Then, we have Bill Newton who is the best contractor in town as a member. He has been wanting to get to work on this place for years. You work with me here, Bruce, and I will also help out with the New Year's Day open house party. I can help make sure your events are serviced properly."

"I can't thank you enough, Brad. And I look forward to working with you on the new Rosewood Clubhouse."

"You won't regret it, Bruce. I can expect our conversation of today to be on the agenda of the January Board meeting?"

"You got it, Partner."

"Also, I will need to be compensated dollar wise, to the degree that I incur labor costs to replace myself at my own restaurant. I will send you a bill."

"No problem. Have a great day."

"You too Bruce."

I was elated. Finally, circumstances had coalesced, and provided some leverage for us to get this long overdue project rolling. I called Marta Koenig and shared my conversation with her. She was almost as happy as I was to go forward with the start of a remodel. But always the pragmatist, she cautioned about the costs of such a large undertaking at this time.

"It isn't going to cost anything to start with. If Ron Atherton helps us, we will just be talking conceptually to start. We may have to pay for the reproduction of some architectural drawings is all."

"Then you go for it, boy," she said.

Go for it I did. We got the Dinner Dance menu planned out. I ordered six cases of Chateau Branaire, one of my favorite little boutique, Bordeaux wines. Costly, but not nearly as expensive as a Margaux, and probably ninety percent of the quality.

We got a deal on some Kobe tenderloins, and they proved to be a huge hit. Although previously frozen, and dearly expensive, we served Copper River for our Salmon course.

The Holiday Dance dinner was divine. Everyone loved it. Before the entertainment started, Larry called our culinary team out from the kitchen, and the members gave us a standing ovation in appreciation for a job well done. It felt rather odd to be standing in the dining room of my own club in Chef's attire, but I was very happy with the results of our efforts. Anything for the team.

While I was busy working with our kitchen crew, Bruce Cranston was absorbed with getting his survey out to the membership. We received our questionnaire via email about the middle of the December, and promptly filled it out, and hit return. It was more basic than I had anticipated, more subjective than scientific, mostly generic in nature, in my opinion. But Bruce apparently felt that it would be an invaluable asset to the Board going forward.

The New Year's Day Open House was anticlimactic. Since the Club had butchered the first two holiday parties, and as that was two thirds of the Proprietary membership, they didn't seem very anxious to waste their New Year's Day on more bad food, and slow service. So, we ended up with lots of the older members, and a bunch of the Social members. That is a bit of a strange mixture of people, as the Socials tend to be a much younger crowd. But everyone gravitated to their own comfort zones, and the party went off well enough. The heavy appetizer and raw bars were well received, and Larry gave Leon the latitude to pour some decent wines.

By the time the January Board meeting rolled around on the ninth of the month, I was barely caught up with myself, and still tired and worn down a little from all of my self-inflicted activities. It had been a very busy season, not only in my being stuck in the Rosewood kitchen so much of the time, but keeping up with our own Jackson Street F & B responsibilities. That is a full-time job in itself, as volume seems to be increasing every year. Then there are all of the year end admin duties, and the monthly and year end reconciliations to take care of. Not to mention dining room and kitchen maintenance, product ordering, fixing equipment, inventory, payroll, taxes due, Christmas bonuses to pay out. Plus, a holiday party for our staff, and my own family to keep up with. It is an insanely busy time of the year. And as if that is not enough, my wife and I share a birthday on the twentieth of December. In reality, I was more than a little worn down, I was exhausted, and in dire need of a week or two off. At least all of our and the club's last two holiday parties had gone well. Too busy, is certainly better than the alternative.

CHAPTER FIFTY-FOUR

Bruce Cranston called our January Board meeting to order, and I gave the agenda a quick perusal. Under the House Committee heading, was a line item referring to 2010 projects. I assumed that would be the entry point for the introduction of the formation of our new Committee and Partnership on the Clubhouse.

Of course, once the meeting has been called to order, and the prior meeting's minutes have been approved, the President's remarks lead off the current meeting's bullet points.

Bruce wished us all a happy New Year, and began with a re-cap of December. He reviewed the holiday functions, mentioned Chef John's untimely accident, and launched into some financial analysis.

"Without overstepping Joe Goldman's monthly P & L report, I am forced to bring our financial position before the Board at this time. And unfortunately, the news is bad. Very bad. The cost of our good will, complimentary parties for the membership has been exacerbated by some unanticipated expenses."

Bruce went on to detail that John's skiing accident had dramatically increased payroll expenses, and we had unfortunately rather severely underestimated those costs. Overwhelming membership attendance at the parties, had sharply increased consumption and therefore our product expenses. An early frost in California's Coachella Valley had tripled the cost of our produce, and we had to buy a new commercial ice maker for the dining room. That cost five grand. Another ill-timed plumbing backup in the kitchen had required an expensive holiday stop gap repair, to name a few problems. The effect of all of our overages, caused our expenses to escalate to approximately ninety five thousand dollars, for the parties alone. Considerably more than what we had budgeted for. 50K for the two disastrous cocktail parties, 25K for the Dinner Dance, and another 20K for the NYD open house. This did include staff gratuities for working the parties, but because of the club's terrible execution on the first two holiday parties, the contributions to the employee fund fell well below previous year's amounts. Therefore, the club was compelled to add another 10K to the employee's holiday fund, or risk a mass exodus by the staff.

Another complication from our holiday bumbles and internal difficulties, was a mini run on memberships. That would be a mini run in the wrong direction, with over twenty members submitting their resignations since the first of the year. It seems that in addition to Charlie's antics, our good will intentions for our members had backfired, and produced negative results instead of the desired effect. Some of these members were abiding by the exit policies of the club, which mandate a five-thousand-dollar buyout of one's surrendered membership. Other members were taking issue with the standard four and one-half percent cost of living dues increase, that had automatically kicked in at the start of the new year, and were just walking away.

"They have been informed that they will be unwelcome at any future Rosewood events, and could face possible legal action, and or negative credit reporting," Paul informed us.

"What was their reaction to that?" Mary Lou Rousseau asked.

Larry spoke up in reply, and informed us that, "the majority of the members who resigned were pretty hostile. They referred to our past President as a disgrace, said we were inept at running this club, and were very upset with a dues increase at this point in time. And to make matters worse, some of the younger members are walking away with a fairly healthy balance due in their accounts."

"This is unacceptable. We should sue them for breach of contract for trying to just walk away," stated the always aggressive Sonny Brown.

As one of our Board attorneys, Toni Duncan spoke up. "Yes, we have the right to sue, under the provisions of a binding contract. However, with all that has happened in the last month and a half, in addition to being time consuming and expensive, a lawsuit would also create another raging public relations nightmare. Imagine that little blond snot from Fox News getting ahold of something like this, and running with it. I can just see it now. Rosewood sues its own membership!"

"The bottom line is our cash reserves are now down to approximately thirty thousand dollars," Bruce droned on. "With the growing exit of Proprietary members, and the resulting decline in revenues, this puts us in a precarious financial position. January payrolls are coming up, the first of which will be escalated due to the holiday parties. We are committed to paying the gratuities from all of the holiday parties, and of course the minimum wage just went up again. Then quarterly taxes are due before the end of the month, and these are all significant drains on cash flow."

Marta Koenig took the floor, and was of the opinion that while our cash was indeed at a disturbingly low level, Rosewood was still debt free, and if need be, could always open an operational line of credit. "All we have to do is to offer our property as collateral to secure a loan," she intoned us.

"But Rosewood has never had to borrow money before in our history," observed Tommy Thompson, one our new Board members.

"This is true. But these are perilous times, my friend."

By this early juncture of the meeting, the writing on the wall was becoming pretty clear. Under the circumstances, there were few if any Board members in the room who were willing to begin a discussion of any clubhouse upgrades or expansions. I would need to put a heavy spin on the conceptual and cost-effective nature of our new subcommittee. And, of course, my suspicions were confirmed, when we got to the House Committee section of our agenda.

Sara Richards made her House report, and basically all she had was a great deal of thanks to the crew of ladies, who had helped decorate the clubhouse for the holidays. When we got to the House Committee line item concerning projects, Bruce Cranston interrupted Sara with an update on anticipated projects for the coming year.

"After a thorough review of the Member Survey which was sent out the middle of last month, I have had the very positive response rate of approximately sixty nine percent of our Proprietary Members. The overwhelming sentiment of the members of this club is to be the very best Golf Club we can be. Therefore, my plan for the direction of Rosewood for the coming year"- drum roll please, I thought- "is to continue on in the time-honored tradition of achieving excellence in our golf program. I have spoken with both our Greens Superintendent, and our Greens Chairman, and we are in agreement, that all of our golf course bunkers should be refurbished, to include improved drainage. Our next, and highest priority this year will be elevating the quality of our greens to be the very best in the State of Washington. Frank Davis envisions greens so pure, with rolls so true, it will bring people from throughout the region to play with us. We feel that with Frank's expertise and leadership, we can attain both of these goals within a manageable time span, and negligible expense to the club."

Not even a word about any kind of clubhouse project committee? I looked at Bruce, and he was busy shuffling paper in front of him, so he wasn't about to make any eye contact with me. You weasel, I thought.

Just to be contrary, I asked our esteemed President if there were any plans to begin reviewing the condition of the clubhouse anytime soon. "No," he replied. "Other than looking into some screening between the bar and the dining room, there are no plans for any more activity or improvements in the clubhouse this year. That was made pretty clear in the responses to our survey." I feigned a migraine, and excused myself from the meeting. I do not have time for this, I thought.

After some discussion later that night at home, I expressed my frustrations, and my wife and I decided not to become part of the members who were lining up to walk out on the club. She and our son loved to golf as much as I did. Also, there was the matter of the swimming pool, which both of our kids loved to death, and spent most of their summers at. So, we would stay golfing members, but just not spend as much time or money in and around the clubhouse. We would start to pull away from the club a bit. In reality, for all of my exhortations about upgrading the club, I was essentially competing with myself, and our business. Who needed it? But by morning time, I was much calmer.

These decisions also didn't prohibit me from reviewing my expenses for the month of December the next day. I was more than happy to rewrite my invoice for kitchen bailout services as yet rendered to President Cranston and Rosewood CC from two thousand to twelve thousand dollars. And I would get that money, even if I had to sue Cranston's sorry ass for it. Hey, just take it out of your new line of credit account.

Next on my agenda was inviting my wife's mother up here to help with the kids for a few days. I wanted to run down to the desert for a little R & R. We both needed to get out of Dodge.

The rest of Rosewood's month seemed to progress haphazardly from what I heard. The club was basically broke, and another thirty members had walked away. This meant a fifteen to twenty to thousand dollar decrease in monthly dues to the club. An amount we could ill afford at the moment, considering the state of our current cash flow. The termination fees were helping with the cash flow, but Larry and Bruce had still secured a one hundred and fifty-thousand-dollar line of credit, which had already been broken into. Larry Easton was into his last two months of service before retirement, and we needed to get going on a search for a new General Manager pronto. The kitchen drainage system continued to backup with raw sewage, and be a problem, as I could personally attest. It was sorely in need of a permanent fix. And Frank Davis was already over his equipment budget for the repair and reconstruction of our course's thirty-nine sand bunkers. Other than that, things were going swimmingly.

Things were also going swimmingly on Magnolia Street and in the Vancouver community at large. Our local media still had the Rodriguez Investigation on the front burner, and exploited it as much as possible. People in our town, seemingly couldn't hear enough dirt. The trials were progressing slowly, and were still in the pretrial stages. Rosewood was fading out of the picture little by little, except whenever Charlie Strong's name came up. He was always referred to as the ex-president of Rosewood Country Club. It was like a neon sign at the entrance to Vancouver. "Rosewood is trouble. Keep your distance."

The Magnolia neighbors had maintained their planned course of action, and a community meeting was scheduled by them for Wednesday evening, the third of February. They would be meeting with the street's brain trust and their personal injury attorney.

The meeting convened at seven pm, and the usual suspects were there. "How is everyone coming with their therapy?"

"Good," was the unanimous response.

It is a pleasure to work with such a conscientious, disciplined group, the lawyer thought to himself. "I have drawn up some preliminary paperwork, outlining our most compelling damages, and suggesting Rosewood's liabilities in monetary terms and amounts. We have several options. A, we can file sooner, rather than later for a more moderate settlement. B, we can gather more data, we can continue to compile our case histories and document our professional evaluations. Then we file for a larger amount at a later date."

"How much larger an amount?" Carol Horn asked.

"For a class action suit of this magnitude and with the amount of emotion this case will naturally generate, I feel that the difference in amounts would be approximately double. Say five to six million dollars, versus ten to twelve."

"Those are both considerable sums. How soon would you be able to file?"

"Should we decide on the earlier filing, I would need about two to three weeks to collect your information, and plug it into my formula for you."

"Will we be filing against Rosewood itself, or the Board of Directors collectively?"

"It will be a combination of the two. Most likely the D & O liability coverage will be in the neighborhood of a million bucks per Director. And the Club will also have liability insurance. I think that we can easily demonstrate the magnitude of the negative relationship between your community and Rosewood. We have evidence which indicates the majority of the hostile actions were promulgated by Rosewood. They operated in complete disregard of the law for the most part. This is evidenced by the numerous noise complaints filed with the City of Vancouver. And the lack of any response to correct those on-going issues by either Mr. Easton, Mr. Davis or their maintenance crews.

Secondly, it is fairly obvious that, even though the Board of Directors was kept in the dark by the VPD to protect their case against Charlie Strong, the Board still didn't handle the situation properly. Charlie should never have remained on that Board. Then there was the Board's egregious handling of Hugh's expulsion. All of his rights as a member were violated, and to make matters worse, the fact that Charlie Strong was still around to poison the issue was deplorable. Next, we have the Board fostering and maintaining a structure of governance which was very hostile. Even if the Board had no overt participation in the actual corpus delicti of the assault on Bob. It was almost as if they encouraged their very own president to commit an act of premeditated murder. If not for the one in a million chance of an undercover agent on this case, Mr. Kudlach would not be here with us today. How much stress has that caused this neighborhood every time the doorbell rings?" The Magnolians shuddered, and nodded their heads collectively. But they liked what they were hearing.

"And finally, the Rosewood Board as much as publicly admitted past culpability. Their public email to their membership about mending fences, and atoning for past wrong doings is a critical red flag. It is almost a signed admission of guilt.

No, I think we have ample grounds to proceed against both the Officers of the Board, and the Organization itself."

"Why don't you let us have some discussion, and sleep on it, and we will get back to you tomorrow."

"That is more than reasonable."

"Great, I'll call you in the morning."

The Magnolians opened three more bottles of wine. It was another therapy session and a mini wine tasting. They began to weigh their options. Hugh Schmidt readily voiced his opinion, and said, "I think we should strike while the iron is hot. All of the involved players are still in place. Who knows what could happen if we wait another six months to a year? The Board will change. I think that Larry Easton is ready to retire. He could leave the area, that type of thing. Also, from what I hear, Rosewood is having some pretty serious cash flow problems. This lawsuit just might be the straw which could break the camel's back."

Carol Horn spoke up next. "I agree with Hugh, and feel we should go ahead and proceed now. Although there is the distinct possibility any defense team would request a Change of Venue in this case. My feeling is we definitely have momentum on our side, and the community behind us here. We should go now."

Bunny, Lillian, and three or four others spoke out. Everyone wanted to go ahead and proceed. Bob Kudlach sat back like a wise sage, and let everyone else speak up. He wanted to begin proceedings as soon as possible himself, but was humble and patient enough to let the group speak for him.

Finally, he weighed in. "Well, the sentiment in this room seems to be unanimous in favor of a quicker resolution. Not that anything will be quick. I have seen Civil Suits drag on for years, however we will continue to wage our small battle against the gorilla in the room, no pun intended. We will continue to snipe at Goliath, until someday, by some miracle, we will bring him down."

Carol Horn had one last comment. "Friends, there will be an enormous amount of preparatory work to do before we can file our complaint with Clark County. I encourage all of us to keep our schedules as light as possible for the next couple of weeks. This will allow us to work as best we can to meet our councilor's needs. I will call him first thing in the morning, and instruct him to start litigation. Rosewood will have approximately three weeks to respond to our complaint, once we have filed. We will need to be extremely alert and attentive during this period, in order to assist our attorney and the development of our case. Are there any questions? No? Well then friends, this thing is happening."

With there being no questions, Carol assumed everyone in the room seemed relatively certain of what needed to be done. In closing, Carol shared one more fact with us. "If everything goes well, the case against Rosewood should be served and filed before the end of this month. We are going on the record, and this will bring repercussions to all of us. Be careful out there, and please email me if anyone has any questions."

"I'll bring my wine glass back tomorrow," she said to Lillian Kudlach, and with that, she turned and was out of the door.

CHAPTER FIFTY-FIVE

Everyone at Rosewood, possibly everyone in the northern world, was happy to see January go away. February starts to bring up the tulips, daffodils and primroses. Valentine's Day splits the month, and is always a fun holiday to celebrate. Plus, it is the shortest month of the year, which accelerates the march towards spring. Finally, we are exiting out of the long, grey winter in the Northwest.

Our February Board meeting was relatively uneventful. Given the fact the club was now virtually broke and also going into debt, there was not too much to chat about. At least the outward flow of members had started to stanch. This was about the only positive take away from our gathering. This and the fact of the seemingly unrelenting barrage of incoming artillery was starting to ease. Rosewood, and also the Board had been inundated with proverbial rockets, lasers, and ICBMs from all directions since Halloween. Then, of course, the major Scud missile of Charlie's arrest, in our own bar yet, and that resulting fallout. But things seemed to be calming down. We were all looking forward to spring, some quality golf, and more pleasant times.

It was decided since Chef John was still recuperating, we would minimize the attempt to offer any theme parties to the membership. The kitchen was barely hanging in there as it was, and didn't need any more stress than they already had trying to keep up with daily operations. I certainly wasn't going to come around and bail anyone out again.

We voted to keep Chef John on the payroll in spite of his inability to work, which would pay off for the long run, but was a burden for the short run on our tight budget. He was helping co-ordinate by phone and with recipe and menu planning, etc. Fortunately, or not, depending on your perspective, our F & B sales volume was very slow to almost nonexistent. Everyone knew the Chef was out sick, and people were staying away in droves. The rest of the droves were having a few cocktails, or snow birding down in the desert.

Whoever wasn't in the desert, must have been coming to Jackson Street Steak House nonstop. Our family business was doing a bash up job for the dead of winter.

The Rosewood search committee, had had several non-descript applications for a General Manager through our preliminary inquiries, but nothing serious seemed to be developing. Larry had intimated to several of us, of his availability should we need him. He said he could probably stick around until May, if we hadn't found anyone else before then.

Joe and Bruce made an announcement of even more expenses incurred from the December parties. Bruce proceeded to glare in my direction. I glared back. It was a glare down. My wife and I were flying down to the desert for a long weekend, after Valentine's Day. And on Bruce's dime yet. So, what did I care if that jerk wanted to glare in my direction? I was a blink away from resigning from the Board anyway.

There being no further business, we adjourned. It was one of our shortest meetings of the past couple of years. We were all glad to get out of there. The onus of our Board responsibilities was beginning to seriously wear everyone down.

My wife and I were looking forward to our get away. While spring was beginning to show her face in our climes, there is nothing better for a northerner, then to hit the desert in February for a shot of brio.

Other than Christmas, and maybe Fourth of July, is there any better time in the world than spring? The birds are chirping, the buds are starting to open, the bodily juices are starting percolate. If you are a golfer, and you don't live in or winter in the desert, spring is a renewal of your vows with the game. Even though we play year-round in Vancouver, fall and winter play is a largely cold, damp, often windy, uncomfortable and British Isles style of game. Contrarily, spring brings warmth, hope and mettle. This is the year. The swing will improve, the putts will drop, the new Christmas driver will turn the tide.

Mexico, Hawaii, Florida, Arizona, Palm Desert, wherever, are even better. Rather than the gradual onset of longer, sunnier days you jump off of the plane, and get an immediate blast of full on non-alcoholic sunny intoxication. Even to sit on the deck in the morning is a joy. The sun embraces you, your body loosens up automatically. While I love the four seasons, that first snow, or the first freezing night spent in front of a roaring fireplace seems hard pressed to compare with our first day of spring in the desert.

The golf balls even like the warmer weather. They roll farther, and fly straighter. They also seem to want to stay with you longer.

We had so much fun and decompression time, seeing lots of friends from our home club. Every day, there was a game with a different foursome, on another course. Relaxing pool time in the afternoons, with a good book and a cold beverage was beginning to be a habit. There were dinners out every night, sometimes under the stars. We can all thank Frank Sinatra and Dean Martin's influence in the Palm Springs area, because the Italian food there is incredible. Not to mention the indigenous Mexican food.

Five days went by in a blink, and we could hardly have had more fun. But the wife was beginning to feel guilty that the kids weren't with us, so it was time to go.

Sui Chang had finally been escorted back to Portland, Oregon. She was being held without bail in a maximum security federal facility. It was cold, noisy, and she was miserable. She was wearing one those ridiculous, orange jump suits. Her skin was dry, pale and starting to crack. Her hair was thick and oily. She had a scratchy wool blanket to call all her own, and curl up in every night. She was allowed to see her husband one hour a week, and was allowed to communicate with her attorney at will. But he worked out of San Francisco, so he was around very little. Other than that, she had no friends, no acquaintances, no visitors, and no other contacts.

She was sitting on the edge of her steel bunk bed, with her head in her hands. She cursed herself for ever relaxing her guard, and trusting any of these miserable white people. Stupid, sloppy, unsophisticated, ignorant white people. Yet here she sat, under their lock and key.

The memories of Tricia Watson particularly haunted and galled her. Usually she could sense trouble or a threat of any kind, from a mile away. It was her intuitive specialty. Her instincts were what had propelled and insured her safe navigation from the treacherous and dangerous streets of Southeast Asia, to the pinnacle she had enjoyed prior to her fall from grace. Yet she had allowed herself to become beguiled by this attractive, yet largely unproven novice of an American woman. A mere child actually, compared to the imperial imminence of Sui Chang. I must think, I must collect myself she thought. There must be a way out of this.

Sui Chang slept fitfully for the next week. She was losing any concept of time and space being locked in her cell twenty-three hours a day. She had no windows, no privacy and the overhead, florescent lights beat down on her 24/7. All she had to cling to, was her ratty, scratchy army issue, green wool blanket. If I can just get out of here, she thought, I can start over. I have resources put away. Finally, on the eighth day she spoke to her matron, "I want to talk with Officer Watson please."

Steve Rodriguez phoned Tricia at work. She had been promoted to Detective on the Vancouver PD, as her undercover days were over, and Chief Farley wanted Larry Larson to spend his last year on the force training Tricia to replace himself as Chief of Detectives. She had also enrolled in criminology classes at Portland State University for the spring semester, and along with her budding relationship with Steve and her family responsibilities, was being kept pretty busy.

"Sui Chang wants to talk with you."

"Really. What about?"

"I don't know. Maybe she misses you, or maybe she wants to flip."

"You think?"

"Why don't you go find out?"

"I will. How about I buy lunch, and then stop by and see her?"

"Best offer I've had all day. Let's meet at my office in an hour."

After lunch, Tricia kissed Steve goodbye, and headed for Corrections. She checked in, and was led to an interview room. As a detective, she was not required to wear a uniform, and was dressed smartly in a black pants suit. So, she felt pretty fashionable when an unkempt Sui Chang was led in in manacles, and her orange jumper.

Sui Chang nodded in greeting, and wanted to rush into Tricia's arms and hold her. Tricia's was the first familiar face besides her husband, that she had seen in over a month, and that overwhelmed her. She began to cry.

Although Tricia felt little remorse for the woman, she reached out and held her hand, in a gesture of friendship and comfort. Sui finally collected herself, and spoke. Her voice was barely audible, "I am so miserable. Why must I pay for sins of my husband? Please help me. I can help you."

Thus, was born another coup for the Rodriguez Investigation. Not only had the Investigation stopped the incursion of a major portion of the West Coast's supply of hard street drugs, now they could hopefully develop another conduit into the international supply side of the dirty business as well. The DEA was thrilled, all the way to the top in Washington DC, and Steve's star continued to shine brightly. He would now have to take very special care of Sui Chang.

From my experience, another segment of Murphy's Law must state, that if you get away somewhere pleasant, and enjoy life for a moment in time, you often need, for some perverse reason, to pay for that brief respite. It seemed like we had no sooner gotten off of our plane at Portland International Airport, when my cell phone rang. It was Marta Koenig.

"Have you heard?" she asked me. "Where were you?"

"I was in Palm Desert for a long weekend. What's up?"

Well, she hit me with what was up. And it wasn't a laser, a missile, an ICBM, or even a major scud. It was an Atomic Freaking Bomb. "The Magnolia neighborhood has filed a civil suit against Rosewood Golf Club and the Board of Directors for eight million dollars."

"What? You are kidding me."
"Nope, that's the gospel truth."
"Holy Cow. Now what are we going to do?"
"I don't know. There is another special meeting tonight."
"When did this happen?"
"Late yesterday afternoon."
"What time is the meeting tonight?"
"Six thirty."
"Is Pete Collins going to be there?"
"I certainly hope so."
"Thanks for the call. See you later.

CHAPTER FIFTY-FOUR

Every time we thought things couldn't get any worse, another disaster seemed to land directly on top of us. We were all assembled in the conference room at six thirty pm, when Pete Collins made his way in.

This was the last thing anyone needed, particularly myself. We had been gone for five days, I wanted to get my desk cleared, and get back to my own duties. I was finally in a relaxed state, and it certainly wouldn't hurt to spend some time with my kids. Instead, here I was at the club, in another stupid, crisis management meeting. The worst part of the situation appeared to be, how we as the Board of Record, would now have to stick around and defend ourselves from this frivolous civil action. Simply resigning, and walking away from the Board was no longer an option for any of us.

And Pete was not the least bit reassuring. "I have read this complaint thoroughly, and from the actions of Charlie Strong alone, there seems to be some merit to the case."

We all let out a collective groan.

"What can we do to protect ourselves?" someone asked.

"Well, the Board was wise enough to have Director & Officers insurance in place. That will certainly help. Also, you have liability insurance to the tune of three million dollars, so the personal exposure on all of your parts, should be shielded for the most part. The problem as I see it, is defending this law suit. That will be very expensive. I do not personally do civil cases, but would be happy to refer you to some very good people I have worked with in the past. However, I must warn you this could be a very costly process. There are no public defenders for country clubs. And to make matters worse, you need to consider Rosewood's current financial status. I might suggest getting an attorney in place, and confer with the insurance adjusters. Try to get this complaint before a mediator, and get a solution defined as soon as possible."

And that is exactly what we did. The Magnolians were as happy to bury the hatchet quickly and deeply in our collective backs, as we were happy to avoid any personal losses. We hired a friend of Pete's, and told him that we quit. As preposterous as it sounded to all of us, we surrendered. Magnolia Street, you win. Our attorney and the insurance negotiators were able to mitigate a lot of the complaints against us. In short however, at the end of the settlements, and due to all of the litigation costs, and our depleted cash position, Rosewood Golf and Country Club settled the case, but we were forced to declare bankruptcy.

The Magnolians, as a class, were awarded some three million dollars. The Insurance Company settled out of court, as they were not about to go into a court of law and defend a case of this magnitude and notoriety. The risk of a jury trial, and all of those potentially greater damages, plus attorney fees was, as we suspected, more risk than they cared to consider.

The Magnolia neighbors paid themselves any expenses incurred, such as psychotherapy costs and attorney fees. They paid off their attorney's percentage of the settlement, and voted to donate close a million dollars to the City of Vancouver Public School System. But they also kept an undisclosed, but tidy sum in a neighborhood trust account. Apparently, a war chest in case they should ever have to go to battle again. Or maybe just a lifetime supply of Pinot Noir money. I don't know.

Once the dust from the lawsuit settled, The United States Golf Corporation won the extensive bidding process, and bought us at the bankruptcy auction. They won out over several local developers, and it looks like we will stay in the golf club business.

The first thing we received from them, was a due diligence letter. It extended us an invitation to stay on with the new operators as proprietary members at the New Rosewood G&CC. Their first order of business was a 1.4-million-dollar renovation of our clubhouse! I like these people already.

In addition to the clubhouse remodel, they brought in a first-class Food and Beverage team, and the resulting facilities and personnel upgrade, along with the vastly improved national economy, has brought in a surge of new membership. We have a waiting list for social memberships, and have recouped all of the proprietary members we lost in the crash. Plus some. The club is healthier than ever now.

The USGC is a private company which operates golf courses. They manage each of their facilities with their own team. There is no longer any need for a Club Board of Directors. Thank God. There is only a Liaison Committee, established for the purpose of maintaining efficient communication with the membership. I like these people even better.

Thirdly, USGC members have reciprocal playing rights at all USGC courses. Nationwide. All two hundred and forty-nine of them. How can you beat that? And there are some pretty nice clubs in the USGC portfolio too.

Six years have expired now, and we are still enjoying life at the New Rosewood Golf & Country Club.

Jeanine and I do our best to hit the fairways the majority of the time. And so far, the liaison committee hasn't called either of us yet.

The End

EPILOGUE

Charlie Strong was sentenced to twenty-five years at the Washington State Penitentiary in Walla Walla, Washington. He was given an additional term of ten years by the Federal Court for aiding and abetting in the Drug Trafficking case, but was allowed to serve his sentences concurrently. He will be eligible for parole in eighteen years. He is well on his way to an online degree from Whitman University in Psychology, and leads a prison help group for inmates who suffer from Post-Traumatic Stress Syndrome. He has also recently formed another support group among his fellow prisoners specializing in anger management. Charlie intends to earn a Master's Degree in Clinical Psychology before he is released from prison. He is reported to be a model prisoner.

Rick Ferin was sentenced to two years in Federal Prison for aiding and abetting in the trafficking of a controlled substance. Federal sentences are very severe as to consideration in their reductions, but because of his complete co-operation with the Federal Prosecutors, he served his time, and served relatively light duty. In other words, he was in a so-called country club prison. After his release, he was reinstated by the ILWU, albeit reassigned to a lesser position, and in the Seattle region.

Nikki is still the receptionist at the ILWU offices, at the Port of Vancouver. She married an electrician, and they have two young children.

Larry Easton retired, and joined the New Rosewood Golf Club. He plays regularly.

Frank Davis was invited to stay on as greens keeper by the USGC. He doesn't play quite as much golf with us as he used to, but many people say we have the finest greens in the State of Washington.

Sui Chang, to the undying chagrin of her husband, co-operated fully with the authorities. Although, unbeknownst to them she was very selective in what information she divulged. Still, she was a star witness for the prosecution. The FBI placed her in the witness protection program after the trials were completed, and moved her to a city somewhere in the Midwest. The option of her ever returning to the Asian continent is dim at best. She would be most unwelcome in her old circles. But she is a survivor, and will surely make the best of her new life. She has started an on-line lingerie business, and it is rumored that she is active in LGBT community.

Unfortunately for them, Mr. Chang and his buddy Bao Thieu got stuck as the bad guys in the whole Rodriguez Investigation. They were found guilty on all accounts, and the Feds have figuratively buried them. They will not see the outside of a prison for a long time.

Steve Rodriguez and Tricia Watson were married a year to the day after their first dinner date in Portland's Pearl District. Steve stayed on in the Portland region for another five years, so Tricia could pay back Ray Farley for all of the training time and money he had invested in her. Steve recently accepted a promotion to Chief Agent in Charge of the Chicago Office of the FBI. They live in a condo on Lakeshore Drive.

Tricia is pregnant, and has temporarily retired from law enforcement. Dean Junior is thirteen years old, and like his mom, he loves to play basketball and baseball.

The Magnolia neighborhood has changed significantly. Bob Kudlach separated from his wife, and moved back to the east coast. Carol and Neil Horn also divorced. Hugh and Bunny moved to Las Vegas. The Magnolians distributed the remainder of the award money before they all went their separate ways.

The street has a much better relationship with the Club now.

AUTHOR BIOGRAPHY